Leaving school at fifteen, Peter Woodbridge began a successful business career and later a family life that allowed him little time to achieve his ambitions as a writer.

Determined to pursue his passion, he has written numerous unpublished short stories and several novels. Born in England, he is a Canadian living in Vancouver. He enjoys time spent in Barcelona, hiking in Arizona and travelling.

Visit at: www.peterwoodbridge.com

Author's Note

The location and layout of police buildings in Barcelona and Ceuta have been disguised.

Dedication

For Trish and Sally, Gill and Rosemary.

Peter Woodbridge

The Girl from Barcelona

Austin Macauley
PUBLISHERS LTD.

A CIP catalogue record for this title is available from the British Library.

ISBN 9781786296788 (Paperback)
ISBN 9781786296795 (Hardback)
ISBN 9781786296801 (eBook)

www.austinmacauley.com

First Published (2017)
Austin Macauley Publishers Ltd.
25 Canada Square
Canary Wharf
London
E14 5LB

عدو عدوي هو صديقي

The Enemy of my Enemy is my Friend.
(Arabic Proverb)

Chapter 1

Catalunya: The Visitor

It was the smell of his masculinity that she remembered, on the days he came to take her.

"Look, I have brought a gift for you."

Downstairs, the back door slammed shut as her aunt hurried away. Then the silence.

He removed his uniform and folded it carefully, placing it flat on the wood table next to her school books. Smiling at her, he sat on the edge of her narrow creaking bed.

"How are you?" he would ask, reaching out and running his fingers through her hair. She did not answer because she knew it was not a question, just a prelude.

The first time, she had shivered—powerless to prevent him. Later, she merely turned her head, fixing her gaze on the metal crucifix nailed to the wall. Underneath, a small plastic font contained holy water. To protect the congregation from evil, the parish priest had assured them. Amen.

She knew all about her femininity, of course. Lewd stares of boys and grown men; furtive glances of wanting and desire. Head down, she had hurried home from the convent school, last year's uniform skirt too short for her long legs; her face flushed, as she felt the lusting, groping gaze of the men—and the brooding resentment of the women.

He was kind and gentle. Yet, she had imagined it differently... The boy next door? A handsome prince? Oh well.

Out of sight and hearing of the nuns, older girls bragged about their lost virtue. She had said nothing. In all those years, not a word to anyone. Our little secret.

"He is a powerful man," said her aunt. "They have needs. It is normal."

"Scandal would not be good for the family," she reminded her at a later time, the metal spoon scraping against the girl's plate as she served out their meal. "Not good for you."

"Besides, who do you think pays for your expensive schooling? For your language lessons?"

All of this she learned to accept as a matter of practicality—in a man's world.

As she grew older, he took more interest in her studies. They conversed in Arabic.

"Languages will serve you well," he told her, acknowledging her progress with approval.

On another visit, he examined her school books.

"Is this what they teach you at the convent?" his voice leaving her in no doubt as to his displeasure. "Those evil black crows continue to dispense the Church's hypocrisy."

"Read this," he suggested to her the next time, handing her a slim well-used book. He cupped her face in his hands and looked earnestly into her eyes. "Keep an open mind, as I have taught you."

"You have a hiding place for it?" he asked, and she nodded.

Over the next several years, he brought more books for her, frequently testing her understanding of them in the brief conversations they enjoyed.

Her aunt had the eyes of an eagle and the bone-crushing poise of a hyena. "His books fill your head with nonsense. They are stupid ideas, not of the Church. Do not think, girl, I have not observed the many times you avoid communion."

Then, one day, it started just like any other. Before, he had been self-assured, confident of his prowess, assured of his masculinity. She had smiled kindly at his clumsiness. Seeing his embarrassment, she sought to reassure him. Yet, both realised his failure marked a transition.

He visited less frequently. Eventually he stopped arriving altogether.

"He has been posted to Madrid," her aunt said one day. Her puckered mouth preluded her vitriol. "If you cannot keep a man like him, what hope is there for you?"

"Will I have to leave school?" she asked.

"No, he still pays for that—and your board and lodging. Precious little else any longer."

Seeing the venom in her eyes, the girl understood her role in the household. Deprived of the extra income, her aunt grew more resentful.

One day, a mistake. Without any money, in desperation she stole a blouse. The Mossos made light of it, understanding her youth and seeking to protect one of their own Catalans. The store owner's wife, a shrew from Seville, demanded full retribution. Too young for adult court, the girl was placed on probation.

Once a week, a mandatory meeting with the youth corrections officer. A kindly man. Twice monthly, a session with the psychiatrist—a middle-aged woman who found her attractive. In the small town, word soon got around.

"You are nothing but a promiscuous thief," her aunt accused. "A brazen slut."

Filling a bag with her few belongings, the girl left town in the middle of the night. In her purse, the business card he had given her—a phone number only to be called in dire need, he had said.

The truck driver could not believe his luck. He would take her all the way to Madrid. There would just be one stop on the way, he smiled.

In the Shadows of the Sagrada Familia

The Metro to Pompeu Fabra slowed as it pulled into the almost deserted Sagrada Familia station. A tall athletic young man stepped out onto the platform. He paused to adjust the positioning of his jacket and glanced around.

Seeing an exit that would take him to the meeting place, he followed the signs for Placa Gaudi, exited the turnstiles and stepped onto the escalator up to the street.

"Follow me," he heard a heavily accented voice alongside him. He recognised the figure—a tall man, his face hidden in a black hoodie, who moved quickly ahead of him.

It was a routine that they had played out several times before in different locations in the city. Just as before, the man carried a bulky yellow backpack which he clasped tightly over his shoulder.

By the time the young man had reached the street his contact already was well ahead.

The younger man realized he needed to hurry his stride. It was late at night. Behind him, he was aware of the bright lights of Gaudi's masterpiece basilica.

He skirted the edge of the park and the grass verge. The man, who by now had reached an unlit phone kiosk towards the end of the street, paused waiting for him.

As he approached, his contact turned to face him. Despite the younger man's taller-than-average height, the man seemed to tower above him. His face, angular and pinched, was overwhelmed by his penetrating blue eyes and the dismissive sneer of his downturned mouth. He wore the same black leather gloves as on previous occasions.

"You have the documents?"

Without waiting for an answer, the man cut into a gap alongside the windowless brick wall at the back of a residential building and made his way into the bushes that marked this corner of the park.

The younger man hesitated. "You have the money?" he called out to the man's back.

His contact spun around and shouldered the heavy backpack.

"The documents are what has been agreed?"

The younger man nodded.

"Let's see what you have," stated his contact, leafing through a bundle of documents the younger man withdrew from the inside pocket of his jacket.

Pausing, the man studied a few of the enlarged photographs. "Hmm," he said after a time. He leafed through several pages and seemed to be examining a list. "Okay," he conceded.

Swinging the backpack off his shoulders, he placed it on the ground in front of the younger man. "Check it," he instructed.

His phone rang. "Hmm," he said again and turned to look at the younger man.

"Check it," he repeated, his voice now hardening.

The younger man unzipped the bag and glanced quickly at the contents before zipping it back up. His movements took only a few seconds before he looked up again. As he did, he was astonished to see a long-barrelled gun now pointing directly at him.

"Caballero. Nothing personal. Mustapha says that our arrangement has changed," said the man.

In the fraction of a second it took the bullet to travel and penetrate his forehead, the younger man was aware that time had slowed to a halt. It passed like minutes. He saw everything more clearly than ever before. His life was there before him, now in slow inexorable motion; he was an objective observer of his own demise.

He arrived at a single thought. It was a regret, devoid of emotion. He felt, in retrospect, that he should not have been quite so trusting of his employer.

Mossos' Headquarters

Deputy Inspector Antonio Valls looked up from his desk. Using his long fingers as a comb, he swept back the long strands of dyed blonde hair that continually flopped across his face.

"Amigo?"

"Homicide at Placa de Gaudi. Opposite the Sagrada Familia," announced Xavi, dropping a thin manila-coloured case file onto the desk and slumping into a chair.

Valls nodded. "I'm reading the crime scene report. Male, probably early twenties. Found early this morning. Shot once at close range. Do we have anything to go on?"

"Madrid is involved," stated Xavi, with contempt. He saw his partner's raised eyebrow. "Already?"

"I talked to a sergeant at the crime scene. He said a senior officer from the National Police called him on his cell phone. The sergeant didn't know how the madridista obtained his number."

"Those bastards have better information than we do—and it's our own backyard," spat Antonio.

The madridista asked a lot of questions," said Xavi.

"Such as?"

"He wanted to know if we had found any documents, and a backpack, with the victim's body."

"Let me guess. The documents and the backpack are missing."

Xavi nodded.

"Did they check the CCTV cameras at the Metro?"

"Yes, and at the Sagrada Familia as well. The victim was seen on the footage coming out of the Metro. So was a taller man carrying a backpack."

"Did we get a good visual on the backpack carrier?"

Xavi shook his head. "You think there was some kind of exchange taking place?"

"It was a rendezvous of some kind," said Antonio. "Did the sergeant say if the madridista gave us the ID of the victim?"

"No. He told the sergeant the victim might be a member of the armed services; he wasn't sure. The sergeant told me he thought the madridista was holding back on information."

"All personal belongings were missing from the body?" offered Antonio, as his partner nodded confirmation.

"The park is a favourite overnight hang-out for druggies. The sergeant says that the body was found by a young tourist sleeping on a park bench, when he went into the bushes for a piss."

Xavi's phone rang. Listening for a few minutes and taking notes, he looked across at Antonio. "That was the sergeant. Two of our squaddies picked up a druggie about six blocks from the crime scene. He had lifted the victim's wallet from the body. Except for the cash he stole and spent on a bottle, we have recovered the rest."

"The victim's a Civil Guard junior officer," continued Xavi. "Cadet First Class David Casals, stationed in Ceuta. Age twenty-four. He has a driver's license with a Barcelona address—in Gracia."

"So, what have we got?" asked Antonio. "I mean, for Madrid to be involved, it has to be drugs, money laundering or people smuggling—so we lose jurisdiction anyway, eventually."

"What do we know about the madridista who called our sergeant?" he added.

"He said he was a chief inspector with the GEO unit of the National Police."

"Madrid's commando unit investigating terrorism and international crimes," Antonio screwed up his face. "Well, right now it's a homicide in our backyard; we have jurisdiction, until we lose it."

His phone rang.

"It's Jose Miguel. The chief wants to see us both right away," Antonio groaned as he called off.

Xavi pressed the elevator button to the eighth floor, scanning his security card to get access.

"How is it with you and Maria?" he asked, receiving a shrug from Antonio in reply.

"She's fine."

Xavi said nothing. Well, that killed off any further discussion, he thought.

The elevator doors opened, easing a potentially awkward silence.

The chief had ordered tightened security on the executive floor, they noted. Antonio followed Xavi, putting his items through the metal detector. "Hey, Carmel," he smiled at the female security officer. "Did you see the game last weekend?"

Antonio knew that she was in her mid-twenties and divorced, with a young son. Her ex, a former Mossos squaddie, had quit the force a year earlier and gone to live in Ecuador. It was hard to figure out some guys, Antonio thought. She was a nice-looking woman, and a good mother; she deserved better.

For an instant, the eye contact between them held a realm of possibilities.

"How's your son? Jose, isn't it?" he asked, shattering the moment.

She smiled again, differently this time.

"He loves preschool," she radiated.

Antonio looked around. "Security seems a bit tighter this morning?"

"Yes. There's some kind of VIP arriving from Madrid," said Carmel.

Antonio's text message alert sounded. It was Maria.

Quickly he texted a reply, promising to call her later. Then he switched his phone to silent.

He waved to his father's secretary and knocked at the door.

"Sit down please, gentlemen," instructed the chief. The two officers took seats close to his large wooden desk. Jose Miguel sat to one side, taking notes on his laptop.

"Xavi, tell me what you know about the homicide near the Sagrada Familia," the chief requested.

He listened while the officer provided a summary of the facts. Xavi told him about the surprise call from the senior officer at GEO to the sergeant at the crime scene.

"Toni?" asked the chief, swinging his chair and turning towards his son. "Anything to add?"

"We have started to theorise a little, sir," answered Antonio. "But nothing concrete to go on, as yet."

"Okay," said the chief. "Let me see if I can add some information. What I will tell you is that this case is—and must remain—at the highest level of national security and confidentiality."

Before continuing, he sat back and twisted both ends of a pen between the tips of his fingers. The brief silence that followed seemed to create the desired effect. He knew he had their attention.

"I had a call early this morning from the National Police in Madrid. That call occurred almost immediately after the body had been found and called in by our squaddies.

"It seems that the National Police, their GEO Special Operations to be precise, have an active case underway. It involves the recruitment here in Spain, and radicalisation, of westerners for jihadist work in Syria and the Arabian Peninsula."

The chief theatrically placed his pen back on the desk and looked at the two officers. "As you know from the identification that was recovered, the Sagrada Familia murder victim is a young border guard, part of the Civil Guard. He was stationed in Ceuta—with the military contingent responsible for security of our border with Morocco.

"That frontier normally is tight as a drum," noted the chief. "GEO was tracking him.

"They think he is, or was, a mule in a cash-for-passports trade. Barcelona, as we know, being a prime source of stolen passports. I got the impression there may be some other things involved—so let's not be naive." He nodded at them. "It's not likely to be as simple as the National Police led me to believe.

"Here's where it gets interesting," said the chief. "We already know that the Romanian, British and Russian gangs operating here sell stolen documents to domestic groups specialising in identity theft. The local groups then sell fully developed and legitimate identities to the highest bidders internationally."

Jose Miguel leaned forward and broke into the conversation. "It's a kind of value-added trade in stolen documents. It's generating big money, and attracting some talented information technology professionals—especially since the economic downturn.

"A few days ago there was a large haul taken from one of the cruise ships returning to Barcelona: over two hundred passports."

The chief was irritated by the interruption, but nodded in agreement.

"Madrid has been working with the security forces, notably the DST in Morocco. They've been tracking the stolen documents supply chain for some time. After the Civil Guard and GEO busted a large document-and-people smuggling operation over there last year, the network went underground.

"They arrested two Spaniards and eight foreigners. Even under pressure, the prisoners have revealed almost nothing Madrid didn't already know. The network went silent—until recently. GEO thinks it has been resurrected, but with a new and sinister twist."

The chief paused again before continuing, the pitch of his voice much lower.

"We know that ISIS and other jihadist factions in the Middle East are no longer content with radicalising ideologically misguided freedom fighters from the West, to fight in Syria and other hotspots."

He sipped a plastic cup of water.

"Our colleagues at the DST in Rabat say that Morocco is being used as a training ground. And as a routing point for siphoning highly trained radicals back into western countries."

"They're using the madrasas for training western radicals to spy from within on their own countries," offered Antonio.

His father nodded. "An increasing number of converts to Islamic extremism are western university graduates and professionals in medicine, the military and other strategic positions. They're in occupations where we are vulnerable to attack."

"Like Hasan in the Fort Hood mass shootings in 2009?" continued Antonio. "He was an American army psychiatrist— a major who turned fanatic."

The chief nodded curtly, still not able to hide his irritation at being interrupted.

"The outcome was that the Americans learned to carry out in-depth profiling and pre-screening at border points—and so did we. But the target group of radical converts we're dealing with today wouldn't be identified by profiling.

"The enemy has become more sophisticated. The objective of their new network is to keep us from identifying who these converts and potential converts are. Their thinking is that, if we don't know who they are, we can't track them through normal procedures." He paused again.

"You've been briefed during our anti-terrorism training sessions on what's been trending, as far as that's concerned.

My point is that, with this homicide case, Madrid is well along the path of identifying the members of an active network—they say it's sizeable and significant.

"The result is that maybe hundreds of sleeper agents, who knows how many, are just waiting to be activated and become engaged in al-Qaeda-directed sabotage activities domestically."

The chief leaned forward. "Here's the plan.

"Madrid will continue to be in charge of the special counter-espionage operation. The National Police have the final say in decision-making. An officer from GEO is on his way here." He consulted his watch.

"He should be arriving at El Prat about now; he's being met by one of our people and will be here shortly.

"There's a significant Catalan element to this case. We don't want to lose complete control. Madrid has jurisdiction. But I think we will be able to assign local assets.

"They agree. It's a good opportunity to prove that we can work together," he beamed.

"That's where you two come in." The chief leaned back in his leather chair. "This is a special op and I want it run through my office. On a reporting basis, you will remain in communication with Jose Miguel. He will be able to assign special funds and resources.

"It's an official assignment, but it's out of your normal scope. You can decline if you wish."

He turned to his son. "Toni, I'll be candid with you. The GEO officer is a deputy inspector—the same rank as you.

"This problem we have with overlapping security and police forces in Spain is an administrative nightmare," he sighed.

"Eventually, we'll get it sorted out. In the meantime, we have to be prepared to make some compromises."

He looked directly at Antonio. "I have agreed with Madrid that the GEO man will be the officer-in-charge."

"Why don't you assign someone else, sir, and avoid the ranking issue?" asked Antonio, looking unhappy.

"Toni, within the Mossos, you are the most qualified person we have for this assignment. You speak French and some Arabic. You can help him navigate his way locally. It's just an unfortunate coincidence that you have the same rank.

"Xavi, I want you to provide backup for Antonio," said the chief, not wanting to debate any further with his son. "You'll both be given temporary special powers and Toni will have the authority to travel outside our patch.

"Now it's decision time," said the chief, clapping his hands together.

"Should I be looking for other officers to do this work?" he asked, his eyebrows raised high on his forehead.

Both officers shook their heads.

"Good," said the chief. "Jose Miguel will arrange the administrative details."

He raised his hand in dismissal, and the two officers started to follow the assistant back to his office.

"Oh Toni," said the chief. "I need just a few more minutes…"

As Antonio lingered behind, the chief shuffled some papers on his desk, delaying until Xavi and the assistant were out of hearing.

He walked around his desk and leaned back, sitting on the front of it.

"Toni, if you don't want to do this…" he began.

Antonio interrupted him.

"Dad, I'm certainly not going to turn down this assignment just because you think my ego might be bruised. There's been a murder in our backyard and it's our job to see the case through and get the guys who did it.

"You've given the job to me and I'll do it. If that means working with a federal officer in charge of the investigation, that's fine. I've done it before. I'm okay with it—really."

His father leaned forward and patted his upper arm.

"Good for you. I just wanted to make sure you're okay with the arrangement."

"I'd better get going," said Antonio with a shrug.

"Just one other thing," added the chief.

He took a deep breath. "Your mother and I, well, we wondered how you and Maria are getting along. You know what women are like, son. She worries about these things. And, yes, I'll be honest. I, too, would be happy if we could have grandchildren at some time." His voice trailed off as he saw Antonio's face darken. "But everything in its own time," the chief added in haste.

"Is there anything more, sir?" asked Antonio, stepping back and giving his father a formal salute.

Xavi was waiting for Antonio. As soon as he saw his partner, he pressed the elevator button to the 6th floor.

"More of the same from my dad," said Antonio as the elevator doors closed. "Plus his usual speech about their need for grandchildren," he shrugged. "You want to join me for an early lunch?"

He heard a buzz from his phone and read the text message aloud. "*Chief wants you to look after GEO Deputy Inspector Diego Abaya and make sure he is welcomed. Chief will meet you both for lunch. Table for three. 1:30 p.m. at Batista's. Confirm with me please.*"

"Sorry, Xavi," he slapped his partner on the shoulder. "I have to babysit the madridista. I guess we'll have to catch up later, amigo."

Chapter 2

Madrid: Monument to Franco

"Does he know anything?"

The question came from a moustached man in his mid-eighties sitting across the café table from Chief Inspector Raphael Robles. Unusual for his advanced age, the older man had straight shoulders; his posture confirmed the bearing of a former military man.

Robles shook his head. He knew he was taking a chance talking face-to-face with the General, but he had made sure his cover story for the meeting was solid. Besides, he was making a significant investment in the old campaigner and his cohorts.

"He knows that we have an ongoing operation in place, sir—and that the murdered Civil Guard officer is somehow connected to the case.

"He also knows the victim was acting as a mule for the jihadists."

The older man said nothing, but kept his unwavering eyes on the Chief Inspector.

"I told him that we suspect there is a security leak—at a high level in the Civil Guard. There's no need for him to know anything more," he continued. "Not unless you instruct me otherwise, sir," he added after a pause.

The two men stopped their conversation. A middle-aged couple, who looked like tourists, sat down at the table close to them and noisily shuffled their metal chairs on the tiled floor. Then, just as quickly, they stood up and walked over to another table across the room near the window. Both men looked relieved. The General leaned over to the table they had vacated and slid his hand underneath. They had not planted any listening devices; still, it always paid to be cautious. In the old days, men under his command had been experts at such ruses.

"Diego can be a hothead," said Robles, who had gratefully noted the General's obsession with security. "But he's a good officer. Operationally, he's one of the best we have in GEO. Let's see what he can do for us in Barcelona."

The older man shook his head. "The Mossos aren't Spain's smartest policemen. They'll probably let the case drop after a few days."

"I don't think so, sir—not in this instance."

Robles could not have failed to see the bushy greyed eyebrow that was raised in his direction by the older man as he reacted to the remark.

"Really? Why?" The older man's eyes suddenly were even more sharp and penetrating than usual.

"I had a call this morning from the Mossos' chief of police. I know him quite well. He's close to retirement and he sees this as a potential test case for interagency cooperation. He's assigned a senior officer to work with Diego."

The older man considered this news for a moment. "It wouldn't be a good thing—if they went digging too far. You know that."

"That's why I chose Diego. In my opinion he is better off, for now, with just a basic briefing. He'll be more effective that way."

The older man digested the information. "Keep me informed, Chief Inspector," he said, getting ready to leave.

Robles was not quite finished with his own agenda for the meeting, but it had to be handled carefully. "Is there anything more you need, sir—in terms of resources, for example?"

"We are ready," the General replied, the emphasis in his voice leaving no doubt. "The question is, Robles, are you confident they will deliver their side of the agreement?"

"They? You are speaking of…" His voice trailed off.

"Yes," interrupted the older man, his eyes flashing a warning.

"I would stake everything on it. I would stake my life on it," said Robles, in turn also leaving no room for doubt. He had been reassured by the older man's caution; the less they spoke openly about Mustapha, the better.

The older man said nothing. After a few moments, he nodded at the chief inspector. Pulling the collar of his coat higher, he rose stiffly from the table. It was cool for October, and these days he was feeling the chill.

Leaving the café, he made a brief cell phone call and walked along the street for several metres. Apparently short of breath, he leaned back and sat on a concrete wall to steady himself. He wiped his forehead with a white handkerchief that he knew would be visible from the apartment opposite. Easing himself to his feet he continued slowly on his journey.

Seeing the grocery store, he entered. Pushing a metal shopping cart, he walked slowly along the shelves directly to the back of the store.

Normally, it irritated him that retail merchants positioned basic food items at the back, forcing shoppers to walk past shelves of tempting items they couldn't afford. He remembered vividly many years of deprivation throughout Spain when only the basics were obtainable—and then not very often. But today, shopping for groceries wasn't his main purpose.

Idly, he picked a small container of half-cream milk, checked its due date and then looked at each of the others in turn. He placed the best one in his shopping basket.

A few minutes later, reflected in the mirrored surface behind the dairy products shelf, he saw a young woman whom he recognised at once. She was carrying a shopping basket and moving slowly in his direction.

He lingered, still looking at the shelves, but watched her as she came closer. She reached past him. "I need a clean phone. Again, no GPS tracking," he said, as she started to move away.

The young woman said nothing and continued towards a shelf of eggs. She seemed undecided and left her shopping basket behind, walking out of the store.

He moved slowly towards the eggs and made a pretence of selecting a small box, shunning the higher priced organic options. Then he chose a warm baguette from the bakery. Making his way to the cashier, his hand clasped the phone he had picked out of the young woman's abandoned basket. He slipped it into his pocket.

Five minutes later, carrying his plastic shopping bag, he entered a thrift store. He made a show of picking through a rack of used clothes. From here, without being seen, he had a good view of the street. He dialled a number.

"It's me," he said, when the familiar voice answered.

"How is our friend?" asked the voice.

"He suspects nothing. He's doing his job. He has assigned one of his men to help in the investigation. The Mossos are involved, but you need not be concerned. You may proceed with the next stage of *Operation FERROL* according to plan."

Removing the back of the prepaid phone, he stripped out the battery and SIM card with surprising dexterity.

Placing the battery in an inside pocket of a well-worn garment on the rack, he picked up his bag of groceries and walked towards a shelf of used shoes. There was a dull thud as he dropped the empty phone down a hole at the back.

No one would find it there, he was sure.

He might be an old man, he reflected, but he was still operationally sound. Yes, he had retired long ago, but he reminded himself he was still a general—one of the most decorated in his era.

As he waited to board a bus back to his apartment, the SIM card dropped from between his fingers and fell onto the damp pavement. With his heel, he crunched it underfoot. A few minutes later, as his bus pulled up in front of him, he used his toe to slide the crushed card down a gutter, watching it disappear from sight. The call he had made could not be traced to him.

The bus driver waited patiently as the old man negotiated the steps up into the bus. He smiled politely, waving away any need for his passenger to show his senior's pass. He did not restart the bus until he was sure that his passenger was seated securely.

The old man stared at his bag of groceries, but his thoughts were focused on the plans he had just authorised. They would be underway already. Spain's experiment with democracy had become jaded and unworkable. Now was their time.

His bus route took him past the monument that had been placed in honour of the victims of the Spanish Civil War. As they reached the monument, he lifted his head to look out of the window.

He knew the place well. On the same spot, many years ago, he had stood in full uniform at rigid attention, standing next to the Generalissimo himself. At that spot, they had unveiled the statue of Franco's North African campaign. Franco's statue had remained in that position of honour for many years—only to be peremptorily removed and cut up for scrap metal, as the country was swept along with the tide of democracy and political correctness.

It seemed to him that progress was a debatable phenomenon. There was no respect these days for the country's history—or for its real heroes, he reflected. His mouth set hard; at least now he could draw some satisfaction from the knowledge that things would soon change for the better.

Catalunya: Diego Arrives

"Diego, get on the next flight to Barcelona," my boss had texted me early this morning.

"An espionage case has broken open. An officer from the Civil Guard has been murdered. You'll be working with the Mossos. Give me a call when you get there."

I got one of the last seats and had to sit at the back of the plane. The day had started badly already. I tried to read the case files I'd downloaded, but that's difficult when you're wedged between the toilets and a mother with a screaming baby.

Sometimes I wonder why I don't just settle for a nice desk job somewhere at headquarters.

There had been no time to pack properly, so I walked off the plane at El Prat with just a carry-on bag. It's a GEO rule that we must have one in the office ready to go. I diverted into airport security and showed them my ID—and my gun. I don't like other people handling it.

It was another annoying experience getting out of the airport.

If the public knew how many people carry weapons—officially—through airports every day, there would be a major panic. That's not to mention the weapons the bad guys are able to smuggle through with the help of airport staff and baggage handlers.

Airport security is an illusion: it's pathetic.

There was one compensation as I walked straight through the baggage reclaim area. The Mossos seemed to be expecting me, at least. A plainclothes and car were waiting for me. He pointed to a Mossos d'Esquadra squad car parked in a no-waiting area.

I told him to give me fifteen minutes. I was anxious to call my boss. This place was as good as any to make the call; my escort could wait. After all, I thought, if the Mossos can't park illegally outside their own airport, who can?

"I've got a lot of questions, sir," I started to say.

Chief Inspector Raphael Robles cut me off before I was able to continue. "Look, Diego, you'll just have to wing it until you get up to speed on the case. I'll have some additional files encrypted and sent to you. They'll help with the background."

I half-smiled as he said this. It's standard procedure for all files within the National Police and other security forces to be encrypted. Otherwise we'd be at the mercy of hackers. What Robles was really telling me was that he hadn't yet decided how much to reveal to me. My guess was that he wanted to whitewash the files before he sent them.

Robles was like that. Spain might have a reputation for not having the greatest levels of efficiency and motivation, but I can tell you that there are a whole bunch of ambitious guys like him who are constantly striving to push their dicks to the front of the line.

"This has political ramifications," he continued, which was no surprise. Everything Robles touches does. He continued with his briefing. There were lots of information gaps, and I had a long list of questions. I said nothing because Raphael Robles is not someone you want to upset. Plus, he's been a sort of benefactor to me since I joined GEO. He was behind my promotion to deputy inspector, and that put a lot of noses out of joint in the department, so I figured it wasn't the smartest move for me to start cross-questioning him at that particular moment.

"It's a great chance for us to work with the Mossos and the Civil Guard," he continued. "All three security agencies working harmoniously." I could almost hear him purring.

"I'll copy you confidentially on a personal email," he continued. "It's from my opposite number at the Mossos. You're going to be working with one of their best officers." He paused to let this information sink in.

"By the way, he's the son of the Mossos' Chief of Police. So, you know, be on your best behaviour Diego."

I hoped my deep sigh was not audible to him. Working with these regional police forces was bad enough. Throw in a dose of nepotism and I already knew things were going to go badly wrong.

Just when I thought the day couldn't get much worse.

"Remember two things, Diego," my boss continued, after he had gifted me with this particular piece of news. "This is a joint effort between our security forces— politically, it has to go right. Secondly, you're in charge of the investigation, but try to be sensitive to these regional people. Now, get going. You may be away for a few days, so you can reassign your other work later."

There was a pause.

"Diego, you have to get on top of this thing and put it to bed as soon as you can." His voice sounded strained.

Not long later, at the Mossos' headquarters, I'm following along behind my escort who takes me quickly up to the sixth floor.

When I saw this young prick Antonio Valls walking towards me, it just confirmed my worst fears.

My escort turns to me as we walk along the corridor. "There he is now, sir," he says, as he points in the direction of a young kid coming towards us.

I'm thinking I don't like this. I mean, just look at him. He struts like a turkey cock getting ready for mating. Total confidence in himself. He doesn't even look like a policeman.

He's dressed like a fashion model. Tall, with blonde highlights in his excessively-long swept-back hair.

My first impression? What a shithead.

"Hola, Deputy Inspector Abaya," he says to me. "I'm Deputy Inspector Antonio Valls." No salute. Instead he gives me a big smile and extends his long arm for me to shake his hand.

I'm the ranking officer here. Deputy Inspector Antonio Valls clearly has a problem with authority. First impressions count. Black mark number one against this kid gets entered into my book.

He looks me directly in the eye—with an amused look, like I'm some lowlife from the backstreets. "Would you like to have lunch?" he asks in that soft voice of his. You'd think we were old buddies. Without looking at my watch, I know it's already past one o'clock. I haven't eaten since I tried to consume that crap they served on the flight.

I shrug and say, "It's your back yard." Then I get a salute from my escort as he hands me over. At least one of these regional cowboys has been trained properly, I think to myself.

Then I follow behind Pretty Boy like an obedient school kid on his first day. Now I'm really starting to get pissed off.

It doesn't make it any easier that some of the young chicks in the building keep looking up and throwing admiring glances at him. Black mark number two. What kind of police force do they operate in these parts, I wonder. Seems far too casual to me. More like a happy family than the top line security force it ought to be.

We ride down in the elevator. In the underground car park, lights flash his car's location. Surprisingly, it isn't a sporty convertible, as I half-expected, but a recent model BMW. Still nice.

Obviously, this kid has money... or daddy does. At least he's parked well down in the dungeons, not in a VIP space.

It's reassuring for lowlife immigrants like me to know that daddy's influence doesn't stretch to bumping up his son's position on the car park rankings. He flicks open the trunk with his remote. Lifting up my travel bag, he fusses with it and places it with exaggerated care alongside his golf bag and tennis racquets. Just a damn playboy.

"We'll drop this off at the National Police hostel on our way," he smiles at me. So far, I've said about five words in all this time.

It's a warm day for autumn, and I'd like to take my jacket off. I'm carrying my SIG P226 in its sheath, so I decide against it. We weave through the downtown traffic, and he seems to read my thoughts and switches on the air conditioning. That's better, I'm thinking. Except that he is a bit of a crazy driver. Skilled, but too fast when it's not even an emergency.

"How do you like the 226?" he asks, to show me that he knows what I'm carrying. Well it's common knowledge that everyone in GEO carries the gun. No brownie points there, Antonio.

Maybe he just wants me to know that he knows what I'm carrying. I bat his comment back to him. Right down the middle. "It's standard issue," I say without any great enthusiasm.

By now we are driving east along the Gran Via, and I wonder where he's taking me for lunch. I'd have been just as happy eating in the Mossos' canteen.

"I read your file on the Alfonso case," he says to me out of nowhere. "Nice job," he adds.

"Thanks," I say. I'm trying to figure out if this kid is genuine or if he's just sucking up. Already, I don't like his attitude. He's casual, almost insolent. Not enough for it to be labelled insubordination. Not yet anyway. Maybe it's just the way these rich pricks in Barcelona are raised.

Next thing, he will want us to be tweeting buddies.

"When did you first know that Alfonso was lying to you?" he asks. Again, I'm a bit surprised. He would have to have read the case file closely to be able to ask a question like that. Hell, maybe he's just been well briefed by someone. So, I chat meaninglessly for a few minutes and let the conversation lapse.

I recognise the Ronda Litoral and we swing west. I get my first good look at the Mediterranean and can't help relaxing a little.

I haven't been to Barcelona for some time: maybe two years, I think. It's October, but the streets are just as full of tourists. We slow down as we enter the Old City.

I glance at my watch, in a way he can't see. Eight minutes for a journey that probably should take fifteen. Not bad. Maybe I can use him as a driver. That's a skill I might need in an emergency.

He pulls up alongside the heavily guarded National Police building on Via Llana. I know the place from previous visits. And I know the correct procedure. I get out of his car and show my ID to one of the armed guards. He examines it, salutes me and stands aside.

Now that's what I call a disciplined security detail.

Pretty Boy doesn't get it. He's acting like a tour guide. As he gets out of the car, I see he is waving his Mossos badge. He takes charge of my travel bag—like it's his most precious belonging—and starts to follow me in. I have to intercede on his behalf with the guard. Now I'm starting to feel better.

The desk officer must have been briefed that I'm arriving. He has everything ready. "I've got a lunch appointment," I tell him.

"My car's on the street," Pretty Boy interrupts to tell the officer who immediately glances at me for approval. I nod an okay to him.

The desk officer looks at him and asks for the registration number.

I lean forward and tell him it's a blue BMW, 5-Series. I give him the licence plate number and, just for good measure, to impress Antonio, I tell him the date that the insurance expires.

I want these regional cowboys to know that not everyone from Madrid is a dumb ass.

Antonio doesn't say anything. From his body language, obviously he's taken note. His tone already is shifting to being more polite.

As he deposits my travel bag at the elevator door he says, "I'll wait here until you're ready."

I nod, and mumble something. So far, he's been very much in charge. He certainly has self-assurance, that's for sure. Don't worry, I'll change all that, I say to myself as the elevator door opens and I start to get in.

"Oh, just a minute sir, please," he says, forcing the elevator doors back open and looking at an incoming text message on his phone.

"It's from the chief, sir," he says. "He wants to meet us at the restaurant in ten minutes." The elevator door closes.

"Fuck these Catalans," I say aloud to myself as the elevator takes me up to my room.

Antonio's Office

Lunch with the chief had been awkward. Glancing across the office, I could see that Antonio was still upset. He'd been giving me the icy cold treatment since we'd driven back from the restaurant. He had his feet up on his desk, gazing out of the window.

I suppose I might have been a bit abrasive. I'd been polite to the chief; it would have been disrespectful of his rank to do otherwise. Even so, I wanted him to know where I stood. I told him that there wasn't any doubt in my mind that, as a Muslim

34

and immigrant from Morocco, my promotion to deputy inspector at GEO was a political move. An experiment, a need by the department to show that it can move with the times. I told both of them that my promotion had unsettled the old boys' club within the National Police. I'm not popular with them, I told him, but I get the job done.

I told him it didn't matter to me if Antonio was his son or not. So long as he was up to the job, I wouldn't have a problem. That much was fine with the chief. I guess where I may have gone a little too far was in telling him that the jihadi extremist threat in Spain needed to be handled by Madrid and the country's international partners. The chief had not liked that.

I can tell you one thing, sir, I had said. Terrorism has got nothing to do with religion. As far as I'm concerned, the people we are up against are a bunch of murderous, callous and uncompromising savages. They'll stop at nothing. Absolutely nothing.

Which branch of the security forces you and I work for counts for dick-all among the vindictive violent psychopaths we're dealing with, I told him.

Pushing back my chair, I walked over to Antonio's desk.

"I don't think your father likes me."

"Can you blame him?" asked Antonio, swinging his legs off the desk. "He was just trying to be reasonable, and you turned on him like an animal."

"I just wanted to make it clear…" I said, but didn't finish the sentence.

"What you made clear, Diego, is that you're an insensitive asshole. If that was your intention, you made a good job of it."

I shrugged. "So where do we go from here?"

"You're the ranking officer, so you tell me," responded Antonio, his tone brooding and obstructive.

"Well, as the local asset on our team, what do you recommend?" I turned it back to him.

Antonio was silent for a few moments. "To respond to that, I need answers to a few questions."

"Fire away."

"This case is about a lot more than a murder. It's obvious that the National Police are involved up to their eyeballs. So what the hell is going on, that we in the Mossos haven't been told?" he asked, not attempting to disguise his anger.

"Okay, fair question," I responded. "I'll tell you what. I'll trust you once with this kind of information. If you ever let me down, and if you're not sacked or shot in the process, I'll make sure you're screwed as a police officer—and your father's influence won't be able to help you."

Antonio shrugged. "You see, there you go again, Diego. Straight into combat. I don't know if this interagency cooperation thing is going to work—not on this case."

"I'm just trying to make it clear that the information I give you is highest security."

"And I have the highest security clearance," Antonio shot back. "So, what's your problem?"

"Okay, point taken," I conceded, holding up my hands in mock surrender.

"My boss briefed me before I left Madrid this morning. Long before the Civil Guard officer was killed, we had an active file open on him."

"Which is why your boss made a personal call to the duty officer at the crime scene—before you left Madrid," challenged Antonio. "And that's also why your boss asked our sergeant if we'd found the backpack?"

I had to smile. "You knew about that?"

"We're not damned idiots, if that's what you're suggesting."

"Right," I said. "I can see that I should have started at the beginning."

Over the next few minutes, I repeated the briefing that Raphael Robles had given me a few hours earlier.

"At GEO, the information we have is that the murdered Civil Guard officer was working as a mule for al-Qaeda. We think he may have been trafficking stolen passports. You probably have a better idea than I do about that particular activity."

Antonio shrugged. "It's big business here."

"We don't have any idea who killed the officer. He was garrisoned at Ceuta—and you know that's a port of entry for illegals into Spain and Europe," I said.

"So why did you agree to seek our help?" asked Antonio.

"The only other item I was briefed on before I left Madrid is that we need your expertise and local cooperation. My boss seems to be high on that, for some reason."

"Again, why do you need our help?"

"We think there is a high-level security leak in the Civil Guard," I told him, keeping my voice low. I watched his face and let the information sink in. "So far, we haven't found out where."

I leaned forward across his desk. "Group 60 at GEO is different from Groups 40 and 50. Those two are the original commando units. They're combat—organised into fully integrated terrorism detection and assault units.

"Group 60 is new. It's a small division of people, including myself. We're not combat. We work mostly on an individual basis, on counterterrorism intelligence."

Lowering my voice again, I said, "We were monitoring the activities of David Casals. He was a rising star in the Civil Guard. From what we know, over the past few months he seems to have been assigned to other special duties.

"He had never crossed the border into Morocco but, somehow in the process of his new role, he met with al-Qaeda recruiters—probably in Ceuta, or maybe here in Barcelona where his family comes from. We don't know if he had been radicalised or not.

"Anyway, the DST operating out of Marrakech tipped us off and we started to track his activities.

"He wouldn't be the first Civil Guard member to go rogue on us. In the National Police, we also have a few problems—and I'm guessing you do too in the Mossos, for that matter.

"After our successful joint operation with the Civil Guard last year at Ceuta, we busted up an ISIS recruiting network. We suspected, after that, the recruiters would change their *modus operandi*.

"We think David Casals's first drop was a test run. That happened a few months ago. After that, his handlers seemed to trust him more—at least until his latest drop near the Sagrada Familia."

"What happened to change things?" asked Antonio.

"That's what we don't know," I told him shaking my head. "We thought the Civil Guard was in control of the monitoring operation. Then we learned he had been murdered. The rest you know."

"Okay," said Antonio. "Second question—how much do your people know about the stolen passports supply chain, I mean the one based here in Barcelona?"

"Probably less than you think we know. We are part of the Cyber Defence Committee, of course. With biometric data implants into modern passports the safety net is closing on the passport snatchers. Most of Europe is now biometric. The States and Canada are slowly adopting this technology. But Canadian passports, for example, still command a premium price.

"Jihadi extremists are moving up the value chain and faking complete identities," I told him.

"Not just them," said Antonio. "The Russians were the first to figure this out, and the fake IDs have been used for laundering billions so far," he added.

"But with the new wave of terrorists, it's not passive identity theft for the purpose of stealing or laundering money," I said, wanting to make the distinction clear.

I wasn't sure how smart Antonio was and I guess I didn't find out the answer until later. At the time, he seemed to me to be in his job because of his family connections. I'll concede that he must have a reasonably effective police officer to merit being promoted to deputy inspector, but I'm sure that being the son of the chief of police didn't harm either.

"These people are succeeding in training and then placing their sympathisers in powerful positions in the West—and globally," I told him. "We believe there's a sophisticated espionage and spy network already in place.

"The worst of it is that we don't know the worst of it," I added, still wondering if Antonio fully understood what he was being told.

"Okay, third and final question," said Antonio. "Why is GEO so willing to cooperate on this case with us?"

I sat back and laughed. "On this case, I suppose you could say we are not sure who we can trust within the Civil Guard. The Mossos is the lesser of two evils."

"At least you're honest," said Antonio without emotion.

"My turn," I said.

"I go back to my earlier question. What do you recommend we do next?" I asked him.

Antonio nodded. "An hour ago, my partner met with the deceased officer's family. His parents are in shock. He comes from a nice home up in Gracia. No one can understand why he was shot. He was a top graduate at school, an athlete and a tennis star. You can never tell with these things, but it supports what you said earlier. Xavi's conclusion is that David Casals seems an unlikely candidate to be an al-Qaeda mule.

"From what you've told me about the security leak at a senior level within the Civil Guard," he continued, "I think we need to pay a visit to Ceuta—and talk to them. Someone must know something. Let's stir things up a bit."

"Not bad," I said. "I like the plan."

As I got up from his desk, my mind was clear. I thought to myself, now let's see if Antonio can perform as well as he talks.

I took a cab back to the National Police hostel. The first thing I did was to carry out a sweep of my room. I'm not paranoid, but I've survived this long by assuming the worst in people—including my own. I would have been surprised if my room had been bugged, and my search revealed nothing.

Looking at my watch, I sat down with my laptop and keyed in a quick report, encrypted and emailed it to Raphael Robles.

Changing into shorts and t-shirt, I went downstairs to the police gym. For an hour, I followed my workout routine. Robles had observed it a few months earlier. He said it would trigger a physical collapse even among the fittest athletes. I liked that comment. So I gave it an extra ten minutes.

I showered, cooled down and went back to my room. There wasn't a lot of space to move around.

I sat at the narrow desk and called Raphael Robles at home in Madrid.

"I hear that you've impressed the Catalans," he said with a chuckle.

"They want to help, but they're surprisingly amateurish," I replied.

I put my bare feet on the bed, my toes playing with the airline's baggage tag on my travel bag.

"You'll find they're a sensitive bunch," continued my boss, "but I suppose you know that?"

I smiled. "I've found that out already. It may be a challenge, but leave it to me, sir. You will have received my emailed report by now. I'll call you tomorrow with an update."

I made the next call, to my wife, even shorter. I love my wife and my children, and the less I expose them to my work the better. A brief phone call was enough. Protecting them is always uppermost in my mind. You never can be certain who's listening in.

Moroccan Connection

Had Diego examined his travel bag more closely, he would have found a well-hidden powerful micro-transmitter that had not been there when he arrived in Barcelona.

In a small room in the Mossos' headquarters, both his phone conversations were duly monitored and transcribed. In compliance with the police transcriber's instructions, the transcripts were emailed without delay to the chief and Antonio.

Quietly, with minimum fuss, the transcriber made a separate copy. This, he placed in his briefcase.

Later, as part of his normal routine, he would drop off the disk, and several others he had duplicated that day, at a dead letter box located on his way home.

His enterprise, he reflected, helped to pay for the apartment of the young Moroccan girl whose exotic charms he inadvertently had neglected to mention to his wife.

Isabel and Julia

"Look at who's dropped in to see us," exclaimed Isabel, as her brother walked into the room. He waved a wrapped bouquet of flowers vaguely in the air.

"I found him on the doorstep," said her partner with a laugh, accepting the flowers. She sniffed at them appreciatively.

Antonio leaned over the sofa on which his sister was stretched, painting her toenails. "Hi sis," he smiled, giving her a warm hug and planting a brief kiss on her neck. "How's business?"

"The usual," she replied with a scowl. It had become a regular exchange of greeting between them.

"Coffee, Toni?" asked her partner, placing her hand on Antonio's shoulder.

"Thanks, Julia."

Toni pulled up a chair and sat alongside his sister.

"Mama and Papa have been asking about you," he announced, repeating another regular exchange.

She shrugged. "I doubt that *he* has."

Antonio knew better than to try defending his blatant lie.

"Obviously, they haven't forgiven me yet. So I should leave it for a while." She pulled her foot close to her face, examining her nails closely. "They're a different generation. They don't understand."

"How's Melissa?" asked Antonio, switching the subject as Julia handed him an espresso.

"Recovering," said Isabel. "She was beaten up badly."

"Are you guys any closer to making an arrest?" asked Julia, sitting down at the table playing idly with her phone.

"She looked at lots of mug shots from the gallery. Nothing yet," said Antonio.

"Sadistic sod," said Isabel, adding for clarification "the guy who did it."

"They think they're above the law, those rich guys," said Julia looking up.

"Most of them are okay," Isabel responded, adding some more crimson lacquer to a big toe. "The money pays the rent, and then some."

Julia stared at them. She started to say something, but then changed her mind. She went back to studying her phone.

"It's dangerous work," she said after a few moments. "I don't like Isabel doing it."

"We've talked it through before." Isabel sounded angry.

"I'm just saying," replied Julia, studying her phone again.

"Coffee's great," Antonio intervened. "But it wouldn't harm if you mended the bridges with our parents."

"What?" protested Isabel loudly. "Is it '*Have a Go at Isabel Day*' or something?

"The economy is in the shits," she continued, now on her favourite rant. "Through no fault of mine, I lose my nice secure job as a teacher. I nearly lose my apartment through foreclosure. So I turn to using the other talents I have. If you guys have a problem with that, blame the damned politicians who got us into this mess."

"Blame the greedy pig bankers," spat Julia getting up and storming into the kitchen. She returned a few minutes later with the flowers, stems cut and arranged in a clear glass vase. "What do you think, honey?" she asked proudly.

"They're lovely," pronounced Isabel, still studying her toenails.

"You could have looked at them at least," her partner scowled. Noisily, she stomped back into the kitchen and slammed the door.

"We wanted to give you the money to bridge you over," said Antonio quietly to his sister. "That's what upsets Mama and Papa."

Isabel gave out a loud sigh.

She swung her legs off the sofa, placing her heels on the coolness of the tiled floor. She put both hands on Antonio's shoulders and planted a wet kiss on his lips. "Toni," she said gently, "think of it as social work. I look after some old men who have money. I make them feel better about their lives. Besides, most of them are as gentle as kittens."

Antonio ignored the thought that came into his head. The guy who had beaten up Melissa certainly had not been a gentle kitten, he wanted to say. But getting into an argument with his sister would do nothing to help change her mind.

"All women do it," she continued. "It's just that I do it for money. At least I'm up front about it."

"I worry about you, sis," he said, taking her hand in his. "All I ask is that you are careful."

She kissed him again and he pulled back sharply away from the too close contact. "At least you don't give me the lectures about morals, the way Papa does," said Isabel gratefully. But she sounded sad.

"He's a different generation. It's hard for him—and for Mama," began Antonio.

"To admit that I'm a prostitute, you mean," she said a little bit too loudly.

"You're not really a…"

"Okay, I'm a courtesan, if you prefer a fancy label on it. It's all the same thing, isn't it."

"I've talked to Mama, and she understands. For her, she just wants to have her daughter back," said Antonio, seeing an opening to say what he'd come to say.

"You see!" exploded Isabel. "It's not understanding that I want from them. I understand the bible. That doesn't mean to say I believe in it. I don't want peoples' understanding and sympathy."

"What *do* you want?" asked Julia explosively, as she re-emerged from the kitchen looking ready for a fight.

"I don't need understanding, for sure. I need clients." Isabel shot back.

"I'm sorry," she conceded, aware of her partner's impending meltdown.

"You know me better than anyone, Julia," she added, her throaty voice sounding seductive. "I want people to accept me—for what I am. Not for what they want me to be," Isabel said, turning to face her.

"I accept you—as you are," said Julia quietly.

"Yes, you do. That's why we are together. That's why I love you." She blew her a kiss.

Julia's face brightened considerably.

Antonio figured he didn't need to be there any longer, and glanced at his watch for the third time in thirty seconds.

"I know," said Isabel, voicing it for him. "You'd better get going."

Antonio nodded. Although she was younger than he—by three years—it seemed to him that Isabel had always been in charge, as far back as he could remember.

"Thanks for the flowers, brother," she smiled at him. Gone from her face were the scowl and the attitude. They were replaced by the dancing brightness of her wide green Catalan eyes—almost a mirror image of his. For a moment, he saw the vulnerable little girl that she rarely allowed anyone to see.

"Now piss off, and let me get ready for work." she said with a laugh. At the same instant, she reached up with her arm and wrestled him down towards her, planting another full-frontal kiss on his lips. He pulled away awkwardly, and she laughed out loud.

"Can't take it, can you, Toni?" she challenged, as she finally released his neck from her strong grip.

Fifteen minutes later, she lit up a cigarette. Julia lay naked alongside her, looking at the ceiling. "You called me Toni again," she chastised.

"Get used to it, honey," said Isabel, punching a pillow back into shape. "You don't think I'm the only one who has fantasies, do you?"

William

At the Mossos' headquarters, a Chinese man in his early twenties sat in front of several monitors and a nest of computers stacked high to the fluorescent-lit ceiling. William Chang was an illegal immigrant. A student in Barcelona, he overstayed the period of time permitted on his visa. That was not an unusual occurrence but, unlike most who had fallen astray in the same manner, he had been unlucky.

He was caught in a Mossos sweep of an overly noisy penthouse party, and found in possession of cocaine. Far too much to be regarded as an innocent small time using tourist, the arresting officers had said.

His hacking talents had caught the attention of Antonio, who became even more intrigued when he discovered William's background. After a few meetings in the interview room, and three days in jail, William was recruited as an unofficial civilian member of the Mossos team monitoring cyber-terrorism.

In return, he was issued a European passport with a Spanish identity. He had no wish to return to China—especially because he had defected from the army. He had been a member of the Beijing's *Cyber Blue* elite hackers.

William's change of identity and this new arrangement, working anonymously for the Mossos, suited him perfectly.

"Hey boss," he said as Antonio entered the room. "What's up?"

"How are your contacts in Morocco?" asked Antonio, sitting down in the narrow space beside the youthful hacker and his towers of electronic equipment. He watched as William's fingers danced, like crab legs at rapid speed across two separate keyboards.

"Kung Fu is a reliable friend," said William, not even hesitating his pace. "We can trust him."

"I'm going to Ceuta," said Antonio. "I'm meeting with the Civil Guard. Can you and your friend monitor the traffic out of there?"

"You give us some filters, boss. What are we looking for?"

"I'm not sure. What I'd really like to find is a connection between the Civil Guard in Ceuta and somebody in Barcelona. Problem is, I don't know who. What I'm hoping to find is a connection that will help us identify the killer of the Civil Guard officer near the Sagrada Familia."

William stopped what he was doing. He pointed to a laptop on a side desk. "That's his."

Antonio looked surprised. "How did you get it? I thought that Xavi had taken it over to the lab for analysis."

"He did. They've finished with it for now. I asked them if I could take a look."

Antonio thought about this for a moment. William was an unofficial appendage to his department. The lab was the official group monitoring and reporting on cyber-terrorism.

Even so, it had not been difficult for Antonio to sell the chief on the advantages of having William's talents at their disposal. He wasn't officially on the books, and he was paid in a combination of ways.

"What did you do to deserve that? Are you dating one of their girls or something?" he asked.

William grinned. "Just did a few favours. You know how it is, boss. Live and let live."

"I guess I don't want to know what those favours were, do I? Anyway, what did you find on his laptop?"

"I got a copy of the report by the lab techs. They did a good job."

"But?"

"I searched the metadata files. They're a favourite hiding place. I got lucky and found a few additional things," said William modestly.

"I've uploaded them here," he added, pointing to the nearest of the two active monitors on his desk. "Plus, I did some checks on his Internet searches. Also, to be quite honest boss, I hacked into his server—and his parents' phone records."

"Holy shit, William. Can anyone trace this stuff back to us?"

"No, it's really safe. I went in through the CIA office here in Barcelona. I used a zombie computer I have set aside for the purpose. It can't be traced to us, don't worry. Besides, we're the white hats, aren't we?"

"I'd better not ask where the zombie is located."

"No, but if I told you it was the American ambassador's residence—his daughter's university laptop, actually—you shouldn't be surprised."

Antonio burst out laughing. "William, I don't know whether I'm going to regret the day I brought you in here or not."

"No regrets so far, boss," William grinned. "Besides, you need me. The bad guys are still winning—by a wide margin."

"What did you find?"

"A few things of interest," replied William. "Most importantly, he was in contact with several people in Ceuta, which I had to look up. Never heard of the place before. One of his contacts also is with the Civil Guard. But he has connections with people who have links with others we have on record. And they have al-Qaeda connections, according to the Americans."

"Who is the Civil Guard connection?" asked Antonio.

"A senior officer at the Civil Guard garrison. Here he is." William displayed a photograph and brief profile of the officer.

"Anything else, maestro?"

"The deceased officer had a girlfriend. Strangely, I can't find much about her. What is interesting is their relationship."

"In what way?"

"Well, months ago, it was just the usual stuff. Boy-girl conversations. Quite a lot of intimate stuff. Then, suddenly, he stopped sending emails and texts to her. He switched to phone calls. None of the security services had a phreak tap on his phone at the time, so we don't know what they talked about.

"The only emails he sent after that were almost always formal. That tells me something changed. Problem is, boss, I don't know what."

"Have you told anyone in the lab about this?"

"Not yet, boss. Not until I've reported it to you."

"Hold on to it for now, until I have a chance to check things out in Ceuta."

William nodded. He liked his lifestyle in Barcelona. He was aware that he had a thin lifeline and depended on Antonio for it to continue. He wasn't about to screw that up.

"Okay, let me tell you what I'll be looking for in Ceuta," said Antonio. "Maybe you and your friend can help me."

For the next five minutes, Antonio identified keywords that would narrow the search and trigger alerts on the system that William had set up.

"What's our site going to be, boss?" he asked.

"Let's do the usual one," replied Antonio.

"This Kung Fu friend of yours is Chinese, right?" he asked, getting ready to leave.

"Yes. He speaks seven languages," said William, raising his pencil thin eyebrows in mock distaste. "Between the two of us, we can cover you 24/7 on almost any platform you'd be interested in."

Antonio patted William on the shoulder.

"Thanks, William, anything I can do for you?"

"Just keep the crack coming, boss. You know the score. Mossos against the bad guys."

"Let's see what the squaddies have picked up from tonight's haul on the streets," said Antonio. "I'll have some sent over to you."

Pilar & Maria Meet for Lunch

"This one?" the hostess asked, pointing to a small round table with a good view of Passeig de Gràcia and Gaudi's Casa Batlló. The girls grinned and nodded enthusiastically to each other.

"I can never get over the beauty of the Casa," said Maria, sitting down. She stowed her bag between herself and the table.

Pilar smiled and wedged herself with care into the other chair.

"You look great," said Pilar. "Things are going well with Toni?"

Their dialogue was interrupted by the waitress placing menus on the table.

"Well, *you* look fabulous." said Maria. "If I didn't know you keep yourself so healthy, I might say that you are pregnant again," she laughed.

"Oh, my God!" she exclaimed, as she saw the blush on her friend's face. "Are you?"

The brightness in Pilar's eyes betrayed her secret. "Ten weeks," she said quietly. "We had it confirmed just this morning. Xavi is over the moon."

"Oh Pilar, that's wonderful. Congratulations. How are you feeling?" Her words came pouring out. On instinct, she pushed her chair back and moved the table to give her friend more room.

"Thanks." Pilar flashed her friend a conspiratorial smile. "But I'm not showing just yet."

"I should have guessed. All the clues were there. Then at dinner the other night, I remember now, you weren't drinking."

"You're the first one we've told," Pilar confided, her eyes searching Maria's face.

"Your news is so wonderful! A summer baby? Do you want to know what it is?"

"We want you and Toni to be the godparents," Pilar blurted out, knowing that she and Xavi had not even discussed the subject. He would be totally fine with it, she knew. But she felt guilty, knowing she should have asked him first.

Maria was nodding her head vigorously.

Pilar was aware that Maria was smiling at her, waiting.

She leaned forward and grasped her friend's hand. "Sorry, I just phased out for a moment."

Maria smiled and squeezed Pilar's hand with both of hers. "It's okay. It's a big change."

"In a way, a shock. A beautiful surprise, yes, but still a shock."

Pilar was surprised to feel tears running down the side of her nose. "Sorry," she sobbed. "I guess we weren't anticipating it."

"Well, now, as her or his godmother, I am going to take charge of your diet—starting with today's lunch," announced Maria.

She picked up the menu with a flourish. "Wine is out—but you're there already. How about still water for both of us? Meat or fish or pasta?" she pondered aloud.

"Nothing too strong in taste. Let's wean her or him into the world of Catalan café cuisine gently," Maria continued, laughing at the same time.

"I've got it," she exclaimed, slamming the menu pages back together.

"I am so happy for you both," she said, leaning forward and squeezing Pilar's hands again. "May I tell Toni?"

Pilar gulped, but managed to nod her agreement. "Of course you can. We'll drop by my sister's place tonight and tell them, and Xavi will call his mum this afternoon. We're just glad that his dad got to see and enjoy our first two."

Their meals arrived.

"You didn't actually answer my question," said Pilar, raising an eyebrow. "About you and Toni, I mean."

Maria played with her fork for a moment. "We get along very well. You know that."

"But?" Pilar asked gently.

Maria shrugged her shoulders.

"The two of you seem to get along just fine. You're naturals together."

"We agree on that. Even Toni and I agree on that," said Maria, still toying with her food.

"Maybe I shouldn't tell you this," Pilar confided, "but Xavi says that Toni is always saying his parents are pressuring him to ask you to go over with him and visit them."

"Well, he seems to be doing a good job of ignoring them," said Maria with a brave smile.

"They like you."

"Yes, I know they do. But I want Toni to want me to visit with them—not just take me because he's under pressure from them."

"He really adores you, you know. It's easy to see."

Maria laughed. "I'm a top-notch defence lawyer. I can find holes in a prosecution's defence without even working at it. But I can't figure out why Toni doesn't want to… well, you know!"

"Commit?"

Maria nodded. "I sometimes think it's my fault. You know… I was married before and it didn't work out. It affects some men."

Pilar leaned over and squeezed her friend's hand. "I don't know what is stopping Toni. One thing I am sure of is that it's not your fault. You've been fantastic for him. He's a much better person when you are around."

Maria lowered her voice. "Maybe I should just pretend I'm pregnant, and see how he reacts."

Both girls burst into laughter. "It's been done before many times... and it nearly always works," Pilar giggled.

Maria shook her head. "No, it's a fun thought. But you and I know that you can't have a lasting relationship that's based on dishonesty."

"You could make a mistake?" prompted Pilar, only half joking.

"I already made one of those by marrying Sergio. Actually, to be really honest, I'd like to have the kind of relationship that you and Xavi have."

Pilar squeezed her friend's hand again.

"You will have, sweetheart. You will have."

After they finished their meal, Maria paid the bill. She said goodbye to Pilar and hailed a taxi.

Her lunch with Pilar had been wonderful in so many ways—but unsettling. She was happy with her friend's great news, and happy that her friend cared about her. Yet, there was something that left her annoyed. She had allowed herself to be lulled into an intimate conversation about herself and Toni.

Her phone rang.

"Hi, it's me," said a voice she recognised instantly.

"Hi," she responded, her voice subdued.

"Sorry, catching you at a bad time?"

"No, it's fine," she responded, aware that she almost always slipped into defensive mode when her ex-husband called her. Her heart sank. It was not a feeling that she enjoyed or wanted to prolong.

"I've been following your recent successes," he said. The admiration in his voice was genuine.

When Maria said nothing, his energised voice continued. "That last case you did—you know, the Pappas case—made everyone sit up and take note."

"The judge was generous. I got lucky," she responded, her brain searching for the real reason he was calling. She really didn't feel like talking to him. After Pilar's news, she was already feeling down.

"Matter of fact," he continued, "our senior partner was very impressed. He *would* like to meet you."

"Sergio, look, this is not a good time. I'm in the middle of things. Maybe some other time?"

"No, Maria. This is not a *you-me* thing. Honestly it's not. I know we're over. It's purely professional. The senior partner is very impressed. He would like to meet you."

Maria smiled. One characteristic about Sergio was that he could never stop selling. In spite of her low spirits, she smiled. Her ex never changed. He was so predictable.

"I really appreciate it," she heard herself saying. "But this *really* is not a good time."

"Okay, babe, I hear you. But don't think we are going to give up. Ramos Sanchez is the top billing firm nationally. We want you. Not just in the courtroom—you'd be on the advisory board."

Maria digested this information for a few seconds. Wow, that really would be something, she thought.

Instead, she heard herself say: "Sergio, I do appreciate it. Really, I do. But it's the wrong time."

"Okay, babe. I hear you. But I'm under strict orders not to give up. Anyway, how are you?"

"Actually, just great—thank you."

"Has he asked you to marry him yet?" he asked, in a mocking tone.

"Bye," she said quickly, and stabbed the end-call button on her phone. "God dammit," she said, as she slumped into the back of the taxi. Now she felt really desolate.

Sergio always made her feel incredibly fantastic—or like shit. "Fuck them," she said loudly.

"Señora?" asked the taxi driver, frowning in his rear-view mirror.

Chapter 3

Madrid: The Condesa

Earlier that day, in a fourth-floor apartment in the Huertas neighbourhood, an attractive woman in her late forties gazed in the mirror as she buttoned up her imported silk blouse. The reflection in the mirror revealed the naked body of a man, possibly in his early thirties, climbing out of the dishevelled bed they had just shared.

She paused for a moment to admire his manhood. Many times, during the past few months, she had reflected that she'd chosen well. He was a magnificent specimen—muscled and well-contoured. Just what she needed. He came well recommended and, so far, had met her all her expectations.

In that respect, however, she admitted that her expectations of him did not extend much beyond the bedroom.

"I'll be away next week," she called over her shoulder, picking up a brush and examining her closely cropped blonde highlights. She squinted critically at her make-up.

The condesa's cut was a new style for her. She was still getting used to it. Turning her head from side to side, she decided she agreed with the majority opinion of her girlfriends at the club.

Shorter hair did make her look younger. It gave her a boyish look, and added a hint of sexual aggressiveness. She was aware that it caught the particular attention of some of her lesbian friends. She liked that.

Even her husband had approved of the new style—not that his opinion would ever be critical of her, she knew.

Carlos had been a good provider when she had needed him early in their marriage. Now she had her own momentum as a minister of the government.

It was widely acknowledged that Condesa Teresa Alvarez Blanco de la Santa Maria was a rising star in the administration. In the most recent election she had expanded her constituency vote—at a time when several colleagues had lost their seats to opposition candidates.

Of course, it didn't hurt her rapid rise among the Madrid power brokers that Carlos' noble family name still carried considerable cachet throughout Spain and among the established families of Europe.

Her male companion was drying off his thick hair with a towel. He came up behind her and cupped his hands around her breasts. He planted a lingering kiss on her elegant neck—which, it seemed to him, stretched forever upwards like that of a disdainful swan. He could not resist running his fingers up through the nape and over the top of her head. She pushed him away.

"Don't," she scolded with a giggle, quickly checking herself again in the mirror.

Looking at him, she felt a pang of jealousy. Really, she wanted him for herself. She didn't want to share him, even if he was discreet about his liaisons. Sometimes, in her office, she just sat and thought about his body and their times in bed together. A few times, she had worried about the risks she was taking. But wasn't that part of the adventure, she wondered.

Flirting, having an affair, was part of staying young. For the condesa, it wasn't a moral issue. It was a basic need. Every day, her still youthful energy propelled her forwards. Just a few years ago, fashion magazines had heralded her as one of the new generation of liberated Spanish women. That was then. Now she was getting older—little by little, and relentlessly.

She needed the physical reassurance that she still had it. Having a presentable figure was important. Being admired was vital. Like all women, she knew there was nothing more powerful and fulfilling for a woman's self-esteem than her ability to arouse the male—inflame him into a frenzied passion and exert total control over every muscle in his body. Or a female.

Actually, she was rather good at that, she admitted.

She turned around and gently pushed her companion backwards. Then she caught his brown chest hairs in her hand and pulled him back towards her. Her face now was centimetres from his. Gritting her teeth, she slid her fingers over his chest and squeezed him hard.

"Ow," he protested loudly, pulling away.

Again she pulled him close to her, and whispered in his ear. "Just remember, Pavel—be careful who you fuck while I'm away."

Suitably aroused, he put his hands on her blouse and began to undo the buttons.

She pushed him away. "Not now. I have to go."

At the front door of the apartment building, the old man who held tenaciously onto his poorly paid job as day-time concierge struggled out of his chair, his arthritic back bent and inflexible, as he shuffled towards the elevator door.

"Condesa," he acknowledged, bending stiffly into a polite bow. She smiled at him in recognition.

Glancing at the Roger Dubuis watch that swung loosely around her slender wrist, an anniversary gift last year from Carlos, she knew it would take her less than five minutes to get to the Cortes. She looked up the street for a taxi.

"Teresa," she heard a woman's voice behind her.

"Eva! How very nice to see you." The two women exchanged polite kisses.

Damn it, thought the condesa. She wished she had taken a few more minutes inside the apartment to fix her hair and make-up.

"You look radiant," said her friend. "Everything must be going well, I assume?"

"Well, with this economy, who knows where we all will end up. It's devastating," the condesa replied, speaking to her friend in a lowered voice.

"Not that we're all quite destitute just yet, are we?" She gave her friend's arm a squeeze. "Tell me, how are your children? Miguel must be around fourteen, and Concepcion? I think I saw that she had won a scholarship, am I right?"

Her friend's face lit with pleasure.

For a fraction of a second, the exchange reminded the condesa why she loved her job as an elected official. Within seconds, she had been able to manipulate the situation. She had been able to divert her friend's attention away from potentially embarrassing questions about herself.

It was one of the gifts she had, of being able to recall names and small personal details, which won people over to her.

Eva threw her head back. "Concepcion works very hard at school…"

"Just like her mother," interrupted the condesa. "And she is destined to become almost as beautiful."

From the corner of her eye, she saw Pavel leave the apartment building. He sat on his moto parked on the sidewalk and searched for his ignition key. She made a mental note to reprimand him at their next liaison.

The arrangement she had insisted upon, and he assured her that he always followed, was that they'd always leave separately. He would wait for thirty minutes after she left and take the staircase down to the street, avoiding the eyes of the concierge. The thought flashed across her mind that, if she couldn't trust him with that, how could he be trusted in other ways?

As soon as she had an opportunity she interrupted her friend, making a show of looking at her watch. "Eva, I simply must get back to the Cortes. Let's get together again soon. Love to family," she added, and kissed her goodbye.

Ignoring the admiring glance of the driver as she settled into the back seat of her taxi, the condesa speed-dialled her secretary.

There was an instant pick up from the young girl. "Si, señora?"

"Zoe, I will be back in the office in a few minutes. Ask Alexander to meet me there."

Shortly after, the condesa swept into her office.

With a curt nod to the young girl who jumped up as she entered, the condesa asked, "Alexander?"

"Yes, señora. He is already waiting in your office." The young girl ran after her employer. "Is there anything I can get for the señora?"

"I'm dehydrated for some reason," said the condesa. Subconsciously, she ran her fingers through her hair. "Perhaps water."

"Alexander," she announced loudly, as she pushed open the solid wood door to her office.

Her parliamentary secretary jumped to his feet. "Condesa," he smiled, displaying a wonderful set of brilliant white capped teeth. His thick jet black hair was swept straight back. It highlighted his deep brown eyes and slim build.

He looked very much the gentleman polo player that he was—when not administering to his boss's parliamentary business.

The condesa looked at him. "I like that blazer on you," she said, sweeping past him to sit at her desk. "It goes well with those grey trousers and your open-neck shirt."

"Thank you, Condesa," he smiled. "And if I might be permitted to say so, you look wonderful today."

"Alexander, that's crap and you know it," she shot back. "You know very well how I spent my lunchtime today, don't you? I can't keep any secrets from you. You spy on me far too well."

"Condesa," he started to protest, but she waved him off with her hand.

"Just remember, Alexander, that I make a wonderful friend and employer." She wagged her index finger at him. "But…"

"Condesa, I fully understand…" he continued to protest. She cut him off again.

"How is that boyfriend of yours, anyway?" she asked, looking up from the desk. "Is he of legal age yet?"

"To vote, I mean, of course," she winked at him.

For an instant, Alexander seemed to blush.

Whatever went through his mind for those few seconds was soon replaced by a less defensive thought—which, to his relief, succeeded in dispatching his momentary facial display of embarrassment.

Perhaps it was his resentment at her reference to his prepubescent preferences. Certainly, it was not the first time they'd had this particular conversation.

Some time ago he had confided to a friend that it was all part of the condesa's command and control defence. She was a wonderful lady really, Alexander had whispered to him.

She means no harm, especially to me, he had explained. It's just her way of maintaining power in a tough macho male-dominated political setting. And we all know how difficult that is, don't we just?

Alexander let the awkward moment with his employer pass. Then, gently, he placed several files on the leather-bound desk mat in front of her. "These are urgent, Condesa.

"Particularly the blue sheets," he added, biting his bottom lip and indicating the drafts of parliamentary speeches from the previous day. "As you know, we have until this evening to make corrections before they become official."

The condesa sat back in her chair, and examined his face. "I'm going to stay with what I said," she ventured, holding up her hands in protest. "What corrections are you proposing?"

"Without actually changing anything you said in the Congreso, dear Condesa, we could insert this word in place of that one," he said, dabbing at the offending sentence with his baby finger.

"Is the man that sensitive?" she protested, referring to an opposition member whose question in debates the previous day quite clearly had been designed to embarrass her.

She had responded to him rapidly—cutting him down to size, even if her words had been somewhat harsh.

"Next month, we face a vote on the roads and highways budget," Alexander continued. "And it's an uphill battle," he observed, indulging himself in an impromptu pun. It flashed through his mind that his friends would have enjoyed the word play, even if the condesa invariably was unappreciative of his wit.

"He is chairperson of the committee. It would be nice to have him on our side, Condesa."

"Alexander, you'll be the death of me," she shook her head. "Okay, submit the revision and see if they will accept it. Maybe they will, and he won't."

"Thank you, Condesa," he nodded. "And perhaps a personal call from you to him—just to smooth out any ruffled feathers... An investment in future cooperation, you know."

She looked at him sternly and raised her eyebrows. "An apology?"

"Absolutely not, Condesa." Alexander made a wonderful pretence of looking horrified. "Just one of your wonderful and diplomatic personal calls. To ask if, perhaps in the heat of the debate, things may have been implied that were not intended and so on…"

She nodded with a shrug. "I'll do it if you insist."

Alexander leaned in front of her and slowly withdrew the file from her view. Then he positioned the next folder exactly parallel to the edge of her desk pad before standing back. Her reaction was what he had anticipated.

"Not this one, again," she said.

"It's become more urgent, Condesa—with the police investigation. They are asking for answers to the questions they have submitted to us in writing. More concerning for us, they have now set a time limit."

There was a knock on the door, and the girl entered carrying a tray of two glasses and a bottle of chilled water.

"Thanks Zoe, just leave it there."

The condesa watched the girl to make sure that the door been closed behind her. "Has Felipe seen this latest?"

"I took it over to his law office personally this morning, Condesa. He doesn't want to risk anything by talking on the phone, of course. He'll arrange to meet with you discreetly. He asked me to stress to you two things. Most importantly, do not go past the timeline for submitting your answers. Almost equally vital, you will have to release the construction company documents the police are requesting."

"Why are they still chasing after this?" she asked. "Isn't there a statute of limitations?"

"Regrettably, Condesa, not in cases involving issues of taxes and alleged tax fraud, I'm sorry."

Although he answered with a glum face, Alexander felt a measure of revenge for her earlier personal attack on him. The legal predicament facing the condesa was hers, and not of his doing. He had been careful, during Spain's housing and infrastructure spending boom, to avoid signing any of those particular documents. He could be subpoenaed, he realised.

But that was an entirely different matter from being a named beneficiary of fees paid by the winning contractor.

"Advice please?" she asked.

"Condesa, I would suggest you authorise Felipe to release the documents to the police without delay—and in entirety. He's already viewed them thoroughly and he advises that there is no benefit to waiting until the last minute. In fact, quite the reverse. We want to be seen to be cooperating with the police."

"And the answers to their questions?"

"Felipe said he would coach you personally on those."

"Best to meet him here," said the condesa. "At least we know that they are not going to take the risk of wiretapping us here in the Cortes."

Her parliamentary secretary smiled and wriggled his eyebrows. "One of the more fortunate outcomes of the Baltasar Garzón case, Condesa."

Three hours later the condesa's car entered the gated premises of her villa in Moraleja. She drove down the ramp to the garage underneath the house. Picking up her laptop and briefcase, she went to the elevator door and flashed her passkey across the security screen.

As the elevator ascended, the condesa could hear the unmistakeable sound of the piano. Carlos was playing one of his favourite Granados sentimental waltzes. As the elevator door opened, she saw that he was almost slumped over the piano, his wheelchair forcing him to play at an angle that most pianists would find constricting.

His back was to her and he did not seem to notice her enter. She waited until he had finished, then she applauded.

"Bravo, don Carlos. *The Oriental*'—that was magnificent."

She draped her arms around him, and kissed his ear. Then she noticed the tears that had wetted his cheeks. "Oh, Carlos, darling, whatever is the matter?" she asked with concern.

"It is just the music," he replied. "I'm just a sentimental old man. You know how Granados always brings back memories of the old days."

"Let me pour us a glass of wine." She swept into the kitchen and extracted the cork from a bottle selected from the rack, carefully sniffing the cork and contents. They sat close together and she reached forward to hold his hand.

"How was the office?" he asked, looking up at her.

"The police are still chasing everywhere—trying to make corruption charges stick to someone."

His face hardened, and she could see in him the old campaigner from a bygone era. "This kind of insolence would never have been tolerated," he growled, withdrawing his hand and using it to grip the arm of his wheelchair.

"We live in a democracy nowadays, my dear," she responded gently. "The authorities—and the people—have all kinds of rights."

"That doesn't make it correct," he protested.

"Not when they are attempting to take good people down. Heavens, they are even trying to besmirch the good name of our royal family.

"I really have to question why we even bother with this political experimentation—democracy and the European Community.

"Look at where it's taken us," he added forcefully.

After a pause, he said, "Fernando visited today. Unlike me, he has no trouble getting around. Not bad for an old soldier. He still has all his advisors around him: myself, our army friends, the former commissioner at the National Police and his banking friends.

"These days, policing is all about illegal immigrants, drug smugglers and terrorists," he added. "That's who they should be chasing. Not loyal servants of the government doing their best to carry out their duties."

"You and your old cronies, Carlos," she laughed, and kissed him again. "If you could have your way, you'd take Spain back to the days of the conquistadores and the Inquisition."

"Spain may have lost her way, rather late in my lifetime, my dear," he replied, in a voice that sounded suddenly much more youthful and determined than the condesa had heard for some time. "There are some of us who feel that the old days may not have been a bad thing for our country."

"That's why I don't take you on the campaign trail with me, Carlos, darling," she laughed again.

He held out his crystal glass as she replenished his wine.

"I don't begrudge what you are doing. Not by any means, my dear. At least, you are part of a government that is trying to do something. But you have your hands tied. Spain's national decisions are being made in Brussels and Frankfurt. The Basques and the Catalans are determined to separate. It's utter madness."

"What are you and Fernando plotting to do about it?" she asked, this time with a note of mock-seriousness. "It's hard to turn back the democratic clock."

He smiled at her. Then, placing his empty glass on a side table, he wheeled his chair back over to his piano. "We have done so before, when the democratic experiment clearly did not work for Spain. In fact, we did it several times—and quite successfully, I might say."

The Conscience

Francisco Rioja took pride in being from the 'old school'. He believed in good old-fashioned investigative journalism—which almost certainly was why he'd lost his full-time salaried job with a national newspaper.

A few years earlier the publication had come under new ownership. The new people were social-networkers. They immediately relegated what he considered the real news to the inside pages, or didn't include it at all.

"Social networking is the way of the future," he had heard the new managing director declare. "People want to tweet and blog their opinions."

Francisco had stayed silent. He wanted to tell the twee bastard that, in his opinion, the world would be better off if most people were silenced at birth. There was far too much personal opinion for it to be healthy.

He had chosen not to stay. In turn, they were glad to see the back of him.

"He's a prickly individual to deal with," his supervisor had told the new management. "A good writer, but a loose cannon. Not a team player."

There were wide smiles around the office when the announcement was made of his immediate departure.

Now he worked freelance, selling stories to whichever editors would buy them. He offered none to his former employer.

In truth, he would admit that he was too much of a loner ever to have fitted into the mainstream media world. He frankly admitted to anyone who would listen that he didn't like people. Two wives had divorced him, and he had little in common with his only child—a now married daughter from his first marriage.

At his advancing age, support payments to his second wife had dwindled to virtually nothing. His sparse studio apartment reflected his desire for the bare necessities.

His only indulgence to himself was his collection of high quality cameras and lenses. They helped generate enough income for his needs, and fed his desire to expose the sins and hypocrisies of fat cat businessmen and corrupt politicians.

The more he could make them squirm with embarrassment, the better. If he could help put them in jail, he was even happier.

If, by chance, they decided to take the easy way out and end their own lives, he considered this to be simple justice. One had recently, when Francisco had exposed the man's nefarious deeds. Not nearly enough compensation for the wretched misery the man callously had wrought on ordinary hard-working people, thought Francisco.

He did not consider himself a vindictive man. Exposing their evil ways was a job that someone had to do, and it suited him to do it. He did it well, he felt.

Today, his green rental car was parked illegally at an expired parking meter in the upscale Huertas neighbourhood. He was keeping a keen eye out for two targets.

Following the trajectory of his camera lens, one eye was sharply focused on the door of an apartment building from which, minutes ago, the condesa had emerged. She had lingered on the street chatting to an acquaintance. She seemed distracted, thought Francisco.

Then a young man emerged whose face he recognised from previous occasions at this location. This was too much of a coincidence, his experience of surveillance told him.

On previous surveillances, he had taken numerous high-speed close-ups of both people, but he had not yet caught them together. Today, he had been able to take several frames where the condesa seemed to be looking over at the young man who was now about to ride away on his moto. Then she got into a taxi.

He noted that his secondary target, a meter maid, was moving along the street in his direction. Carefully, he stowed his camera with its 500 mm zoom lens. He started his engine and drove off. He followed the condesa's taxi for several blocks, but saw that she would be returning to her office at the

Cortes—just as she had last week when she had made the same lunchtime rendezvous.

He looked at his watch. If he returned the rental car now, he could remain within the twelve-hour special rate limit offered in the offseason by the rental companies. After dropping off the vehicle, he could catch the Metro to the Cortes and continue on foot with his surveillance. Nevertheless, he considered, it might be prudent to have a car on standby, just in case it was needed.

He placed a reservation for later that day on the lowest price vehicle available. He declined any insurance. It was a rip-off, he considered. Exposing rental companies' insurance scams had been one of the more enjoyable highlights of an article he'd authored some months ago, for a left-wing magazine.

On the way to the Cortes he still had enough time to stop off at a fast-food place for his favourite dish. It was an imported hot spicy noodle, of which he had become increasingly fond—and the price was right, he reflected.

Chapter 4

North Africa: Ceuta Civil Guard Garrison

It was hard not to be impressed.

I'd already felt much better after we left Barcelona. Getting out of the police territory controlled by the Mossos lifted my spirits. At last I felt in control of the case, exuberant that I could focus on what Raphael Robles had detailed me to investigate. Now, looking down from the helicopter transporting Antonio and me to Ceuta, it was fascinating to see how close the continents of Europe and Africa are to each other.

At one time, Africa was connected to Europe by dry land. Scientists speculate that, around five million years ago, tectonic movements caused the land bridge to subside—on several occasions. The Mediterranean Sea was formed by a sudden inflow of seawater from the Atlantic Ocean.

They tell us that the initial breach built into a massive flood.

Powerful surges of seawater and rock scoured a deep channel yet only a few kilometres wide. It would become the Strait of Gibraltar. Directly opposite from Gibraltar and Spain, the landmass which exists today is Morocco.

Just as the Moors once occupied Iberia and profoundly shaped Spain's politics and cultures, imperialist Spain later occupied Morocco. The tiny eighteen square kilometre landmass of Ceuta is one of Spain's few remaining territories in North Africa. It is claimed by both countries, but remains firmly controlled by Madrid. That made me feel good.

Our chartered helicopter from Malaga touched down at the Ceuta heliport in the mid-morning. Neither of us had visited the enclave before, so we retrieved our carry-on luggage from the hold of the aircraft and walked towards the terminal. The heat of the day was already intense.

By mutual arrangement with the local Civil Guard, there was no official welcoming party to meet us. We wanted to keep a low profile.

As we entered the heliport terminal building, I couldn't help putting myself in the position of a casual observer. Anyone seeing us at that moment might conclude that the taller of us, with blonde highlights in his flowing hair, designer shades, strolling with a relaxed swagger, might easily be a movie star or a sports celebrity.

I'm conscious that I'm the smaller of the two of us. I'm darker skinned, my business suit wasn't fitting me very well. Antonio and I didn't look like natural companions. With my muscled torso, anyone could be forgiven for thinking that I might be Antonio's hired bodyguard. Well, I was determined to put that image right.

What we didn't know was that, observing our arrival from the shelter of the second floor of the terminal building, a middle-aged man in a short-sleeved shirt had been waiting and duly reported our arrival by cell phone to his controller.

Exiting the terminal, we caught a taxi to the National Police building on Paseo de Colon.

Tourist brochures describe downtown Ceuta as an attractive old Spanish city. Away from the tourist-focused central area, I can tell you that it transitions quickly to a North African identity. It's a border town, and people on the two sides of the high-security, constantly guarded and heavily fortified double-wire fence live in stark contrast. As an immigrant from Morocco, I had mixed feelings about how Moroccans at the border were treated by the Spanish authorities, but I wasn't going to let my emotions get in the way of my job here.

Just a few kilometres to the east of us, contingents of armed police and military forces patrolled the border separating the enclave from Morocco. Six months ago, more than a thousand illegal migrants had tried to scale the wall—some successfully. Twelve had been killed in the process.

The short taxi ride to the National Police headquarters was completed in silence, both of us lost in our own thoughts.

Ceuta: National Police Headquarters

I showed my pass to the security guard and motioned for Antonio to follow me.

The perplexed guard spent more time than he should have trying to determine where in Spain the Mossos d'Esquadra were located. I was amused. I didn't need to treat Antonio like a poor cousin; I'm sure he felt that way already.

A National Police colonel came out to greet us. "Have you visited Ceuta before?" he asked.

Antonio shook his head, feeling grateful for being included.

"There seem to be a lot of Civil Guard officers, even in the downtown area," he commented.

"They run the place, frankly," said the colonel. "I understand you two have an appointment over at their headquarters this afternoon?"

I was impressed by the bank of CCTV monitors mounted on the colonel's wall. "How far away is it?" I asked.

"About twenty minutes," replied the colonel, walking over to a wall map and tapping it with his finger. "They're very close to the border. That's the focus of everyday life in Ceuta. All of us are aware of the frontier. It's just a question of when there are going to be attempts to breach it again.

"I realise you're dealing with a confidential case," he continued, looking directly at me. "If you can explain what you need, I'd be pleased to help—as much as I can."

I looked at him and took an immediate liking to the man. Clearly, he was at ease with himself. He was a middle-aged long-term service officer. Nothing much would faze him, I would guess.

Antonio seemed content to let me do all the talking, so I gave the colonel a credible synopsis of the case so far. He listened attentively.

"You're here to see what you can find out from the Civil Guard? Good luck with that, by the way. They, and we, tend to keep our distance," he observed without emotion. "At the senior levels, we're polite. I can't always say the same for the boys on the ground." He raised his eyebrows, and picked up a file from his desk.

He waved the file at us. "Last weekend, some of ours and some of theirs got into a fight in a local café. That's what happens when you put testosterone-driven young men in a situation of potential conflict. You can't blame them, really. They're trained to fight. We create the situation, so no surprise when they go over the edge every so often.

"I just have to find a way to make sure these incidents don't appear on anyone's permanent record."

I enjoyed the colonel's explanation. To be honest, I've always relished a combat role.

"Boys will be boys," I grinned, with a knowing look at the colonel.

"We don't know who we will be meeting," said Antonio, who seemed anxious to steer me away from my unabashed attempt at comradery.

"Colonel, what can you tell us about al-Qaeda operations here?" he asked, and I gave him a frown.

The colonel sat leaned forward. "I don't know how far you've been briefed on that score. The Civil Guard tends to work very closely with the SVA customs people. We get dragged in when necessary.

"I can tell you one thing. Al-Qaeda is certainly becoming more active here. Up until recently, they've taken a non-aggressive approach—keeping a low profile, in a sense.

"Ceuta has always been a conduit into North Africa and vice versa. It's getting busier all the time."

Antonio was listening, anticipating that the colonel's statement would lead to more detailed and possibly valuable information. But I had already decided to cut right to the point.

"We think that if we can push the Civil Guard, and find out exactly what the murdered officer's assignment was, it may show there's an al-Qaeda connection," I said.

"But the vital question is, what kind of connection is it?" I added.

"I really don't know," answered the colonel. "That's something you will have to ask the Civil Guard.

"I can't speculate," he added. "However, it may be useful to your enquiries to know that, in the joint operation against al-Qaeda that we conducted last year, several Spanish nationals working here in Ceuta were arrested. They are still in custody. Not here in Ceuta, of course.

"Both the Civil Guard and we have interrogated them," he continued. "They were low level operatives. Al-Qaeda is effective in isolating its networks. They talked, but what we learned from them did not reveal much that was new to us."

"Has anyone else interrogated them?" I asked.

"If you're referring to our European allies, the answer is no," replied the colonel quickly, as if he had been anticipating the question. "And if you are asking about our friends, the Americans, I can assure you that our methods of intelligence gathering—and persuasion, if you wish to call it that—are just as effective as theirs."

"Is there much of an American intelligence presence here, sir?" asked Antonio, who received a raised eyebrow from the colonel.

"Gentlemen," he said in response, rising to his feet and pulling up the venetian blind on his office window. "Across the strait is Gibraltar. It's occupied by the British. This is a fact of life that, as Spaniards, we know very well. We don't like it—but, as I say, it is a fact of life for us."

He let go of the cord and allowed the metals blinds to drop, making a sharp rattle in the process.

"Wherever the British are, the Americans are there too, in their inside pocket, and vice versa. This, too, is a fact of life. We have to contend with it."

There was silence for a moment, as the colonel returned to his desk.

"Was there any American, or British, direct involvement in last year's operation?" asked Antonio, anxious to pursue his point.

The colonel kept his eyes fixed on the surface of his desk. Then he looked up at them. "Do you have any information that there *was* any American, or British, involvement?"

"Frankly, sir, we don't have any information at all on those you interrogated," said Antonio.

"But your question was more than… more than just a shot in the dark?" asked the colonel, examining him closely.

"We," began Antonio, "the Deputy Inspector and I," he added, aware that I was watching him with suspicion, "we had speculated that perhaps you had been able to turn one or more of those you interrogated. Perhaps putting them back into the field of operation."

"You have a cynical mind," responded the colonel with a wry smile. "In this case, your suspicions are well founded." He slid a file across the desk towards them. It was labelled high security.

"Michael O'Flaherty," he announced. "You can look at this. Then it goes back into my personal security files. He was one of those arrested in last year's sweep. He's CIA. I interrogated him personally. He's the most fearsome, wild-looking undercover operatives I've ever encountered. If he hadn't been authenticated by the Americans, I wouldn't have believed he was one of ours. Flaming red hair, bearded and unwashed—you'd have to go a long way to find a more authentic looking jihadi extremist. And he has a temper to go with it."

"Irish American?" I suggested. I had reached for the file and was staring at the operative's photograph.

"Wherever he comes from, he's straight from hell," said the colonel, "and I don't scare easily.

"We and the Civil Guard decided not to disclose in the official records that he was one of those arrested. The Americans wanted him back in the field quickly. So we agreed with the Civil Guard to smooth things over to look like he had escaped the sweep."

"So the Americans are still running him?" I asked, and received an affirmative nod from the colonel.

"Was he able to tell you anything useful about al-Qaeda operations here?" asked Antonio, again receiving a respectful glance from the colonel.

"Without compromising himself, he couldn't give us much." He glanced this time at me, then at Antonio.

"You can share the information with my colleague," I said flatly. "He has top level clearance."

The colonel seemed to consider his next words.

"One thing the American confided to me, and it's not on the record, is that he thinks there's a high-level double-agent working within the Civil Guard. Naturally, I expect you to keep that information to yourselves," he added.

It did not sound like a request.

Our drive to the border was quick. On the colonel's advice, we travelled in a heavily armoured National Police vehicle. It pulled inside the Civil Guard compound overlooking the border with Morocco. As we exited the vehicle, and walked inside the main building, it seemed to me that the heat had risen by about ten degrees. Despite the intense climate, heavily clad Civil Guard patrolmen and fully laden personnel vehicles seemed to be everywhere. It was the most active and tense border crossing I had ever experienced.

A muscled security officer checked our IDs before we went through the metal screener; then we were ushered into a waiting room. The facilities were impressively modern and well equipped. I had the feeling that it reflected the intimidating power of the Civil Guard at most of Spain's border points. They are more army than we are in the National Police, and they seem to have an aggressive attitude of superiority to go with it.

Opposite our waiting room, a door was ajar and I caught a glimpse of a CCTV control room. I'd guess it had over forty active monitors. The room was packed with young uniformed personnel. They seemed hardly older than teenagers, I thought. There was a buzz of excited activity to the place. I could almost feel what the colonel had meant when he had talked about the high level of testosterone among his troops.

After a few minutes, the door opened and an older man entered. His movements were slow and deliberate. Antonio glanced at the man's uniform; I think he was trying to determine his rank.

"Adjutant," I said from behind him, guessing the nature of his dilemma.

The old man bowed slightly in our direction. "If you would follow me, gentlemen," he asked, immediately walking back outside and proceeding to shuffle down the corridor.

I glanced at Antonio and shrugged my shoulders. We followed the old man, slowing our steps to match his diminished pace.

Our short journey took us to the end of the main building, where an elevator transported the three of us to a lower floor. Away from the glare of the sun and the fluorescent lights of the main floor, this area of the building seemed much cooler and quieter. More like an annex, it seemed to me.

The adjutant tapped gently and entered through an office door which bore a green metal sign identifying the occupant as Capitan Alfonse Primero. The room was dark, using mainly natural light. Heavy wood shutters covered one entire window, shutting out even the small amount of sunlight which reached down to this floor of the building.

The capitan was sitting behind his large wooden desk. He did not immediately look up when the adjutant knocked and ushered us into his office. The adjutant marched much more briskly than his normally slow, laboured pace and stood to attention on one side of the desk.

"Thank you for seeing us, Capitan," I said after several seconds, breaking the silence. Slowly he finished what he was doing and walked with deliberate steps around his desk. Although in his mid-sixties, he looked a lot older.

He returned our salutes, without enthusiasm.

"I understand that you were the deceased's commanding officer, sir?" I ventured.

"Yes, Deputy Inspector," he said without smiling. "But perhaps you could first enlighten me as to the precise purpose of your visit here to Ceuta?"

I explained the circumstances of the murder, leaving out large parts of what we already knew.

"Forgive me, but for what seems to be a very unfortunate—but regrettably commonplace—homicide, I am puzzled why the investigation requires a team of two such senior officers." He looked at both of us in turn. "A deputy inspector from GEO and another from the Mossos? Are there some other issues involved, perhaps?"

I nodded. "You're correct, Capitan." I paused and took a breath. "You will recall very clearly the incident last year when we at GEO worked with your team here to intercept a large smuggling ring linked to Moroccan jihadi extremists and al-Qaeda. They are now held in protective custody, of course."

"This is well known, Deputy Inspector. But, again forgive me, how does that relate to your visit here?"

As he spoke, the capitan moved closer towards us. Antonio told me later that he could smell musk perfume and stale tobacco. I noted that, in contrast to the standard issue blue Civil Guard uniforms, the capitan's was a well-worn sage green tropical uniform of the Spanish Legion. His sunken chest displayed the aging insignias of a distinguished army career. Alongside were more recent ones from his police service.

As he came closer, we saw more clearly the man's opaque yellow vacant eyes, like those of a lizard, and his sallow-skinned sunken face, the texture of dry parchment. His eyelids were surrounded by multiple folds of darkened skin. A thin pencil moustache covered his upper lip. A specimen from a bygone era, it seemed.

His bearing was predatory and, as he stood in front of us, I could tell that Antonio was experiencing a creepy level of discomfort at the close personal examination to which he was being subjected.

To Antonio's relief, I addressed the capitan to divert his unwanted attention.

"We believe that the deceased officer—Civil Guard first class David Casals—may have been involved in a similar activity." I said, "We would like your permission, sir, to speak to any close friends he had here in the force."

The capitan bristled, and seemed to grow higher by a centimetre—which might have been comical except for the obvious rage that now caused his face to flush a deep purple.

"You are suggesting that one of my officers committed treason?" he demanded.

"We are carrying out a homicide investigation, sir," I responded as politely as I could. "A crime has been committed and there are reasonable grounds for us to conclude, at this stage in our proceedings, that the officer was playing an active role."

"And what evidence do you have for this?" the capitan asked in the same demanding voice.

Quickly, I explained the circumstances but omitted any mention that the deceased officer's activities were under GEO surveillance.

"You have found the documents and backpack, of course?" he asked, looking up keenly at both of us. He seemed to be searching our faces for any clues as to the answer.

I admitted that we had not.

"Sit down, gentlemen," he said at last, as he walked back behind his desk.

The tension in the room seemed to subside a little. He spoke in older Spanish, with the strong Castilian accent of the monarchy. He nodded to his adjutant, who left the room and returned a few minutes later with a young uniformed cadet; the poor lad's hands shook as he served a glass of mint tea to each of us.

Drawing in his breath, the capitan looked at us and said, "You may think I am uncooperative. That is not my purpose. I would ask you to place yourself in my position, and ask yourselves if you would have a different response," he said rhetorically.

"Here at Ceuta, we are sitting—as they say—on a powder keg. Tens of thousands of migrants—some, the victims of oppression—along with many others from Africa and the

Middle East see this as a gateway into Europe. In addition, as you are well aware, we are an espionage point, in which the Government of Morocco is an inconsistent friend.

"They, and we, cooperate at certain levels and on some issues. On others, there is a regrettable lack of foresight—among our forces as well as theirs—about the magnitude of the threat that faces both our countries. I tell you this because it is important you know why I will tolerate your questioning of my men only under strict conditions.

"If you spend any time here, you will readily understand why. Only through strong and confident enforcement of the law—and here we are talking about a dangerous and volatile frontier—can we guarantee to Madrid that the borders will hold."

He stood up and turned away from us, his hands clasped together behind his back. He looked out of the narrow ledge window. He seemed to be studying the mountainous terrain surrounding the enclave.

"Any attempts at subversion of our forces are met with a steel hand," he said, swirling around and facing us. He punched a clenched fist into his open hand. To both of us, it seemed a theatrical move, probably created for our benefit.

"The morale of our forces must be maintained," he continued with a raised voice. "With respect, gentlemen, speculative forays into the activities of the deceased officer will serve no purpose and might well cause a weakening of our garrison's resolve."

"We have no such intention, sir," I said quickly. "Our focus is entirely on the deceased officer. Whatever you can tell us about him, we would be grateful."

The capitan suddenly seemed tired and sat down with an effort, even though his gaunt frame seemed to carry almost no weight. "I don't know what I can tell you that will be of any interest," he said, reading from a folder on his desk. From it, he recited various facts with which the two of us were already familiar. "He seems to have been a young, but promising, officer. It is an unfortunate tragedy, of course."

I glanced at Antonio, and said, "Was the officer on a special assignment, or other duties, sir?"

The capitan shook his head. "I would know about it, if he was."

"What about his friends, sir?" I probed, trying to keep my tone measured.

"He must have had some, I suppose," the capitan answered, and then suddenly coughed. It was a long hacking sound. We waited while he recovered.

"Would it be possible to speak to them, sir?" I asked, repeating my earlier request.

While we waited for an answer, he made a show of brushing off a speck of dust that had settled on his tunic.

"What purpose would that serve?" he asked after a delay, his eyes now seeming to withdraw even further into their ancient sockets.

"It could help our enquiries, sir. We may be able to bring closure to his family—which we would like to do as soon as we can," said Antonio.

"His duty was firstly to his country, not to make his parents feel better," the capitan bristled.

"Even so, sir," I persisted. "We would appreciate the chance to talk to his fellow officers and friends."

He walked up and faced us. "Very well. In that case, you will submit your questions to my adjutant, and we will arrange the necessary interviews for tomorrow morning. I trust this is acceptable to you?"

"We understand fully, sir. Your help is appreciated. We can work with your adjutant in preparing the questions," I said, knowing it was probably the best outcome we could expect.

"We have some lunch being sent up from the officer's mess," said the adjutant as he escorted us out of the office, taking us to a small meeting room at the far end of the building.

An hour later, strolling outside together in a wired compound for an exercise break, Antonio and I were able to voice our thoughts without, we hoped, fear of being overheard.

"In a way, he's right about not letting us loose on his officers," I said.

"How much do you think he's covering up?" asked Antonio, ignoring my assessment.

"Difficult to say," I replied. "What intelligence we can retrieve from this visit will depend on who he parades in front of us. I wouldn't hold my breath."

"You think our visit here could be largely a waste of time?" asked Antonio, turning to face me.

"They're not being very cooperative. Maybe we can find out something more from his buddies tomorrow."

"In that case, maybe I'll try to grab a tennis game," said Antonio suddenly. "It's cooling down, and I could do with some exercise."

My initial response was surprise, followed quickly by annoyance. "Look, if we're working as a team, there probably are some things you could do that would be more helpful," I shot back.

"Such as what?" asked Antonio. "Such as following the script that's being written for us by these guys?" he said in answer to his own question.

"Do you have a better idea?" I asked.

Antonio shrugged his shoulders. "Maybe. We came here to stir things up. Why don't we do just that?"

"What do you propose we do?" I scoffed. "That old Spanish legionnaire runs his officers like his personal fiefdom. I'd be surprised if he wasn't one of Franco's buddies!"

"He was probably one of his cadets at least," said Antonio without any emotion. "You saw that monument to the dictator on the ride up here?"

I nodded. We had both seen the *Monument del Llano Amarillo*, a tribute to Generalissimo Francisco Franco, marking the beginning of the Spanish Civil War. The monument had been rescued from Moroccan territory when it became independent.

"We could split up," suggested Antonio. "You could ask for an escorted tour of the frontier, and see what you can find out in the process."

"What do you plan to do?" I asked.

"After we've finished with the adjutant, I'll look around here and ask him if I can get a tennis game. I noticed some courts on the way in."

Antonio was aware of the sneer I directed towards him.

"Why not treat yourself to a hammam and screw one of the local women while you're at it?" I asked in disgust. "After all, it's not as if we're here working on an active assignment."

The Adjutant

Our meeting at the Civil Guard garrison put a damper on the day. I'd been feeling optimistic when we had met with the colonel. Having met the capitan, I wasn't so sure.

After we had finished preparing our questions with the adjutant, Antonio took off to play tennis. I headed for a guided tour of the border. I didn't find out anything new, so I asked the driver to drop me off at the hotel and I checked in. It wasn't much of a place, but it was on the approved list of accommodations. Downtown, there seemed to be Civil Guard patrols everywhere.

Antonio didn't get back until early evening. He was flushed in the face, I guess from his tennis game. He had dropped his bag off in his room. I gave him a cursory account of my tour of the border, but he seemed very anxious and excited to brief me on his own activities.

"I found this hidden in David Casals' locker at the tennis club," he said to me. He handed me a clear plastic bag containing a CD.

"What is it?" I asked, worried about his mention of the locker.

"It only has two files; both of them are encrypted. It might be a novel that David Casals was writing, but my guess is it might have something to do with our investigation," said Antonio.

"Where did you find it exactly?" I asked, aware that I might sound more interested in the process than the new evidence.

"I can explain that later. But don't you think we should report it to the colonel?"

"I don't know," I said, thinking aloud. "You say you found it in David Casals' locker. That's Civil Guard property." My voice was scolding.

"Frankly, I'd be a little less concerned about whose turf it was on, and a lot more interested in finding out what's on the disk," Antonio shot back, becoming exasperated.

Backing off, he adjusted his tone. "Diego, why don't we let the colonel decide how to handle it. Let's just get it deciphered."

"Okay," I said reluctantly. I didn't want to get on the wrong side of the Civil Guard.

I reached for my phone and sighed. "Antonio, I just wish you'd let me know what you're doing when you're out there acting like Sherlock Holmes."

Ten minutes later I handed the CD to the officer the colonel had sent over.

"Is there anything else you have up your sleeve?" I asked Antonio. It really wasn't a question.

He saw no purpose in arguing the point and helped himself to a whisky from the mini bar.

We were getting hungry and decided to venture out and eat at a local restaurant. The clerk at the desk had recommended one known for its authentic Moroccan food. Antonio seemed excited and a bit jumpy.

The place was noisy and frequented that night by a few late-season tourists, but mostly locals. I started to feel a little bit better when we ate, but the CD was worrying the hell out of me. In the end, I just picked at the tagine lamb cooked with prunes and almonds, which Antonio seemed to find delicious and ate enthusiastically.

There were long silences between our brief snatches of conversation. When the karaoke began, Antonio took the opportunity to dance with a group of Dutch girls sitting at the bar. He seemed to think there was no reason to be subdued. For him, flirting with the girls was fun. The girls seemed to enjoy his company; after all, he is handsome and tall. They teased him about his blonde highlights.

Suddenly, I was aware of someone standing at our table.

"Deputy Inspector Abaya," the man began. I said nothing. "The adjutant would like to meet with you. Urgently, please, sir."

The man was not in uniform, and appeared to be some kind of local messenger. He was quite old and seemed of Bedouin extraction.

"Why can't he meet us here?" I asked.

"The adjutant apologises, sir. He has some confidential matters to discuss."

It didn't take me long to decide. We needed some kind of break in the case, and I was reluctant to let Antonio take all the limelight, so I agreed to go with the messenger. Wait outside, I told him. We'll be there in a minute or two. I was carrying my SIG, so I was ready for anything.

"Someone you know?" Antonio asked, as he sat down.

"Maybe our first break here," I said quietly. "Pay the bill and follow me outside. We may have to walk for a time. No questions," I added.

There were a few people on the street, and a heavily-manned Civil Guard patrol cruiser. If we were being followed, I thought, it wouldn't be hard to track our movements. We walked at a distance behind the old man. He skipped over the stone roadway like a teenager, his hands keeping his robe out of reach of his sandals.

He seemed to make no effort to shake off anyone who might be tailing us. Antonio said it all seemed a bit melodramatic to him. Why not get a taxi, he asked.

We passed along the outskirts of a souk, ignoring the attention of street hawkers. Soon, we left the high rises of the Andalusian section and found ourselves in one of the poorer neighbourhoods. Here, the streets were much narrower. The lighting was sparse and the buildings were older; they leaned inward towards each other. Several dogs barked at us, and I thought the glances from the locals became more hostile.

There were few Europeans to be seen, but more Africans. Most were Moroccans—some wearing djellabas and a few men with kufi caps. We had to walk faster to keep up with the old man and, as he turned a corner, he beckoned to us. The darkened doorway was out of sight from the street.

"Follow me," he said rapidly, now speaking Arabic. Leading us past hemp sacks and wood crates along a narrow corridor to the back of a windowless building, we could smell the odour of sewage from bad plumbing and a strong smell of spices. I felt re-energised.

We emerged into a narrow alleyway, and the older man continued to gesture to us—this time with greater urgency. I was impressed at how quickly he could move. Glancing behind, I didn't think we were being followed, but couldn't really tell. Climbing up five or six steep steps in a narrow alley, we entered a warehouse converted into a residence. A large wooden door closed noisily behind us.

In the murky light, we did not recognise him at first. No longer wearing his uniform, the adjutant seemed somehow even older, more frail and vulnerable. He sat at a small round metal table to which two additional chairs had been added in anticipation of our meeting.

He waited while Antonio and I sat down.

From his inside pocket, he took a map and put it on the table, spreading the paper flat with his hands.

"In three days' time, the Moroccan security services will carry out simultaneous raids on three al-Qaeda madrassas— one in each of the locations shown here on the map," he began. "We know this from reliable sources inside the DST.

"We also know that that these madrassas are training elite operatives, radicalised professionals from various western countries, in the final stages of an al-Qaeda programme. A terrorist 'finishing school' in most respects."

I nodded. "Yes, we know that Iranian and other funds are being used for training of al-Qaeda. It's the brainchild of an al-Qaeda facilitator named Muhsin al-Fadhli," I said without emotion. The adjutant's eyes widened slightly as he heard this.

"You are well informed," he said.

"It's no secret," I shrugged. "Al-Fadhli's operations are largely non-classified information within GEO. The Americans have named him publicly on their wanted list. His death was widely publicised some time ago."

"What we really want to know," I said, "is how this is related to our investigation into the death of the Civil Guard officer in Barcelona?"

The adjutant took a moment to consider the question. "One of the radicalised westerners at the locations I've pointed to on the map is a Spanish citizen—a woman. She is the fiancée of the deceased officer," said the adjutant.

"They were both radicalised?" Antonio asked.

"No, it's a bit more complicated than that," replied the adjutant. "They're both working undercover for us."

Antonio and I exchanged glances. That was just the start of things. I became increasingly concerned as the adjutant explained the details of the Civil Guard's undercover operation. My phone began to vibrate in my pocket; I ignored it, focusing my attention on what he was telling us.

"The capitan has close contacts within Morocco. It was he who masterminded the recruitment of David Casals and later recruited his fiancée. She was selected personally by the capitan, with officer Casals' full cooperation. She agreed to act as bait for the al-Qaeda cell that we know exists here in Ceuta. Believing that officer Casals was already turned to their cause, the al-Qaeda cell here quickly accepted his fiancée."

"He was working undercover for the Civil Guard and she was too?" asked Antonio seeking confirmation of this new information. The adjutant nodded.

"Does the DST in Morocco know this?" I asked.

"For various reasons, including protecting her undercover status, the capitan decided not to share this information with our friends in the DST," said the adjutant.

"Placing her in even greater danger?" my voice rose in concern. "Especially if the DST raid goes wrong and she gets killed. After all, they won't know that she's one of ours, will they?"

"Well, we didn't know until this morning about the raids the Moroccans have planned. We assumed she would complete her finishing school training in Morocco and return to Spain as a double agent—a sleeper agent for al-Qaeda, but actually under our command at the Civil Guard," explained the adjutant.

"What does Madrid plan to do?" I asked, annoyed that I had not been told of this. I ignored the repeated vibrations of my phone.

The adjutant's face seemed to drain of colour. "The capitan decided that it was a local operation, and that it was not necessary to bring Madrid into the loop at this stage."

I felt my face turn white, then a sudden rush of blood as it reddened. I pushed myself up from the table, my chair falling over behind me.

"Why didn't he give us this information when we met him?" I demanded, my voice rising in anger. "Why this charade? Why waste our time?"

"The capitan is a cautious man," the adjutant started to say, and held his hand up when I started to interrupt him. "Please, let me finish, Deputy Inspector."

"No, I won't," I shot back.

I dragged my chair back up and sat down close to the table. "Let me see if I've got this right. The capitan took it upon himself to recruit officer David Casals, and later his fiancée, to penetrate an al-Qaeda terrorist cell. In the process, one of them was killed and the second is in imminent danger and in the hands of savages.

"Do I have that about right?" I demanded of the adjutant, who now was shifting in his seat, understandably looking extremely uncomfortable.

"With respect, sir, what was he thinking?" I said loudly.

When I didn't receive a reply, I said, "Let's face it, sir, it's a complete botch-up of an operation." I stood up to leave; I couldn't believe what he had told us.

The adjutant remained silent and avoided eye contact with us. "Things are a bit different here on the frontier," he said eventually, his weak voice now almost squeaky.

I sighed loudly and ignored him.

"You're running a maverick covert operation here," I told him, pronouncing my words deliberately. I breathed in, my chest feeling constricted and tight. This is crazy, I thought.

"By law, and by the chains of command that each of us works under, Madrid must be centrally involved in any terrorist operation," I told the adjutant.

"For reasons only known to you and the capitan, you risked the lives of Civil Guard officers—two young and inexperienced officers—in an unauthorised undercover operation that, without any official support, now seems doomed to fail. One of them is already dead—murdered."

The adjutant licked his dry lips. "Let me try to explain. We chose this meeting location for a purpose. The capitan wanted to ensure that what we are talking about would not be overheard and would be, so to speak, off the record."

This was really unbelievable. I considered answering my phone, now vibrating almost constantly, but decided to ignore it.

"When we learned that two police officers would be visiting Ceuta to investigate the killing of officer David Casals, the capitan was expecting two regular officers—not, with respect, you two. Clearly, you are both abnormally well-qualified officers with the Special Forces. The capitan was taken by surprise and needed to think through the situation to his next steps."

Again he held up his hands as I began to speak.

"The capitan is proud of his long career here in North Africa, and proud of the performance of the men under his command. This began as a border smuggling operation…"

I couldn't take any more, so I interrupted him. "Madrid must be informed at once," I commanded. "We don't have any time to waste."

"If the Moroccans said this raid is planned for three days' time, that means Friday. Do you have any precise information about the timing?" asked Antonio, speaking for the first time.

"No," replied the adjutant, "we asked them to confirm when the raids would take place. They would tell us only that they were planned for some time on Friday."

"Which could be accurate, or they might be covering themselves for an earlier strike," Antonio suggested.

The adjutant bowed his shoulders, but said nothing.

"What is the capitan's plan?" asked Antonio.

"There seems to be no other option now than to advise the Moroccans," the Adjutant replied without enthusiasm.

"If there's a leak on their side, that's as good as finger-pointing her as a target for al-Qaeda," I said, almost spitting out my words. "If they find out she's a spy, who knows what they will do to her!"

The heat in the room continued to build, and I realised we had been there for quite some time. I was feeling awful. Antonio, I guessed, was not much better. Having played two games of tennis earlier, he was feeling dehydrated. Both of us struggled to think clearly.

I was straining to think of a way to get the girl out of danger. The other part of me was seething with rage about the stupidity of the aging capitan. I could not believe that such an experienced officer would carry out a maverick operation—involving al-Qaeda—without it being cleared with his senior officers, and without the support that regulations mandated.

"There is," the adjutant began to speak slowly, "another option."

"What?" I snapped, no longer able to hide my intense anger.

The adjutant shifted his position, and seemed embarrassed about what he was about to propose.

"There is the possibility of rescuing the girl—before the DST raids take place," he began cautiously.

"I can't imagine them wanting to compromise their own operations," Antonio started to say.

"No, not the DST," intervened the adjutant. "The capitan was thinking about our own forces."

"GEO?" I asked. I was stunned.

"To work outside our national boundaries, GEO would have to have permission from the senior levels of government in Madrid. Probably from the prime minister himself," I told the adjutant. That's just not going to happen. For one thing, even if it was a good idea—which it isn't—time is too short."

The adjutant bit his lip before venturing into the next stage of his suggestion. "The capitan has something more modest in mind." The room went silent. "A small commando force—nothing official, of course. A quick in-and-out, as the British call it," he continued.

Clearly he was oblivious to the shock that was spreading across my face.

"You are suggesting that *we* could be part of this unofficial, covert operation to rescue the girl?" I asked in a mocking, exaggerated tone.

"The capitan feels that it has a good chance of success," offered the adjutant.

"This is crazy," I said. "I can tell you, for both of us, that our answer is absolutely no. The capitan created this mess and he can dig himself out of it—if that is possible, which I doubt.

"I have to tell you, sir, that we are bound by duty to report what you have told us to our superiors—without delay."

The adjutant nodded slowly, his features signalling defeat, his hollow eyes now devoid of life.

He stood up unsteadily. "Thank you, gentlemen. I understand your position. I apologise that we have wasted your time. Abdul here will escort you back to your hotel."

Then he shuffled slowly to the door, and left us sitting at the table—in stunned silence.

The Brigadier

The next several hours seemed to go very quickly.

As soon as we could, we found a taxi and dumped Abdul. It took us fifteen minutes to get to the National Police headquarters.

"I've been trying to reach you, Diego," said the colonel with a sigh of relief, as soon as his office door was closed. "That CD contains valuable information. It's been classified, so I can't tell you much, but…"

"Sir, with respect, we have something you must hear about without delay," I interrupted and told him about our meeting with the adjutant.

"Just a minute," said the colonel, looking concerned. "I need to have this on record. Follow me," he instructed, leading us to an interrogation room. "Excuse the melodrama, but given the nature of what you're telling me, I think it's necessary."

As we spoke, the frown crossing his forehead grew deeper. Part way through, he put up a hand to stop us, and made some brief calls. Soon, we were joined by two younger officers on the colonel's staff. A few minutes later, a stern looking Civil Guard brigadier entered the room and was introduced briefly.

"Please repeat for the brigadier what you have just told us, and continue," instructed the colonel.

As I spoke, occasionally referring to Antonio for details, I described everything that had happened since we arrived in Ceuta. There was silence after I had finished.

"Officers," said the colonel addressing us both, "clearly, we are dealing here with a serious national security issue. I am sorry, but your homicide investigation must be set aside. I have to discuss with my colleague in the Civil Guard how we will proceed. For now, we ask you to remain here in this room and not attempt to make outside contact until you are cleared to do so."

He held out his hand. "Your phones and electronic equipment, please," he asked.

"These are not being impounded. They will remain untouched in a secure place, until further notice. I regret this, but it is necessary under the circumstances. You will have an opportunity to talk to your respective superiors later."

For the next several hours, Antonio and I sat in the interrogation room, saying little. Fresh coffee and cold water arrived, along with some snacks. We picked at the food, hardly saying a word to each other. I felt we were being treated badly—imprisoned like criminals. After an hour, one of the junior officers on the colonel's staff returned.

"The colonel apologises," he said pleasantly. "He has asked me to brief you on the current status."

I was unimpressed. As a National Police GEO officer, I naturally had anticipated that I would be part of the action. Antonio also seemed to be in an ugly mood.

We listened as the junior officer described the operation now taking place in Morocco. "We and the Civil Guard are working jointly with the Moroccans," he told us, giving away little detail.

"What about the information on the disk?" I asked the young officer.

"I don't have any information on that, sir. Is there anything else I can get for you?" he asked, before leaving the room.

The new information was doing little to lighten our spirits. I felt slighted, like an outcast.

Sometime later, there was a noise as the colonel and brigadier returned to the room.

"Again, gentlemen, I apologise," the colonel began.

"What we can tell you is that the Moroccans launched a joint operation of their security forces. They raided three madrassas. We do not know the full status of the operation as yet. We are working in full cooperation with them," he glanced at the brigadier. "At this point in time, we are reasonably hopeful of success.

"In the meantime, we have some additional questions—if you are willing to help us?"

I nodded to the brigadier, who turned to face Antonio.

"Tell me again, why did you go to the tennis club?"

Looking at him, Antonio could not detect if he was being criticised or not. He knew that he was on potentially shaky ground. The Civil Guard was powerful. They could make his life difficult. I guess he knew that his Mossos status could protect him only so far.

"I wasn't very interested in playing tennis, actually," he began. "But I remembered being told that David Casals, the murdered officer, was a champion tennis player at school in Barcelona. It was a reasonable guess to assume he would also play tennis where he was stationed—here in Ceuta.

"I didn't share this thinking with Deputy Inspector Abaya, because I had nothing to go on but a hunch. Frankly, if I had asked the capitan or the adjutant for permission to search his locker at the tennis club, they almost certainly would have said no."

He paused, seeking feedback from the body language of his listeners. He received none.

"From all the indications we'd received, everything we knew pointed to David Casals being a first-class officer and a model guardsman. It occurred to me that he might have left a trail of evidence of some kind—in case he didn't survive. I tried to think what I would do if I were in his position. I thought that a professional like him would leave behind information that his colleagues would need. Somewhere safe. Not obvious."

"Why the tennis club?" asked the brigadier.

"Well, if you play tennis, or squash or golf, sir, you'll know that guys keep all kinds of things in their lockers: photos of girlfriends, condoms, porn, cell phones. Anything they might want to hide from their wife, or from anyone else.

"The CD was taped to the roof of his locker. If I hadn't been searching for it, I never would have found it. I had to ask for a game of tennis, so that it would be natural for me to be in the showers and locker room. His name was still on his locker, and the rest was easy."

"You didn't think we were capable of finding the CD ourselves?"

"Well, sir, if you knew about officer Casals' mission, I would imagine that your people would have searched his locker already. It's twenty-twenty hindsight because now you probably know many more details about his mission. But when we arrived here in Ceuta all we knew was that his homicide involved some unusual elements."

"Possibly involving the Civil Guard and, under the circumstances, you didn't know who to trust?" the brigadier prompted, completing Antonio's thought process for him.

Antonio nodded. He could imagine what some of the others in the room might be thinking—and it wasn't likely to be complimentary. Nevertheless, he was determined to plough on.

"From the evidence we had, the al-Qaeda mole, or moles, are entrenched somewhere in the Civil Guard at Ceuta. I guessed that they might figure out the idea of looking in his locker fairly soon. I thought it was worthwhile checking it out."

"Did it occur to you, officer, that we might be aware of the CD's existence—and left it in place to see who would attempt to retrieve it?" asked the brigadier, his eyebrows raised in question.

Antonio's heart sank. That had not been a scenario he'd considered.

"For the record, and in your defence," continued the brigadier looking directly at the colonel, "I want you to confirm that you brought this evidence to our attention at your earliest opportunity, through my colleague the colonel here?"

"Yes sir, I did," answered Antonio. His voice sounding deflated as his body slumped.

For the first time, the brigadier allowed the briefest of smiles to escape his lips. He glanced at the colonel as if seeking his confirmation to speak.

"Of course, there will be internal enquiries into what has transpired. I can tell you, speaking for our service, that we do not take kindly to other security agencies, including regional police such as the Mossos d'Esquadra, going outside the confines of their jurisdictions—particularly on our turf."

Looking at me, he added, "I am aware, Deputy Inspector Abaya, that you had no prior knowledge this action was being taken by your colleague at the tennis club. Therefore, GEO is in no way implicated.

"On the other hand, I am aware that—within the Civil Guard—on this occasion we have been caught with our pants down. One of our own senior officers is guilty of perpetrating covert operations. We and our allies are trying to rectify this error of judgement as we speak.

"I am also aware that the jurisdictional issue is far from clear, and that you acted in good faith. Candidly, the Civil Guard may be at fault in Catalunya for not keeping our colleagues at the Mossos better informed of our activities—on your turf.

"To set your mind at rest about the question I asked earlier about the tennis club," he said, continuing to look directly at Antonio, "we were not aware of the existence of the CD. It was good police work on your part to find it, Deputy Inspector. We have taken the precaution of returning it to its original position inside the locker. It's under observation, and we will see what we might yet catch in that particular net."

Antonio looked relieved. I guess that he had been dreading the criticism that he expected me to deliver when we got through this night. Now, at least, I would have to moderate my anger at his unorthodox sleuthing.

"Can you tell us what is on the CD, sir?" I asked.

"I am afraid that has to remain classified, Deputy Inspector," responded the brigadier. "We are not able to disclose any details at this time. I'm sorry."

He stood up, nodded at the colonel, shook hands with them and left.

The colonel glanced at his watch. "Your possessions will be returned to you in a few minutes. I assume you will want to report to your respective superiors. I have arranged for you to have a private office for the next several hours. Our phones are fully encrypted, and the offices are not bugged." He smiled at us reassuringly.

"Deputy Inspector Abaya," he said to me. "Perhaps we could have a word in private?"

****

Two hours later, feeling tired and disheartened, we sipped without enthusiasm at the fresh coffee that had been brought into the room. We hardly spoke or looked at each other. Our orders, coming from the most senior levels in Madrid, were clear and unequivocal. The case was closed and our work on it was finished.

Around five o'clock in the morning, the door opened and a perky young staff officer breezed into the room. He had the mannerisms of a senior boy in high school and spoke to us as if we were first form juniors.

The capitan was operating outside his jurisdiction, he told us. It was a regrettable state of affairs, and he could reveal to us that the capitan had been relieved of his command. His superiors had no knowledge of what had been going on.

Despite his distinguished service record, he could be court-martialled. However, it had been decided in Madrid that he would be allowed to retire on a full pension.

The adjutant? Regrettably, he had committed suicide. His body had been found just a few hours ago. It was tragic really, crooned the staff officer. By all accounts, he had been a wonderful aide to the capitan. Something must not have been right. You know. Not quite right in the head.

It would be up to the Civil Guard to decide but, most likely, there would be a full enquiry, of course.

In the meantime, the staff officer assured us, the most urgent priority was to protect the girl. The DST had been informed at the highest level in Rabat, and plans for the raids on the madrassas had been advanced. I am sorry to have to be evasive about the details, he explained. However, we are confident that, with luck, the Moroccans will by now have secured her safety.

After being rescued, she would be repatriated to Spain as soon as possible. The staff officer apologised for any inconveniences we may have been subjected to during our time in Ceuta.

The homicide investigation involving the death of officer David Casals was being taken over by the Civil Guard. As far as the Mossos and the National Police were concerned, the case was closed. Antonio and I should return to our respective bases, he confirmed. Naturally, the Civil Guard would require that this unfortunate matter must remain under the Official Secrets Act.

Travel arrangements were being made and we could return home, he said, with an exaggerated look at his watch, probably by the late morning flight from the Ceuta heliport through Malaga. And thank you again for your excellent work in helping uncover and resolve this regrettable case.

Chapter 5

Catalunya: End of the Road

"The Moroccans did a good job," said the chief, beaming. "They arrested thirty-one people at the madrassas. Two were injured in gunfire, but our girl is safe.

"They've separated the jihadist converts they captured. They're in solitary confinement, out of contact with each other. When the Moroccans return the girl to us, no one will suspect her involvement.

"Altogether, it's a successful operation. Well done, you two," he said to Antonio and Xavi.

"And, of course, Diego and our colleagues in Madrid. I've conveyed that to my opposite number.

"Chief Robles at GEO and I are particularly pleased that we have been able to work collaboratively together on this case," he continued, with a beaming smile.

"Sir, we didn't get any closer to solving the homicide," said Xavi.

"No, but I have every confidence. Well, maybe not right away, but I think we will solve it eventually. As for the information on the CD, that's now classified.

"We may never know what was on it. The Civil Guard has iron grip control on it," added the chief, shifting his body awkwardly in his chair. "That's one area where I'm not so happy. The feds seemed a bit too glib in the explanation they gave us for the senior level leak. Still, I guess we can't do anything about it now."

"Maybe we can," said Antonio with a mischievous smile, holding up a memory stick between his fingers.

There was stunned silence in the room.

"Let me guess," said Xavi, half-dreading what his partner's answer might be. "You made a copy of the CD?"

"Toni," said his father loudly.

"No one asked me if I'd made a copy," Antonio grinned. "I thought they would, but they didn't. They probably searched our belongings while we were out of the hotel."

"Where did you hide it?" asked Xavi, the smile on his face reflecting his delight.

"The more obvious the place, the more secure it is," said Antonio. "I left it at the front desk at the hotel—in an envelope I addressed to myself."

"Well, officially, we can't have a copy," protested the chief. "It's Civil Guard property."

"Sir, you just said you thought the feds have not told us everything they know about this case," countered Antonio.

"Whatever was being covered up before is still being covered up—despite the soothing assurances of our colleagues in Ceuta and Madrid," he added.

"This information can't find its way into our mainstream channels—I mean here within the Mossos," cautioned the chief wagging a finger in the air.

"We have William," smiled Antonio. "He's a secret weapon against the inexorable tide of federalism."

"Okay," said the chief after a few minutes. "Let's find out what was on the CD. For goodness sake, keep it off the record."

"William's existence is completely off the record, sir," Xavi reminded him. "Everything he does for us has to be kept that way. For his sake and ours."

Puzzling Information

"What do these mean?" asked the chief, looking mystified. He rubbed his eyebrows and looked again at the two sheets of paper the sergeant had placed in front of him.

"The one you're looking at, sir, is a series of six numbers. They are matched against dates on which something has happened or will happen—like a transaction or quantity of something. There's no indication that it's sourced from a government, organisation or an individual, so it could be almost any type of activity.

"The other page is a list of six names. Put the two of them together and it tells us a little bit more," continued the sergeant, leaning in front of the chief and placing the two pages side by side.

August	5	Alpha
November	20	Zaragoza
December	20	Cuenca
April	20	Delta
June	20	Marbella
September	20	Pimentos

"They look like coded shopping lists to me," said the chief, throwing up his hands. "Don't we have deciphering experts for this type of thing?"

"Deciphering experts are good at identifying *patterns*, when something has been coded or encrypted," said the sergeant, anxious to please the chief, but wanting to display his expert knowledge. "But usually they don't know, or aren't aware of, the *context* for the data or information. We can take both approaches."

"The thing is, we know we are dealing with al-Qaeda," Antonio intervened. "Therefore, if we try to interpret the information in the context of what al-Qaeda does—in terms of terrorist activities—we can start to make some guesses about what it means."

The sergeant nodded.

"I like that thinking," said the chief. "What you're saying is that we should remember that the context relates in part to who else is involved and the circumstances behind their activities."

Antonio nodded. "Maybe one of the first context questions we should ask ourselves is why the feds in Ceuta reacted so strongly to the existence of this information."

"And why the murdered Civil Guard officer felt it was such valuable information that he burned it onto a CD and hid it in his locker at the tennis club," added the chief. "I mean he could just as easily have written or typed it on a piece of paper."

Antonio was impressed by his father's insight.

The sergeant intervened. "What may be helpful, sir, would be to create scenarios. It's a technique we use. Scenarios provide a structure and context for the information."

Over the next ten minutes, they identified a series of situations which might explain the circumstances for the transactions.

"I like the terrorist target scenario," said the chief after they had reviewed them all. "That one resonates best with me. What do you think, Toni?"

"I'm a bit cautious," replied Antonio, his voice drawled deliberately. "We know that this is really valuable information. We don't want to get drawn too quickly into supporting one particular scenario and one theory."

The sergeant nodded his agreement.

"I won't express an opinion just yet," Antonio continued. "What I think I should do is to act as a devil's advocate and look for weaknesses in each of them."

"Try to pick holes," said the chief. "So that we don't get carried away with our theories? I like it, Toni."

"Working on your favoured scenario, sir," Antonio continued, "if these are terrorist targets, what does the information tell us?"

"Let's start with the dates," said the chief, only half-listening and running with his imagination. "Whatever year it was, or is going to be, overall it's a fifteen-month period during which some transactions take place, or events happen. Now that worries me."

"You mean, because we're almost into November?" asked Antonio.

The chief nodded.

"Well, if August refers to this year, we can easily check to see what al-Qaeda and the others were up to during that time. I'll get Xavi on that right away," said Antonio keying his partner's number into his phone.

"What about the numbers?" the chief mumbled.

"They could be quantities of something. Alternatively, they could refer to amounts of money," offered Antonio.

"Five of something, followed by twenty of something—repeated several times," said the chief.

"The 'somethings' could be the same, or they could be different," noted Antonio, leaning back in his seat. 'For the sake of simplicity, let's assume they are the same."

"Whatever they are, they have to be significant," said the chief, starting to joke. "I mean, they're not traffic fines in euros." He smiled again at the sergeant and received another enthusiastic laugh.

"If they refer to sums of money, the amounts would be large. Banks must have been involved somewhere," suggested the sergeant, seeking an opening.

"Well, not necessarily the western banking system," suggested Antonio. "There's always the hawala. "

The sergeant nodded his agreement. "The hawala system is particularly relevant with some of the money transfers we've seen from Gulf-based financiers."

The chief looked puzzled.

"Explain to me how the system would work in this case," said Antonio to the sergeant, seeing his father's discomfort.

"*Hawala* is a money transfer that doesn't require physical transfer of the money," the sergeant began, pleased to be able to display his expertise. "It's a trust system. In our case, someone in Morocco, for instance, would pay a local hawala broker a commission to arrange a credit transfer. The broker would issue a promissory note—usually involving a secret code, known only to the parties involved in the transaction."

"That could be an agreement to transfer funds to al-Qaeda in Damascus, for example," said the chief, now explaining it to the others. "But no actual money moves across the borders. The broker in Damascus would pay the money to al-Qaeda in Syria—if they could give him the secret code."

"The broker in Morocco would owe the broker in Damascus the same amount of money," added Antonio. "He would now be in debt for that amount to the hawala broker in Damascus."

"Which he could discharge by paying the cash in Morocco to someone who is owed money by the hawala broker in Damascus," the sergeant beamed. "It's used a lot in money laundering."

"All of it based on trust," the chief emphasised. "Avoiding transfer and other taxes, and laundering the money without it having to actually move anywhere. Which is why it's highly illegal," he added.

"But effective when it works," said Antonio. "And if you're dealing with al-Qaeda, or ISIS, I wouldn't imagine they are people you would want to scam."

"That still leaves the problem of getting the money to a place where the hawala system works," said the chief.

"Well, one way would be to transfer it in a backpack—from Barcelona to Ceuta," said Antonio.

"Ha," exclaimed the chief. "If that young Civil Guard officer made several trips, as we know he did, he could make the crossing to Ceuta in uniform and maybe even avoid detection. Ingenious!"

"But that doesn't explain everything," said Antonio. "There would still have to be some kind of trusted courier to take the promissory note and secret code to al-Qaeda. It would be too risky to send any other way."

"That is the usual way for large amounts," said the sergeant. "The types of people who use this system have used it for thousands of years. There's not a lot new. They are very conservative."

"You know, if these are millions, they would add up over a hundred million euros," observed the Chief.

"If we are talking about millions of euros, or some other currency, then it would fit quite well with money laundering," said the sergeant. "I mean, we are not England where it's estimated that the Russians alone have transferred the equivalent of ten billion euros a year of dirty money into the London property market."

Antonio whistled. "Now that's a lot. But somehow, in the context of al-Qaeda, I don't think we are talking billions—more like millions. What do you think?" he asked.

"You're right, sir. Among all the terrorist groups operating in the region, ISIS is the one with most money. They get it from looting banks, from oil sales and from kidnapping ransoms.

"ISIS kidnappings bring them revenues of nearly two million euros a year. It's a big business for them. Unlike al-Qaeda, they generate their own revenues—they have a better business model, so to speak.

"Al-Qaeda is a poor cousin, when it comes to wealth. In the past, they have relied on Islamic charities, rich families like bin Laden's and Islamic-linked companies operating in the west," the sergeant continued.

"Recently, we have been picking up signals that al-Qaeda is trying to develop a more sustainable revenue base."

Antonio was amused by the sergeant's statements. He guessed that the man was not speaking from first-hand experience. His confident statements sounded like he was echoing news snippets picked up at one of the international seminars on terrorism financing some of the staff guys in the Mossos had attended. He decided to let the man bask in the glory of his moment in the sun.

The point he made was a good one, thought Antonio. "So you think that al-Qaeda could be branching out in some ways?" he asked.

The man nodded his head vigorously, and drew in a sharp breath. "Absolutely, sir.

"Look at it this way. If we think about it in business terms—as the terrorism business, if we could call it that—a lot of these terrorist organisations, the ones that survive, rather than the ones that are forced to merge with others or whose operatives simply leave to join another group, are the terrorist equivalent of technology start-ups."

The chief raised an eyebrow, and the sergeant picked up a warning signal that he had better not allow his enthusiasm for the subject to get the better of him.

"Go on," said Antonio, observing the man's dilemma and not wanting him to retreat into defensive mode. He knew that his father could be intimidating for many of the Mossos' lower ranks. Even if the man's information came directly from a seminar, it was proving valuable in understanding the information on David Casals' CD.

"They need sustainable financing," said the sergeant treading forwards carefully and with a searching glance at the chief.

"So these could be payments for something?" offered the chief. "But for what?

"I mean, if we are talking about payments of twenty million euros, those kinds of amounts are associated with weapons and smaller scale armaments and military vehicles. They are deals where there is a lot of risk and the need for cash up front," the Chief offered an answer to his own question.

Again, Antonio was impressed by his father's analysis.

"Yes, sir," the sergeant added. "Very big illegal deals—when major pieces of equipment are involved, such as planes and warships—usually are country-to-country."

"Like Russia supplying Syria's Assad?" suggested Antonio.

"Then there is technology theft and smuggling," said the chief speaking his thoughts aloud, "but that's not what we are looking at here, is it?"

"Actually, that's a perceptive thought, sir," intervened Antonio. "The Americans, Brits, French and Israelis are the big suppliers of so-called defence hardware and software to our side. The Russians and Chinese supply the other side.

"Between them, they have fostered the growth of terrorist organisations. In the process, there are a lot of groups out there now able to offer terrorist services for sale.

"It wouldn't take much imagination to suggest that what we are looking at here might be payments for smaller scale armaments or payments for terrorist services, or both."

"Okay," said the chief. "Let's hold that thought and see what else we have." He looked at the sergeant.

"The other sheet of paper has a list of items and names on it. They don't make much sense either," he added before the sergeant could muster an answer.

"They're code names, if they mean anything at all," continued the chief, picking up the sheet and reading the list for the third time.

Finally, the sergeant spoke up. "The language is ours, not something foreign. Three of the names are places within Spain; two are Greek words standing for the first and fourth letter of their alphabet. They're also mathematical symbols and values. Pimentos simply means peppers."

"It looks transactional, that's for sure," commented the chief. "Whatever Alpha was, or is, seems to be worth less than later months. Anyway, I'm not a cipher expert. Do you think we can take the risk of getting it to the lab for analysis?"

Antonio sucked in his breath between his teeth, making a sound that expressed extreme caution.

"We certainly don't want to risk the feds knowing we have it. We will have to be very selective to whom we give it." He looked at the sergeant, who nodded his acknowledgement of Antonio's thought process.

"How about if I ask William to take a look at it?" suggested Antonio. "He's got a mathematical, off-the-wall brain."

"Okay, see what he comes up with. If we can't make a breakthrough, I'm going to suggest to the sergeant here that we need to bring in a deciphering expert and see what they can make of it. If there's a pattern or code, they should be able to break it."

The sergeant nodded. "Okay, thanks, Geraldo," said the Chief, receiving a smart salute as the man rose and left the room.

Antonio's phone rang.

"It's Xavi. He did a quick scan of the internet. August this year was an active month for the jihadists; one significant event stands out."

The chief looked concerned.

"ISIS went to a lot of effort to blow apart the ancient ruins at Palmyra in Syria," said Antonio. "If you remember they seemed quite determined—yet those places have no strategic value in the war."

"Well, in the propaganda war, they do," countered the chief. "ISIS is winning that one."

Antonio pushed back his chair and held his folded hands up to his mouth in contemplation. "At Palmyra, ISIS seemed to be working on a trial and error basis—possibly using locally available explosives. Perhaps they finally managed to get it right, from their viewpoint at least. The monuments there have been almost totally destroyed."

"We know that one-third of Muslims in Spain live in Catalunya," stated the chief without emotion. "Obviously, we are a target. The arrests we made last month—that was a Salafist cell we had been monitoring for months."

"Salafist jihadis aren't the only ones we have to worry about," said Antonio.

"What we have to remember, Dad, is that al-Qaeda and ISIS compete with each other, or they have so far. But they have the same objectives—the jihad. We know that al-Qaeda's agenda is global. ISIS has focused mainly on Iraq and Syria to date. It wants to dominate the territory. Al-Qaeda wants to have a global impact.

"If al-Qaeda and ISIS worked together globally, the outcome might not be nice."

"Meaning?" asked the chief, sounding agitated.

"Well, just as we have been talking about, al-Qaeda in the past has relied on trained operatives—volunteers and new recruits—for its dirty work. You know, 9/11 and all the other massive terrorist acts to destabilise western countries.

"ISIS has become a trained army. If our suspicions are correct, and they started to work outside the Middle East, al-Qaeda money could hire full-time ISIS vigilante operatives to carry out its destructive activities."

"You mean we could see more of them here?" asked the chief. "That's nothing new. We have before. But why Spain in particular, and who would provide the money?"

Antonio said nothing, but tapped his finger on one of the pages sitting on the Chief's desk.

"If you're right, and those are millions of euros being paid to al-Qaeda, there would have to be some people here in Spain willing to pay the jihadists a lot of money to help destabilise the country, politically and economically," he continued.

"I don't like it," the chief's voice boomed. "That means domestic targets here in Spain."

Antonio shrugged his shoulders.

"It all supports your scenario, Dad. It might also explain why the feds jumped onto the information so quickly and shut us down from any further investigations."

The chief digested this information for a moment. Then he asked, "What about this month? Have there been any significant events anywhere?"

Antonio shook his head, looking concerned. "Not yet, anyway."

The chief's raised eyebrows gave emphasis to his reaction. The N9 celebrations flashed across his mind.

"Damn," he said, looking troubled.

"It's frustrating in so many ways," he added after another pause. "I thought we really had something on that disk—intelligence we could understand and act upon. We know the feds have this information and they've attached a lot of importance to it. It must mean something to them."

"It's big enough for that young officer to have lost his life over it," said Antonio shaking his head.

"It's just one part of a very significant puzzle. We need to find more pieces," he added.

"And quickly," said the chief.

Dinner with Friends

Antonio had arranged a dinner for the four friends. Maria was excited. She and Pilar had talked by phone.

"Do you think it's something really special?" Pilar asked.

Maria thought it risky to presume anything; they had been together for seventeen and a half months, but Antonio had not shown any sign of moving ahead. She shrugged her shoulders, but later at the office found herself daydreaming.

"Best not jump the gun," she had cautioned Pilar, although it was nice to speculate. She picked up the phone and made a hair appointment. "What do you think of the red dress?" she asked her friend. "I haven't worn it for a time, but it still fits well."

Antonio had been moody in the past week or so, but now he seemed much happier—and arranging the dinner was out of character for him.

"Good signs," giggled Pilar.

"I've got an announcement," said Antonio when they were well into the dinner. Pilar flashed a look in Maria's direction.

"I've organised tickets for skiing in Andorra at Christmas—for all four of us. It will be great for us to take a break together." He looked at them, clearly pleased with his surprise initiative.

Maria managed to force a brave smile.

Pilar was not nearly as generous. Her face crumpled as she saw the pain on her friend's face. The girls waited for a few moments before heading to the washroom.

"What do you think, amigo?" Antonio was asking Xavi. "It's years since we went up there for winter sports."

Inside the washroom, Maria finally let down her guard and sobbed on Pilar's shoulder. Her friend could feel her shaking with emotion; the disappointment was just too great to bear.

Later, helping Maria fix her makeup, she attempted some encouraging words. "Maybe not tonight, *carinya*. But he adores you. It is so easy to see. I'm sure he will ask you soon."

"Soon?" blurted out Maria. "Soon?" She began to cry. "Riding across the Pyrenees on a three-legged donkey would be quicker."

Pressure on the Chief

"How is the girl?" asked Antonio. "Is she back in Spain yet?"

"Still in Morocco," replied the chief. "The security forces there are doing a detailed debriefing of all the detainees. Can't blame them really. They had three active al-Qaeda cells, those that they know of, operating in their country."

"The girl should be able to help them," suggested Antonio.

"I'm not sure she wants to do that, Toni," said his father. "Apparently, so far she's been non-cooperative with our Moroccan colleagues. She has just clammed up under interrogation and isn't saying anything."

"Well, until she's instructed by our people to talk to them, she's probably doing the right thing from a security point of view," ventured Antonio.

"Anyway, for now, they're holding her for questioning. At least she's safe, and we will repatriate her as soon as we can," said the chief.

"They'll take her straight to Madrid and they can go through a full debriefing there."

****

I hadn't heard anything from Antonio since Ceuta, and I'd become busy with other work piling up on my desk in Madrid while I was away.

Raphael Robles seemed delighted with the results we had achieved. I'm not sure why; certainly, I wasn't very happy about the outcomes. It still stung that my colleagues over there had chosen to exclude me from the action.

It was easy to understand why the Civil Guard wanted to hush things up. The episode with the capitan must have been a major embarrassment for them. To me, it smelled like a cover-up.

I was just about to head off to the gym for a lunchtime workout when I got a surprise call. It was from someone on the brigadier's staff.

"Officer Daniela Balmes was shot to death this morning," he told me. "She was still in the custody of the Moroccans and had been transported to an army base for repatriation to us in Madrid," he said.

My first instinct was that the Moroccans must have been very careless with their security.

"We think it was an al-Qaeda operation," he told me. "One of her guards at the Moroccan army base shot and killed her, then he shot and killed himself."

I took the information straight upstairs to Raphael Robles. He had just returned from a meeting with the government at the Cortes. He seemed devastated by the news from Morocco, and turned white with shock. I agreed with him that officer Balmes' death was really unfortunate. She was a brave young officer and had been our best remaining lead in the homicide case.

An hour later, he surprised me by calling me back to his office. He looked upset. "Diego, I have talked to our colleagues in the Civil Guard, and they agree. I want you to fly over with one of their people and bring the officer's body back here to Madrid.

"In many ways, she was a hero—going into the field like that. This is all the fault of the capitan. The least we can do is make sure she is buried with full military honours, here in Spain."

Chapter 6

Madrid: Carlos' Reunion Party

The condesa had expected that Carlos would be having a few old friends over to the house for the reunion he had been planning. As she pressed the remote to unlock the tall iron gate, she was surprised how many cars were parked along both sides of the driveway.

Steering her vehicle between the tightly packed vehicles, she noticed a white construction van with a roof rack and ladder. It caught her attention because it stood out—seemingly a poor cousin among a class of gentrified thoroughbred limousines. She wondered if Hortensia might have needed to call in a repairman.

The array of cars was impressive, she thought. Their drivers were standing in a group, some smoking cigarettes. They stood to attention as she drove past. One of them quickly hid his cigarette behind his back—like a guilty junior schoolboy caught smoking by the head prefect.

Manoeuvring between two vehicles parked at an awkward angle, the condesa steered her car down the ramp to their underground park. She took the elevator upstairs. She could hear the buzz of voices coming from Carlos' den.

"Hola, Hortensia," she said entering the kitchen and smiling at their middle-aged housekeeper. "I see that don Carlos is entertaining. Do they have everything they need?"

"They told me not to disturb them, señora," the housekeeper replied. She had been quite relieved when the master had given her this instruction. She disliked the smoke from their cigars, and some of those old men were quite creepy, she thought.

"Did we need a repairman?" the condesa asked. "There's a contractor's van outside on the driveway."

The housekeeper looked puzzled. "No, señora. It must be one of the master's guests."

The condesa went to her study and checked her cell phone and emails. There was a confirmation from Zoe that she had been booked on the flight she wanted to Barcelona. She wrote several quick emails and heard a car engine start at the front of the house. Carlos' meeting seemed to be coming to an end, she guessed. A few minutes later she heard other car engines start and drive towards the gate.

She went back into the kitchen, where Hortensia was preparing their evening meal. "Mmm, that looks good," she complimented the housekeeper. "Don Carlos' meeting looks like it's finishing. I'll go down and help him."

"The master said that he will not need dinner tonight, señora."

This news surprised the condesa, who suddenly felt the need to cover up her ignorance of her husband's plans. "No problem, Hortensia. At least I'll be here to enjoy your masterpiece." She received a big grin from the housekeeper.

Cigar smoke permeated the far end of the house. The condesa reflected, not for the first time, that she was glad her husband confined his bad habit to an area well away from their living space. It appeared that almost everyone had left. Carlos was talking quietly to a former colleague in the Army. They stopped talking when she entered the room.

"Teresa," said Carlos, turning his wheelchair and moving swiftly towards her. "You know General Bastides, of course."

The General smiled and bowed slightly. "Condesa! Always such a pleasure."

"The General is just leaving," Carlos said, looking at both of them. "He has very kindly offered to give me a lift to our class reunion get-together tonight. I'm really sorry, my dear. I completely forgot about it. Hortensia has packed my uniform in an overnight case—so I will have everything I need. I can change at the club. Are you sure you'll be alright without me for one night?"

"Of course, darling," she replied, kissing him on the forehead. "I have lots of work to do. It is a pleasure meeting you again, General," she added, starting to offer her hand to Carlos' former army colleague, but receiving instead a salute from him. She may have been wrong, she reflected later, but did she also hear the faint sound of heels clicking together?

She took the handles of Carlos' wheelchair and pushed him to the elevator. "Let me know when you're returning tomorrow, darling. I plan to be here for a few hours in the morning. Then I'll go work at the office and get ready for my speech in Lleida."

"My goodness, I completely forgot," exclaimed her husband spinning his wheelchair around to talk to her. "I'm really becoming very forgetful in my old age. Please forgive me. And, of course, have a wonderful trip."

"You are not old, darling," she smiled. "You just have a lot on your mind." She caught a sharp glance from the General who then quickly turned away.

Teresa watched as the General's car drove down the driveway. She decided on a quick walk around their garden to clear the tobacco smell from her clothes. It really was a disgusting habit of Carlos', she thought. Harmless enough at his age, and he enjoyed it. Still, it was unpleasant for others.

She frowned as she thought about the General's visit to their home. And it was so unlike Carlos to forget to tell her about something as important as a military class reunion.

By the time she'd returned to the smoking room, the worst of the cigar smoke had dissipated. She replaced the top of a brandy bottle and flushed the remainder of several cigar stubs down the toilet; she knew how Hortensia hated that particular job.

A phone rang and she looked around. She traced it to an armchair. A cell phone had fallen down the side of a cushion. She glanced at it and saw that it did not belong to Carlos. The call display indicated a long-distance number. She let it ring out, and took it back upstairs with her.

"Hortensia," she called. "One of my husband's guests has left his cell phone behind. I'll let don Carlos know but, just in case I'm not here, it will be on the hallway table."

"Si, señora!" the housemaid called from the kitchen.

"Oh, and most of the smoke has cleared. So it's okay for you to clean his smoking room. I have cleared some of their stuff away."

"Gracias, señora," answered the housemaid, coming out of the kitchen and wiping her hands on her apron. A few minutes later the condesa could hear her footsteps clumping down the wood steps in the direction of the smoking room.

The phone rang again. The condesa decided to ignore it and the sound soon stopped.

She was walking back to her study to call Carlos, when the cell phone rang again.

She went back and glanced at the call display. It was the same long-distance number and, from the caller's insistent ringing, clearly it was urgent. Picking up a pen, she made a note of the number on a notepad and took the sheet with her, intending to call Carlos.

There was no reply from his cell phone, so she left a message for him to call her. Pocketing the sheet of paper, she went back to her study. It was getting dark. Walking around each window, she closed the curtains. Then she walked over and studied a reproduction Picasso on the wall. Reaching over the frame, she pressed a button and the picture swung outwards revealing a wall safe.

She keyed in her password and the door released. Reaching in, she removed a sheaf of bound papers, then closed and locked it with a spin of the dial. Going back to her desk, she placed the papers in an overnight bag.

Some time later, her phone rang. It was Carlos. "I got your message. The phone you found belongs to the General. It's really important that it remains secure. Do you have it with you?" he asked, his voice rushed and lathered with concern.

"Of course, Carlos darling. It's here. I have it with me. He's been receiving calls. Do you want me to…"

"No, don't touch it. Don't answer it," Carlos shot back. "The General's chauffeur will be there soon to pick it up."

"Okay," the condesa started to say.

"I'm sorry, Teresa," said Carlos, intervening, "but there's sensitive material on that phone; you know how it is."

"It's not a problem, darling. I'll have it ready for the General's man. Now don't worry, Carlos. Are you alright? You sound stressed. Are you managing okay?"

The General's chauffeur arrived. Watching him through an upper window, the condesa confirmed her earlier impression that he was more than his role implied. For certain, he was former military. She found him menacing: he had deep piercing blue eyes and his mouth bore a permanent sneer. Then there was what seemed to be a burn mark on his arm. Perhaps that was why he always seemed to wear those black leather gloves, she thought.

Tonight he was polite, but she felt she was being interrogated about the loss of the phone. No, she assured him, she had simply heard it ring. Actually, several times. Otherwise, the phone had been left securely on the hall table. No one had touched it, she assured him.

The General's chauffeur softened his manner and thanked her. He bowed to her in almost the same manner as his employer.

Still thinking about their brief conversation, the condesa watched as his car moved slowly down the driveway and through the automatic gate, turning left on the road that would take him in the direction of Madrid. The condesa poured herself a glass of brandy. Then she slumped into a thickly upholstered easy chair and sipped her drink. The chauffeur certainly seemed very full of himself, she reflected.

Hortensia announced that dinner would be ready shortly. "Would the señora prefer it on a tray in her study?" the housekeeper enquired.

"That would be a good idea, thank you dear," she replied.

She couldn't get the cell phone incident out of her mind. Carlos' and the chauffeur's over-reactive response seemed almost on the verge of paranoia, she thought. She hadn't even checked to see if the phone had been security locked. She was too young to remember much about the days under Franco, but this seemed to have a tinge of the same feeling of oppression.

Her phone rang. It was her parliamentary secretary. "Condesa, do you still wish me to come by?" he asked.

Teresa's mind refocused on the papers she had taken out of the safe. She rubbed her forehead, in an effort to clear her thoughts. "Yes, of course, Alexander. You know the gate code. Let yourself in."

She looked at her laptop and tried to prioritise her list of things to do: three urgent items from the Cortes, two from the charity that she chaired and several outstanding emails—some of which, she decided, could wait. In addition, she had to review the presentation she would be giving in Barcelona, the day after tomorrow.

Hortensia knocked and wheeled in a trolley with her evening meal. "You are always working, señora," she said. "I have made some soup, to start. It will do you good." The condesa smiled at her housekeeper.

About half an hour later, her parliamentary secretary buzzed her from the gate. "Just approaching the house, Condesa. Is it convenient for you?"

Minutes later the doorbell rang and Hortensia showed the visitor into the condesa's study. The personal assistant smiled and sat in the chair that the condesa pointed towards. A few moments later, without speaking, she rose from her desk. Taking the night bag, she handed it to him. "These are what you need, I think, Alexander. You will, of course, ensure they are delivered safely. I can trust you on that, can't I?"

"Naturally, Condesa," he replied. "I will guard them with my life. Felipe is expecting them tonight."

The condesa nodded her approval. "May I offer you any refreshment?" she asked, more from politeness than any wish to see him linger any longer in her home. He declined and left.

The condesa sat back in her chair and thought about the sequence of events that she anticipated. Felipe would receive the construction contract papers tonight and would scrutinise every detail before handing them over to the investigating authorities tomorrow. Of course, he would make a duplicate— just as she had done, and secured them at a safety deposit box at her bank.

Although she would be implicated in the construction bribery scandal, she knew that she had not benefitted—at least not financially. It was true that she had been able to meet a campaign promise to her constituents. Surely, that was not a criminal offence, she reasoned.

Felipe's view had been the same. But in the world of politics, and the witch-hunt that the investigators were pursuing relentlessly throughout Spain, she was concerned that an over-zealous official might not see things quite that way. These days, it was difficult to know from whose pay book those officials might be enjoying their rewards. If things did not go well, she knew she would need every powerful friend she had.

It was then that she put her hand in her pocket and took out the notepad sheet on which she had written the number of the long-distance incoming call on the General's phone. She was about to put it through her shredder. Instead, out of curiosity, she Googled the area code. It was the international code for Marrakech.

On instinct, she folded the sheet and put it in her handbag. Generals, whether retired or not, have friends in high places. She and Carlos did too. But these were different times. If the authorities investigating the construction contracts became too officious, she reflected, it might be useful to have some leverage with the General and his powerful friends.

Catalunya

Antonio had been called out late on a homicide case. He crawled into bed alongside Maria. She woke briefly and hugged him. Then she turned over and started to go back to sleep. It was 4:00 a.m.

He could feel her soft skin press closely against his, as she wriggled her backside and spooned hard into him. Her naked body carried the fragrance of gardenias, and her hair smelled fresh. These sensations, along with the adrenaline and coffee from the night's operations, created in him a potent cocktail of lust and desire.

For a few minutes, he tried to stave off his passion. Finally, he could stand it no longer. He reached forward and stretched his arm around her body. His hand cupped her breast and his thumb caressed her nipple.

She turned suddenly to face him, a wicked grin on her face that he could sense even in the dark. She crawled on top of him and stretched her open hand between his legs. Her long hair covered his face.

Then she laughed and said, "What took you so long, top cop? I was worried for a moment you might be training for the priesthood."

Moroccan Girl

The church bells from Santa Isabel's rang the second time that day, summoning to mass those who had missed the early morning service.

Manuel, waking from a deep sleep, thought that the bells sounded louder than usual. Then he realised that the doorbell of the apartment was ringing. He glanced at his watch, and then at his wife's still sleeping and shapeless form—mouth open wide and loudly snoring.

Shuffling to the door, he peered through the spyglass. In dismay, he slumped with his back against the door. He had told her never to come to his home. How had she found out where he lived, he asked himself. How had she been able to get into the apartment building?

The bell rang again, insistent for immediate attention.

He unlocked the door and put his finger to his lips to quieten her. She looked terrible. Her clothes were torn and her hair was dishevelled. She had been crying and her eyes were wet and blood red. A large dark bruise was forming on one cheek, and she had what almost certainly was a cut from a knife at the corner of her nose. Blood was seeping towards her mouth.

"Madre de Dios," he exclaimed. "What happened to you, Saida?"

She began to cry. "You must come with me. At once. If you do not, they will kill Omar. Please, Manuel, please!"

"Shhh," he implored, pleading with her to keep her voice down.

The Mossos transcriber tried to think how he could get her out of the building before his wife awoke. His heart beat loudly and his face flushed.

"Wait in the stairwell," he told her, pointing to the fire escape at the end of the corridor. "I will be out in a few minutes."

The girl started to push her way into the apartment, but he held her narrow shoulders and turned in the direction of the stairwell. "Honestly, Saida, please wait. I will come out in a few minutes. I have to get dressed."

He saw her dark eyes, wide and moist with fear. In that moment, he was aware how young she was.

Manuel did not remember the journey to her apartment. It was located in a poor area of the city. They had selected it together because it was what he could afford, along with some spending money for her family. After all, he told her, he only had his salary from the Mossos. He did not mention that it was supplemented by his other earnings. She and her family were glad to accept whatever he gave them.

Before, whenever they had met to be together at the apartment, Saida's mother had taken Omar away for a discreet interval. Today, as they entered, the older woman was sitting on the floor against the wall. She was holding the boy close to her—trying to protect him.

Two men were in the room. The first, he recognised at once. He was the one who had recruited him. The man had given no sign of recognition as Manuel had entered, and picked at the dirt in his fingernails. He seemed indifferent—almost bored about what was taking place. Manuel had never liked the man. He was a coarse fellow from the country, with the manners of a pig.

The other man, sitting in reverse on a kitchen chair, was smiling at Manuel—although the smile did not suggest any element of friendship or goodwill. It was a self-satisfied smile which indicated events were falling into place just as he had expected.

He was of stocky build with a well-trimmed beard. In a way, the man was quite handsome, conceded Manuel. For a moment, the thought crossed Manuel's mind that the man might be a relative of the girl. Perhaps an older brother, unhappy with his sister's liaison with an aging man.

Quickly, he dismissed the thought. In his hand, the man held a gun—pointing directly at the boy's head. The man's stance clearly was intended to threaten the child.

What was the gunman doing, and what was his contact doing here, Manuel looked puzzled.

He stood motionless as Saida shouted out her son's name and ran to him, kissing him and shielding him with her body.

The boy was just over five years old, Manuel knew. He realised that in all the time he'd been seeing the girl, he'd never asked much about her about her family. It was for his own pleasure that the arrangement had been made, and he did not see why he should not enjoy the full focus of her attentions.

The gunman spoke to the girl in French. Manuel did not understand what he was saying. Standing in the middle of the room he listened—trying to guess at what was taking place. He tried to piece together what might have happened.

In any case, it was increasingly clear to Manuel that he had made a serious error.

He was sure there was no connection between the Moroccan girl and the copies of materials he provided to his contact through the dead letter box. But somehow, he realised with a growing sense of dread, the two things had become related.

The girl looked up at him, and said in a barely audible whisper, "He wants you to provide some things from the Mossos."

"What things?" asked Manuel, his stomach feeling a sudden sharp spasm of pain.

The gunman continued in French, without waiting for the girl to translate.

"He wants access to the Mossos' underground car park."

Manuel shook his head. "It can't be done. Security is incredibly tight. The pass code changes every week. Not just that, they have fingerprint scans at the underground parking entrance."

The gunman spoke to the girl for a few minutes. "He asks how delivery vehicles get into the building?"

Manuel swallowed hard. "They must have a visitor's pass, and be escorted in."

"Are you an escort, he asks," said the girl.

"No, I'm not. I'm just a clerk in the office," conceded Manuel in a low voice, fearing that worse was yet to come.

The boy started to cry and the Moroccan girl pulled him close to her, stroking his hair. The gesture of love between the two affected Manuel in a way he did not expect. The girl was a casual affair. Yet he had thought that somehow their relationship would last—maybe until he could save enough money that they could go away together.

It was a ridiculous notion, he knew. Yet, the thought of it had kept him focused at work and willing to take some risks that really didn't harm anyone.

"He wants you to get him a security pass and tell him the entry code," said the girl.

"But that's impossible…" Manuel began to protest—until he saw the gunman raise his arm and take direct aim at the boy's head. The girl and her mother screamed.

Manuel threw up his hands. "Okay, don't shoot. I'll find a way," he pleaded with the gunman, who smiled at his quick acquiescence before slowly lowering his arm. Then he spoke again to the girl.

"He says you can go," she said. "He says to tell you that you are not safe. If you confess to the Mossos, your life will be over. So will ours. He says that if you cooperate with him, he will leave us all alone. That is his sacred promise. He will have no further use for you. You will be free to live your life as you wish."

The gunman spoke again in rapid French. When she turned to speak to Manuel, there were tears streaming down her cheeks. She sobbed before she could catch her breath to speak. "He says... he says that if you set a trap, everyone will die. They will kill us all—as they would execute common criminals. They will slit our throats."

She buried her head in her hands and tried to wipe away her tears. "Do you understand, he asks?"

Manuel could feel his heart pounding in his chest. He nodded helplessly. "Saida, I'm sorry... " he started to say to the girl, but she abruptly turned away from him. Her normally beautiful eyes were now blazing with a hatred of him that he could not have believed was possible.

Slowly, he turned around and walked out of the door. He did not fear being shot in the back and, for an instance, almost wished that fate on himself. As he walked out to the street in a daze, he tried to clear his mind. How could he accomplish what the gunman had demanded? He tried to force himself to think. There was nothing. He could not concentrate. The look of hatred in Saida's eyes stayed with him. He couldn't rid himself of the image.

Without being aware of his direction, he began to wander the streets. He was not conscious of how long he walked, or how far. Then he realised that he was sitting on a park bench. The metal was still cold from last night's frost. Vaguely, he was aware of some passers-by, but his focus was on his image of the hatred on Saida's face.

If he could find a way to get what the gunman wanted, perhaps no one would find out, he reasoned. Maybe he could keep his job after all. Maybe he could still save the girl and her family.

Maybe they could go back to the way it had been. Their times in bed together; the good times. Laughing together over the little jokes he made, which she found so amusing. The fun they had even in the confines of her small, overcrowded flat. Their lovemaking after the boy had been taken outside for a walk by her mother. The discreet knocking sound on the front door when it was time for him to leave. That was what he most wanted, he reassured himself. It was worth fighting for.

He stood up from the metal bench and walked. His head throbbed with pain. More painful to him, however, was what he would tell his wife. He hated living with her. He recoiled at the mere thought of her coarse habits. Gladly, he would leave her if he could.

But, in truth, he dreaded her wrath almost as much as he feared the consequences of his indiscreet actions.

Mossos' Headquarters

It was God's merciful deed to him that Manuel's fear of his wife's fury turned out to be unfounded.

Without being fully conscious of his actions, before returning to their apartment, and as a matter of habit, he had purchased a newspaper and two bars of her favourite food snack from a nearby Pakistani-owned store. As he let himself into the front door, he saw her sitting in front of the TV. She was engrossed in watching a popular game show.

She said nothing to him as he handed the snacks to her. "I'll need the newspaper," she said, her eyes fixated on the screen. "Don't go taking it to your office again. I need it for kitty litter."

The cat was as miserable a creature as his wife, and he resented both animals equally. The cat clearly felt the same way about him, and frequently tried to scratch him. He had dreamed several times about throttling it, hiding it in a strong plastic bag and throwing it in a contractor's garbage bin somewhere well away from their apartment building.

This morning, he had deeper concerns to worry about. Disposal of the miserable feline could wait another day. He felt surprisingly upbeat. Despite everything, there was still the prospect that if his plan worked, he could abandon his wife to her coarse habits and be happy again with Saida.

"I have to go to the office," he heard himself saying to his wife. He had his next line of explanation ready, but she showed no interest. For him, working on Sundays was quite normal—even though he never actually travelled anywhere close to his place of work. After all, Sunday was the day he normally would visit the girl. Working at the office was a perfect cover.

"Bring me back some cigarettes," she called to him as he opened the apartment door—on which, just a few hours ago, the girl had been hammering her slender fists. "I'm on my last package."

He screwed up his face into a mask of hatred as he shut the door behind him. The woman was vulgar and vile, he muttered to himself. What a bitch!

The security guard at the main entrance to the Mossos' headquarters recognised him. "Sunday overtime?" he asked, with a slight begrudging tone.

"Backlog of work," replied Manuel, wondering if in future it would be to his advantage to get to know the man on a more-friendly basis. It might come in useful, considering the task ahead of him. On an impulse, he offered the guard the morning paper, still unread.

"Finished with it?" the guard asked with a surprised half-smile. Manuel nodded and walked through the swing doors which the guard had opened for him. "You could try the Sudoku. Usually it's quite good."

In the past several years, since Manuel had acquired his supplementary extra-curricular job, he had made a continuing study of the security system at the Mossos headquarters building.

Security was designed to stop people from bringing certain items into the building. He posed no danger in that respect. Carrying nothing but the lunch he prepared for himself, and occasionally some fresh blank CDs, he was in no danger of being intercepted when he entered the building.

There was less concern among the security people about persons exiting the building, when he was most at risk.

Long ago, he had memorised the location of the building's CCTVs. He had learned to look out for the random spot checks that the security people carried out—which could be a mild irritant any time he had any CDs for the drop box. He always had a cover story ready in these circumstances.

Today, in the lobby, he slowed his steps. Bending down to tie his shoelaces, he scanned the area and refamiliarised himself with its exact layout.

There were four elevators to the higher floors and two to the parking area underneath the building. One of the elevators was in use by a building maintenance crew doing electrical work above the lobby ceiling lights. Several paperboard packages containing replacement light fittings were strewn on the floor.

He walked carefully around them, and flashed his ID card at the scanner to open the elevator door. Travelling to his floor, he saw that there were a few people working at their cubicle desks in his section, but his presence was not noticed.

For once, he was grateful for the obscurity that his insignificant physical bearing conveyed. He slumped into his chair and switched on his computer. He opened his home screen, making a pretence of studying the display in the eventuality that anyone might question his presence there on a weekend.

In the quietness of his cubicle, he sat back in his chair and racked his brains for a solution to his dilemma.

He knew of several colleagues who used the car park. He did not. The Metro was much cheaper and on a special occasion he might take a taxi. Surely there must be a way to steal someone's ID card, he pondered. There were strict rules in the building about wearing ID, but he knew that not all his colleagues were prompt about returning visitor cards to security.

Lost IDs had to be reported without delay. Then there was a long process of enquiry and an equally long process of getting a permanent replacement card. Two years ago, despite objections from the police union, a system of fines had been introduced. Most employees had become careful after that.

The security people were paranoid about these things. Most people he knew would rather enter the elevators under cover of someone else's ID than go through the pain of reporting a lost ID card—which they probably would find later in a piece of clothing at home, or occasionally one that had gone through the wash.

Then there was the problem of random fingerprint scans at the entrance to the underground car park. If that unit could be disabled or bypassed, he supposed, the backup security system was physical ID—usually inspected by security people who would know him by sight.

Slowly, the outlines of a plan came into his mind. It was risky, but it could work.

He got some files out of his locked desk and idly leafed through them, his attention focused elsewhere. Sipping the water he'd carried over from the cooler, he checked his watch. It was already near lunchtime. Usually at this hour on a Sunday he would be at the girl's place, he reflected with disappointment. He allowed his imagination to drift into an erotic scene with her. It was a fantasy he thought about often, even here at his desk.

Her dark-skinned body, slender and smooth. Her mouth, at first resistant to his advances, would suddenly yield to him—inviting further aggression and building his passion to an almost unbearable tempo. Then, with a low guttural laugh, she would slow him down.

Pushing his body back onto the bed, she would move slowly up his body dragging her tight pointed breasts provocatively over his chest, gently rubbing and relaxing him before encouraging him again, repeating this cycle several times before forcing her hand around his modest manhood and making him feel like a god.

Slowly the fantasy faded. He glanced around the office. It seemed emptier now than before, as people headed home or out to a local café for lunch. He was alone as he took the elevator down to the lobby and walked around the ladders and safety scaffolding being used by the maintenance people. He felt the need to use the washroom.

Fortune, ever fickle, was to present him with an opportunity that day.

As he entered the washroom, one of the maintenance guys came out. Manuel stood aside to let the larger and more powerful man through before he went in. He received no thanks for his politeness, but that was not unusual. He had found early in life that he did not inspire confidence in other people. Often, he felt pushed aside. Years ago, he had come to accept it and no longer resented being dismissed as inconsequential.

There were other things he was good at, he reassured himself.

In one of the stalls, another maintenance worker was making heavy weather of the meal he had eaten the previous night. On the counter by the washbasins, the man had taken off his leather tool belt before entering the stall. Manuel could not believe what he was seeing.

In a pouch on the leather belt was an ID card.

Without even glancing around, he pocketed it.

He left the building as soon as he could. With luck, it might be some time before the owner found it was missing. Back on the street, he smiled in relief.

Feeling exhilarated by his clever sleight of hand, he hailed a cab and instructed the driver to go to a shopping mall that was a block or two away from the girl's apartment. He sat back in the taxi and relaxed. The day had started badly, he reflected, but things were getting better. Much better.

He reflected again on his own cleverness. He had been smart to tell the taxi driver to drop him some distance from his actual destination. It was the kind of quick thinking of an undercover man that set him apart from others, Manuel commended himself.

He began to feel that, if things continued to go his way, this unfortunate situation might yet be resolved in his favour. In truth, he admitted to himself that the gunman had terrified him. As he walked the remaining distance to the girl's apartment building, he felt satisfied that he had achieved so much, so quickly. The gunman would be pleased with him. More importantly to Manuel, he would find a way to regain Saida's confidence in him.

Things would go back to normal. He was determined now that he would leave his wife. He would take the girl and her son away somewhere with him. They would work out the details later. They didn't need luxury, just somewhere where he could be a good husband to the girl and a father to her son.

He could do it, he knew he could. First thing he had to do was to get past this immediate crisis, then everything would be fine.

Permitting himself a smile, he walked up the stairs to her apartment. The elevator in the building had been out of use for some time. He was enjoying the exercise.

Yes, everything is going to turn out just fine he reassured himself.

Santa María la Virgen Church, Near Lleida

Rays of light from the late autumn's mid-morning sun penetrated the ancient stained glass windows of Santa María la Virgen. Transformed into a myriad of colours, they came to rest near the scuffed wooden pews where Father Damien Aracruz de le Misericordia was kneeling

Close observation would indicate that kneeling might not be the most accurate description of the priest's pose at that particular moment. His last snort of the magic powder had been a day ago. He had exhausted his supplies and the prospect of obtaining more seemed dim.

During the night he had woken in a cold sweat, and now he felt depressed and irritable. He had fallen onto the floor in an attempt to steady his tremors rather than with any thought of penitence or devotion. The glass of vodka he had consumed just shortly before seemed to have no effect. He struggled to organise the scattered thoughts that formed, then burst like bubbles, in his head. One pervasive thought stood out clearly to him: he had to get a grip on his mind, and soon.

It was difficult because the brightness of the morning light was distracting him.

Above the altar, there was a slight imperfection in a small triangular panel of the glass window. It had happened several hundreds of years earlier when molten glass had been poured into a crude mould by faithful artisans of the parish helping to build their church.

Now it acted like a prism. In obedience with the eternal laws of God and of physics, the imperfection refracted a single ray of pure natural white light—a solitary island of white in a sea of the captivating colours of a rainbow.

In the stillness of the church, a shaft of indigo blue light caught tiny specks of dust floating aimlessly. A microcosm of our pointless existence in this world, Father Damien reflected, allowing himself to wallow in his own despair. His right hand holding the wood rail shook, and he steadied it with his other hand until the tremor stopped.

The movement was involuntary and was something he could not easily hide. So far, he had been able to pass it off as nerves. Then he wiped some dampness coming from his nose with the back of his hand.

He cast his eyes downwards, silently reciting a prayer embedded in his brain for almost all his fifty-seven years. Father Damien observed, as he had many times in his long tenure, that the indigo blue light from the window rested in an almost perfect formation on two particular stone floor tiles in the nave, almost as if it were indicating a treasure hidden under the floor.

Faint and almost imperceptible, the vestige of a hopeful smile passed fleetingly across his face. He sighed aloud. He had prayed, without avail, many times for such good fortune. He had long imagined that hidden in a secret place somewhere in the church, possibly under those very stones, lay a fortune in treasures stashed away years ago by one of his predecessors. A secret act carried out perhaps at a time of great crisis, or a time of persecution, he speculated. A treasure hidden for safekeeping, somehow overlooked and then forgotten until this day.

Yet he knew they were simply dreams—mere fantasies—fed by an excess of chemicals that too quickly had decomposed into unhelpful by-products now coursing through his veins.

His dreams were false prophets of hopes and yearnings that were without any likelihood of substantiation—and without any prospects of a divine response. The lack of heavenly recognition was much like his life, he thought. His thoughts hinting of bitterness were quickly assailed by his spiritual defences, reminding him that evil thoughts were the work of the Devil and must be cast out.

Chastised by a feeling of guilt and now, as the vodka lost its potency, beginning to feel remorseful, he reminded himself of his modest station in life. He thought sternly about the oft-taught lesson that he had no right to refuse, or be resentful of, the path that God had chosen for him.

He had often gained solace from the Beatitudes. They were even more reassuring to him in their modern form. For the meek shall inherit the earth, he murmured.

To seek a hearing with the Holy Trinity, Father Damien directed his prayers—offering them all almost exclusively and respectfully to the Blessed Virgin. It was a lesson he had learned young. Do not permit yourself the conceit of addressing thy Creator directly, the monseigneur at school had cautioned him. For we on Earth are not worthy, the devout old man had said. Rather, beseech the Virgin Mary, the Mother of Christ. Beseech her to be your supplicant. Pray for her to intercede on your behalf with her son.

These words had guided Father Damien through childhood and later taken him into the priesthood—ultimately to his position of spiritual guardian of this impoverished parish.

He lifted his eyes to look upon the statue of the Blessed Virgin positioned on the wall just three metres from where he was kneeling. She looked down upon him, her outstretched arms reaching out to him. It was a divine invitation. Come with me, my child, she seemed to say.

Yet, no matter how hard he tried, he could not dispel the harsh sense of abandonment. He knew deep depths of despair and depression. Loneliness, in many ways, was his closest friend; he feared it not.

He knew he should be grateful for the gift of his life and all its blessings. Yet, if he were to be honest with himself, he would admit that almost all of his prayers over the decades had gone unanswered. Not unheard; not necessarily even ignored. But just as surely, in effect, as if they had been rejected and arbitrarily dismissed.

A sudden sound behind him caused him to turn around. Except for Sunday Mass, holy days and other special occasions, the heavy wooden door at the entrance to the church remained locked. He had not heard the Narthex door open, although he had left it unlocked for the few devout parishioners who may wish to gain early access to the church and offer prayers, or light a candle.

He recognised the two men who walked towards him. His stomach tightened, and the feeling of anxiety he experienced every time they returned. Composing himself, he threw up his arms in welcome. "Bless you," he exclaimed.

One of the men he knew well, the other through association. Both scared him.

The man he knew as a builder from the village addressed him first. "Good day, Father. We thought we might pay you a quick visit," he smiled, revealing tobacco-stained teeth. Just as quickly, the smile disappeared.

Father Damien was aware the church was empty of parishioners. Scared, his eyes looked past the two men and swept the back of the church. He did not like being seen with them. "Shall we go to the vestry?"

"We're okay right here," said the second man abruptly. His tall, thin frame and threatening demeanour did not encourage social chatter. Not that Father Damien thought he had much in common with them. He was constrained, however, by the business arrangements they had with him, a situation he had rushed into and almost immediately regretted.

The builder addressed him. "There's a rumour going around that you're being replaced."

"Replaced? No, no. The bishop has reassigned me to a new parish, that's all. Look, it won't make any difference— you know—to our arrangement," he smiled reassuringly at both of them in turn, searching their faces for signs of response.

"When's the new one arriving?" asked the tall man, using his fingers to push his leather gloves deeper onto his hand.

The priest looked flustered. "There's no rush the bishop has told me," He smiled a generous smile that seemed out of place in the conversation. "I'm to take my time. You know, finish off here what I have to do. Tie up loose ends, and all that. I have a very nice new parish…"

"We're not interested in where you're going, Father," said the builder loudly. Then he added more softly, "I'm sure you'll do a good job there. What we need to know is when you leave and when your replacement arrives."

'Look, everything will be fine here…" he began to say.

"When the hell are you leaving?" shouted the tall man, taking a threatening step towards him.

"Two months. That's as soon as my replacement can get here," blurted out the priest. "And, of course, I myself have to get ready. For my new assignment, I mean. It's really quite exciting. And you needn't worry…"

"What date exactly?" demanded the tall man, losing his patience.

"He will be arriving January 1st. I'll stay until then," answered the priest, the energy disappearing from his voice.

He looked at the two men, who seemed to relax with this news. "Okay, that will do," said the builder. Father Damien bit his lip and reminded himself these were not the types of men who would tolerate any questions from him. He waited patiently for them to speak.

After a few moments, and without consulting his colleague, the builder said, "We will be coming around in a few days' time for our merchandise. You can find something else to do while we are here. Thursday evening."

"Absolutely," said the priest, with pseudo pleasure. "Whenever you'd like."

He received no response.

"We'll take a look at our stuff now," said the builder. "We have our key."

The priest looked down at the ground. Then he clasped both hands in front of himself, as if resolved to talk about something painful. "Will I still be able to get…" his voice almost squeaking.

"You'll get your stuff, Father," said the builder. "We look after our own in the Church. You know that." As if to substantiate his point, he withdrew from his pocket a small bag of white powder. He put his hand on the priest's shoulder and gripped it firmly. "You'll get a guaranteed supply of this."

The priest took the bag and slipped it quickly into a pocket inside his cassock. "Thank you," he said with evident relief. "Thank you."

"You can go," said the tall man. They watched as the priest scurried back towards the vestry. He didn't turn to look back at them.

The priest retreated to his bathroom. Locking the door with shaking hands, he took out the white powder. Wetting the tip of his finger he picked up a few grains, placing them on the side of his tongue; then he sprinkled a thin line of the powder on the side of the sink.

Blocking one nostril with his thumb, he inhaled it through the other. He leaned back his head, breathed in heavily and waited. The effect was immediate. He felt his body relax and his blood flow quicken. He felt a surge of energy and optimism.

Most of all, he felt strong. Renewed like this, he knew he could face anything.

Aladdin's Cave

At one time, Father Damien's church had been the centre of a prosperous peach and pear growing community. Several of the outbuildings at the back of the church, now unused for a long time, had housed agricultural equipment and stored crops.

The advent of irrigation, higher crop yields and centralised storage led to the decline of the smallholdings scattered around the village. Rich landowners from Madrid now controlled the business. Trucks drove the produce directly from the field to large-scale centralised cleaning and grading facilities thirty kilometres away.

The two men unlocked the heavy doors to one of the stone outbuildings. It was secured by two robust locks they had installed themselves. The structure had been kept in good repair by the diocese—a fact the builder had noted when he'd scouted the area.

His white construction van with the ladder was parked next to the building. Hidden from the road, they were confident it would not create comment from anyone passing by. From the back of the van, the builder lifted out two parcels of empty paper sacks. They were labelled 'cement'. The tall man lifted out a machine that would seal them once they were filled.

They secured the door shut behind them. Using a flashlight, the tall man located the light switch. In place of the dim bulb, he inserted a large wattage version which they stored for their visits. Both men blinked as it created a harsh bright light. The building was ideal for their purposes. Built of thick stone, it had no windows. Under the shade of the trees outside, it was always cool and well sheltered.

"Let's check it," said the tall man.

The builder walked over to a pile of plastic bags and took a penknife from his pocket; he made a small slit in one of the bags.

"How is it?"

"It's fine. Nice and dry," he said, looking closely at the contents and squeezing the white crystalline contents between his fingers. "Yeah, they're good," he added, after checking two other bags at random.

"What about the other stuff?" asked the tall man, nodding his head in the direction of several wood boxes painted with a red skull-and-crossbones and the words "Danger Explosives".

"That's the stuff I don't like," he said with distaste, as the builder opened one of the boxes of yellow granules.

"You needn't worry. It's not going to harm you. You can treat it pretty rough," the builder smiled. "Just make sure you wear gloves while we're mixing these two."

"How far away are the detonator caps?" asked the tall man, remembering the list of required materials he had been given.

"Ten minutes. We'll transport them separately, of course," he smiled with the smug self-assurance of an expert, again revealing his tobacco-stained teeth. He recalled his theft of the explosives from a limestone quarry that summer.

"Okay, let's not waste time," ordered the tall man.

They took off their jackets and, for over an hour, they worked slowly but steadily. At first, they were hesitant about the mixing process—aware that their instructions had to be carried out exactly.

"The ratio has to be exactly as we've been instructed," said the tall man.

"Yeah, yeah, I've done this before," replied the builder with obvious irritation in his voice.

One by one, they rebagged the freshly created mixture into the paper sacks then sealed them. As each one was finished, they stacked it in the middle of the floor.

"How stable is this stuff now?" asked the tall man, pausing for breath. It was not the first time he had asked the question.

"I've told you. It's mostly fertiliser with the granulated TNT. Without the detonators, it's not going to do nothing. We can take it anywhere," said the builder. "Just treat it like sacks of cement or sand. So long as you don't drop it, we'll be safe transporting it, don't worry."

When they finished, both men were sweating.

"Okay, you can wait outside," said the tall man. "Just remember…" he said without finishing the sentence. His threatening demeanour made it unnecessary as the builder scurried quickly towards the door.

From his pocket, the tall man took out a key and appeared to examine it. He waited until he heard the door of the van open then close shut. Satisfied that the builder was doing as he'd been told, he approached a second door leading off the first and unlocked it.

With narrow wood beams, the inside room was smaller—and less well lit. He took a flashlight from his jacket pocket and scanned the room. It always gave him a special kind of pleasure to be here, to know that he was the guardian of such riches.

Stacked in neat piles, ingots of pure gold gleamed as they were caught in the light. He could not resist running his fingers along the bars, feeling a light film of dust. He took comfort from their roughness and loved the dull clunk sound they made when lifted and dropped back into their place. He knew the precise number of ingots, and their total value—a calculation he had made frequently. With rising gold prices, each now was worth almost a half million dollars.

He found peace in this room, and had described it to the General as Aladdin's Cave. The General liked the name. This vast store of wealth funded Operation FERROL. It was a good omen.

Brushing aside a dead fly caught in a cobweb, he reminded himself of his sacred duty to his cause. The fly, wrapped in a cocoon of web, became stuck to the back of his leather glove.

He recalled that, many times as a child, he had removed the wings and legs of flies while they were still alive. It had given him satisfaction to count how many times the limbless insects would attempt to escape—sudden bursts of activity from their dismembered bodies before they would finally succumb.

He had wanted to share his scientific findings at school, but his classmates always avoided him. Even his teachers, fearing his awkward looks, would stay out of his way.

When it had come time to join the army, he found outlets for his proclivities that school had never offered. After that, most of his more extreme acts carried a veneer of official legitimacy. Those which didn't, he hid very well.

His eyes clouded for a brief moment. There had been one time; it was during his days in the army. It had not gone well. Perhaps it was the most serious mistake he had made. Certainly one he would never repeat. Fortunately, it had come to the attention of the General. The incident had been smoothed over. The parents of the boy had not pressed charges, and the General ensured that the police recorded nothing on the official record. After that, he was protected.

Of course, any time the General needed a special assignment carried out, he was chosen. Almost always these were unofficial, and often violent—a circumstance that appealed to him immensely. When the General retired, he had been offered a job as his chauffeur.

Along with special duties.

His flashlight beam panned over to a neatly piled stack of wooden boxes; they were the focus of his attention.

Prising open the lid on one of the boxes, he extracted three bundles of used, clean euro banknotes of varying denominations—with a total value, he estimated, of well over a million dollars. These bundles he stuffed individually inside his jacket pockets. It was precisely the amount that the General had authorised him to take for the drop-off to the next courier, plus some also approved by him for incidental expenses, to meet the working capital needs of the project.

He recounted and confirmed all nine of the wooden boxes containing euros. The money had been withdrawn from the bank in Andorra when the government clampdown had started in earnest. It had been a wise move by the General and his supporters. Nowadays, the police were checking vehicles coming over the border.

Satisfied with his work, the chauffeur locked and double-checked both doors before getting into the van. "I told you not to smoke," he told the builder. "It's a disgusting habit."

The builder scowled and lowered his window to throw out the butt.

"Not here, you idiot," said the chauffeur, grabbing the builder's arm.

"Are you certain we can trust that fucking priest?" he asked after a pause.

"He's terrified of us," said the builder. "Anyway, he depends on me for his stuff. We have enough time on our side. I'll take care of him when we have to. Just leave it to me."

"I don't like it," said the tall man. "He's too creepy and unstable for my liking."

"We'll be okay for a few more weeks," said the builder with confidence. "You heard him. His replacement doesn't arrive until January."

The tall man did not look convinced. The stash was far too valuable to take risks, he reminded himself. He didn't trust the priest, and he didn't trust the builder for that matter. He would speak at once to the General.

Unseen to the men, Father Damien pulled back into the shadows of his bedroom at the back of the house alongside the church. Minutes earlier, the room had echoed with the rhythmic sound of the electric shutter of his expensive camera taking multiple frames per second of the two men. It had been a wise investment of parishioners' funds, he reflected.

Expertly, he took out the camera's memory stick and secured it inside the shoe he was wearing. After replacing it with one containing photos of local wildlife and architecture, he placed the camera back on his bedroom table, on top of his collection of ornithology books.

Father Damien had no misgivings. If the bishop was determined to put him out to pasture, he wanted to make sure that he'd have enough fodder on which to graze.

As for the two thugs, he didn't want to know exactly what they were planning. He had an electronic trail of photographs—he preferred to think of it as photographic evidence—of them unloading the bags and wooden boxes under cover of darkness. They were not the actions of a legitimate building contractor, he told himself. He had taken the precaution of recording on film each of their visits.

Whatever was in the bags and the boxes, he suspected it was probably evidence enough for him to seek shelter in the Civil Guard's witness protection programme.

After all, he reflected, as the chemicals coursing through his body made him feel bolder, hadn't the Church in Spain and the Civil Guard been allies for generations?

Call to the General

The General called him back very late that night.

"What is it, Luis?"

"Aladdin's Cave must be moved—urgently."

"You are sure of this?"

"I am certain of it, sir."

"Are we betrayed?"

"No sir. It is just a precaution. Relocation will be sufficient."

"Very well. You have my authorisation to do it. Is there anything else?"

"The other merchandise was delivered to Mustapha's people in Barcelona this afternoon."

"Good. You will explain later the reason for Aladdin's relocation?"

"Yes, sir, of course."

"Be careful."

The General cut the connection. Luis looked at his watch and tried to calculate how long the transfer would take. He knew that he was being overcautious, but something told him it was the prudent thing to do. The General had assigned this mission to him; he would not fail his commander.

It was past midnight. Leaving his apartment, he walked south along the street. A taxi slowed alongside him, speculating on a possible fare. He turned his head away, and the cab driver drove away at a gentle pace that would not consume petrol unnecessarily.

Luis turned the corner onto a quiet street. He would need a vehicle and glanced around for a suitable target. Time was of the utmost importance, as he had told the General. He needed something fast to get to his destination, a vehicle that would not attract attention. He had considered a plan to drive out of the city, dump the first vehicle in the suburbs and find another one. It would reduce the risks of detection, but waste time. The General's warning words still echoed in his ear. He would take the risk and hope he got it right.

Jumpstarting the BMW had been easy; it was something he had done several times before. The fuel gauge showed almost full. That was a good omen, he thought. On instinct, he reached under the dashboard; within seconds, his gloved hand found what he had suspected. It was plugged into the on-board diagnostic port. His fingers gripped the GPS tracker and yanked it out of its socket. As he drove down the street he laughed cynically and threw the device out of the window.

He would have to stay off the autopistas because of the toll booths; it wasn't a problem for him and posed fewer risks of being stopped for speeding.

Once he got close to Lleida, he would enact his contingency plan—a low-risk scheme that he had worked out previously in some detail. The only variable was the human one, he reflected—the builder. He would take care of that flaw later.

Clearing the outskirts of the city, he eased back the driver's seat to accommodate his long frame, and settled in for the drive.

Hours later, he approached an address on the outskirts of the town. He was in luck. As he slowed the BMW, he saw that the stonemason's truck was parked, as usual, in the unlocked yard. He had noticed the sturdy vehicle on several previous visits to the church. It was old and battered, and he was confident—because of its age—that it pre-dated the era of tracking devices. Equally important, its chassis had been reinforced to carry heavy loads of stone and building materials.

Those features were important to his plans.

He drove past the yard and parked the BMW at the end of a quiet street. He knew the Madrid license plates might attract attention, but that was a risk he would have to take.

The stonemason's truck was easy to start, although a little noisy for the chauffeur's comfort. Revving the engine as little as possible, he drove off in the direction of Father Damien's church. While driving, he called the builder.

"Yes?" The man's voice sounded thick and sleepy.

'You have to meet me at the church."

"When?"

"Twenty minutes."

"It's four o'clock in the morning; can't it wait?"

"No, it can't. This is top priority and urgent. Orders from him."

Dimming the truck's lights to avoid arousing the attention of the priest, he geared down and eased the vehicle into the driveway leading to the stone building at the back of the church. He glanced at his watch. Hmm, a well-executed operation so far, he congratulated himself. Getting out of the vehicle, he stretched his long legs and waited for the builder. He would need the man's help to carry the heavy cargo out of the buildings.

He planned to wait until the second load to move the gold ingots and wooden cases of euros. The builder would be astounded by the riches they would be loading into the vehicle. Luis had no intention of letting the man's base nature get the better of his judgement. He, Luis, not anyone else, was the sole custodian of Aladdin's Cave.

Minutes later, the builder drove up in his van. "What's up?" he growled irritably, the smell of garlic and cigarettes still lingering on his breath.

The two men loaded the paper sacks they had filled previously, splitting the bulky load between their vehicles. The chauffeur knew that it was less than a half hour's drive to the isolated farm, where the merchandise would be stored in a barn, well-hidden from sight.

Glancing at his watch, he calculated how long it would take to unpack the first load and safely transport the precious second one.

Time was tight, but he thrived on the spikes of energy that his adrenaline created. On the second trip, they would load the contents of Aladdin's Cave into the stolen truck; it would be safe until further orders were given to him by the General.

He would instruct the builder to follow him in his van on the second trip to the farm—an instruction he anticipated the greedy and nasty man would obey with enthusiasm. After all, he coaxed, who would not want to know the new location of a massive fortune in pure gold and used, non-traceable and perfectly negotiable currency?

For the builder, it would be a one-way journey. The man had been useful, but his job was almost done. For this vital stage of Operation FERROL, they had to narrow the risks. Luis had a special reward planned for the builder. Yes—overall, a good night's work.

The General will be pleased, he felt sure.

A Surprising Development

I thought I should let Antonio know, as soon as I got back to Madrid.

"The girl who was shot in Morocco was not the Civil Guard officer," I told him.

From the silence over the phone, it was obvious that he was as surprised as I had been. I could imagine the surprised look on his face. "Oh," he said slowly. "Tell me more."

"I had my suspicions while I was there," I said.

"Hmm, this gets interesting, Diego," said Antonio. "If she's not our girl, then who the heck is she? Number two, where *is* our girl?"

I had been wrestling with the same questions. Then, just over an hour earlier, a phone call from the Civil Guard had given me the answer to one of them. "The deceased girl's name is Ana Puentes. She was from Cordoba—about the same age and build as officer Balmes. The Americans have a file on her; she was being trained as a jihadist operative in Iraq."

"You think that the two girls must have switched places?" asked Antonio, his mind now running ahead with this new knowledge.

"Which means there is still a chance that our girl is still alive," I added.

151

"But where?" he asked, posing the obvious question. "And how did you find out?"

"When we got to Morocco, we did a simple fingerprint test. That information wasn't available to the DST and, when she was in their custody, she claimed to be Daniela Balmes. We had confirmed that to them. So we can't blame the Moroccans for the mix-up," I said.

"Diego, this tells us that the two women must have been in contact—and probably in the same location—at some time for the switch in identities to have taken place," said Antonio, the tone of his voice indicating that he was still wrestling to understand the implications of the new information.

I was already ahead of him. Before calling, I had spent a gruelling hour with Raphael Robles grappling with the same issues. He had been elated with the news, which he said kept the case active for us. We had come to the conclusion that officer Daniela Balmes almost certainly had been in Iraq, and might still be following the capitan's orders to infiltrate al-Qaeda but under a different identity—that of Ana Puentes.

There seemed to be no harm in sharing our conclusions with Antonio, so I did.

Chapter 7

The Bishop

The market town, some distance from Lleida, had been decorated cheerfully for its special day. Streets had been hosed clean in the early hours. Banners hanging across its narrow streets swayed in the cool morning wind coming down from the hills. Catalan flags flapped in large numbers alongside a few national flags which, in near pristine condition, rarely were displayed in public, except on special occasions such as these—when the existence of Madrid reluctantly had to be acknowledged.

The boom times had come and gone. Many in the condesa's constituency had witnessed the false prosperity of the construction frenzy. It had meant temporarily better times for some, but few could boast any lasting legacy from it.

Madrid had delivered a tangible asset in the form of a new city hall. She would perform the opening ceremony and had a speech to make. In the face of severe austerity facing the country, any promises for their future would have to rely on making them feel good.

They drove past the basilica. What was it that she had learned at school, the condesa asked herself. A saying, attributed to Seneca—the Roman statesman of Iberian origins— *'Religion is regarded by the common people as true, by the wise as false and by the rulers as useful.'*

Yes, she would take her cue from the teachings of the Church itself. Hard work and sacrifice on Earth were linked to eventual rewards elsewhere—a better life for future generations of children and an assurance of the eternal life.

Her final appointment before lunch was to attend a reception being given for the recently appointed new bishop.

He was an impressive figure and had been recognised by many—including, she had been told, several influential advisors within the Vatican—as a promising new image for the Church. The new pope seemed determined to make dramatic changes, and the freshly minted bishop already had been summoned to Rome several times.

With his ceremonial red gown flowing behind him, he strode forward energetically to greet her. He seemed to her more like a Hollywood celebrity than a modest shepherd of his regional flock. This was perhaps a sign of the New Spain, she thought, as he made direct eye contact, held her gaze for far too long, and reached forward to clasp both her hands tightly in his.

She was impressed. He must be very bright to have risen so quickly through the church ranks, she reflected, drawing a parallel to herself in the government.

He was personable. She found herself captivated by his charm. He was unreasonably attractive, she admitted to herself. As a man of the cloth, there would be nothing carnal about it. Perhaps his intense spiritual power simply added to his physical mystique.

Even without the pomp and ceremony surrounding him, she had the feeling she was meeting a young and most likely ambitious new prince of the Church.

It was evident that he reciprocated her admiration of him. He continued to let his dancing eyes speak for him. She felt that, in those few moments, although he had said almost nothing to her, they had known each other all their lives.

She felt a surge of exuberant optimism. He had swept her along. She had not resisted, of course. He had an eminence and carriage which seemed to sweep every obstacle out of his way and attracted an entourage of enthusiastic followers, pulling them in like iron filings to a magnet. She found herself quite breathless.

The young bishop, treated like an adored movie star, seemed keen to provide his blessing to the many parishioners who grasped for him and kissed his hands.

Feeling a sudden chill down the nape of her neck, she was aware of someone staring at her. It was not a glance, not even an intense stare. It was almost a look of adoration. With a frown, she turned to face an older looking priest with long grey hair that really needed to be better groomed.

"Father Damien," he said with a grin, gently but hesitatingly offering his hand to her. She noticed it was cold to the touch. It was an unsettling feeling, almost as if she were touching a corpse.

"Father Damien of *Santa María la Virgen*," he elaborated, leaning his head to one side like an inquisitive turkey, and raising an eyebrow as if to enquire if she was familiar with his parish.

She wasn't, but long used to such incursions, the condesa bequeathed him with a smile so radiant that it would easily have lit a thousand church candles. "Of course," she answered. "How are you, Father?"

He did not have a chance to answer before he was pushed aside, far too abruptly, by one of the bishop's handlers. The condesa resented the clumsy intrusion and called out to him as he was manhandled to the back of the crowd.

"Lovely to see you. We will catch up later." Then she herself was swept onwards and quickly returned to the bishop's inner entourage.

She was unsettled by her meeting with the priest, and was left with a strange feeling of foreboding.

A Message from Turkey

"Why me?" asked Antonio. "Isn't it a Civil Guard matter?"

"She has insisted that a Catalan officer from the Mossos be there," replied the chief. "You know, Toni, it's quite a feather in our cap. We need to work alongside the feds more often."

"It hasn't worked out that well so far," Antonio shot back, only to encounter a frown from his father.

"The Turkish authorities have said she is suffering from deep trauma. She has been under fire, and held captive both in Iraq and Syria. We need to handle our part of her repatriation in an exemplary fashion," the chief insisted.

"And my involvement has approval from Madrid?"

"Yes, Toni. From the Interior Minister, himself."

"I bet you the Civil Guard is not happy," said Antonio.

"Well, she is one of their officers and they are a bit touchy—especially after Ceuta. But with Madrid supporting us, there's really nothing to worry about."

Turkey Military Base, Near Istanbul

Their planes arrived separately in Istanbul. The Civil Guard commandant arrived early, his Spanish Air Force jet landing at the Turkish military base routinely used by NATO forces. Antonio's scheduled flight from Barcelona arrived at the public terminal at Ataturk airport.

Emerging from the gate area with the other disembarking passengers, Antonio saw the flicker of recognition on the face of the Turkish army officer. He was standing a short distance away, next to an electric shuttle.

"Deputy Inspector Valls?" he asked, stepping forward to greet Antonio. "You have carry-on, no checked luggage, I understand. Come with me please."

He indicated a seat on the shuttle, and sat down beside Antonio. The driver bypassed the disembarking crowds and drove directly to a customs priority lane. Minutes later, exiting the main terminal, they arrived at a guarded military vehicle.

"Your colleague from Madrid, he has arrived already actually," announced the Turkish colonel, glancing at Antonio as if anticipating a reaction.

He suspects that there's a turf war going on, thought Antonio, making no comment, but noting that the colonel was from the security service MIT.

"She has been through incredible experience," the colonel said, as their driver negotiated the perimeter road, moving with speed towards the helicopter terminal. "I, myself, admire such women. They are very strong. More than most man, I would say."

They entered a secure area and pulled up alongside a military helicopter waiting on the tarmac.

"This is more quickly than the roads in Istanbul," said the colonel as they strapped themselves in.

"What has she told you?" asked Antonio, shouting against the noise of the engine starting up.

"Ah yes, straight to the business. I understand your concern," the Turkish officer shouted back, allowing himself the briefest of smiles.

"Actually, from our president himself come the orders to my boss and me that the girl must receive only the best treatment."

"We are grateful for that, sir."

"So we not torture her or anything," he smiled, while handing Antonio a set of ear protectors.

His personality was engaging, Antonio conceded.

After the leading edge of its rotor blades pitched up to full speed, the helicopter began to lift off gently, immediately swinging east. Any further conversation would be impossible with the noise. Ten minutes later, it touched down at the military base. When the rotors stopped, they strode towards a waiting vehicle.

Antonio was impressed with its luxury and security features. There was a sealed glass partition separating the passengers from the two military police drivers—young boys with cropped hair and fresh faces.

"We have common enemy," said the Turkish officer leaning over to Antonio. "Al-Qaeda and ISIS not good for your country. Not good for mine."

Antonio nodded his agreement.

The Turkish officer looked at him with a mischievous grin. "Also, we remember that Spain was Muslim caliphate for many hundreds years. Many interests we have in common, yes?"

Antonio nodded his head. "Sir, you have the uniform of an army officer, but the flair of a politician."

"Sometimes in Turkey these are same things," he replied, his voice becoming more serious.

"Your officer, she is safe—and my government promise expedite travel her to Spain. When? It is your choice."

"Forgive me, sir," said Antonio. "Normally, there are official channels to handle repatriations, usually through our embassy. I think, in this instance, my colleague, the commandant from the Civil Guard, will request how the girl should be repatriated."

The Turkish colonel nodded. "Yes, this much he has made clearly to me," he said. "He is senior man from Spain, I understand these things. Big powerful."

From his briefcase, he removed a copy of *Hurriyet*. He passed it over to Antonio who read the headlines.

The colonel said with distaste, "The newspaper, it says many foreign peoples they believe Turkey bombing the Kurds and the rebels, to help the ISIS. This is not true. Not true.

"Our president himself, he has authorised that your female officer must receive top dog, best grade treatment. We not harm her. We not cross-examine. Western peoples must see Turkey is good NATO ally," his eyes wide with emotion.

"Sir, that is out of our hands. I am simply a policeman. I know nothing of politics," said Antonio.

"Our president himself, he has said this," insisted the colonel. "We show we fight on same side as you. The officer girl will be safe. We not harm. We not interrogate."

"I am the junior officer here, sir. Protocol is involved. There is not much I can do…" Antonio started to say.

Interrupting, the colonel wagged a single finger in the air in a wide arc. "No. She says the Mossos different. Maybe you communicate Turkey cooperation to your people. The commandant, he does not listen. Shouts a lot. Not a nice man. I trust you help us."

The vehicle slowed and the colonel announced, "Now we are arriving. Tell me what you want for the girl, please."

"Has he interrogated her?" asked Antonio, knowing that the Civil Guard commandant would not hesitate to impose his seniority.

"No, he has shouted many times at us that he wants to talk to the girl alone. But she say no to us. She is not want that. She talk to Mossos most urgent of all, she tell us. She scared of powerful officer from Madrid. So, we wait for you."

The commandant was sitting at the table. He barely acknowledged Antonio when he entered with the Turkish colonel. A few minutes later, the girl entered the room surrounded by two Turkish female military police. She wore drab grey army fatigues issued to women in the Turkish army. They were oversized and the sleeves were folded back over her wrists. Over her head, she wore a hijab. Antonio was

159

surprised how young she looked. In her early twenties, at most, he guessed.

She stood at attention, and saluted the Civil Guard commandant. He returned her salute without enthusiasm. Then she looked at Antonio, who thought he saw a glimmer of a smile. "Please sit," invited the Turkish colonel.

Antonio introduced himself to the girl. The relief on her face was unmistakable. It seemed to him that in that instant she lost ten years of stress. They spoke a few sentences of greeting in Catalan.

Antonio turned and asked the Civil Guard commandant, "How would you like to proceed, sir?"

"I have already informed officer Balmes that her orders are to travel with me back to Madrid. I have a plane waiting. There really is no need to waste any more time here," he said testily, glaring back at Antonio.

"We are grateful to our Turkish allies," he added, addressing the colonel, his voice becoming a little bit more respectful. "However, we are anxious to repatriate our officer as soon as possible.

"Is there any reason we cannot leave immediately?" he asked, looking directly at the colonel.

Glancing at those seated around the table, the Turk shook his head. "If you wish…" he conceded.

Hearing this, the commandant gathered the papers he had in front of him and stood up.

"Sir," said the girl, speaking quietly but remaining seated. "I am under your orders. If you say so, I will of course leave immediately with you. But there is something you may wish to hear first."

Antonio saw the anger that flared in the commandant's face. The man seemed to struggle with his thoughts for a moment, and remained standing.

"I am carrying out my duties as an officer of the Civil Guard, and I am not able to discuss many things with you," the girl continued, turning to address the Turkish colonel. "I am only able to discuss confidential things with my commanding officer and with the commandant here." She glanced in his direction. "However, I am in possession of military information which might impact the safety of Turkish people and their allies in Syria. With the permission of the commandant, I should provide this to you without any further delay."

Antonio was impressed by the girl's choice of words and he saw the impacts they were having. He watched as the commandant's eyes flickered and glanced towards the colonel. The colonel's body stiffened at this new development, and he directed a harsh look in return to the commandant.

"I insist," he said emphatically. "Continue please."

With a heavy sigh, the commandant sank back down into his chair. His mouth remained hard set. As if looking for a target to bully, he shot a look in Antonio's direction, clearly intending to question why the Catalan policeman's presence in the room was required. Antonio returned his hostility with an impassive stare.

"The reason I asked for a Mossos officer to be present," said the girl, observing the exchange between the two men, "is that I have learned about the murder in Barcelona of my fiancé, Civil Guard First Class David Casals."

There was a hush in the room, as if the air suddenly had been sucked out. Again, it was not just her words, thought Antonio. It was the way she delivered them. Each of the men in the room now had their eyes on her. She was not unemotional, he noted, but certainly she was not a hysterical young female officer overwhelmed by the trauma of her experiences.

Her formality, speaking of her fiancé by his rank, conveyed to each of them that she was very much in control of her emotions. There was nothing the commandant could do to silence her, Antonio observed with satisfaction. He had taken an instant dislike to the man. He wanted to help her, if he could, to protect her from this over-bearing oppressive senior officer from Madrid.

"Daniela," said Antonio quietly, giving her a reassuring smile, "perhaps you'd better start at the beginning." Then, glancing at the commandant, he added, "If there are things you cannot tell us, we understand, of course. But the colonel urgently needs to hear whatever military intelligence you are able to provide to him—and I certainly would like to hear what you know about the circumstances of the murder of your fiancé."

In the corner of his eye, Antonio saw the resentful glare that continued to be directed at him by the commandant. Ignoring it, he looked only at the girl.

"I was in northern Syria," she began, with a glance towards the commandant. "I am not a jihadist, which I think you already know. My assignment…" she paused and looked again at the commandant, "was to pose undercover as one.

"It was not difficult. I was recruited by the same al-Qaeda agent in Ceuta who recruited David, my fiancé," she added. "David was not a jihadist either. But he had been successful in infiltrating an al-Qaeda cell in Ceuta. He had carried out missions for them. They seemed satisfied with his loyalty, and appeared to trust him. I think that gave me special status with my recruiter."

Antonio was aware that she was still continually glancing at the commandant, as if searching for his approval to continue. The man gave no indication of his feelings and sat stone-faced at the table—his arms crossed stiffly across his heavily decorated Civil Guard tunic.

Eventually the girl looked down at her hands clasped tightly together on the table. It seemed to Antonio that she was struggling for words to continue. "My commanding officer, Capitan Primero, had information that large amounts of money were being transferred to al-Qaeda in Syria and Iraq. The money was coming from unknown sources in Spain. My assignment was to gain acceptance, train as a jihadist and find out what I could about the sources and purpose of the money."

Antonio saw that she was now avoiding looking at the commandant and he guessed that, as a serving officer subject to the rules of court martial, she was being careful about the consequences of alienating him. He could see that she was struggling to give the Turkish colonel only the minimum essential information about her assignment. From what little Antonio had seen of the colonel, he doubted this had gone undetected by him. He seemed like a smart man.

"Al-Qaeda had other ideas for me," she continued. "I had expected to be sent overseas for training with other western jihadist volunteers. Instead, like David was, I was told by my recruiter that my services would be more usefully deployed in other activities.

" 'You speak Arabic and French,' they said to me. 'That can be useful to us.'

"They said little else, but told me to be patient and not say anything to anyone, including David. Then, one day, my recruiter, Fatma—a Syrian woman in her thirties—instructed me to return to my home in Barcelona. Fatma said I must take my passport and they would contact me there with further instructions."

"You reported this to your commanding officer, Capitan Primero?" asked Antonio, aware of the sharp glance he was receiving from the commandant.

"Yes, the capitan arranged for me to take special leave. He also provided me with contact numbers that I could use in case of emergencies. We have a code name for my identification."

The girl continued to avoid the now hostile glare she was receiving from the commandant.

"From Barcelona, I travelled to northern Syria and was delivered to the custody of an al-Nusra rebel commander. His unit was fighting, at that time, north-east of Aleppo," she continued, clearly missing out a large part of her story. "He knew all about me—that I am an active officer with the Civil Guard in Spain. I worried about it, but he seemed to think it was a good opportunity for his cause. His name is Jamal Ismet."

"How you got to Syria?" asked the Turkish colonel.

The Civil Guard commandant started to interrupt. "That is not important..." but he stopped speaking as the Turkish colonel waved away his interruption, saying, "Okay, no questions now. Okay later."

Daniela paused to allow the negative impacts of their adversarial exchange to subside before she continued speaking. "Before becoming a rebel commander in the north, Jamal had been a surgeon in Homs. He was a lecturer at Al-Baath University. He came from a prominent Sunni family. At the beginning of the conflict, his family had been killed by Assad's regime forces. All of them. Only a few cousins survived, he told me. I thought he must be motivated by revenge. Yet he always seemed calm.

"Jamal is connected with al-Qaeda high command. He is well-informed. He knew about the money coming from Spain. He told me that it was important to them because al-Qaeda has almost no financial resources remaining. He said that, when bin Laden was alive, it received substantial funding from the Arab League and from Gulf investors. He said that, since then, ISIS had become rich and powerful and that Al-Qaeda needed to change the way it operates—to become more of a business, generating its own taxes and revenues.

"I was quite surprised that he was willing to provide this information to me. I had expected to meet Islamic zealots. It was not that Jamal is not a strong believer in the jihad—he is—but he was talking to me like a business person.

"He told me that al-Qaeda was interested in me because I came from Spain. He spoke about Mustapha, and he asked what I knew about him. I told him I knew nothing, which was not true. The capitan had told me that Mustapha is al-Qaeda's chief operative in Spain. Part of my orders were to find as much as I could about him."

" 'But I am told you are well connected in Spain,' Jamal countered, 'with Mustapha.' Jamal seemed so certain that I had a special connection with Mustapha that I dared not deny it further. Perhaps it was because of my relationship with David, I don't know. One thing was obvious to me. Without the connection to Mustapha, I might not be quite as valuable to Jamal.

"Instead, I diverted his question and asked him, 'Why should I help you?' "

The commandant interrupted. "I don't see how any of this is related to releasing my officer and allowing us to return to Madrid. As our NATO allies, we can inform you of these things later."

"Continue please," said the Turkish officer, ignoring the commandant's outburst. His tone conveyed to Daniela his displeasure with the commandant's truculent behaviour.

"Jamal told me nothing more that day about Mustapha. He was courteous and said that I must eat and rest after my long and stressful journey. He told one of his men to show me to my tent. But then he called me back inside. I remember it quite vividly.

" 'Daniela, you must remember this is a war zone,' he told me. 'This is a vicious war. Today, I could kill you, and you will be nothing. The beasts and the carrion will carry away all traces. Or you can help us,' he stated flatly. 'The choice is yours.'

" 'I am going to trust you,' he said, 'but if you are a spy, I will give you as a wife to one of my men. If they know I have discarded you, your treatment will be far less hospitable than if you remain under my care. You understand?'

"He said that I should think about what he had said, and that I should read the Koran. 'It will help you decide, should you be torn between conflicting masters.'

"I am not religious, but that night I prayed to Mohammed. I admit it. The Christ I learned about at convent school seemed so far away and unimportant in that desolate, hostile land."

Daniela stopped talking and looked in turn at the men sitting at the table.

"I slept for only a few hours. It was cold and I could hear gunfire. I had become terrified about what would happen next. I didn't have any idea of how I could help Jamal and al-Qaeda, even if I had wanted to.

"Eventually I must have fallen asleep because I woke late in the morning. Jamal and his men had been out on a mission. Some of his men had been wounded. They had several prisoners. I found out later that prisoners nearly always were executed on the spot. Except, sometimes, if they could be sold for ransom or other purposes, they would cut off the prisoners' leading fingers from both hands, so that they could not fight with weapons again.

"Jamal was treating the wound of one of his men, when I was taken to his tent. He was upset and looked up at me as my guard pushed me inside. 'Yesterday, Daniela, you asked me why should I help you?' he said.

"He told me that he would show me why. He said that he would keep me with his unit and show me what was happening in that region of Syria. He told me that I would see the impacts of barrel bombs dropped on civilian targets by the regime. Many women and children had been killed. 'That was terrible,' he said. 'It is genocide. Many more have very bad injuries. I am a surgeon. It is my job to help these people. But Assad is killing Syrian people, targeting Sunnis, faster than we can save them.' "

Antonio watched in fascination as Daniela's face became strangely vacant; it was as if she had transported herself back to the past and was speaking to Jamal.

" 'I will take you to many villages,' Jamal told me. He said that, at one time, they were thriving and prosperous, but now they are destroyed and deserted. Everyone has left. Civilians, and even some fighters, seek asylum through Turkey and in Europe. They seek shelter anywhere in the world where it does not rain everyday with bombs from the regime. Then you can decide, Daniela, if you want to help us.'

"For two or three days I did not see much of him. I was allowed to get up and move around, except my every action was watched carefully by his guards. I could tell they did not like me. It was only because of Jamal that I was allowed to remain alive. It was on the third day at his camp, I think, when I felt that I did not care any longer if they shot me. I had eaten something that was really bad. I was sick and could not control my bowels. There were flies everywhere in the camp and the smell of sickness and death.

"Jamal had me brought to him, where he gave me medicines and sent me back to my tent to sleep. After that I felt better. Actually, I was still weak and fatigued, but it felt good to be alive. Later, I was able to eat a little food.

"The next day, we broke camp and drove for several hours to an abandoned village. It had a drinking well that had not been contaminated, so we had fresh water. Jamal commandeered the headman's vacated house and compound in the village centre. It was still in usable condition. And he gave me a room—unfortunately with the same hostile guards stationed outside.

"That night, I had dinner with him at a table in his room. It was obvious that he believed very strongly in the jihad. He said that ISIS wants to fight regional battles and establish a new caliphate, but that al-Qaeda must fight a global war.

" 'We have the same objectives as ISIS,' he said, 'but our methods are different. For this, we need money,' he told me. 'That is how you can help us, Daniela. The West will supply it to us. The West has no morals. It will buy what it needs and what we can supply. It is not just oil you buy.'

" 'What else would the West want from Syria?' I asked him. I was not being antagonistic. It was not easy to understand what he wanted from me.

" 'You buy our services as terrorists,' he said. 'We are good at such enterprises. It is a simple business transaction for us.' He told me that the money from Spain was coming from some powerful and rich Spaniards. He said they wanted to overthrow the government—and take Spain back into a dictatorship.

" 'We are good at undermining this precious institution that you call democracy,' he told me with a smirk. 'So what if you get a vote? What good it does for you? It does nothing, I tell you. The politicians, they change, but it remains still the same. You have your freedoms and you do not live always in danger of being killed at any time, at the will of some tyrant. So what? It does not matter who your masters are—the outcome in your country is the same.'

" 'For a payment to us, we will help one group or the other in your western democracies. Your regimes change and you are able to carry on with your lives. Here we cannot. We fight against genocide. I, myself, know this only too well. Mustapha says to us that what he is doing in Spain can be done in other western countries. He has sent you to help us. So, now, tell me please, how will this take place? How will you, and other westerners who believe in the jihad, assist us?' "

Once again, Daniela stopped talking and looked at the men sitting at the table. Antonio had been expecting a further outburst of protest from the Civil Guard commandant, but the man seemed as fascinated as the others by her story.

"I had no idea, of course, how I could help him—let alone set up for al-Qaeda in other countries what Mustapha had set up in Spain. I mean I am only a junior officer—and a female—and he was talking to me as if I was a powerful leader from the West.

"Just to play for time, I asked Jamal, 'How is the arrangement with Spain being handled here in Syria?' At first, he did not understand me. So I kept talking. 'It is difficult for me to make any recommendations unless I understand how you are able to deliver on your side of the bargain.'

"Instead of flying into a rage, which I half-expected, Jamal nodded and rubbed his forehead with his hands. 'You know about the hawala, of course you do. We have received some of the payment you have promised. Now you have to trust us that we can deliver,' he said in a low voice. 'Mustapha will have his results very soon. Then you will see. But, here on the battlefront, we do not have time to wait. ISIS is getting stronger.

" 'Daniela, a Syrian saying is that you cannot wait until the rains arrive to see if the seeds you have planted will bring new crops. By then, it is too late to plant more seeds. You must have faith that we will deliver what Mustapha is buying for the money we are receiving from Spain. If we are to achieve the jihad, we must have more money from the West— much more money—very soon. We need hard currencies... dollars, euros and gold. Just like the hawala money we are receiving here in Syria from Spain. Please tell this to Mustapha. He will be pleased very soon with the results we deliver. Together, we must think beyond Spain. Other powerful people with money will want to buy our services. To help them achieve power in their own countries.'

"What about ISIS?' I asked.

"Jamal snorted with contempt. 'Daniela, listen to me. ISIS is strong today—this is truth. Things will change. History will prove me right. Our civilisation exists for more than ten thousand years, actually. We have many rulers and many names. We survive what is taking place—the terrible, terrible things—and we will still be here as a people. Al-Qaeda will survive. It will represent all people in a better society, I believe, if Allah is willing. That is what we pray for. Not for the death of infidels. Not for the executions by ISIS. Not for the senseless violence.

" 'Now, tell me please, how you help us.'

" 'Do you know Mustapha?' I asked, the question coming from me without any preparation. 'Do you know who he is?'

" 'Why would you ask a question to which you already know the answer?' asked Jamal. 'It is to test of my loyalty perhaps?'

"At this, I shook my head vigorously. 'No, Jamal, it is not a test of your loyalty. Mustapha trusts you. He trusts al-Qaeda'

" 'Then what, Daniela? Explain to me please.'

" 'If Mustapha's true identity is revealed, Jamal, it will mean the end of his operations. You understand that?' I told him."

She looked at the men sitting around the table, and seemed to feel the need to give them an explanation. "At the time, it seemed quite an obvious thing to say. I knew I had come as close as I could to get Jamal to reveal Mustapha's identity— just as the capitan had ordered me. Now I would have to create another way of finding out his name from Jamal.

" 'Your loyalty—and silence—is vital to all you want, Jamal,' I told him.

"Then, a day later, something unexpected happened. Jamal called me to him. He asked me to sit down, and he sat next to me, very close. He put his arm around my shoulder. 'I have some bad news, Daniela. Your fiancé in Spain has been killed. I am sorry.'

"I asked him what had happened, but he had no more details. I asked him how he had obtained the information, but he would not tell me. It seemed a bit unreal. Maybe I was a bit in shock, but it did not upset me—not right away. One thing I knew for certain—if David had been killed, it was not an accident. He had been murdered.

" 'It is time for you to return home, Daniela,' Jamal told me. 'You must talk to Mustapha for us.'

"For a moment he seemed to reflect on his own past. He looked desperately sad. 'Grieving is a difficult process,' he told me. 'Yet, it is necessary, Daniela.'

"Two days later he told me that he had arranged for me to go back to Spain. He said it was no longer safe to travel back the way I had come. He had made a deal with ISIS that I would be given safe passage to Iraq. He would send two of his men along to make sure I was not harmed. In Iraq, I would join up with a group of western jihadists who had graduated from their training school and were being sent back home.

"I was quite happy with the news about going home. It meant the end of my assignment, and I would be able to report some success to Capitan Primero. I had not found out about the sources of the money, or the identity of Mustapha, but I had found out that it was being used by Spanish nationals to buy terrorist services from al-Qaeda. I had found out that ISIS was cooperating closely with al-Qaeda. I had found out that more money would be transferred very soon from Spain.

"I will tell you honestly, I was scared. I wanted to get home. I needed to find out more about David's death and see his parents. So I agreed.

"The journey across northern Syria was terrible. If it had not been for the men that Jamal had assigned as my bodyguards, and the letter I carried signed by an ISIS commander, I never would have survived. In Iraq, the harassment continued—even though on the journey I was well-disguised. When I arrived, I was placed in the training school for my own protection.

"At the school, the women were always separated from the men, except for the classes. Always, of course, we prayed separately. We ate separately. We slept on floors in a different room. But in classes, we were allowed to talk together. That is how I met another girl from Spain, and the American."

At the mention of her meeting with the American, Antonio noticed that the Turkish colonel raised an eyebrow. He said nothing and the moment passed quickly.

"The girl's name is Ana Puentes. For the brief time we were together, she and I became friends. I felt sorry for her. She hated being in Iraq and she was appalled at the way women were treated—even the western women who had volunteered for the programme. She was desperate for the training to be over, so she could get home. She was scared about what they might do to her."

"What about the American?" asked the Turkish colonel.

"I don't see how that is relevant," protested the commandant, jumping into the conversation. But he stopped talking when the colonel lifted his hand.

"He was terrifying," the girl answered. "Everyone whispered that he was an ISIS spy within the group. You know, to weed out unreliable westerners and traitors. He was a giant of a man with flaming red hair and beard. His teeth were large and uneven. He was a wild man. A street fighter. No one liked him."

"And you?" the colonel pressed. "What did you think of this man?"

"I was scared of him. I did not trust him.

"Soon afterwards, I was told that I was part of a group that would be sent back to the West. I told Ana, of course, because I was so happy. She was not selected to go with the group, and she cried. Because she is a petroleum engineer, they wanted her to stay behind and assist them. She begged me to let her go in my place. I said that I was sorry for her, but it was a ridiculous idea. They would find out and punish us both.

"She said that she could not take any more, and wanted to end her own life. She said we looked alike, and it would not be difficult to trick our instructors at the training school. She said that I had not been there long, and no one would discover the deception. She kept begging me. I wanted to help her if I could, but I said no.

"The day I was told I would be sent back to the West, I was trapped in a corridor by the American wild man. He pushed me against the wall, and told me not to scream. 'I know about your mission, Daniela,' he whispered in fluent Spanish, his face up against my ear. 'I have met Capitan Primero. He knows I am with the CIA.'

"I tried to push myself away, but he was very strong. He said, 'We need to know who Mustapha is. Have you found out who he is?'

"Of course, I suspected he was a spy and struggled to push him away. But he was persistent.

" 'We know about Jamal, but we must find out about Mustapha. If you know, you must get the information back to your commanding officer as soon as possible. You can trust me.'

"I knew I couldn't trust him, and eventually he let me go. I began to worry that I had been found out. Jamal was no longer there to help me, and his two men had gone back to their camp. What the American had told me made me scared. But it also made me think. Even if he was an ISIS spy, he was right. Mustapha is the key to the money coming from Spain, and the link to senior people in al-Qaeda. If Mustapha's identity can be revealed, we would find out how the money being funnelled through to them is controlled within Spain.

"Apart from al-Qaeda leaders themselves, the only person who knew Mustapha's identity must be Jamal. I was convinced now that he must know Mustapha and be in contact with him. How else could my recruiter get me so close to Jamal so quickly? Only because David worked for Mustapha and authorised it. Who else could have found out so quickly about David's death and my connection to him? It had to be Mustapha who had told Jamal.

"I didn't say anything to the American. But, to succeed in my orders from Capitan Primero, I knew at that moment that I could not return to Spain without getting Jamal to reveal Mustapha's identity to me.

"After that it was quite simple. I agreed to trade places with Ana. She was so excited that I had to plead with her to remain calm. At the last minute before the departing group left the training compound, I cut my hair to look more like hers. They had taken our passports, but I knew that our photos would look similar. We changed into each other's clothes. Our shoes were different sizes so we kept wearing our own.

"I also knew I had to get back to Jamal as soon as possible."

Antonio glanced over at the commandant, whose stern face had relaxed, and it seemed that he was now studying Daniela with renewed respect.

"After Ana and the graduating group had left, the rest of us felt depressed. It was a let-down for us to be left behind. Maybe our instructors picked up on our despondent mood, because they cancelled training classes that afternoon and our evening prayers were not enforced as strictly as usual. They gave us extra food.

"Then I had a nasty shock. A group of soldiers arrived and they demanded to see Ana and the American. I had been thinking only of how to get in contact with Jamal, and I had neglected to rehearse my new identity as Ana. I could recall some of her background, but not much. My first concern was that our ruse had been discovered, but that was not what the men wanted. They were engineers from an oil refinery captured from the regime by ISIS and they wanted help from the two petroleum engineers in our group. That meant me and the American. I was terrified."

174

The colonel put up his hand at this point, and called for fresh water and tea to be served. Please take a few minutes to rest, he told Daniela. Everyone stood to stretch their legs. The air in the room had become stale and the colonel opened one of the windows. "We continue in five minutes, please."

As he moved around the room, Antonio brushed past Daniela and gave her shoulder a squeeze. He whispered something quietly in Catalan, and she gave him a weak smile.

A few minutes later, the colonel nodded to Daniela and she continued her story.

"We went with the men. It was several hours drive over roads where there had been heavy fighting. Our vehicle was an old Humvee captured from the Iraqi army. The oil refinery had been damaged and was heavily guarded by the time we arrived. Our vehicle was unhindered because it was flying the ISIS flag.

"The American knew immediately that I was not Ana, but he said nothing. Once he gave me a grin and wink. It was a weird sensation, but made me feel better. I was still scared of him. His eyes looked fervent and wild, just like all the other ISIS fighters.

"We met Iraqi refinery officials, who were angry that a woman had been brought to help them. They shouted abuse and were very antagonistic to me. The American surprised me. He was very protective. I didn't hear what he said to them about me, but eventually the senior official allowed us to tour the site. A couple of times, the American turned to me and spoke quietly in Spanish telling me not to speak, that it would be alright.

"By now, I began to trust him—but not completely. We spent a lot of time in the control room at the refinery, which was very hot. Their engineers had managed to get only part of the damaged equipment working. He spoke to me on several occasions, but I knew it was only for the sake of appearances. He handed me a printout of computer data, which I pretended

175

to look through. I kept my eyes down. It was wise because it saved me from raising my head and looking up at the men, which they did not like me doing. They were hostile and resentful.

"We got back to the training compound later that night. They allowed us to eat together, and the American put some printed spreadsheets on the table, which we pretended to study and discuss. 'I will help you get a message to Jamal', he told me.

"Two days later, the men sent as bodyguards by Jamal arrived and I was taken back to his camp. I didn't have time to see the American before I left. By then, I knew for sure he was CIA.

" 'But why?' Jamal asked me when I arrived back at his camp. 'Why did you come back, Daniela?'

" 'I can help you here,' I told him.

" 'You can help us too in your own country.'

"I walked over to him, and put my arms around him. 'I want to be here with you, Jamal.'

"That night I gave myself to him," said Daniela without any emotion. "He was older, and he wasn't very good in bed. He fell asleep soon afterwards. I was happy for him anyway. He was exhausted and he never allowed himself much rest. He was unselfish, always trying to do good—for his men and for his people.

"Jamal wasn't any good as a lover, but I made him a hero among the men he commanded. It isn't very hard for women to fake orgasms, and I faked a lot for him. I spent a lot of my time with him. Mostly in his tent when we were on manoeuvres, but sometimes in a room in abandoned homes that our unit would occupy for several days at a time.

"He enjoyed his newly earned reputation among his men for being a powerful warrior and lover. I made sure of that.

"He was quite different from the others, but he could have a violent side too. One of his men took the wife of another.

176

Jamal convened a court and listened to the evidence. 'Even in warfare, we do not kill people without a trial,' he told me, exhibiting his profound distaste for western civilisation. When the man confessed, Jamal took out his pistol and shot off the man's penis and testicles. The man wailed and screamed. Jamal shot him through the head. 'It is Sharia law,' he said to the group that had assembled. 'Allah is great.'

"Most of the time, when he was asleep, it was too dangerous for me to search among his papers. He kept his military radio-phone close at hand, and also his cell phone—even though there was no service most of the time. Sometimes, when I was sure he was deeply asleep and not just pretending, I was able to look for information that might help lead me to Mustapha. I guessed that he might be using a codename, but I could find nothing in his phone log. I decided I would have to find a different way to get Jamal to tell me about Mustapha.

"There was one day when he was sleeping, I was lucky. He was careless about where he left his things. I can read Arabic. Although some of his military papers were in a regional dialect, I was able to understand a lot of them. The rebel forces were secretive about the location of their own units and ammunition stockpiles. Jamal had developed a string of informers and he was accumulating information on ISIS strongholds and fuel and ammunition supply dumps. One of the documents described the ISIS chains of command and the location of ISIS command headquarters in Raqqa."

Daniela gave a hollow laugh, as she recalled something from the past. It was a laugh without humour, almost bitter.

"I even used his watch to take down the coordinates of where we made camp and where the ISIS stockpiles were located.

"His men did not like me. I could tell from their eyes that they thought I was an infidel whore. Given the chance, they would have raped and killed me—but they feared and

177

respected Jamal. There was one of them in particular who I knew did not trust me. I could see it in the way he looked at me. He was fiercely loyal to Jamal. Several times, I was aware he was watching me—spying on me.

"I had made up my mind that, if they discovered what I was doing while Jamal was sleeping, I would take his gun and shoot myself through the roof of my mouth. I did not want to suffer what they would do to me. Twice I practiced with Jamal's gun, making sure I knew how to turn off the safety switch and kill myself before they could reach me."

Antonio glanced at the others in the room. Daniela's story was powerful. Sometimes, when she paused to recall a particular event, the room was held spellbound in the kind of respectful and almost fearing silence that grips a congregation at the most solemn moment of the Consecration of the Mass.

Several times, she seemed to be speaking in a state of trance. Her eyes not moving as her words came slowly and deliberately, as she saw something in the distance, perhaps recollecting a painful memory, a sadness coming from some precious thing lost that could never be regained, a moment of fear, sometimes a slight movement on her face displaying a loathing, revulsion or sickening disgust.

At other times, when she looked at them, her eyes became bright and animated, moving in a dancing duo with her eyebrows, as she described a moment of triumph or told an anecdote. Such moments were too brief—short pauses, the calm in the midst of a storm, too soon followed by a return to the wild, unrelenting, destructive acts of war.

Many times, Antonio was struck with how young she was. Too young, he thought, to have been part of such trauma. Yet, he knew that what Daniela had experienced was mild compared with the brutal realities that were taking place every hour in the warzones. Horrible, harsh atrocities, unimaginable in any world, except one controlled by so-called civilised human beings.

"Did you find out the names of the ISIS commanders collaborating with Jamal?" barked the Civil Guard commandant, finally asking a question.

Antonio glanced at him. In recalling her story, Daniela had suffered a lot of additional stress and he thought she needed a break in the questioning. But she shot back at the commandant.

"Names?" she asked. "I think I can do better than that, sir."

She stood up. Then she astonished everyone in the room by pulling down the trousers of her army green fatigues and kicking them away. With both hands, she lowered her panties, letting them drift down her legs to the floor.

Lifting one leg onto the table, she exposed her crotch and pushed the fingers of her right hand into her vagina. Slowly, she pulled out a thin plastic film—like a condom—which she placed in the middle of the table.

"Excuse the crude method of delivery, gentlemen," she said without any obvious indication of embarrassment.

"Inside, you will find my shorthand notes about the places I was taken, with GPS readings taken from Jamal's wristwatch. It will give you estimates of the numbers of ISIS troops and their allies. It will give you the location of supply dumps and car-bomb factories."

She paused for a breath. "In three cities, there are large fuel and ammunition dumps. In the case of Tal Afar and Raqqa, you will find the precise GPS coordinates of ISIS command headquarters—as of three days ago."

She looked around the room at the astonished faces of the men. "I slit an artery on my leg several times a day and smeared the blood on rags I stuffed between my legs. Al-Qaeda and ISIS have no respect whatsoever for women. They treat us worse than dogs. But, like most men, they won't molest a woman who is having her period."

179

She waited for the silence to be broken. When none of the startled men said anything, she continued talking. "I'm tired. I'd like to take a shower."

"After that, with your permission, sir," she said, addressing the commandant, "I'd like to go home."

Lleida: Father Damien

He was used to getting up early and going about his work, but this morning Father Damien had been startled when he was awakened well before his normal time by the noise of a vehicle in the courtyard outside his bedroom window.

He had stumbled out of bed. Stubbing his toe against a side table, he muttered an expletive and steadied himself as he pulled gently back on the curtains.

Even in the pre-dawn darkness, the priest could see the builder's van had parked away from its normal position, and the driver's door was opening. He had reached for his glasses, groping for them in the darkness. His head hurt; his sinuses felt dry and tight.

Usually both men arrived together, but this time he could see only one. It was the tall man—the one he feared more than the other. The tall man was joined several minutes later by the builder. They had worked under cover of darkness, without any lights, loading things into both vehicles.

Father Damien had come down from his latest dose earlier that night. It was not the usual stuff they gave him—much weaker, and it had no lasting benefits. He knew right away that he would need another fix soon. If he had felt better, he would have taken more photographs of them. The nauseous feeling in his stomach forced him back to his bed. He would let them get on with what they were doing, and he had fallen back into a fitful sleep within minutes. That was hours ago.

Now the tall man was approaching the house.

It would be a relief when this business arrangement was over, Father Damien sighed. He knew the men were criminals. It didn't matter—as long as they kept giving him his supply.

He was taking a risk trusting them, he knew. He didn't have many options. They had scared away his regular dealer—a troubled, but willing, youth from his parish. It was a regrettable state of affairs.

He took comfort in the knowledge that he still had his insurance policy, a powerful bargaining tool. He was reassured by his own astuteness.

Over the past few weeks, he had taken the precaution of downloading all the photographs he had taken of them onto a separate memory chip. This he had taped onto a piece of paper and placed inside a stamped envelope.

He had no hesitation in knowing to whom it should be addressed.

The image of his meeting with the condesa still burned brightly in his mind. The smile and direct look she had given him when they had met at the bishop's reception had been breathtaking. She had noticed what happened when he had been pushed aside by one of the bishop's assistants, who were all too well aware of his human frailties.

He loved her for that. The condesa had even turned and called out to him. It was that moment that the realisation had dawned on him. She and the Blessed Virgin were as one. She had reached her arms out to him and thanked him for all his great work. He knew he would be able to trust her. She was purity and goodness itself. At last, his prayers had been answered.

He had left the letter in a safe place for his housekeeper. He had given specific instructions that, should anything happen to him, the woman should mail the envelope to the condesa—without opening it. It was ready to post. The good woman always had been reliable and he was confident that she would do as she had been instructed.

He pulled out of sight of the window, as the tall man approached the house.

Some moments went by. Possibly the man had knocked on the door. Maybe he hadn't. Father Damien wasn't sure.

His uncertainty was quickly resolved. The tall man had climbed the stairs and was now confronting him. As usual, he was wearing his black leather gloves and seemed to be unconcerned that he was trespassing on the priest's domain.

"Personally, I don't like you," he said, moving close. "However, my colleague the builder assures me that you have been of good service to us. Your loyalty will be rewarded."

He handed the priest a plastic bag of white powder. "Here you go, Father. Make this last. Stay ready. We will have further need of your services soon."

This was by far a better outcome than the priest had been expecting. He took the bag and thanked him.

"Anything," he said, unable to control a wide toothy grin. "Anytime. Just ask. Thank you, and God bless you."

"You know, of course, not to say anything to anyone about our business arrangement?"

"Of course: you can trust me. You know that, señor."

"I do," said the tall man. He had wandered over to the window and was examining the priest's camera. Without asking, he clicked it on and began scrolling through the memory chip.

"I'm so excited," volunteered the priest as he watched the man scroll through the photo memory. "Just yesterday, I saw a jay finch. By now, it may have flown south."

He watched intently as the tall man lost interest in the camera's gallery of photos, and replaced it on a side table.

Turning to the priest he said, "Remember… loyalty," and he held two fingers together in the shape of a gun pointed at the priest's forehead. "You understand?"

The priest nodded his head vigorously, and clutched the plastic bag of white powder close to his chest.

He watched as the tall man got into the builder's van and drove back down the driveway.

Inside the van, the tall man shook his head. "Stupid fucker," he laughed. "He actually believed that crap."

He glanced at his watch. "Ten minutes should do it," he said aloud to himself.

He would drive to where he had parked the stolen BMW, near where he had stolen the stonemason's truck. Having disposed of the builder's body in a disused well at the farm, he now needed to get rid of the builder's van.

The stonemason's truck would be reported missing, he reasoned. But he doubted its owner was an early riser. He was taking a slight risk going back there, but so long as the police linked the builder's abandoned van with the disappearance of the stone mason's truck, he reasoned, they would have no reason to look for him. Later, it would be a simple matter to dump the BMW he'd stolen in Madrid, and find a new vehicle. Nice and tidy, he reflected, satisfied with the results of his mission.

Father Damien had spent most of his adult life preaching with profound sincerity about life after death. Whether it exists or not, no mortals know, he had been fond of telling his congregation.

He had sniffed a rather generous portion of the white powder, unaware it was uncut high grade. Now the unfortunate priest was well along a one-way journey.

Soon he would find out for himself the truth about the afterlife.

Daniela Establishes Her Credibility

The painful memory of Ceuta had started to fade. I'll be honest: it still bugged me that I had been kept out of the action. If it had been just the Civil Guard which didn't want me involved, I wouldn't have minded so much. But when your own people shut you out, that hurts.

The Barcelona homicide case was no longer foremost in my mind. The Civil Guard had wrestled it away from us all. In retrospect, I could understand that; there was no immediate terrorist threat, so GEO would be expected to stand down.

Anyway, since I got back, Raphael Robles had assigned me to other work, so I didn't have much time to dwell on the personal and professional slight I had received.

I had heard a little about the girl's rescue from Turkey. Actually, Antonio had texted me, and suggested we talk by phone so he could brief me. Then I got so busy, I kept putting it off.

The phone call I received this morning from the Civil Guard jogged my memory. It turns out that the information the girl brought back from Syria and Iraq was useful; in fact, it was first class intelligence, according to the officer who called me.

It was a late, but I returned Antonio's call. At the back of my mind was the thought that we hadn't parted on very amiable terms. It was mainly circumstantial—the homicide case had not gone well for either of us. And I wasn't feeling that I needed to suck up and make friends with the Catalan regional police. By calling him, I would like to think I was just being courteous.

"I thought I would let you know," I told him. "Our American friends sent in Reaper drones and the Turks did some on the ground surveillance. What the girl gave us was first class intel."

"That's good to hear," said Antonio; he sounded genuinely pleased.

"You'll be interested to hear that all the targets in Syria were destroyed," I continued. "Not just that, but the Americans and Turks seem to have kissed and made up—after their very public spat about the Kurds."

"I assume all of this remains off the record?" he asked me.

"For now, yes. It has to," I confirmed.

"There's one other thing, Antonio," I said, not anticipating the change of tone that crept into my voice. "As part of our internal review, we couldn't find out much about the girl. Before now, she seems to have led a very uneventful life. It's unusual for us not to be able to find something in her past."

"I suppose the Civil Guard has all of that," Antonio replied.

I didn't want to tell him that the girl's file had been sealed by the Civil Guard; no one could get access.

Antonio sounded a bit distracted, so I decided to close off our conversation.

"I'll see what I can find out about her," he said, as we rang off. "I'll let you know as soon as I can."

Chapter 8

Madrid: La Condesa's Heavenly Gift

"Señora, this came for you," said Zoe, handing an envelope to the condesa. It was marked personal and urgent.

The condesa examined it, feeling something small and solid inside. She recognised the name of the sender—Father Damien, the strange old priest from her constituency.

Sliding a letter opener through the well-sealed package, she laid the contents on her desk. A memory chip taped to a thin piece of paperboard dropped out. There was a short undated note addressed to her, with the initials of the Blessed Virgin Mary drawn in an elaborate exaggerated scroll alongside her name.

Excelentísima Señora,

> *Forgive my intrusion, for I have no one else to trust. I have sinned grievously and beseech you to ensure this letter is placed safely into the hands of the authorities.*
>
> *I am involved in a crime. Yet I do not know fully what crime it is. If you are reading this letter, it is because something unpleasant and unnatural has happened to me. I have instructed my housekeeper to forward it to you in the event of my sudden demise.*

In an out-building alongside my church, the authorities will find evidence of materials that either are the proceeds of criminal activity, or have been procured for the purposes of crime. I cannot identify both of the two men with whom I have been in collusion, but one is well known to me as a man from the village—Ramon Garcia.

You should not trust this man. He is a building contractor whose family are members of my parish. Formerly, he was a member of the Civil Guard. The other is a very tall man; I do not know his name. Be careful, please, because he is pure evil. The activities of these men are recorded in the memory chip of photos attached to this letter.

I pray that nothing nefarious will result from my weakness. I have failed everyone and I ask God's forgiveness. Please help me, good lady.

Your devoted follower,

Dedicated to the Immaculate Heart of Mary,

Damien Aracruz de la Misericordia (Fr.)

Using her intercom, she summoned her assistant.

"Zoe, as quickly as you can, search online for Father Damien in Lleida. He's the parish priest of Santa María la Virgen. I need to know if he has been in the news in the last few days. And when you come back, bring me the digital camera please."

The condesa re-read the note and then placed it on her desk pad. Then she prised the memory card away from its moorings.

"It wasn't difficult information to find, señora," said Zoe, coming back into the room after a few minutes. "It's all over the local papers. Apparently, he committed suicide." She handed the camera to the condesa, who pushed the memory card into its slot and switched it on.

The first few frames were photos of the church of Santa María la Virgen. Then there was a series of night-time photos taken from inside a room, not using a flash. She caught her breath as she recognised the white construction van with the roof rack and ladder.

She saw a photo of the van's owner unloading into a brick building what looked like bags or sacks. She recognised him from the meeting in Carlos' smoking room. The next photo frame caught her full attention—and she felt her blood pounding. Helping the van's owner load the van was an unmistakable figure—the General's driver. She scrolled through the remaining frames. There were several close-up shots of the pair. One frame gave a clear image of the van's licence plate number. If these had been taken by Father Damien, he had done a capable job of the photography, she thought.

The condesa sat back in her office armchair. What did these really mean, she wondered.

By themselves, the photographs said nothing. They had been taken over a period of time. To a casual outsider, they simply would be photographs of two men loading and unloading what looked to be agricultural supplies.

Yes, it could be said they looked somewhat furtive, appearing to check if they were being watched. They could have been stealing the materials, she reasoned. Their actions easily could be explained away.

Yet if you knew, as she did, who the men were—and if you knew which influential people they were connected to—you could put a very different interpretation on the priest's photos, she reasoned. Both men were closely connected to Carlos and the General and, by association, eventually linked to her.

The condesa knew that she needed to think this through before doing anything.

If there had been no connection to Carlos and herself, she asked herself, what would she have done with the letter and the photographs? She answered her own question. She would simply have given them to the police. In any case, she knew she would have to do so fairly soon, otherwise it might constitute withholding evidence.

What would the police make of the priest's letter and the photographs, she wondered. In the hands of a junior policeman, especially one with knowledge of the locale, it might become buried in a case file. Scandals involving the clergy were not welcomed—especially in Spain's rural parishes.

The old priest had not seemed fully mentally stable when she had met him. Was this letter to her just a figment of his imagination? Possibly evidence of paranoia, she speculated. Was the letter as simple as to be a rather elaborate and perverted form of a suicide note?

The thought that nagged at her was one she refused to admit, even to herself, had any significance. It was the connection between the two men and Carlos. She hoped that the whole thing was a coincidence and had nothing to do with him.

She admitted to herself that she was not convinced.

She was concerned about the construction corruption scandal hanging over her head, and the spectre that, no matter how innocent she might be, the investigators could ruin her political career. She would have to consider her actions carefully.

It was unrealistic to pretend that Carlos was not somehow involved. Something was not right. If not Carlos, certainly the General was involved, she was convinced. Maybe that was it. Carlos might be an innocent party to something in which the General almost certainly appeared to be a central figure.

Then she remembered the phone number she had written down on the scratch pad. She looked in her purse, and located the scrap of paper. Then she Googled the dialling code for confirmation. Just as she had found out before, it was a Marrakech phone number.

By itself, it meant nothing. Yet, the same uneasy feeling came over her. She remembered Carlos' concern when she had told him about finding the General's mislaid phone. Come to think of it, she reasoned, he had not been acting normally for several weeks now.

Deep down, she loved Carlos. She needed an opportunity to speak to him about the letter and the digital photographs. Once she knew Carlos was innocent of any direct involvement, she could speak frankly with the police.

It was a question of priorities, she felt. It was the duty of a wife to give her husband the benefit of the doubt, gently remonstrating herself for questioning his honour. And, of course, it was prudent to proceed with caution, she concluded, because she herself could become a casualty in the process— collateral damage.

In the meantime, she was aware that she was holding potentially important evidence in a situation in which someone apparently had committed suicide. She was duty-bound to report it to the police as soon as possible. Failing to do so was not only withholding potential evidence, it also could affect her career.

She summoned Zoe again. "I need a photocopy of this letter. In fact, make it two," ordered the condesa. "Then I want you to take all of this over to the National Police headquarters. I'm going to make a call to them right now."

Zoe made the photocopies. Meanwhile, the condesa had downloaded the photos from the camera onto her laptop. She made a separate memory stick copy. Walking over to the bookcase, she taped the memory stick to the back of a legislative manual. It was well hidden. Just an insurance policy, she told herself.

Then she picked up the phone and called the National Police. She explained to the officer in charge how she had received the letter and a memory card of what appeared to be photos. No, she didn't really want to speak to anyone more senior at this point, she thanked him. After all, this might be some kind of prank.

She made a note of the officer's name in her phone. It never harmed in life—and politics in particular—to have a good line of defence. She smiled at her astuteness. Then, of course, there was the matter of the corruption investigations unit. With that hanging over her head, it would be wise for her to be seen by the authorities to be more than cooperative, she reminded herself.

Here is my cell phone number if you need me, she told him. I will send my assistant over with the letter and contents right away. Where should the girl go, and whom should she ask to see, the condesa asked.

She was fully aware that the letter might take some time to be processed by the authorities. In the meantime, she felt reassured by the knowledge that she had acted like any responsible person would be expected to do, in contacting the police without delay.

If asked, she could always plead that she had not looked closely at the memory stick. It was quite plausible for her to claim that she had not recognised the two men and the white construction van, she reasoned.

In the meantime, she would go home and talk to Carlos.

She picked up her office phone and dialled his number. There was no answer. She called Hortensia on the house phone, but the housekeeper did not pick up.

She tried calling again.

This time, Hortensia answered. Señor Carlos had left several hours ago, she told the condesa. She personally had packed his bags for him. Where was he going? She thought the señora knew. He had told her that he would be spending a few days at their hunting lodge in the country. Was everything all right, she asked the señora.

Don't worry, the condesa reassured her. I must have forgotten that he'd told me he was leaving to go there today. No, no message, thank you. I may not be home until late, so don't worry about making dinner for me.

"Oh, who is driving him?" she asked the housekeeper, almost as an afterthought.

"They are travelling in the General's car, señora."

"They?" asked the condesa, fearing the answer.

"The chauffeur was driving the car when they left the house, señora. In addition to Señor Carlos and the General, there was the retired policeman—the close friend of the señor."

"The retired policeman?" asked the condesa, her voice beginning to crack. "You mean from the National Police?"

"Yes, I think so. I made them some food to take with them. There will be nothing at the lodge when they arrive. And I reminded Señor Carlos to ask his guests to ignite all the log fires when they arrive. It is already quite cold in those mountains. The fires will take the dampness out of the rooms."

"Thank you, Hortensia, that was very considerate of you," said the condesa. Aware of the strain that must be obvious in her voice, she said with a dismissive laugh, "I'm sure all those big strong men can take care of themselves."

"Si, señora," the housekeeper replied with a polite chuckle, but with an edge to her voice that indicated she was concerned about her.

The condesa replaced the phone. It was quite unusual behaviour for Carlos, she frowned. Usually he was considerate about letting her know his plans and movements. She checked her texts—nothing from him. He had been quite proud of himself recently, when he had mastered the skill of texting and, for a few days, had inundated her with them.

She checked her email, and a brief message from Carlos showed on the screen. He would be fine, the message told her. He was driving up to the lake with the General, and staying overnight at the lodge. No need for her to worry. He would be back in a few days. She should take some time for herself, he said, and rest. He loved her very much.

The condesa re-dialled his number. Again, there was no answer. She decided against leaving him a message. After all, even if her parliamentary office at the Cortes may not be bugged, she was unsure if her cell phone was being tapped or not.

She needed to see him—urgently.

The Lodge

The condesa normally liked driving the little Fiat they kept at the apartment, but it did not accelerate well up steeper hills. Now she was stuck behind a truck. Worse still, in the wet conditions, the truck was throwing up clouds of spray and she could not clear her windshield long enough to see the way ahead.

Her journey up the A6 from Madrid had passed quickly. Had she not been thinking almost completely about Carlos, she would have enjoyed the drive. The most recent occasion when she had made the same journey, she had allowed herself

193

the luxury of gloating, just a little, at the progress she and her government colleagues had made in advancing Spain's road and high-speed rail networks.

As a comparatively recent addition to the Cabinet, handpicked and appointed as Minister of Infrastructure by the Prime Minister himself, it was widely acknowledged that the condesa had worked hard to secure large increments of funding from the European Union.

Her charm in Brussels had paid off. She had obtained money for rural road upgrading and removal of tolls on some stretches of autopistas, which now were toll-free autovias. The government had created jobs at a time of austerity and high unemployment. That meant votes to keep it, and her, in power.

Being in opposition—without any influence over events— would not be fun, she reflected.

Today, none of those thoughts crossed her mind. As she drove, she created scenarios about Carlos' recent actions. She could explain most of them as being quite innocent. Yet, several questions still nagged at her.

Until she had more answers she would not be able to explain his actions any further, she concluded. It was really up to Carlos to trust her and put her mind at rest.

As the driver of the truck in front of her signalled his intention to pull off the narrow road leading to the next village, the condesa saw her opportunity to accelerate and overtake the vehicle. She shifted gears and swept past, grateful that no other traffic was in front of her. Within fifteen minutes she was approaching their lakeside lodge.

Carlos' family had owned forestland and had maintained hunting rights in the area for centuries. At one time, a local sawmill supplied oak timbers to Madrid. The heavy oaks, along with old pine, provide the framing of many of Madrid's heritage homes.

Before it became a public park, hunting of ibex and deer was popular. It is even said that Franco himself used to enjoy weekends at the lodge. The condesa disapproved of any talk on this subject. Unlike Carlos, she had chosen to spend little time there.

As she neared the unpaved approach roads to the lodge, she slowed down.

There was no other traffic on the country road. She pressed the remote which opened the high wrought-iron gate. The long gravel track that led to the lake wound its way unevenly between large boulders of the Sierra. There were stunted pines, which had not fared as well in the damp ground closer to the lake as others had in the better drained soils higher up the mountain.

As she approached the lodge, even in the dark she could see that the men had taken Hortensia's advice. A thick plume of wood smoke was coming out of the main chimney of the lodge. During the summer, the woodsman had stacked firewood against the outside wall, under shelter of the wide overhanging roof—a structure well-designed to keep snow away from the main entrance.

Above the wide entrance door was mounted the head of a giant antlered ibex.

It was a haunting sight. When she had first seen it, the condesa had felt intensely sad. She was staring at a near-extinct species. She had said nothing to Carlos, of course; he would not have understood. Some things in Spain needed to become extinct, she had muttered quietly to herself. These beautiful animals deserved better.

The condesa conceded that it was a perfect getaway for Carlos. The mountain air was clean and crisp. The deeply rutted sides of the valley shut out the world and created a silence that only those who love mountains can fully appreciate. There was good fishing in the lake. They had no neighbours for several kilometres. She could understand why he loved the isolation of this place so much.

Today, it did not seem that isolation was what he wanted—assuming that he had made the choice, thought the condesa, with an image of the General forcing itself into her mind.

She had to admit her growing resentment of the power of decision-making over their lives that her husband increasingly seemed to be yielding to him. Not to mention his sinister chauffeur. She shivered at the thought of the creepy man.

She parked her car in about the only parking place available and shivered as she felt the evening mountain coldness bite into her skin, barely covered by her light jacket. She should have come better prepared for the climate she admitted to herself as she closed her car door.

They must have seen her lights coming down the driveway, she reasoned. But no one came to the door to meet her.

She avoided looking at the mounted head of the ibex, and rapped loudly on the heavy wooden door. After two more attempts, the door opened.

"Condesa," said the General's chauffeur, clearly surprised. "We were not expecting you." He hesitated for only a fraction of a second. It was enough for the condesa to bristle with indignation.

"We?" she thought, but said nothing. You're just a damned employee. Carlos and I own this place.

The chauffeur could not have mistaken the message in her blazing eyes. "What a pleasure. Please do come in," he invited, stepping aside and making a great flourish with his arm. "I will tell the Count you have arrived. May I help you with the luggage from your car?"

She shook her head and turned away from him. The wood fire in the main room looked inviting. She went over to it and stood with her back to its intense heat, appreciating the heavy smell of wood smoke.

A few minutes later, Carlos pushed his wheelchair into the room, his two hands deftly steering it over the large carpet covering much of the planked wood floor.

"Teresa," he said, almost in a half-shout. "This is wonderful. I didn't know you were going to drive up."

He wheeled up to her side and raised his arm for a hug. She obliged him, but without any great enthusiasm.

The condesa glanced around to make sure they were alone. "Carlos, I have been trying to get hold of you. We have to talk."

Carlos breathed in through his teeth. "That might be a little difficult right now, darling. As you can see, we have a little get-together of old comrades." He nodded towards the drawing room,

"Why didn't you tell me you were coming up here, Carlos?" asked the condesa, now close to tears.

"I know how you must be feeling. I'm sorry. I've had a lot going on recently, darling." He tried to hold her hand to reassure her, but she pulled it away quickly.

"There's a lot we have to talk about," she continued.

"Are you staying overnight?" he asked, looking around for her suitcase. Then he continued to speak. "I know I haven't been at home much recently, and I'm not being a good husband to you at present. I know that. But I love you and, well, once I have this business out of the way, we can spend a lot more time together…"

"It's not that, Carlos," the condesa snapped. She moved away from the fireplace aware that the heat had raised her core temperature more than she had intended.

She looked at Carlos. He seemed shocked at her outburst, his cheeks draining of colour. His eyes had widened. Then, just as quickly, they seemed to retreat inside their sockets. He seemed to diminish in stature and his once-noble face looked distressed.

"What could it possibly be, darling?" he asked after the pause, a deep frown furrowing his forehead.

"We have to talk, Carlos," she repeated, "but not with them around," she motioned to the drawing room.

He glanced at his watch, and seemed to be trying to arrange events in his mind. "Can we talk in the kitchen?" he suggested. "It's quieter in there."

She shrugged her shoulders and, without thinking, took the handles of his wheelchair and pushed him towards the door into the kitchen.

He took his hands off the wheels, looked up and smiled at her: "It's a long time since you did that."

The casual remark shocked the condesa. She had not been aware that she had been any less dutiful recently to her husband. A knot formed in her throat, and tears started to well up in her eyes. Then in a torrent they began to fall alongside her nose. With her two hands already in use, she was powerless to stop them from dripping off her chin.

"Condesa." She heard his voice behind him. Unmistakably it was that of the General.

"It is wonderful to see you again." He beamed a smile in her direction. Bowing slightly, he asked, "How are you?"

She was embarrassed by her tears and struggled to think of an answer.

"Don Carlos," said the General, immediately switching his attention to him.

Then he turned to address the condesa. "Would you mind, dear lady? I have to steal your husband, just for a moment." His voice indicated it was less a request than an instruction.

Carlos looked at his wife with a pained smile. "I won't be a minute, darling—honestly." He leaned forward in his wheelchair and clasped her hand.

He spun his wheelchair around and followed the direction of the General, who by now was striding half way across the floor in the direction of the drawing room.

The condesa had never really relaxed at the lodge. At that moment, she began to hate it. It had a heavy atmosphere of something she could not describe. She had not driven up here with the intention of staying the night. Now her mind was clear. She would drive back to Madrid just as soon as she and Carlos had talked. She needed to know what was going on. How had their lives changed so quickly without her being aware of it?

Carlos' innocent remark, and the almost childlike joyous smile he had given her as she had started to push his wheelchair, had cut her to her emotional core. It had been so unexpected. Had she been too selfish in the pursuit of her career, she began to question herself. Had she been a neglectful wife?

She remembered his tears when he had played his favourite piece from the composer Granados that night she had come home late. Carlos had been a kind man to her. She knew he was a good man: honourable and true.

She felt guilty about some of her own actions, her affair with Pavel. It had seemed so innocent at first, but over time it had begun to worry her—like a ghostly evil character in a macabre play, waiting in the wings to come forth and spread its poison. She had brushed the awful thoughts away, but still they haunted her dreams.

Despite the fun, she felt stained and besmirched by her actions. Her betrayal. There was a large gap in their ages, but Carlos deserved better.

She had not been to church in a long time, at least not in any meaningful way. Now the guilt was eating away at her; she felt the need to physically rip away the sin from her body, to cleanse herself. To feel again, with Carlos, the communion of more innocent and better times.

Wiping a warm tear from her face, she saw what she had feared—that her makeup was running. Standing up, she looked in the mirror over the sink. She looked awful. Taking a paper towel, she daubed at the worst of the damage. She was not the hysterical type of wife and would have to pull herself together if she was going to talk calmly and rationally to Carlos. Please, just please, don't let those men see me like this, she asked.

Pulling her jacket over her shoulders, she opened the back door of the kitchen and went outside to dry her tears. After the intense heat of the fireplace, the coolness of the night caught her by surprise. In a way, it was refreshing. Her eyes dried. She felt strangely better—almost like she had been to confession. Clenching the lapels of her jacket close, she moved slowly along the wooden deck at the back of the lodge.

The voices she heard were clear and unmistakable, resonating in the cold night air.

"Hide the flag until the condesa leaves, Luis," the General instructed his chauffeur. "You can put it back up as soon as she's gone."

"Do you think she suspects anything, sir?"

"I don't know. She's clever, that one. If she does, we will have to take care of her, won't we?"

The condesa was shocked by the guttural laugh that came in response to the General's threat. Already chilled, she shivered again.

A cloud of cigar smoke drifted from the open French doors of the living room. "Okay, let's go back inside. Carlos must have finished signing those bank papers by now," said the General. "We have to find a way to make the condesa leave soon. We need to be ready for the arrival of our guest. He should be here shortly," he added, as he glanced at his watch.

The condesa remained rooted to the spot, hardly daring to breathe. When she was sure they had gone back inside, she moved carefully back towards the kitchen door, ducking underneath the light that beamed out of the kitchen window.

Then she saw the man. He was standing in an area of flat land about two hundred metres from the lodge. She watched as he lit some oil flares and placed them in a roughly square shaped piece of flat land.

He hadn't seen her, and she opened the door and slipped back into the kitchen.

"Teresa, there you are. I've been looking for you," said Carlos, wheeling over to see her. "Are you alright?" he asked.

"I just slipped out to get some fresh air," the condesa replied, trying to force a smile.

"You look like you've seen a ghost," said Carlos, clearly concerned about her wild appearance.

The condesa's survival instincts kicked in. "Carlos, there's a man out there lighting some flares. What is he doing?"

"Nothing to worry about, darling," said Carlos with a forced smile. "He's a guest of the General and he's probably just getting some air."

"But he's setting up something," insisted the condesa.

"Well, we are expecting a special guest tonight, darling."

"Isn't he driving in?"

"Well, no, actually. He's too well known and we don't want to draw attention to his presence here," said Carlos, looking awkward. "It's nothing to worry about. Now, what did you want to talk to me about so urgently that you drove all the way up here?"

The condesa made a quick decision.

"Carlos, I have been worried about you. Really worried. I suppose that I just panicked when I couldn't get hold of you. It's stupid of me to have arrived without warning. Now I've spoiled your dinner party."

She looked earnestly at her husband. "I think it's all this pressure from the investigators over the corruption scandal. I haven't said anything to them, if that's what you're worried about," she added, when a look of concern crossed his face.

"Now that I can see you're okay, I'm fine. Really I am. Please, darling, next time let me know that you're okay. You were becoming so good at texting me and everything."

He took her hand. "Look, you're not to worry about me. I'm an old campaigner. These are my friends. We can look out for each other." He kept hold of her hand. "It's you I'm worried about, Teresa. You've been working far too hard for too long. You need to take a break from the Cortes. Have a rest, relax and get back to being yourself again."

She laughed and started to cry again. "Is it that obvious that I'm run down?" She placed her hand on his shoulder and squeezed it.

He glanced at his watch. When he replied, his voice sounded reassuring, but the condesa thought it had a distinct sense of urgency to it. "Nothing that a bit of rest won't look after, darling. We can talk about it more at home, if you like? Now, would you like me to ask the General's chauffer to drive you back to Madrid? It will save you the drive this time of night."

The condesa hoped that her shocked reaction to his suggestion had not registered on her face. Spending any time at all in the company of the chauffeur was the most distant thought from her mind. He was repulsive. "No, it's fine, darling. I'm perfectly okay," she heard herself blurt out. "The drive back to Madrid is less than an hour at this time of night."

She noticed the relief on her husband's face, and that again he had glanced at his watch.

"Please ask everyone to excuse me. Say goodbye for me. Tell them your wife is very, very fond of her husband," she smiled and kissed him on the mouth. "Tell them I was worried about you. They'll understand."

Although he was preoccupied, almost certainly thinking about the imminent arrival of their special guest, she hoped that Carlos had listened. She hoped he would repeat to his cronies the script she had just created for their consumption.

Pushing his wheelchair with his gloved hands, Carlos escorted her to the door. She kissed him and quickly got into her car. Glancing in her rear-view mirror, she saw him wave. Seconds later, the tall silhouette of the General emerged alongside of him. They went back inside. The condesa pressed the remote for the big iron gate and drove off at perhaps too fast a speed in the direction of Madrid.

Ten minutes later, as she entered the village, she pulled off into an empty car park. The village hotel had closed for the season. The place looked more run-down than she remembered. In the old days, before the national park had been created, and when hunting had been allowed, the hotel would have been full at this time of year. Now it looked like a sad relic from the past.

Out of sight from the road, the condesa pulled out her phone; she checked for messages. There were several, but none were vital at this time of night.

There was a text from the prime minister's office. It was not urgent. She would get back to it later, she decided. Besides, she now had a lot to talk about with the PM. She needed to see him face-to-face.

First things first: she speed-dialled her personal assistant.

"Alexander, it's me. Listen very carefully and do exactly as I tell you," she spoke urgently. She could hear a young man's voice in the background, asking who was calling at this hour.

"Yes, of course, Condesa. I'm listening," replied the PA.

"I am in considerable danger," she began. "I need you to contact the National Police for me. It is a matter of national concern. Confidentiality is essential. I need to speak to the most senior police officer you can locate. I cannot tell you exactly where I am, but I am here in Madrid," she lied.

"I need an appointment at…" she looked at her watch, "at 11:30 tonight at National Police headquarters."

Her parliamentary secretary had begun his reply, "I know the assistant to…" when she cut him off.

"Alexander, say as little as you can. I repeat, this is a top priority national security issue. I will call you at 10:30 p.m. to find out what arrangements have been made."

The condesa cut the line and sat thinking. She looked around. The village was still deserted. She was thankful for that.

Her next call was to Felipe. The conversation was equally brief. It helped that Felipe was still at his office working. He was much quicker to understand her predicament than her PA had been.

Inside her jacket, her fingers brushed against the envelope of Father Damien's photographs she had brought to discuss with Carlos. She sighed. Had she been discovered at the back of the lodge by the General and his chauffeur, and had they searched her pockets, tonight may have turned out very differently, she reflected with a shiver.

Now this evidence would help her establish her credibility with the National Police—and substantiate her story—if, in the process, she could somehow extricate him from involvement. He was being duped by these men; she was certain of it.

A thought nagged at the condesa. As she developed it into a fully-fledged idea, she started to feel more in control of herself. She was not a person to panic, she reminded herself. After all, it was not for nothing that she had risen so quickly up the ranks of her profession.

She mulled over the outline of the plan that was forming in her head. Some of the possible actions she quickly dismissed as being far too risky. For a moment, a wave of panic started to return. She was about to abandon the plan and go straight to the police. Then she thought about Carlos. A feeling of sadness swept over her again. For a moment, she felt lonely and helpless.

There was no credible way she could return to the lodge and extricate him from this situation. After all, she counselled herself, she really didn't have much evidence to go on. He would be embarrassed if she made a scene. But she had to find a way to help him get out of there.

She was a middle-aged woman. Yes, a minister of the government too. She reminded herself that both were very good reasons not to proceed with the hazardous course of action she was now contemplating. It was stupid. Forget the idea and hand the evidence she had compiled, however fragmentary, to the appropriate authorities. Let the professionals take the risks.

Then Carlos' words can back to haunt her. 'It's a long time since you did that.' Again, she brushed away the tears that were beginning to form. Then, deciding her course of action, she started the engine of the little Fiat and drove back in the direction of the lodge.

Lodge Revisited

As she neared the automatic gate leading up to the lodge, the condesa slowed the vehicle and switched off her headlights. The clear night, with a crescent moon, offered her little help in navigation. Until the very last moment, she did not see the lights of the small black sedan driving rapidly from the opposite direction.

A brief glimpse of an older man. She had quite clearly seen the index finger he'd thrust at her in anger as he swerved to avoid her. Nothing became of the incident and the small black sedan had continued on its journey down the unmade road without stopping. Her heart rate, already very fast, seemed to spike, pumped by the adrenaline now coursing through her veins.

Driving past the iron gate to the lodge she took note of several forestry trails. When she had parked as close to the lodge as she thought was safe, the condesa reversed into one of the trails and hid her car out of sight of the road.

Leaving it unlocked, she was careful not to activate the flashing parking lights with the remote. She took out her cell phone, and changed the setting to silent. It would not be a good time for Alexander to return her call, she warned herself. The adrenaline now helped dispel the cold that she had felt earlier.

Returning to the lodge in this way was a stupid course of action, she knew. But it was necessary if Carlos was going to be protected.

She climbed over the wall at the side of the driveway. She was wearing flat shoes and was thankful for that, at least, she muttered to herself. What if the General had posted a lookout? She shuddered at the thought of the evil chauffeur lurking somewhere in the trees—gleefully waiting for her to return. Did they suspect anything, she wondered. She would have to take that chance.

Inventing a cover story, she decided she could say that her car had hit a rock on the road. That she had lost her cell phone in the process, and that she had been forced to walk back to the lodge for help. It wasn't a completely plausible cover story, but it would have to do, she decided.

She stumbled on the stones along the driveway that lead to the lodge. Pausing to catch her breath, she tried to keep to the rough grass that edged the driveway. That would cut out any sound of her approach, she reasoned. But there was also a risk that she might stumble on the steep hill and fall into the scrub and rocks below.

As she drew closer to the lodge, she moved into the protection of the edge of pine forest. She paused frequently. She couldn't see anyone keeping guard outside the lodge.

Perhaps they felt so confident that they didn't think it was necessary, she hoped fervently.

Then she heard the unmistakable sound of a low flying helicopter. She pulled herself closer into the protection of the forest, recalling that the fire service maintained a helipad and helicopter nearby during the fire season. At this time of year, there was no longer any danger from forest fires, but she remembered hearing that they kept the helipad open during the snowshoeing and skiing season.

She had to admire the boldness of the General and his friends. The locals would be used to the sound and presence of a helicopter. It was a clever way to bring in their special guest. Now more than ever, she was determined to find out who he or she was.

The helicopter switched on its landing lights at the last minute, then it touched down and allowed its engine to cool. The landing pad was on the other side of the lodge. She couldn't see what was happening once it had touched down, but now was a good time to complete her journey up the driveway to the lodge. On foot, it took another five minutes.

Avoiding the front door, she circled the lodge. A breeze was rippling through the pine forest. She remembered the cigar smoke. It had drifted from the east, she recalled. That meant that approaching the lodge from the west would give her the greatest protection from her footsteps being heard.

She paused for breath, feeling a strange mixture of terror and exhilaration. This really was a crazy idea, she told herself. She still had time to abandon it and get back to her car. She could be safely back in Madrid in just over an hour, she told herself. The thought of Carlos drove her forwards.

Keeping close to the unlit area provided by the timbered wall of the lodge, she was glad now that he disliked dogs. He was adamant he did not want them near him. Tonight this was fortunate for her, she acknowledged gratefully.

Her nerves were already tight as a bowstring. She edged closer to the closed French windows.

As she peered through a crack in the curtains, she immediately recognised the man at the front of the room. Her mouth gaped open. Of course: now it all made sense. It was a shock—but no longer a surprise to her.

It was no wonder that Carlos had not wanted her to stay. She shook her head in disbelief. At the head of the dining table was the former leader of one of the country's now-outlawed minority parties. He was talking passionately to the rapt assembly.

Behind him, the Spanish fascist flag that the General had insisted should be in place, in honour of their distinguished guest, had been pinned to the wood walls of the dining room. As familiar as she was with the historic nationalist emblem— the 20-N flag—the condesa was appalled to see it here at their lodge.

She did not know whether the flag was a celebration of Franco's life—everyone knew he died November 20th 1975— or a commemoration of the day in 1936 when the Falangist leader Primo de Rivera had been executed. To the condesa, the flag's symbolism could only mean one thing: fascism was alive and well in this room.

Still more terrifying to her, there were various maps on the wall. The General—who, like the speaker, also was standing—was in the throes of pointing at the maps. Several men around the table were nodding their heads.

Worst of all, the men sitting around the table, including Carlos, began to applaud the General.

It was obvious now to her; these were not old men reminiscing over old times. The influential banker whom she recognised, the military men, the former Madrid police chief, a celebrity who was well known as an apologist for the monarchy, and an archbishop. All of them were there—clearly for a far more sinister purpose than a reunion.

It was so horrible to her. This was not a meeting of the old gang; these powerful men had a well-developed agenda—and probably, between them, the means to carry it out. They were planning something political. Surely she had not stumbled upon the existence of a coup? That would be impossible in modern Spain; the thought raced through her mind. But was it so unlikely?

Times were hard. The economy was struggling. Despite the hard work of the prime minister and herself and government colleagues, millions of people were still without jobs. Youth unemployment was over fifty percent. A lot of Spaniards would not be sorry to go back to the Franco days. At least his dictatorship put food on the table, she had heard many older people say.

Surely they could not be planning a coup, she asked herself again. Why was the General there? Why was everyone in the room treating him like an ascending monarch? If the army took control of the country, it would involve an overthrow of the government—the government in which she was a senior minister.

For the condesa, the cruellest blow was that her husband, her darling Carlos, had not been duped into participating. Clearly, he was a very willing ringleader.

Her heart was pumping so fast that she knew she was in danger of making a serious mistake. Before moving, she thought through her escape route. She would retrace her steps and move back along the rear of the lodge to the driveway.

Her heart was pumping but her mind was crystal clear. She had the presence of mind to check the sky. Clouds now obscured the moon. From the driveway, she would use the cover of the pine trees and exit near the gate, as she had done when she entered. She gave one last glance through the window into the dining room.

To her horror, the General's chauffeur was approaching the French doors—clearly intent on opening them and coming outside. Quick change of plan. The condesa took large strides and ran to the far side of the lodge. She was only just in time before the doors were swung open. Not wasting a minute, she walked swiftly into the cover of the pine trees and hid herself for a moment behind one of the vehicles parked in the driveway, breathing deeply to provide oxygen to her shaking body.

She made it to the road and half-ran up the slope to her car. She stumbled on the loose gravel of the driveway and her shoe came off. She felt the hard gravel and stones bite into the flesh of her foot. It hurt. She swore out loud, and hurried to put her shoe back on.

Her journey to the car got worse. She felt panic for a moment when she couldn't immediately find the vehicle. Someone had moved it, she was convinced. She stopped and leaned against a stone wall, forcing herself to calm her nerves. The moon was now behind the clouds and the place seemed very different from when she had arrived. Had she come too far up the hill?

Finally, she found it. Not wasting a second, the condesa fought to control her urge to cry. With shaking hands, she finally started the engine. Without headlights, fearing they might alert someone, she guided the vehicle painfully slowly back onto the rough stone road. It seemed to take hours.

Thinking later about the journey back to Madrid, the contessa could not recall a single part of it. Before tonight, she had been worried. At the lodge, she had been scared. Now she was terrified. All her doubts had disappeared. Carlos was plotting against everything for which she stood. She had been plunged into the middle of a diabolical subversive plot. She had to get to the National Police as soon as she could.

It was only when she drove onto the A6 towards Madrid, with the reassurance of other vehicles on the highway, that she was able to breathe more deeply and calm her nerves. Then she thought about her appointment. It was already 9:30 p.m.

Within an hour, she would make the calls to Alexander and Felipe. She would have to trust that they had done their jobs properly.

Trust these days was in short supply.

Back to Madrid

Earlier that evening, as she drove northward on the A6, the condesa had been unaware that a vehicle had been following her for some considerable time. It was a black compact budget rental, less than two years old and indistinguishable from any other small car travelling on the highway that evening.

The driver of the compact hadn't wanted to get in front of her. At any time, he figured, she might take any of the several exits available. On one occasion, he had pulled in sharply behind her, cutting in front of a truck—in the process annoying the truck driver, who responded by tailgating him.

Francisco Rioja was unfazed by the trucker's aggressive behaviour. Truckers could piss off, he declared loudly on several occasions during the drive, with his driver's window open to the night air. His surveillance pursuit, he was certain, would prove far more important to the Spanish people than a truckload of agricultural produce arriving a few minutes late at its destination.

He followed the condesa's Fiat as it pulled off the autovia. Not wanting to lose sight of her, he overtook a slower moving vehicle and accelerated fast, coming up too close behind her. After that, he dropped back several more metres—intentionally leaving too small a gap between them for other vehicles coming up behind him to pass safely on the narrow two-lane road.

As the condesa drove through the smaller villages, Francisco narrowed the gap. It was dark, and hard to see ahead. Even so, he had dimmed his headlights several times when he thought he was driving too close to her vehicle.

When she finally slowed down to turn off the main road, Francisco was driving solely on sidelights. As a consequence, he almost crashed into the back of her Fiat when she turned up a side street.

He had cursed several times. It would have helped, he told himself several times that evening, if he'd known in advance where she was going. Then a thought hit him.

She's going to their hunting lodge, he said aloud, pleased with his inspired detective work.

In his research, he had read about the place. It was a hunting lodge sometimes used by General Franco. Up until now, Francisco had forgotten about the place. Until she turned off the main road, it had not occurred to him that this was her destination.

Now another piece of the puzzle was starting to fit into place, he congratulated himself.

Driving past the turnoff, he waited until the lights of the condesa's Fiat were ahead of him by a safe distance. Then he reversed his vehicle and, with its lights off, he followed in the direction she had driven.

It had not been hard to track her. He could see the lights of her Fiat rise and dip, and negotiate sharp corners, as she wrestled with the difficult terrain.

He watched as she used a remote control to open the large iron gates, which barricaded the property and was clearly designed to intimidate and ward off intruders. Then he had driven past the gates and hidden his car at the end of a forestry track.

Getting out of his vehicle, he had a difficult time clambering over the stone wall which bordered the estate. He was not getting any younger, he reminded himself. With camera and zoom lenses in hand, he followed the driveway.

Wary in case he caused any guard dogs to bark, he moved carefully at first. But there seemed to be no sign of any. In his years of sleuthing, he had acquired various skills aimed at silencing barking dogs and other more vicious animals he sometime encountered. Tonight, he was relieved that would not be necessary.

He quickened his pace, and was just in time to see in the distance that the lodge door had been opened for the condesa, and that she was stepping inside. Expertly, he got his camera into action. Later that night, he would review his haul of photographs. When he did, he would conclude that he had at least ten clear frames of the face of the man who had opened to the door to admit her.

He planned to sort through them, and perhaps run one, maybe two, through an ID check—courtesy of a woman friend at the National Police headquarters.

Circling at a distance behind the lodge, and reluctant to get too close, he had been able to take several long-distance photos of the occupants of the lodge. It was evident from the number of vehicles parked in the driveway that some kind of gathering was taking place. He could not identify any of the men inside but, with luck, maybe he would be able to do that later.

Moving back carefully to the front of the lodge, he smiled at his cleverness. He had been able to take close-ups of the vehicles' registration numbers. It had been just so easy, he thought.

His over-confidence was premature. He had to run for cover when the lodge door suddenly was thrown open and the condesa left—obviously in a hurry. His instincts told him to follow her.

It took him a long time to get back to his car. He'd hidden it almost too well down the logging road. In the darkness, he cursed. He had wasted precious time.

Trying to catch up with the condesa's little Fiat, Francisco gunned his engine and was almost forced off the road by a stupid driver coming the opposite way without lights. As his car flashed by hers, he recognised the driver as the condesa.

To avoid detection, he had pretended to continue in the direction he was going.

What on earth is she doing, he had asked himself, mystified why she would leave in such a rush, only to return soon afterwards with her car lights switched off.

Only when he had felt it was safe did he slow down and drive back towards the lodge. This time he was more cautious. Eventually he was able to make out the familiar shape of her Fiat hidden in the woods. Cutting his engine, he watched as she tried to scale the wall. After a false start, he was impressed as she negotiated the obstacle with a lot more flexibility than he possessed.

She had a remote to open the gate, so climbing the wall could only mean that she wanted to avoid detection, he reasoned.

After she had disappeared from sight up the driveway, he used the same hiding place as before for his vehicle.

Climbing the stone wall for the second time that night, he followed the condesa at a safe distance up the driveway. This was getting interesting, he thought.

For months, he had been looking for evidence that the condesa and her husband were involved in corrupt construction project involving government funds in her parliamentary riding near Lleida.

He had a strong feeling tonight that he had stumbled onto a motherlode of evidence. It was the part of his work that he relished. He smiled with satisfaction as he manoeuvred through the pine forest towards the lodge.

Over the next half hour, making sure that he gave the lodge a wide berth, he circled the property and took over fifty frames of photographs. He was amazed; he could not believe his luck. Even from a distance, he recognised most of the occupants in the brightly lit room. This was going to be much more than a national scoop, he realised. It was sensational. But now he must get away.

Back at his car, he paused to make a duplicate miniature-disk of the photos, and sealed it in a pre-stamped envelope. Above all, he must protect the incriminating evidence that he stumbled upon.

He was crouched down low in his car when the condesa returned to hers and, for the second time that night, she drove off in the direction of the A6 and Madrid.

Making a hurried stop at a mail box in the village, he drove fast and caught up with her vehicle well before it entered the autovia. He followed closely behind her—all the way back to Madrid. He was exhilarated by his brilliance and success. For sure, this will be a front-page international story, he congratulated himself.

He had worked hard in life, he reasoned. This was his opportunity to cash in. He didn't care if he became just one more pig guzzling at the trough.

It was his time, and he deserved it.

National Police Headquarters

At 11:15 pm that evening, the condesa walked past two heavily armed policemen through the main doors of the National Police headquarters. Felipe was already inside waiting for her. He gestured to her and they went back outside.

"Are you alright, Condesa?" he asked with concern, alarmed at her dishevelled appearance and several cuts on her knees.

They talked for a few minutes before going back inside. Proceeding through security screening, they were escorted into an interview room.

The room, she guessed, was bugged and would have a one-way mirror system. Felipe nodded to her in encouragement.

It was hard to relax, and she wanted the meeting to proceed without wasting any more time. She was aware of her nervous movements, tapping her foot on the floor. It was the adrenaline, she told herself.

She recited in her mind what she had already decided to say. It all came down to the same basic statement: "*I think my husband, Conde Carlos de la Santa Maria, is involved in fascist activities. He and some very powerful friends are planning something big. I don't know what it is, but one person has already died—possibly murdered—in the process.*"

It would be important not to exaggerate what she knew. She had cautioned herself on this point several times on the drive back to Madrid. Give the police the facts as dispassionately as possible, she had counselled herself. Hysteria was not in her nature, but she knew that she would quickly appear unstable and out-of-control if she allowed herself to stray from the facts.

She breathed in deeply to steady her nerves—not for the first time that evening.

Bottles of water had been provided on the table. She uncapped one. The water was warm, but she drank almost all of it on one swallow.

****

I had been at home earlier that evening when the call came through from Raphael Robles. He told me about the phone call he had received from the condesa's attorney. He seemed unusually agitated, and told me he wanted to meet at his office without delay.

My wife was used to these incursions into our private life. She simply smiled, kissed me and told me to look after myself.

The kids were already up late, and she would get them to bed. Don't wait up, I told her, giving her a prolonged hug. She is a wonderful woman, that lady.

Raphael Robles was sitting at his desk, deep in thought, when I tapped on the glass door into his office. He gestured for me to sit down.

"Diego," he started off, "have you heard of the conde and condesa de la Santa Maria?"

"Isn't she Minister of Infrastructure in the government?" I asked.

"Yes. The corruption squad is investigating them, relating to the construction scandal. We haven't been able to connect them with anything yet," he added.

I waited while he got to his point.

"Tonight, I received a call from the condesa's attorney. A fellow named Felipe Zavalos. They want to meet us tonight. He said it's urgent."

"If it's corruption-related, why don't we just hand it over to the Corruption Squad? Why does GEO need to get involved?" I asked, still wondering why he had wanted to see me in the office so urgently, late at night.

"The attorney said it's nothing to do with that. He said the condesa has highly sensitive information. She wants to talk to us urgently. She'll be here around eleven tonight."

Now this was interesting, I thought, as I leaned forward to hear what else Robles could tell me.

"All he said is that it involves her husband, and a number of powerful people in Spain," he volunteered. Robles was not in a good mood, and was bouncing one knee up and down repeatedly. It was annoying to watch.

I looked at my watch, which indicated 8:15 pm. "If it's so urgent, why doesn't she come in now and talk to us, sir," I asked, "instead of making an appointment near midnight? Do we know where she is now?" I added as an afterthought.

"I got the impression she was travelling into Madrid from out of town," said Robles. He sounded distracted and was not paying attention to my question.

"It might be wise, sir, to track her movements—don't you think? At this time of night, it's unlikely she's arriving by train or plane," I said. "If she's driving here, we should be able to track her vehicle. I can make a call to the motor vehicles unit; they are bound to have the license plate numbers of the family's vehicles. That way, we can put ourselves in control of the situation—without apprehending her."

Robles nodded his agreement, without much enthusiasm. I made the phone call.

"Is there anything more we know about her, sir?" I asked.

Robles stroked his chin, hesitating with his answer. I had often seen him do this when he wasn't sure how much information he could trust me with.

"We have an active file on her husband, Don Carlos, and some of his friends," Robles said at last. "In fact, I've been keeping an eye on them myself. I don't know what the condesa will tell us, but the assessment we have made so far suggests they're a harmless bunch of old boys living in the past."

"It wouldn't be the first time that suspected fascist groups have been reported to us," I said. "There are lots of them in this country and most are just full of shit. In any case, we have to check them out."

"Of course," said Robles. "Especially as this involves a senior member of the government, it might have some credibility. But I'll want to check out all the facts before we start to mobilise any resources."

I agreed with him there.

The Condesa is Interviewed

"Condesa, thank you for coming here late at night. You have something to tell us?" invited Robles without any formalities.

The attorney spoke first.

"I would like to place on the record that the condesa has come here—of her own accord, and without any requirement or pressure from the authorities—to provide the National Police with information she believes might be critical to national security."

"Duly noted," said Robles without hesitation. He sounded abrupt. "Condesa?" he said, turning to her.

The condesa's voice was calm and strong. She began with her rehearsed opening statement.

"I think my husband, Conde Carlos de la Santa Maria, is involved in fascist activities. He and some very powerful friends are planning something big. I don't know what it is, but one person has already died—possibly murdered—in the process."

She proceeded to give us a full account of what she had witnessed, naming several of the well-known people meeting at the lodge.

As she gave us a physical description of the General's chauffeur, I saw the look on Raphael Robles' face. It was just a momentary raising of his eyebrows—a movement so quick that it disappeared almost as soon as it appeared.

I am sure the condesa did not miss it either.

"Excuse me, Condesa," asked Robles. "This is interesting. But what makes you suspect that this is no more than some old friends getting together to talk about the old days?"

"Several things, Chief Inspector," the condesa answered, presenting a well-rehearsed sequence of events.

"My purpose in driving to the lodge, unannounced, was that this morning I received this in the mail." She placed a copy of the memory stick sent to her by Father Damien on the table.

"What is it?" asked Robles. I thought he looked annoyed.

"It's a series of photographs taken near Lleida, in my parliamentary constituency. They were taken recently by a priest who was found dead soon afterwards. I can't be certain, but I think he was murdered.

"I also received this at the same time," she said, placing a copy of Father Damien's letter on the table. She smiled at him. "You have the originals of both."

"I have them…? Pardon, señora?" said Robles.

"You have the originals," she repeated, taking out her smart phone and scrolling through it. "I sent it by courier from my office this morning to… to a Sergeant Alvarez, here in this building."

I was witnessing an interesting exchange between my boss and the condesa. She seemed pleased that she was placing him on the defensive. Robles, for his part, was puzzled and clearly irritated.

The female officer we had in the room reached for the memory stick and inserted it into her laptop. Without speaking, she passed the display first to Robles and then to me.

I observed the condesa's face as she watched Robles scroll through the priest's pictures. I have no doubt she was watching for any signs of recognition in his eyes—especially as he zoomed up on several photos.

"Among the pictures, you will see a white contractor's van. It belongs to a man who attends meetings between the General and my husband. The other man, I think you might recognise, Chief Inspector," she said to Robles. "It's the General's chauffeur, of course. But I think you know him already, don't you? I don't know what is in those paper sacks they are carrying to the van, but I doubt it is sand for the General's grandchildren to play in," she added, her tone sounding tart.

Robles slid the laptop across the desk to me and I scrolled through the photos. I was particularly concerned about the earlier ones showing the bags of fertiliser. Tonnes of it were sold each year for legitimate purposes but, in the hands of the wrong people, there was no doubt in my mind of the purpose for which it was intended. I knew the same thoughts would be going my boss' mind.

"You asked why I think there is something serious happening," she continued, addressing her remarks to Robles. "Let me explain my initial concerns."

She described to us her feelings about the secrecy surrounding the meeting at the lodge, its remote location and her husband's evasiveness with her over the past several months.

She talked about the General, wearing his uniform to the meeting at the lodge. She described how he clearly was in charge of events.

Next, she told us about the General's cell phone and the call from Morocco. At this, Robles shrugged his shoulders and said that such calls were commonplace.

"I know that, Chief Inspector, but it was the circumstances which aroused my suspicions." She described her husband's near-panic about the loss of the General's phone—and about the chauffeur's anxiety to recover it without delay.

It was obvious that my boss was not convinced.

Opening her bag, the condesa retrieved a piece of paper and slid it across the table to him. "I don't know if this is relevant or not, Chief Inspector. It is the Morocco number that was calling the General's phone when I found it in Carlos' den."

Robles did not try to hide his exasperation, and slid the paper over to me.

"Anything else, Condesa?" he asked, looking at his watch impatiently.

The condesa leaned forward—as if she still had an ace card to play. She described to us the arrival by helicopter of the right-wing minority party politician. Robles did not make any comment, but I sensed his body stiffen and now he seemed to be paying closer attention to her.

She told us how the General had stood in front of the map indicating various places to the assembled group, and that she had seen enlarged photographs of some buildings.

"Could you hear what he was saying?" Robles asked.

"No, none of it."

"Did you recognise the buildings in the photographs?" he pursued.

"No."

While this exchange was taking place, I was busy texting on my phone. Although it was late at night, I knew someone would be working on our North Africa desk. I got the results from my enquiry within a couple of minutes and slid the text message over to Robles. He studied it for a time before looking up at the condesa.

"Please tell us again how you came to be in possession of this phone number," he instructed sternly, indicating the piece of paper she had given them.

She described the circumstances in more detail for us. "The phone rang three times while I had possession of it—I mean, before the General's chauffeur arrived to retrieve it."

"Why did you copy the number down?" asked Robles.

"It rang three times in quick succession, so I thought it must be urgent. I was going to give the number of the caller to Carlos, to relay a message to the General. But his manner that night was so strange and demanding that I forgot about it until afterwards."

"To your knowledge, has your husband ever received a call from this number?" asked Robles, leaning across the desk.

"Carlos? Not that I know of." She shook her head.

"Do you think they will still be there at the lodge?" he asked.

"At least some of them will be, I would think," said the condesa. "He was planning to spend the night there. The General too, I'm sure."

Robles stood up quickly. "Diego, come with me," he ordered. "Condesa, excuse us for a few minutes please." Robles and I left the interview room.

The text message I'd passed to him said that the DST in Morocco had confirmed the location of the phone number; it was one of the madrassas that had been raided. The implications were clear to us.

The General's group somehow were linked to al-Qaeda in the Maghreb.

"I don't know what's going on here, Diego, but we have to treat it as a genuine threat. We have to put the people meeting at the lodge under immediate high-priority surveillance. Let's get on it right away."

"But?" I asked, sensing his concerns.

"Despite the condesa's evidence, we don't have enough to arrest them. Not a group of such powerful and well-connected people as they are. We need a lot more evidence."

I showed him another text I'd received while we were in the interview room.

"Who the hell is Francisco Rioja?" he asked.

"Our traffic guys picked him up. He was tracking the condesa's vehicle on the autovia. He's an investigative reporter—chasing a story trying to link the condesa with the construction scandal. We have him in custody, sir."

"Your instincts were correct, Diego," Robles managed a begrudging half-smile. "Where is he?"

We walked down to the interview area where Francisco Rioja was being interrogated and received a briefing outside from one of the officers. Robles' face turned pale when he saw the photographs the journalist had taken.

"We have to keep a lid on these," he told the officer. "I'm going to hold you personally responsible to make sure they aren't released. Understood?"

"If you tell us he's linked with your enquiries, sir, we can keep him in isolated custody for several weeks," he assured Robles.

Robles turned to me; he looked deeply troubled. "Diego, if those photos were to be published by the media, I can't even start to imagine the problems they'd create. If they're genuine, we could be sitting on a political time bomb. We have to keep them under wraps—until we've investigated this thing further.

"I share your concern about explosive-making materials," he added. "If the General and his group are planning to use those, there's a major terrorist initiative under way.

"Diego, I have to report this upstairs. I want you to organise immediate surveillance of every member of the group at the lodge. It is important that you do not apprehend anyone at this stage, you understand?"

I hurried off, while Robles made a brief call and returned to talk to the condesa.

"Thank you for that information, señora," he nodded to her. Turning to her attorney he said, "The condesa has provided us with significant information, and our GEO units already are taking urgent actions to investigate it further. I am not at liberty to tell you what those actions are, but clearly this is a very serious matter—potentially with terrorist implications."

"I must report to the prime minister," said the condesa.

"That, señora, is a decision that will be made by the police," Robles bristled.

"Are you telling us that we are under a gag order?" It was the first time the attorney had spoken since his opening words.

"At this stage, yes," said Robles. "You must know that."

"It places the condesa in a very awkward and risky position," the attorney persisted. "With the knowledge that she has, she is in great personal danger."

"We have no wish to place her any more at risk than she was, and we can offer her our full protection—if that's what she wishes," offered Robles. "Now if you will excuse me again, I will be back as soon as I can. I must ask you to remain where you are."

He nodded in the direction of the female officer. "Please arrange to provide the condesa with refreshments."

After a time, Robles returned.

"Again, Condesa, my apologies for detaining you this late at night," he began. "Thanks to your information, and willingness to come forward so promptly, we have taken the necessary steps."

"The prime minister?" the condesa began to ask.

Robles nodded. "We have a proposal to make. The fact is, Condesa, we need to know much more about the terrorist network we might be dealing with. Our role at GEO is preventative, if at all possible. If a domestic terrorist attack is being planned, we need to know where and when they plan to carry it out."

"If you are asking me to spy on my husband, the answer very definitely is no," she shot back angrily.

"It is late, and perhaps I am being clumsy with my words," said Robles. "I would ask you, Condesa, to consider the national security issues involved."

"I am not going to spy on my husband," she repeated emphatically.

"Can you tell us more about your proposal?" the attorney intervened after a pause.

"Unit 60 at GEO is new," Robles began. "It has been formed to carry out certain non-traditional duties which are required in the fight against domestic and international terrorism.

"While it is clear that the people you have told us about may be involved in something very serious, we need to find out more, as I have explained. It is difficult for me to express my next statement without causing offence…"

"Considering the circumstances, nothing you could say would offend me," interrupted the condesa.

"Thank you. Then to state it bluntly, it would be far better for our security forces—and for the condesa—if it was clear from her actions that she is helping us, actively, to prevent any terrorist incidents that may be underway."

"Why would the condesa even consider taking such risks to her personal safety?" asked the attorney looking shocked. "Why is it even necessary?"

"You asked about informing the prime minister and interior minister," said Robles. "We also have a duty to inform them of the risk to national security. We must alert our regional security partners, based on what we know."

"Your point is?" asked the attorney.

"What the Chief Inspector is saying, Felipe, is that my credibility, as a member of the government, would be far greater if the police were to be able to inform the PM and my colleagues that I am not just cooperating…" began the condesa.

"But that I am a vital and willing participant in our efforts to resolve this threat—and hopefully prevent any incident and loss of life.

"With the minimum of political embarrassment to the government," she added.

She paused for a moment before Robles spoke again.

"Condesa, do you know a freelance reporter by the name of Francisco Rioja?"

"I meet many media people in my work as a minister of the government, Chief Inspector," she answered.

"But you don't recall ever having met Señor Rioja," Robles continued.

She shrugged her shoulders.

"Of what relevance is this?" asked the attorney. He had noted that, on his return, Robles carried a file into the room.

Robles passed the file across to the condesa. "Señora, tonight you were being followed by an investigative reporter. His name I have given you. He took these photographs at the lodge tonight."

As they looked through them, it was Robles' turn to observe the condesa's reaction.

"Are these in the hands of the media?" she asked after a few minutes.

"No, we have simply apprehended the source. There is no need for them to become public. Not yet anyway. Not until we have completed our investigations, and not until..." Robles let his words trail off. He shrugged.

"I understand," said the condesa, drawing in a deep breath and straightening her back. She was aware that her cuts and bruises from earlier were beginning to hurt. "What do you want me to do?"

"Condesa," the attorney began to protest. "This is not necessary..."

She held up her hand to silence him.

"With the help of the phone number in Morocco that you gave us," Robles began, "we now have a tap on the General's phone—at least until he gets rid of it. He may not do that because it is an important contact number for his incoming calls. Anyway, we will continue to monitor it.

"We must have access to the computer he uses," continued Robles. "And to your husband's, Condesa. Right now, we are unable to identify them through our monitoring activities."

It was true, thought the condesa. Carlos' laptop had been a gift from the General. There would be no trace of where it had been purchased, or any handle on his encrypted communications.

The female officer spoke. She placed a memory stick in the middle of the table. "This is a rootkit, Condesa. I don't know if you are familiar with the technology," she continued, "but when this drive is inserted into a computer, it will allow us to monitor everything that takes place. Importantly, once loaded up, the program is almost undetectable."

"Almost?" questioned Felipe. "If it's like a Trojan horse, that still leaves a risk."

"It's much more effective than a Trojan horse. Rootkits are very difficult to detect," she answered in a well-measured friendly tone. "They are activated before the operating system has been fully booted up. This particular rootkit is advanced. It takes control of the software that is designed to detect it."

"How do I use it exactly?" asked the condesa, deciding the issue and picking up the memory stick.

"Señora, you put the memory stick into a USB slot on the computer," answered the female officer.

"After it's been switched on?"

The female officer seemed pleased with the question. "No, that is not necessary, señora. The microchip has its own built-in power source. It bypasses the need to switch on the computer and it bypasses security firewalls and passwords. It feeds itself directly into the operating system. It just needs to be inserted for a few seconds. Then it's done."

"Okay," said the condesa. "I suppose you will know when I have been able to activate it?"

The female officer nodded. "You can insert it into any number of computers. We will be able to identify each of them very quickly."

"Okay," said the condesa pocketing the memory stick. "I'll do it."

"I have a question," said the attorney. "You said that a freelance reporter has been following the condesa. How do you know he won't talk, and put her life in danger?"

"Yes," said Robles. "We too are concerned about that. But you need not worry. He will be held for a time, in protective custody under the emergency laws we have in place."

"This is something to which he has agreed?" asked Felipe, knowing something about the topic.

"He has agreed, and willingly," said Robles. "In practical terms, he has only a partial story to tell at this time. We will arrange it so that, at the appropriate time, he will have a much bigger story. That will be his reward for his silence at this time."

"What assurances can you provide to the condesa that she will not suffer any adverse consequences as a result?" asked the attorney.

"There can be no guarantees," said Robles. "After all, in a democracy we cannot keep him muzzled forever. But please keep in mind that he could have sold his story, such as it is, to the highest bidder. In which case, it would have been front-page news tomorrow. Instead, he is being wise enough to cooperate with us."

Felipe looked at him with a puzzled expression.

"I don't understand. Why would the reporter, with this huge scoop, come to you voluntarily, if it involved a risk that you would put an embargo on his story?" he asked. "Why not go straight to the media with it?"

Robles smiled. "Actually, we apprehended him and managed to persuade him to our way of thinking."

"But how were you in a position to apprehend him?" pursued the attorney, wishing—not for the first time that night—that he knew, in advance, the answers to the questions he was asking.

"One of our patrolmen on the A6 detected the reporter tailing the condesa's car," said Robles. His tone was matter-of-fact and unemotional. "After we had received the condesa's request for an urgent meeting here in this building, we simply monitored her vehicle and all the main roads coming in this direction."

"And to achieve that, you would have done a police database search of the vehicles she owns," said the attorney. "Your patrolmen knew which car to look for."

The condesa shook her head. "Is there anything that is not known these days to our security forces?" she asked. The contempt in her voice was obvious.

"Alas, far too much remains unknown," said Robles, without blinking an eyelid.

"All in the name of protecting democracy," spat Felipe, waving his hand in dismissal as the Chief Inspector began to protest.

Visit to Lleida

I'd been spending a lot of time in the office, so the opportunity to drive out to Lleida came as a welcome break.

I wasn't planning on going. We have a good local force of National Police out there; they seemed to be working well alongside the Mossos who have jurisdiction for the area. At GEO, we were being kept in the loop because the spectre of a domestic terrorist cache of explosives had been raised by the condesa.

It was Raphael Robles who wanted me to go, so I leapt at the chance of a drive and a break from the Madrid routine.

The boys had already gone over the church and its outbuildings thoroughly by the time I arrived. Most significantly, the sniffer dogs had picked up the strong scent of TNT. It's unmistakeable for them, and they went wild. There were some empty crates, which we traced back to a theft from a local mining operation. There must have been a large quantity stored there in those buildings at the back of the church.

Forensics also found evidence of ammonium nitrate, which is available commercially to farmers as a fertiliser. That confirmed the evidence of the Father Damien photos that the condesa gave to us. It's a harmless compound by itself, but, with the TNT, it forms amatol—a high explosive.

Our worst suspicions were confirmed, and that persuaded Madrid that GEO would have to stay involved. That meant me. Robles told me to continue to report every single detail to him.

The big questions, of course, still went unanswered. Number one, where did they move the stuff to, and number two, what are they intending to use it for—and when?

That was the theory we were working on, but there were other interpretations of what we found. Cynics—and defence lawyers—could argue that the buildings simply had been used for legal storage of explosives by a mining or quarrying outfit.

I didn't buy that for a minute, but Raphael Robles is a politician and he was not happy about authorising arrests that might not hold up in court. The boys upstairs listened to him, and ordered a surveillance-only follow-up on the General and his gang.

One of them had gone missing – the General's chauffeur. We had Father Damien's photos, and the condesa positively identified him. Apart from that, we had nothing else to go on. We continued to monitor the General's phone, but he had no communications—at least that we knew of—with his chauffeur. That, in itself, was strange.

Forensics found a few other things. There were tyre tracks by the buildings that we matched later with a stolen van—which, we theorise, was used to move the materials. There's a national and international search going on for that right now.

A few miles away, the local Mossos found an abandoned white van belonging to a local builder. He had gone missing too. There were fresh traces of explosives material all over the van.

We knew the builder had been at the church, from various pieces of evidence. He was the same man in Father Damien's photographs. Local people confirmed that he was often up at the church. In addition, we found tyre tracks from his van all over the area by the church buildings.

Forensics also found two cigarette butts that matched a brand he used, and that has given us a DNA sample for follow-up.

They also found something interesting in the old buildings: specks of refined gold. They could have been hundreds of years old—traces from gold mining that took place just to the north. The samples are at the lab being analysed.

The gold find got my thought processes going, and my theory is we will find they are from recent ingot castings. I think that whoever stored the gold there had amassed a treasure trove—one they are planning to use to achieve the same goals as the explosives.

Raphael Robles told me my imagination was running wild, but let's wait for the lab results and see. I didn't tell him, but I copied Antonio on my internal report.

One thing is for certain: the priest did not commit suicide. Someone was supporting his habit. The dose he took was lethal, and his dealer would have known it. Father Damien had been a real junkie. Who knows why—that was his business.

Following its doctrines on suicides, the church hierarchy initially refused to bury the priest in sanctified ground. Weeks later, the new evidence swayed opinion within the Church. When the local judge changed his verdict to murder, the bishop overruled the earlier finding.

Father Damien received a decent burial alongside the church, and among the parishioners to whom he had dedicated most of his life.

Strange people, these Christians, the way they treat their own.

Chapter 9

The Trap is Set

"You're back," exclaimed the condesa, as the elevator doors opened and Carlos wheeled into the room.

"How was the rest of your evening at the lodge, darling?" she smiled at him, planting a lingering kiss on his forehead.

"You sound much better than last night," he observed, looking cautiously at her.

"It was stupid of me to have worried," she continued to smile, pushing his wheelchair over to a side table where the sun was streaming through the windows. She pulled the blinds so that the late autumn sun, now entering the room almost horizontally, was deflected away from his eyes.

"Actually, I found it quite touching…"

"Well, you're back and that's all that matters," she beamed. "Hortensia can make you a late lunch if you like."

"No, I'm not really hungry. But I do have some business things to catch up on."

"Carlos, I've been thinking about what we talked about last night. I don't think I've been a very good wife to you recently. I want to change that—so we can spend more time together. Perhaps we can take a trip abroad, or something?"

"Teresa, you are a wonderful wife," he protested.

"I can do better, Carlos," she kissed his neck. "I think I've been working too hard."

"I would agree with that, my dear. You have been looking tired recently."

"I have decided to give up my job with the government, and spend more time at home with you," she announced triumphantly.

"You've decided to do what?" asked Carlos, clearly astonished that so much had changed since their brief conversation at the lodge the previous evening. "Isn't this a bit sudden?"

"I was thinking about what you said last night, and you're right. After all, I don't really need the job, do I? Not financially, I mean."

"Well, you've always seemed so happy about it. You took it to get out of the house, remember?"

"Well, darling, I've made up my mind. I've already talked to the prime minister. He's concerned, of course, and he doesn't want me to go. I've agreed to a press release that says I've been working too hard. You know how it is in government. It's all about the public spin."

"Well, if you're absolutely sure my dear…"

"I am, Carlos, I am. Actually, I feel so much better already. Now where is your luggage?"

"The general's man will drop it off later," he replied. "Do you know, I might ask Hortensia to fix me a quick bite to eat. I'm hungrier than I thought."

"Let me do it for you, darling. After all, I'm going to have more time now to look after you." She swept off to the kitchen. He could hear her humming a tune as she went.

"Carlos, maybe later we can take a stroll through the garden?" she called, avoiding the word *walk*, as she was always careful to do. "Then we can discuss the gardener's plantings for springtime."

She was unaware, in her subterfuge, that simultaneously he was elaborating his own pretence; the two of them anticipating vastly different outcomes from events yet to come in the days ahead.

He wanted to, but did not, tell her that in a very short time ahead momentous events would occur that would define the destiny of Spain—and possibly of Europe. For the moment, he simply smiled at her newly found happiness.

Carlos was grateful to the General for many things. The two old friends looked forwards eagerly to the realisation of their dream. He was even grateful to the General's man. It was he who had informed Carlos about the gigolo, a man named Pavel—his wife's lover.

The Russian certainly had good looks, he had conceded when the General's chauffeur had placed the compromising photographs in front of him. Carlos did not blame his wife. She was young and pretty. She had sacrificed much to marry him. Understanding her needs, had allowed the affair to continue.

Now, it seemed, the condesa had realised the errors of her ways. He could forgive her flirtations with democracy: she was young and naive. He could even forgive her affair with the Russian.

But it was time to tidy up such distractions, he resolved. He would have a word with the General's man. Carlos knew that he could not compete with youth and physical prowess. He could at least have the last word, he smiled. The Russian wouldn't enjoy life's carnal pleasures for much longer. In fact, he doubted that the General's man would permit the Russian any future pleasures whatsoever.

"Good idea," he shouted out to his wife, in reply to her suggestion. He would enjoy a stroll in the garden.

Message for Antonio

When Antonio received her text message, at first, he didn't recognise the name of the sender.

"Important we talk," it said. He thought for a minute. Then he texted her. "When?"

"Tonight, can you make 7:00 p.m.?" came her almost instant reply, along with an address.

It was Saturday and Antonio had not yet discussed with Maria what their plans for the evening would be. He had assumed that, as usual, they'd meet friends for dinner.

Rethinking his impulsive first reply to her text, he felt guilty about agreeing to meet the girl. He slumped into his office chair and propped his feet onto his desk. Her text was not unwelcome. He was even prepared to admit to himself that he found it flattering. Actually—more than that, to be truthful—he found it exciting. If he was honest with himself, he had known for a time that he wanted to see her again.

Now it began to trouble him. It was probably better to suggest an earlier meeting time.

At the back of his mind was his still vivid memory of the girl in Istanbul. The image still haunted him. He knew that arranging an earlier time would be the wiser thing to do, yet…

This was stupid, he chastised himself. Surely he was reading too much into her message? Aware that he was starting to think with his male ego, he scolded himself. Was a meeting with her so urgent? He looked again at the text. She had not said it was urgent, only important. She had not suggested that she was in any imminent danger or anything.

The policeman in him reviewed the situation objectively. He could suggest a meeting at his office, say early next week. If she needed to meet him earlier, she would have to come up with a reason.

He visualised a review of his conduct with a senior officer. There was every reason to offer a meeting during normal office hours, he imagined himself explaining. It isn't an issue, he imagined his superior's reply. You did the right thing.

Still uncertain, he hesitated in his reply to her.

After all, any woman who proposes a meeting on a Saturday evening, especially with a man she does not know well, must know she is encroaching on his personal time. Antonio was certain she knew exactly what she was doing. He thought again about Istanbul. For her, this was entirely in character.

Yes, for sure, there was something flattering about it. If he was honest with himself, something potentially intimate—almost complicit—in agreeing a rendezvous.

Still holding his phone, he was uncertain what to do. He dropped his feet from the desktop and took a deep breath. But his mind quickly drifted. He imagined himself with her.

He had not planned to meet her again after Istanbul. That part of the case was over. Now her text message had stirred up in him some feelings he'd preferred to ignore. Yes, he would admit that he'd found her attractive. But she was very young—only twenty-two, he remembered.

She had been through a lot of trauma in Iraq, and Syria before that. He admired her courage and brave actions under incredible pressure. Certainly, she was an excellent field officer—cool, and in control.

That made her even more irresistible, he admitted. She was decisive, and she knew what she wanted. He began to imagine how that would play out if they were together.

Uninhibited, and allowing himself the luxury of abandoning his normal rational thinking, Antonio was willing to admit that, from the first time he had seen her, she had provoked within him a yearning that he had not been willing to define.

Had he failed to recognise the early signs of an infatuation with her, he asked himself with a low laugh. He was amused that at least he recognised the portents and was now willing to admit his feelings to himself. In fact, if he was really honest, he told himself, ever since he'd met her, he had not only allowed—but had willingly submitted to—the flourishing of his feelings for her.

It was a deep primeval yearning.

You're being stupid, Antonio, he told himself. He cast a glance around the outer office. Few people worked at the weekends and, other than the duty officers, most of his colleagues were happy to be on call. The quietness of the office was contributing to his mood, he reflected. The stillness, the laziness. Easy to dream.

In a way, it was like a soft summer's day relaxing by the river when nothing in the world seemed to matter.

The thought of being with her was not love, but lust. And he knew why. Sexually, she was provocative. She had been explicit with her body in the interview room in Turkey. He guessed that she'd probably had exactly the same arousing effect on each of the men in the room that afternoon.

He didn't care. It didn't matter that her sexuality had not been directed explicitly at him, he reminded himself.

Or had it? It was vain of him to imagine so, he told himself. He had said nothing to anyone about that particular scene. He didn't want it sullied. It was almost as if, by leaving it unspoken, he would be able to preserve it—buried deeply in his mind—as a brief, intimate moment they had shared, just the two of them together.

But was there more to it than that?

Glancing again at his phone, Antonio still hesitated. He sensed this was a moment of decision for him. He was not naive. He already had a shrewd idea of what she wanted: it was obvious. She certainly was far from innocent; that much was clear. But how should he respond, he challenged himself. Was this what he wanted? What about Maria?

His phone indicated another incoming text from her.

"Please," it said simply.

Like the animal urges to which he now admitted, her plea was equally primeval.

As with generations of men before him, across numerous civilisations, this simple word, coming from a woman to whom he was intensely attracted, rendered Antonio impotent in his ability to resist. His male arrogance compelled him forward, even though he knew that she knew exactly how to play him.

His submission was immediate and complete. "Okay," he texted back.

****

It seemed to Maria that Sergio always knew when she was at her most emotionally vulnerable. She was shopping at the market when he called.

Just a few minutes earlier, Antonio had called to say that he would have to work late.

Up until that moment her afternoon had been successful and enjoyable. As a special treat for Antonio's dinner, she had selected two pieces of freshly caught white fish from Norway. In the market, she had found some recently harvested broccolini which she would steam tonight, as he liked, for no more than two minutes. As a bonus, she found some fresh capers—all of which would go well with the bottle of Catalan white she had purchased earlier.

They could have a romantic night at home, she planned with rising expectations.

Now she felt deflated. It seemed to mirror her life with Antonio. She really didn't want to talk to Sergio at that moment, yet found herself accepting his call.

"You sound depressed," said Sergio, picking up on her mood.

"It's nothing," she said. "Just a tough week of work."

She hated Sergio's ability to make her feel defensive. When they had been together, he always seemed to find a way to force her to make excuses. She resented the feeling. She had

239

no reason to be defensive. Damn it. He had no right to rattle her emotions the way he did.

"You're in town, I see," she added, having seen his Barcelona phone number come up on her display. "What's up?"

There was a slight pause before he replied. It crossed her mind, knowing how Machiavellian he could be, that he was quickly rethinking his tactics of what to say next.

"Well, it's really a business call," he said.

Maria smiled. She could read Sergio very well. He was straight back onto the attack. Even so, she admitted to herself a slight feeling of disappointment.

"You're on business? Here in Barcelona?" she asked, scepticism showing in her voice.

"We had a partners' meeting yesterday, in Madrid; I flew here this morning."

"Taking a vacation?" she probed in a cavalier tone.

"No, I came to see you."

Maria caught her breath. "Business? On a Saturday?" she managed to blurt out, perhaps a little too quickly.

"I was going to wait, and try to see you Monday," said Sergio, his voice strong and confident. "But I thought you would be busy at work. And what I have to say can't wait."

"Sergio, I have to…" she heard herself starting to say.

"Maria, wait. Please hear me out. This is not about us." There was a brief pause when neither of them said anything.

"I'll get straight to the point, Maria," he continued. "The advisory board and partners of Ramos Sanchez want to offer you the position of senior partner.

"And before you say anything, Maria, we also invite you to chair the advisory board."

Maria said nothing. The job offer with Ramos Sanchez was not a surprise. Sergio had put it on the table before. The advisory board chair position was a new offer—and she was aware of the prestige it would bring her. After all, Ramos

Sanchez was Spain's number one legal firm; she did not need to remind herself.

If it had been an offer to join the firm in Barcelona, where she lived, she would be crazy not to accept, she knew. She had thought about it several times. But, in Madrid, and in close proximity to Sergio—and miles away from Antonio—even if she commuted each weekend, it would not be the same. And there were other things.

Her head was in a whirl. She was still mad at Antonio for his lack of sensitivity to her feelings about the evening she had planned for them together. She had not told him that she was preparing a surprise meal. Even with that, she felt it was still partly his fault for not having anticipated she might want to spend some "together time" with him tonight.

"The partners have asked me to present a financial offer to you," said Sergio, interrupting her thoughts.

Maria felt a twinge of panic. "I don't think I'm ready," she heard herself say. "I mean, this is all such a surprise."

"I understand," said Sergio. "We are not trying to put you under pressure. It's a lot to think about. But I do want to tell you this, Maria. Ramos Sanchez really wants you. You can virtually write your own ticket."

Maria's nervousness subsided, and the scope of the opportunity she was being offered flashed across her mind. If only other things were different...

"Look, I am not supposed to tell you this, so keep it confidential, but the senior partner in litigation will be retiring soon. The advisory board wants to groom an understudy to replace him," said Sergio.

"You're probably not familiar with the organisational structure at Ramos Sanchez, but it will be a very powerful position," he persisted.

"Honestly, Maria, I promise this is not about you and me," said Sergio, lowering his voice. "While I'm here, can we meet—for a coffee—so I can pitch the job to you?"

"I don't think that's a good idea…"

"Maria, be objective," Sergio counselled her. "This is a once-in-a-career huge opportunity for you. You know that. You're a professional, and a very successful one. You owe it to yourself to find out what you would be getting into—and what the potential is—so you can make the right decision.

"After church tomorrow, can we meet for coffee?" he added.

While he had been speaking, Maria had toyed with the idea of meeting him this afternoon, before she had dinner with Antonio. She considered herself to be a reasonably smart woman. At this moment, she was acutely aware that smart women know it's not a good idea to have rival men anywhere near each other.

Not unless you were planning a showdown. Then who knows what might happen.

Sunday would create a problem, because she would be with Antonio. They had planned to go to the countryside to see his grandfather.

Maria decided quickly.

"Okay, I'm busy tomorrow. But I'll meet you for a coffee later this afternoon. But Sergio…"

"I know," he replied quickly. "This is strictly business—I promise you."

****

At the office, Antonio had tried to refocus his mind on work. Within minutes of sitting back at his desk, he had to admit it was a useless effort. He felt excited about the girl, and he really didn't want to think about work.

He'd already concluded that meeting with Daniela probably was not a wise idea. Professionally, there was no reason why they should not be in contact. She had asked for a meeting; he had accepted. Nothing wrong with that. The problem was the timing—on a Saturday evening.

Antonio also admitted to himself feelings of guilt, but why? Why should he feel guilty, he asked himself. It was irrational. Neither he nor Maria were in the habit of talking much about the details of their work. There was no reason why he should have told Maria he was meeting with the girl that evening. But still, he felt deceitful.

If he kept the meeting on a purely professional level, he concluded, no harm done.

Even so…

He speed-dialled Maria's number.

"Hi, it's me again," he heard himself say when she answered. "I'm sorry about tonight. I won't be late," he reassured her, and himself.

Maria's voice was bright and cheerful.

"Antonio, don't worry. It's okay. Look after your work. I know you're worried about that case you're on. I'll be fine."

"Will you go over to your parents?" he asked.

She hesitated. "I'll be fine," she repeated. "I'll probably have a glass of wine and an early dinner with a girlfriend. I'll see you back at the apartment later."

****

Antonio decided that taking a gift to the girl's place would send a wrong message. Now that he was at the front door of her apartment building, and about to press the buzzer, he was not sure.

He took a breath and keyed in her number. She buzzed him up almost immediately.

Half a minute later, he came out of the elevator and knocked sharply on her door.

She opened it just a crack, making sure it was him. For a moment, he didn't recognise her. In Turkey, she had looked strained and much older. Now she wore makeup and had dyed her dark brown hair with red highlights. It was cropped short at the sides and spiked towards the centre. She looks like a teenager, he thought.

The door and her eyes opened wide at the same time. "Thank you for coming; please come in."

The door closed behind him, and she led him inside.

Antonio saw that she had made no effort to dress up for his visit. She had on a warm floppy-top with loose pyjama slacks tied at her waist with an oversized cotton cord. Her feet were bare, and she seemed much shorter that he had remembered her. The sight of her was refreshing, but made Antonio feel old.

He was relieved that he had not brought any flowers, or a bottle of wine.

"This is Pancho," she said as he followed her inside the room. She motioned towards a young man about her age sitting at the kitchen table. "We work together."

The young man stood up, smiled and shook hands with Antonio. "Pleased to meet you, sir," he smiled.

"We're having tea," she said over her shoulder. "Would you like some?"

Antonio remembered he had not eaten lunch.

"Yes, thanks," he heard himself say. He regretted the authoritative sound his voice produced. As she went to the shelf to get a cup for him, Pancho sat back down at the table and pulled his chair forward, straightening his back at the same time.

Antonio used the moment to glance around. Her apartment was quite small, but neat and tidy. She has a flair for interior decoration, he observed. The walls had been repainted recently—in bold colours. He could still smell the fresh paint. Several oil paintings—vivid abstracts—were fixed to the walls. Partly finished canvasses, and a tall clear glass jar of well-used artist's brushes were propped up redundantly against a cupboard.

He assumed she was the artist. Unless, of course, it was Pancho. Somehow he didn't look the type, thought Antonio. Too clean cut. Too establishment. His cropped hair was a giveaway. No artist there, thought Antonio.

"Sit down, sir," she invited as she handed him a glass of hot tea. "Do you take anything with it?"

Her formality cut hard. He had allowed himself to be seduced by his own arrogance. He felt himself flush slightly, embarrassed by the recent memory of his over-zealous imagination. Not bringing her a gift had been a close call. He had been lucky this time.

"How are you feeling?" he heard himself ask.

She shrugged. "I'm back at work, and it's fine." She gave him a grateful smile and her vivid eyes caught his with a flash of warmth, which made him feel better. This time, however, he would keep a tight rein on his emotions, he cautioned himself.

He smiled a thin smile that he knew would convey this was a purely business visit and nodded, leaving a silence which invited her to explain the need for this meeting.

"Pancho was a friend of my fiancé, David Casals," she said.

She spoke without any display of emotion over her loss, Antonio was relieved to observe.

"We all worked in the same section. Pancho had been garrisoned at Ceuta the longest, and he knew David long before I got there. Anyway, he has some things to tell you. Things that I think it's best you hear directly from him."

She glanced at Pancho, then back at Antonio. He noticed that she bit her lip nervously.

"Also, he has not reported them to anyone else. This is kind of off the record for now—at least as far as we are concerned. I don't know what the rules are within the Mossos,

245

so I suppose we can't ask you for the same courtesy. Anyway, we both thought that you should hear what Pancho has to say."

"Why me?" asked Antonio. His tone was friendly, and he smiled as he asked the question. But it was clear that he was there as a policeman. Her answer surprised him.

"We don't know who to trust. Except you, that is. You're straight."

Antonio saw the flash of suppressed humour that Pancho's face allowed to escape.

"I'd like to think so," smiled Antonio, amused.

"Oh, I didn't mean it that way," she laughed, putting her hand on Antonio's arm. She laughed again. It seemed to Antonio that she kept her hand on his arm for a long time.

It was nice for Antonio to see her embarrassment. He felt superior. It was the innocence of a young girl who had said the wrong thing, he thought. Her smile was wonderful and her eyes sparkled with good humour.

Pancho laughed at her embarrassment, further helping to ease the mood. Then, facing Antonio, he told his story.

"He took his job very seriously, right from the start. He always wanted to be a policeman or a soldier. Even at school, he was a law and order guy. He was our top graduating student and he could have chosen a career in almost any field."

"But he chose to be a policeman?" prompted Antonio, aware that his profession attracted all types—but not always the top students. His irony was lost on Pancho, but he saw the girl give him a knowing glance.

"He chose the Civil Guard," Antonio prompted again, wanting to get to the point.

Pancho nodded. "I don't know if you know much about Ceuta, sir," he asked rhetorically. "It's kind of, well, quite traditional. Even for the Civil Guard. He isn't there any longer, but we had an old-school commanding officer— Capitan Primero. He was in charge of training most of the new

246

recruits like David." He glanced over at the girl. "He trained Daniela and me too."

"The capitan had set up a clandestine operation, which later was found to be unauthorised. It involved David," said Antonio, continuing to try to focus the young officer on telling him something he didn't already know.

Pancho nodded, and continued to glance at Daniela. She was idly twisting an errant strand of hair, watching the two of them carefully.

"Don't worry," said Antonio, seeing his discomfort. "You're not going to get into trouble with the Mossos for telling me this."

The young officer seemed reassured. "David was being asked to do some things. Things that he was willing to do for the service. He told me he was involved in an unofficial operation."

"He wanted to make sure that he'd be covered—if things went wrong?" suggested Antonio.

"Not really," said the young officer. "He really wasn't concerned for himself. I think he had stumbled onto information that implicated some very senior people."

"Did he tell you who they were?"

"Yes. He said he would tell me only because he knew his life was at risk. He was worried that, if he reported the information to the wrong person, it might be suppressed."

"And?" asked Antonio sharply, unapologetic for his dogged pursuit. "So what did he do?"

The young officer took a memory stick out his pocket and slid it across the kitchen table in Antonio's direction.

"What's on it?" asked Antonio without picking it up.

"It's a scan of the documents that David took to his meeting—the night he was killed," said Pancho. "David was in a hurry that night. He said he wouldn't have time to scan the documents before his meeting, and he asked me to do it."

"This is a complete set of scans of the documents?" asked Antonio.

"Yes, there were two sets of documents. David told me to be very careful not to mix them up. One set was photographs and some other papers, mostly written in Arabic. Most were handwritten. He said they came from Syria. The other set was all in Spanish—mostly copies of emails and some other documents.

"To make sure I kept them separate, as David had insisted, I labelled the first file 'Syria' and the second one 'Spain'," said Pancho, with a meek smile that suggested he was embarrassed by his choice of file names.

"He was fine with that. I think he just wanted to make sure that, when he handed the documents over to his contact, there was a backup copy on record somewhere."

Antonio looked at the memory stick for a moment. "You have another copy of this in safekeeping, right?"

The young officer glanced at Daniela, then nodded.

"Did you read the documents while you were scanning them?"

"I didn't have time. As I said, some were in Arabic and some were photos; I saw them briefly. That's all."

While they were talking, Daniela had shuffled over to her desk. Returning, she placed a tablet in front of Antonio and pressed a few keys. "I've uploaded the contents of the memory stick."

Scanning through the scanned photographs from Syria, Antonio saw pictures of Palmyra and other settlements destroyed by shells and explosives. Examining them carefully, he saw that most were "before-and-after" photos.

Each had data scrawled in the margins, along with chemical formulas. He guessed that the data gave a detailed explanation of the explosives and quantity needed to bring about the destruction shown in the "after" photos.

He didn't remember a lot of his chemistry from school, but he saw that the explosives, compression equipment and detonators were made from basic materials—ones that could be found almost anywhere.

Turning to the documents in Arabic, he leafed quickly through them. They could be studied later. One in particular caught his attention. He had never seen hawala documents but, now in his hands, he was staring at a copy of a receipt for a hawala payment of two million euros.

Antonio knew that was far greater an amount than was normal. He turned rapidly to the other folder.

"That's a list of the people involved in some very large money transfers to al-Qaeda," said Daniela looking over his shoulder. "At least, the names of some of them—the ones that David found out about."

Antonio studied the list for a moment.

"What is the evidence that these people were involved?" he asked eventually.

"These emails," she said, moving to a different file. She opened up several in succession and let Antonio read them from her tablet.

Antonio's surprise showed on his face, but he said nothing and sat motionless.

"Where did David get these documents?" he asked Pancho.

"David gave the memory stick to me," said the young officer.

"I know that," said Antonio. "My question was, where did David get them?"

"He didn't tell me," said Pancho. "He was in a hurry to meet his contact at Placa Gaudi, near the Sagrada Familia. He said it was to be a routine drop-off and exchange. He had done it before.

"He said he understood the meaning of many of the documents. He had good reason not to trust the people he was dealing with, he told me. He was certain about that."

"Why didn't you report this, and hand it over to the police or security forces?" asked Antonio.

"Which ones?" interjected the girl with a derisive laugh. "You saw the names on that list."

"Did you know anything about this, Daniela?" asked Antonio, turning to face her.

She shook her head, as he expected she would. He already knew the answer to his question.

"I was out of the country, involved in my part of the operation. You know that. So why do you ask?"

"Because I'm being an asshole," said Antonio with a thin laugh. "This is the most important piece of physical evidence we have in the homicide case so far. I need to know exactly how you both came to be in possession of it."

He turned to the young officer. "Pancho, what did David tell you to do with the memory stick documents? What did he tell you to do with them, in the event something happened to him?"

There was a brief pause while the young officer thought about his answer.

"David told me that his chain of command had been compromised. He didn't know who to trust any longer in Ceuta—at least, not among his senior Civil Guard officers. He told me that he had to complete his mission and keep the rendezvous with his contact. The al-Qaeda people he was dealing with were beginning to trust him, and he didn't want to lose their trust.

"He'd already recruited other agents for them at the Civil Guard garrison, including Daniela. By that time, she was on active assignment. David was working with al-Qaeda in Barcelona. He had heard about a senior al-Qaeda operative

250

named Mustapha. David said it was obviously code; he didn't know the person's real name."

Antonio said nothing, and let the young officer continue talking.

"He knew al-Qaeda would never trust him completely. They were watching him closely, he said. So he did everything by the book. He told me that after his third drop," the young officer paused, "the one before the Sagrada Familia meeting…"

Antonio nodded, indicating for him to continue.

"Well, after his third drop, David said he was approached by an al-Qaeda operative in Ceuta. The man told David that he had information to sell."

"Did David say what the information was?" interrupted Antonio.

Pancho shook his head. "David said that the operative was desperate to get his family to safety. He wanted to live somewhere in the West, with a new identity. He gave some documents to David as a partial payment; an advance, he said—an example of the quality of information the operative claimed he could deliver."

"What else?" Antonio prompted again.

"David told me that, at first, he thought it was an al-Qaeda test of his loyalty. He said that he told the operative he would have to check things with his superiors in the Civil Guard."

"Why do you think the al-Qaeda operative would approach David in particular?" Antonio probed. "I mean, he already knew that David was committed to al-Qaeda, and was actively working for them. If David was genuine, the operative must have known he was taking a risk, offering to become a traitor."

Pancho stared at Antonio, giving him a look of respect.

"That's exactly what I asked David. He told me that he had asked the same question of the al-Qaeda operative. The man was stationed at our garrison. His answer was that he knew David and Daniela were engaged. He said that if David was willing to put not just himself at risk, but also his future wife, he already had a lot at stake."

"That doesn't make sense…" Antonio began.

"It might if you think like al-Qaeda," interrupted Daniela. "If David had betrayed the agent to his al-Qaeda superiors, their response would be to eliminate the whole cell—including Daniela and David. It was a risk the agent was willing to take."

"You mean, like the saying, 'keep your friends close, but your enemies even closer'," said Antonio, still not fully satisfied with Pancho's explanation.

"David wasn't convinced any more than you are," said Daniela, leaning across the table. "Go on, Pancho. Tell the Deputy Inspector what happened next."

Pancho leaned forwards and dropped his voice. "David had to take a chance. On the one hand, with the list he'd been handed, he'd been offered the opportunity to bring important intelligence about al-Qaeda to the West. If David handed it to his Civil Guard superiors, and the intelligence proved to be valuable, the al-Qaeda informant would be able to bargain successfully for his family's safety in the West.

"But, if he did that, al-Qaeda would know they had been betrayed. Daniela almost certainly would be killed," he continued.

"For Daniela's sake—and perhaps for his own safety—he chose the other option. David figured he was being set up by the al-Qaeda informant. So he decided to pass the evidence through his handler to Mustapha. Within a few hours, David heard later, the informant had been decapitated.

"David's credibility with al-Qaeda and Mustapha must have risen immeasurably. He said that, after that, he was given even more important work to do," continued Pancho.

"Let me confirm this," said Antonio. "David gave the documents to his handler, who in turn gave them to Mustapha. But David made a copy?"

Pancho licked his lips again, and glanced over at Daniela. Observing these movements, Antonio thought that the young officer would not make a great liar and certainly not a good undercover agent. He's far too honest, Antonio said to himself, his face gives away everything.

"David and I talked about what he'd done. He felt guilty about the informant's death—and the knowledge that, almost certainly, he had caused it. He was worried too about not having consulted his senior officer before making the decision to send the information up the line to Mustapha."

"Anything else?" asked Antonio.

The young officer studied his hands, clasped together on the kitchen table.

"Another reason why David Casals did not want to trust the guy was that Daniela was already active in the field, sir."

"Meaning that he didn't want to put her life in danger," suggested Antonio, "which would have happened if David had accepted the al-Qaeda informant's bait and told the capitan."

Antonio waited for the reply, and observed the tightening of the young officer's hands, which were now turning white with tension. He was biting his lip again. The pause became longer.

"Not really," he said eventually. "David was a tough soldier," said Pancho. He glanced nervously at Daniela.

"May I, sir?" asked Daniela.

Antonio shrugged, and nodded without enthusiasm.

"Pancho has already told me that David wasn't so much concerned about putting my life in danger. He was, but that wasn't what worried him the most."

"What was?"

"David was trying to decide what was best. He thought that the quality of intelligence the capitan had hoped I would bring back from the al-Qaeda front lines would be more valuable than what the al-Qaeda informant had to offer.

"It was a gamble he had to take," she continued. "Who knows if he was correct? He didn't have the luxury of time. He made a decision, and he ran with it." Her tone was matter of fact, and trailed off.

Antonio looked at her again, and nodded absent-mindedly. He was impressed by David Casal's hard-nosed thinking. At the time, David had to find a balance between many dangers, almost certainly without any concern for his own safety. Daniela was the same. He wondered how someone as young as she could remain so dispassionate—and objective—about the risks the situation had posed for her.

Both were very good officers.

"I see," Antonio said at last. He glanced at Pancho. The boy looked exhausted, he thought.

Catching his breath, Pancho continued talking. "After David's murder, and after what he'd told me, I didn't know what to do with the memory stick. I just kept it. When Daniela returned from field duty, I gave it to her and asked her what I should do about it."

"Do you think this was why David was killed?" asked Antonio. "Because he was in possession of this information?"

"Well, yes," said Pancho, surprised at the question.

"Knowing that the backpack contained timely and valuable intelligence, you still didn't think you should have given it immediately to your superior officer?"

"I was trying to make up my mind about what to do," said Pancho, his voice subdued. "Then some things happened at the Garrison. The capitan was suddenly relieved of his position, and his adjutant died." He looked at Daniela. "We think he was murdered."

"You don't buy the story that the adjutant committed suicide?" shot back Antonio.

"No one at the Garrison believes that."

"Why not?"

"Everyone knew he was totally loyal to the capitan. He would never voluntarily have left his master."

"You should have seen him," added Daniela. "He was an old North African campaigner. As faithful as a dog. Suicide was not even in his psyche."

Pancho nodded his agreement.

"But," said Antonio, with a hint of chastisement for the young officer, "instead of turning-in the evidence, you took it upon yourself to withhold it—without any clear plan of how to proceed, at least until Daniela returned. And, for all you knew, Daniela might not have returned home safely," he added. "Then what would you have done?"

"Well, I…" began the young officer.

Antonio held up his hand to stop him speaking. As he did, his long hair flopped over his forehead. He brushed it back with his hand.

"Anything else?" he asked.

Both of them shook their heads.

"Okay, well here's my plan. It's too late for you to turn-in this evidence," he said, addressing Pancho. "You should have done it immediately. But you didn't. So, let's deal with realities.

"Daniela," Antonio continued, now facing her, "I don't know how this will affect your career in the Civil Guard, but you will just have to take that chance," said Antonio.

The quick glance that the young officer threw in her direction alerted Antonio.

"What?" he asked.

"I've already resigned from the service," said Daniela.

"Because?" asked Antonio.

She shrugged. "Personal reasons."

"Well, maybe it's just as well," said Antonio. "But I'm sorry to hear that the service will be losing a very fine officer. I mean that genuinely."

"Thank you," she said in a quiet voice and bit her lip again.

"We are in the jurisdiction of the Mossos," Antonio continued. "I will take possession of this memory stick. You can be assured, Pancho, that depending on what we determine about the contents, we will be informing our sister organisations at the Civil Guard and National Police of the essential facts."

"But they don't have to know how the memory stick came into your possession?" volunteered Daniela.

Antonio shrugged but said nothing.

"What do you propose to report to your superior officer?" he asked the young officer.

"Nothing—unless you want me to."

"You can't put the Deputy Inspector in that position, Pancho. Can't you see he's trying to help you?"

The young officer looked at her, then at Antonio and back to her. Antonio felt sorry for the boy's confusion. The girl was sharper, he noted. Much sharper.

"There is one possibility," she began. She looked directly into Antonio's face, and raised an eyebrow preluding a question.

"I've resigned from the Civil Guard. But I could come to work with you. At least for the duration of this case."

"What, as a consultant?" he asked with surprise. "You know there's an official recruitment process involved?"

She raised her eyebrow even higher and looked directly into his eyes. The provocation was unmistakable.

"If you want me, you'll find a way," she challenged.

Antonio felt the same tension in his groin he'd felt earlier at the office when he'd been thinking about her. Holy saints, he thought to himself. This lady can turn men around her small finger at will.

He was aware that his heart rate had become elevated.

He scrunched his mouth into a shape which indicated deep thought.

"Sir, if you don't mind, I really have to get going," said Pancho.

"Unless you order me to, I won't report anything about this to my senior officer," he announced, getting to his feet. "If the whole story ever comes out, I'll take responsibility for my part in it. That's the least I can do for David."

He looked at Antonio. "Sir, if Daniela is willing to keep contact with me, maybe there could be things I might assist with in the investigation."

He stood up erect, as if to salute, but Antonio put up his hand and waved away the formality.

"You are a good officer, Pancho," said Antonio, with a resigned air of finality. "Who knows what any of us would have done under the same circumstances. One thing I can tell you is that loyalty does count for something. Your friend David Casals would have been proud of you."

Pancho started to leave the apartment and Daniela walked with him to the door. She kissed him on both cheeks and gave him a long hug. Then she shut the door deliberately, and went to the kitchen to put water on for tea.

"You weren't very kind to him," she said over her shoulder to Antonio.

"Pancho was way out of line, and you know it," he shot back.

"Well, you're not too displeased about the outcome," she continued. "Now the Mossos has key physical evidence in the investigation. It was a gift to you. I think you know exactly what you're going to do with it."

"That probably isn't the wisest comment to make to your future senior officer," he challenged.

She handed him a mug of fresh tea and slumped down on the sofa, nursing hers under her chin. She sat cross-legged opposite him. Her loose pyjama top was baggy around her legs. The cord around her waist needed to be retied, he mused. Perhaps loosened altogether.

He pushed the thought from his mind. He needed to get the memory stick documents into the hands of colleagues who would know what to do with them. If they'd had this evidence earlier, they'd have been much further ahead, he reflected with a deep sigh of frustration.

For now, the girl would have to wait.

****

Antonio called me early the next morning at home.

"I want to send you the files," he said, after he had explained his meeting the night before.

"Holy shit, Antonio," I blasted him, "don't you people do anything by the book?"

"Ease off, Diego," Antonio pushed back, "we just got the information ourselves last night."

"Your message says the information comes from sources within the Civil Guard. Do you mind telling me who they are?" I asked.

"I will explain in detail, but later," said Antonio. "Daniela put me onto it. For now, what you have to know is that those photographs are a duplicate of what David Casals took with him to the meeting near the Sagrada Familia."

"And now most likely are in the hands of the people who killed him," I added.

"They weren't the only ones who were interested in what David Casals was carrying that night," said Antonio. "Your boss, Raphael Robles, called our duty officer—he called him directly, just hours after the murder."

That made me think. There had been a few things about Robles' behaviour, and some of his actions, already going through my mind.

"Diego?" asked Antonio gently, when I didn't reply.

"Yes, I've got it," I said. "Thanks. Leave it with me please," aware that my voice sounded strained.

I gave Antonio my wife's email at home to send the files; I hated to do it, but it was the only way. "Toni, do me a favour," I said. Don't mention this information to anyone. Not until I get back to you. Will you do that?"

After Antonio had mentioned Raphael Robles' name, I was aware that the tone of our phone conversation had changed.

"Okay, Diego. I'll wait until you call," I heard Antonio say.

Both of us hung up.

New Recruit

"Daniela has had a difficult life," the doctor began; his voice was objective and clinical. He spoke about the significance to a child of the loss of both parents simultaneously.

"As we now know, it's not just initial shock but the delayed effects throughout life of which we have to be aware. The suppressed emotions."

When he spoke of the probation officer's report, normally a closed file because of her age at the time of the shoplifting offence, his voice faltered. For several minutes, he avoided mention of the psychiatrist's report. Then he consulted his notes carefully.

"The sexual abuse, and the extended time for which it continued, added a new level of trauma to her already troubled life," he began. "From the report, we cannot tell what age it started. It continued, I think, up until she was sixteen. As you will see from your other notes, sir, she ran away from home soon after her sixteenth birthday. After that, there are no further records of her within our jurisdiction."

259

"But you know about her service as a junior officer in the Civil Guard?" questioned Antonio. He knew the doctor was trying to remain objective, but he needed answers, candid answers—off the record, if necessary.

"There was a long gap, after she ran away from home, until she came back up the radar," noted the doctor, studying his notes.

Antonio was slightly irritated. "We know she attended university in Madrid, and she appears to have been a normal student."

"She wasn't involved in sports," countered the doctor.

"She was in an arts and languages programme. They're not all sports jocks, you know," shot back Antonio, who saw the doctor's face flush slightly.

"I can speak to the potential trauma and possible lasting effects of her time in Syria, Iraq and Turkey," he offered.

"That's not what I'm trying to ascertain," said Antonio, screwing up his face. "Isn't it possible that a person can go through emotional traumas in their early life and still come out normal?"

"Well, we don't use the term 'normal' as a benchmark..." the doctor began, but Antonio cut him off.

"Hell, doctor. Just help me understand this, will you please. Is it possible that officer Balmes can have experienced all that trauma and still function as a seemingly normal person?"

"Well, some people have the capacity to..."

"Answer the damned question, please, doctor," said Antonio, a little too loudly.

Adjusting his glasses, the doctor said, "No, in my opinion there will be serious effects—immediately and over the longer term."

"Okay," said Antonio. "Thank you doctor. Now what I would really appreciate knowing is what these effects might be. Firstly, and most importantly, is it likely to affect her performance as a police officer?"

It was out of character, but the doctor smiled. "Police officers have to be a little bit crazy to do this kind of job."

Antonio responded to the joke with a laugh. "Seriously, doctor, what other kinds of impacts might there be?"

"Based on my experience with comparable cases, she would have difficulties with emotional loyalty. Perhaps difficulty to commit to a relationship. Often these kinds of patients latch onto one person, or a cause. In a way, they live their lives through them."

"An emotional immaturity?" asked Antonio. "Lack of self-esteem?"

"They can excel at certain tasks—sometimes going to extremes—as an approval-seeking behaviour," nodded the doctor.

Antonio considered this comment for a moment. He thought the doctor's interpretation certainly seemed to be supported by Daniela's displays of extreme courage and bravery in her active duty. Not a lot of people could have pulled off what she had done.

"You wouldn't preclude officer Balmes from her police duties just because of her background?"

"No, I wouldn't. In any case, I can't foresee how she would be a danger to others. Her traumas might cause her to punish herself—if she thought she was not meeting expectations."

"Even unreasonable expectations?"

"Yes."

"Would you be willing to write up a report of our conversation, doctor? Specifically, just as we have talked about. I respect your opinion. It's just that sometimes there is a tendency—for all of us—when we have to formalise our opinions, to cover our backsides. I'm not saying you would.

It's just that I would not want to read a report which differs significantly from the discussion we've just had."

"Deputy Inspector," the doctor replied, "I know exactly what you mean, and I don't think you have to be concerned on that score. I stand by my opinions."

Antonio got up and shook hands. "Thank you again, doctor. I really appreciate it." He watched as the man headed towards the elevator. Then he called the manager of human resources and asked her to draw up a short-term services contract, just as an interim starting point.

He was determined to bring Daniela onto the Mossos' Homicide Squad—as soon as possible.

Xavi Worries About His Friend

Sitting at his desk, Xavi turned his shoulders and waved his arm without enthusiasm. Antonio had walked past him and had delivered a playful slap on his partner's shoulder.

"How was lunch?" he asked Antonio.

He received a wave from Daniela, which he ignored.

Xavi's watch showed past four o'clock. He supposed that Toni could do what he wanted with his time. Still, this was the third time this week that those two had dined out together.

He didn't feel slighted. Actually, it gave him a chance to catch up on his backlog. Nevertheless, he was worried about his friend.

Daniela was on a temporary staff appointment, the Homicide Squad bulletin had announced a few weeks earlier. The bulletin didn't need to go into a lot of detail. In spite of an embargo on much of the information about the case, news had quickly got out about her work in the Civil Guard. There was a lot of admiration for her, for the bravery she had exhibited in certain combat zones—which weren't officially acknowledged.

Antonio had introduced her to the Squad, and to the other departments at the Mossos' headquarters. At each stop, she had been given a warm and enthusiastic reception. She had shown that she had a flair for casework, and she seemed eager to assist whenever there was an opportunity.

"She's fitting in very nicely," said the chief one day to his personal assistant. "She brings a lot to the table."

"She's a bit young, sir," said the PA. Then, when he saw the chief's frown, he quickly added, "To be given too much responsibility so early, don't you think, sir?"

It was clear that the chief shared no such reservations. "Nonsense," he shot back. "These young people nowadays can handle it. They're technologically savvy. Not like us—we're just old dinosaurs."

The PA thought it would indiscreet of him to mention that, before the dinosaurs had been choked to death with layers of fine dust, they had risen to the top of the food chain. Probably would have stayed there too, the thought crossed his mind, except for the impacts of a large meteorite or two hitting the Earth's surface.

He felt the chief was far too glib about the former Civil Guard officer's combat experience, and far too willing to reward it excessively with choice assignments. Antonio seemed to have the same affliction, and there were the beginnings of office gossip.

That was never a good situation, said the PA to Xavi. Maybe there was a way to head it off, he wondered aloud to Antonio's partner. The message had not been lost. Xavi had talked it over with Pilar.

"I don't like the sound of her," said Pilar. "She's just trouble."

"I don't think Maria would be very happy about it," Xavi continued. "Daniela is following Antonio around like a doting understudy."

"Maybe I'll give his sister a call," he ventured.

"Well, that certainly wouldn't hurt," replied Pilar, warming to the idea. "Having family close by is always a good thing."

Xavi had to wait until the next day for Isabel to return his call. "Sorry, Xavi," she said apologetically. "I had a late night."

"My brother walks around with his brain between his legs sometimes," she laughed, after Xavi broached the subject of his concerns. "If it's puppy love, he'll soon get over it. How old is this girl?" she asked.

"Twenty-two?" she added, answering her own question. "She's barely out of her teens."

"Twenty-two going on thirty-five," said Xavi. "She's light years ahead, in her maturity, of others the same age."

"Well, let me know what I can do to help, Xavi," said Isabel before calling off.

Chapter 10

Catalunya's Independence March

Police presence on the streets of Barcelona was intense. It was still early morning, but their orders were clear.

In groups, and in long lines of barricades located at strategic points throughout the cities and towns of Catalunya, security forces had been gathering. Patrol cars cruised the streets. Mounted patrols reined in their well-groomed horses, allowing them only short bursts of exercise. Teams of well-armed squaddies stood closely together, watching. All of them cautious, speculating quietly amongst themselves how the winds of change might blow. An historic day in the making.

During the past weeks, they had been training for the event: they were ready.

Days before, the marches and demonstrations leading up to today's 'vote' had been subdued. The region's separatists no longer seemed to project the same intense anger that had forced more than one million of them onto the streets in protest against the Spanish government, just a few years earlier.

If the September 11th 2012 protests had surprised and frightened Madrid, they had delighted and encouraged the Government of Catalunya. The protests had captured a popular sentiment in favour of the region's full independence from Spain.

"If that is what the people want," a Catalan minister had said, "it will be our number one priority."

The caveat was "If".

Behind closed doors, the Catalan government had agreed within the party ranks that re-election would, of course, always be their most urgent concern. Forget that and, at best, you might become the official opposition; at worst, relegated to political oblivion.

In Spain's fledgling new democracy, the road to separatism is long, complex and dangerous, they reminded themselves. There are laws and there are the lawmakers, those in power in Madrid kept reminding them—and we are both.

Demonstrators taking to the streets acknowledged that today was not a true vote—not in the formal sense. Those in favour of separation came out willingly and made their 'yes' voices heard. Those against, simply stayed away.

"It's all about the numbers," the political strategists had reminded everyone.

"It's not even how loud their voices might be," they had added. "It's a simple head count."

The president of the regional government had listened carefully. He knew that a large turnout today would reinforce the message they were sending to Madrid.

That meant they needed a million and a half voters on the streets, all enthusiastically shouting "Yes".

As a youthful and popular regional leader, Jose Buenaventura represented the aspirations of a large number of separatists. He and his government had promised independence for the region.

In the past few weeks, he had been receiving stern warnings from the Spanish government about the illegality of the separatist course of action upon which the Catalan government was now firmly embarked. Those laws were created by Madrid, he countered.

Spain's royal family, themselves still struggling with self-created corruption scandals, stayed away from the fray and watched democracy teeter unsteadily on its uncertain course.

The Civil Guard and the army had remained subdued. Like the region's riot police, they lingered in their barracks, armed and ready for a call to action. They could be mobilised quickly against the demonstrators.

As President Jose Buenaventura knew only too well, Spain—despite its brave face of democracy—was never far from feeling the strong arm of political authority.

Yet, few of those thoughts were foremost in the minds of citizens in the streets.

They were driven by a passion carried in their blood, linked to their ancestors, and which would be passed on to future generations—collective actions expressing their shared heritage, their culture. Catalan culture.

They were not people bent on destruction. Today, most were happy and laughing. Merry and good humoured. Not all united, but driven by a common resolve. Their flags of independence; their placards; their costumes and symbols of emancipation—each an individual expression, merged into one shared and indisputable message.

Today was a rallying call for independent statehood and self-government for Catalunya.

They were not demanding concessions from the iron fist of Madrid; yet, they were not politely asking either. They were here to demonstrate their rights. For them, it was simply a question of time. This was N9—November 9th, yet another marker along the journey; one that would end only when they threw off the yoke of Spain. A choking, stifling yoke that had been around their necks now for five hundred and fifty years.

Their culture of independence had pre-existed the creation of Spain itself, they claimed. They had been patient for much longer than before the first history books had been written. Some believed they had been an independent nation before Charlemagne, and even before the Romans.

They could be patient longer.

For these Catalans, independence and autonomy were inevitable—of that they were absolutely certain.

With Franco gone, and the monarchy restored, they sensed a new path forwards… through democracy.

The right to a formal vote for separation would come—if not immediately, then sometime soon.

With intense passion, they believed the vote would bring their cherished dream—survival of their language and preservation of their culture for future generations of sons and daughters, and their grandchildrens' children.

For Madrid, too, it was a question of numbers. The federalist strategists echoed the words of the separatists' advisors, knowing that time was on the side of Madrid.

From the political pundits came the stark facts. True Catalans born and bred in the region, those in whose hearts and minds their culture was embodied, increasingly were fewer, their numbers diluted by the growing immigrant population. If we can just hang on, the Madrid strategists whispered to their masters.

But that's years away, said many.

Water down the "secession crowd"? …too risky to wait for that, said others.

Better to make a pre-emptive strike against Catalunya, said a few powerful advocates.

As Madrid politicians slept fitfully with these thoughts, separatist Catalans dreamed of future glory.

The day was now moving towards mid-morning. With forces fully marshalled, the demonstrators and security forces soon would meet face-to-face on the streets.

The mood was that of a festival, in a way that only Latinos can fully comprehend. Noise, togetherness and fun. If they could not win the day this time, they would at least enjoy it.

Squaddies and the urban guard, mildly fearful at first, relaxed as the good-natured crowds gathered in front of them: some taunting, others sharing a joke together, the more brazen ones goading the troops to disregard their uniforms and join the popular movement.

The noise of loudspeakers was deafening. Flags and banners, in the red and yellow, white and blue of the *Senyera Estelada* flag of independence, swirled over the heads of the demonstrators. Above, police helicopters monitored the rising tide of emotion.

Intrigued and sympathetic tourists were swept up in the excitement. Amateur photographers' phones and cameras fired off at a rapid pace, their videos recording the events of the historic day. TV cameras scanned the jostling crowds.

Standing in the recesses of a shuttered shop on a nearby plaza, an old man moved his walking stick to his left hand, seeking to relieve the stress that his aged and wizened body placed on his tortured spine. His was a generation, the common people, unable to drive out the still-oppressive memories of times when Spain was much less magnanimous—and tolerant.

A photograph could mean a door forced in during the early morning hours; a whisper from a soured neighbour might bring an arrest: a disappearance—one less opponent for the regime. Times had changed, of course. Yet, for him, democracy was a fickle mistress: he knew it to be a seductive balm; a sugar-pill; an opiate for the masses. He spat on the ground, preferring to remain in the obscurity and relative safety of the shadows.

At a building not far away, President Jose Buenaventura was preparing for a full day of activities.

He had risen early at his apartment in Eixample and followed his normal routine of exercise—jogging several kilometres around his neighbourhood. This was followed, back at his apartment, by fifty push-ups. After that, he had taken his usual cold shower.

Today, Jose Buenaventura knew that he would be the focus of the separatists' adoration. With his easy smile and charm, he would spend much of his day among the party faithful in the company of his dedicated phalanx of supporters, later parading together through the streets.

Ever the consummate politician, he was mindful of his larger agenda—meetings with local and international media—and aware of the power of his separatist message.

His wife also had risen early. His freshly dry-cleaned grey blue suit, along with his hallmark blue shirt and tie, were ready waiting for him.

Fully dressed, he inspected the result in a mirror. His taste in exquisitely tailored suits was a legacy from his father's teaching when he was much younger—that he must "look the part". The Catalan president made a final inspection. Looking confident, he strode into the family dining room.

In truth, he was nervous about the outcome of the day.

His two phones had been ringing all morning. As was his habit, he had been selective about which he answered.

Glancing at the display for an incoming call he passed the phone over to his political aide. The middle-aged man was a veteran of several campaigns and a trusted advisor.

"It's Manuel," the president mouthed. "Tell him I'll call him later."

He listened as his aide did a masterful job of making the caller feel he was the most important person on the president's mind that day.

"Let's go over the list again," the president said, as his aide got off the phone.

"Before you do that, sir, we have to do something about your Mossos bodyguards. They've been waiting downstairs for you."

'More than one?" the president grimaced.

He was well known for disliking high levels of personal security, but knew it came with the office.

"Apparently, they weren't thrilled about your jog this morning. You probably saw a lot more squaddies on the street?" the aide queried.

The president shrugged in response. "They weren't exactly what was on my mind at the time."

"I received a call from the police chief's office. The squaddies had to scramble to make sure you had adequate protection during your run. He wants to talk to you personally later."

"Are the mayor and others getting this level of protection too?" the president asked.

"Well, your wife and family will be glad of the security detail around you today, sir, that's for sure," said the aide, wanting to move on.

For the next ten minutes, they discussed his commitments for the day.

"Alright," the president said eventually. "Bring in the bodyguards; let's hear what they have to say."

Half an hour later, his chauffeur had driven both of them to their first event. Their escort of Mossos and urban police were still less than happy about the risks the president would expose himself to that day.

"A good crowd, and it's still very early," noted the aide as the car speeded through the increasingly empty streets away from the main demonstrations.

The president nodded in agreement and smiled. They had reviewed their plans for the day's events late into the night. His organisers had arranged for crowds to gather in several locations throughout the city. The plan was to march towards a central point at Placa de Catalunya where the demonstration would reach its peak and culminate in a series of speeches.

The president himself would be the highlight in front of worshipping crowds and the less adoring, naturally more cynical, media.

The two men stopped talking while a police helicopter swept low overhead and drowned out their voices.

"I need headcount numbers throughout the day—ours, not the public relations peoples' glassy-eyed exaggerations," the president reminded the aide.

"I want to know what Madrid knows, before those bastards know it," he added.

The aide nodded. "We have fifteen minutes before your next speech," he said, looking at his watch. "Do you want to return some of those calls, Mr. President?"

****

The Chief was standing in the communications command post at Mossos' headquarters, being briefed on the deployment of security forces. The main detachments had been ordered south as the demonstrators at the main rallying-points congregated and then swept towards the Diagonal and Gran Via Catalanes.

"They're trying to repeat the success of the September victory march," said a senior officer.

"Not a problem for us," said another.

The chief nodded his agreement.

"What about the diversionary targets—the banks, the government buildings—are we well covered?" he asked.

A female officer replied. "Sir, we have all of them under surveillance; several backup and reserve units are on standby."

"Anything unusual happening?" questioned the chief, addressing her directly.

Her reply was confident and brief. "No, sir, we are ready if anything happens."

The chief turned to his assistant.

Covering his mouth with his hand so that others could not hear him, in the way footballers often do, he said, "Jose Miguel, I don't like these things. They just give an excuse for our usual miscreants to cause mischief. Make sure that we have eyes at the back of our heads."

The assistant nodded, but screwed up his face as he left the room; he was thinking hard about how he could implement the chief's command.

His task might not have been so difficult if the assistant had been aware that, at that exact moment, an open bed construction truck, loaded ostensibly with sacks of cement and sand, had been waved past the police barriers and was proceeding cautiously down the ramp of the underground parking garage at the Mossos' headquarters building.

The two occupants of the van could hardly have looked more different.

The driver, a man adept at disguise, had transformed himself into a convincing version of a Catalan labourer. His companion, still sweating from the tension of the gun that, well out of sight, was thrust into his ribs, wore the same cheaply tailored suit he used for the office.

"Damned demonstrators have delayed us again," said the driver as he handed their identification cards to the security guard.

The guard swiped the cards into his machine.

He held them in his clipboard, and looked inside the cab. Then he walked around to the back of the truck, poking at the paper sacks.

"Why the urgency?" he asked, returning to the driver's window. "No one's working today."

"If I don't drop it off ready for the crew tomorrow, I won't get paid," complained the driver.

The guard glanced across at the passenger, who seemed anxious to say something.

"I work here—on the fourth floor," he volunteered.

"He's my brother-in-law," he continued, feeling the barrel of the gun prod into his body. "The Metro is full of demonstrators. He has to drop off this load. I got a ride from him."

"What is it?" asked the guard.

"Construction sand," said the driver. "I'm already late on my rounds. Believe me, I'm out of here as soon as this lot is dropped off." He thrust his thumb over his shoulder.

"Well, you'd better be quick," said the guard to the driver. "Security is really tight today."

The driver's grip on his gun did not loosen as the truck proceeded carefully down the ramp into the parking area.

"We're not there yet, my friend. If you want to see your girlfriend again, just do exactly what I say. You understand?"

His passenger nodded, wanting to assure him that he would do anything he was told.

The driver steered towards a cement column that he had observed on his previous visit. It was not in the middle of the building, as he would have preferred. However, he was in luck. The regular construction crew working on the lobby had cordoned off two parking stalls alongside. One was used to store their scaffolding.

To his relief, the driver saw that the other stall had remained empty. Moving the orange plastic cones, he reversed the truck into the space.

Switching off the vehicle's engine, the driver thrust his face close to his passenger. "One wrong move," he said with a laugh. He thrust his gun barrel into the man's nose.

His passenger was unable to control the sweat on his forehead and underarms.

The driver, planning to abandon the truck in its current location, got out of the vehicle and looked around for a suitable escape car. His eyes settled on an older model that he correctly guessed would not be alarmed or have a GPS tracker. Within thirty seconds, he had opened the car doors and jimmied the engine.

****

Three floors above the parking garage, in the Mossos' security control room, Carmel was taking her break. It had been a quiet day so far; most of the active Mossos officers had been deployed to the demonstration sites.

She sat down at a screen, reviewing the security tapes from the past few days.

Puzzled by what she saw, she played back a tape from the previous Sunday morning. One of the frames had caught her attention, and her instincts told her something wasn't right.

"Ernesto, take a look at this for me, will you?" she asked her colleague.

As he took her chair at the viewing screen, Carmel leaned over his shoulder and played back a section of tape.

"What do you think they are doing?" she asked him.

The senior security officer took out his close-up glasses and squinted at the screen.

"I don't know. One of them is measuring something," he offered. "That's where the construction crew is storing its stuff. It's okay. I checked them a few days ago."

"But the other guy," Carmel said quickly. "He works upstairs as a transcriber. What was he doing working on the weekend?"

"Maybe he got overtime, lucky sod," he laughed, and got out of the chair. "I don't know. You could always ask him."

Carmel went to a computer. She keyed in some codes. "He wasn't at work yesterday. But he clocked in at car park security five minutes ago. I wonder what that's about. Is Roberto around?" she asked.

"I think he's upstairs at a briefing," responded her colleague, his face now buried in a crossword puzzle.

Carmel got up from her chair and went to the active screening panel. She scanned the monitors.

The monitor showed a partial picture of the construction crew's cordoned-off area. She saw that a flatbed truck was parked in the area, but it was hard to see what cargo it was carrying.

On a hunch, she reversed the tape. Five minutes earlier, the truck had not been there.

As she scrolled the tape back to active real-time, she was horrified to witness the scene unfolding. The truck driver was jimmying a car. She gasped aloud as she recognised the Mossos transcriber, and saw him stumble away from the truck.

"Oh hell," she yelled to her colleague. "We have a problem. This is an emergency. Get Roberto down here fast— I mean now."

She pulled open the desk drawer and ran her fingers down the internal directory. She grabbed the phone and dialled.

"Antonio Valls," came the swift reply.

"Sir, it's Carmel at Security on the second floor. I think we may have a major security breach. It could be a terrorist incident…"

"Stay there, Carmel. I'm coming down," Antonio interrupted.

Three minutes later, Carmel had presented her evidence to him.

Antonio dialled a few numbers into his phone. "Xavi, we have a major security breach in the building. Get the bomb squad to meet me on the top level of the underground car park. Level P1. I'm heading down there now. Quick as you can, amigo. We may not have much time."

Ignoring the elevator, Antonio used his pass card and ran down the connecting stairs. Carmel followed him. They looked around, trying to spot the delivery truck.

"It's over there," Carmel pointed.

They ran to the vehicle. Using his fingers, Antonio tore open the thick paper wrapping of one of the paper sacks.

"Damn," he said as a mix of white and yellow granules poured out of the sack through his fingers. "This isn't sand—it's some kind of explosive."

The thought raced through Antonio's mind that the truck might be booby-trapped.

"Carmel, this might be rigged," he said quietly. "Don't use your phone. Get back upstairs and evacuate the building. Code Red 1. Do it now," he said rapidly.

As she ran to the stairs, Antonio walked cautiously around the vehicle. There was nothing obvious that would indicate an improvised explosive device. Without touching the vehicle, he could tell from the heat of the radiator that it had been driven very recently. There was a clicking sound, like the engine cooling down.

Then he heard the sound of running feet.

Two members of the bomb squad came running up, followed by a handler with a sniffer dog. "What have we got, sir?" shouted the most senior officer.

"It's some kind of explosive. Take a look here," shouted Antonio. As he spoke, the sniffer dog started to jump around and bark.

"Damn, it's amatol," said the officer. "We will have to find and disarm the detonators," he shouted to his men.

"Stand back, sir," he ordered. "We have to test for booby-traps."

"I don't think we have much time," Antonio added.

The senior bomb squad officer spoke quickly to his two colleagues. One of them, carrying a number of pieces of equipment, stepped forward and switched on an electronic device that Antonio didn't recognise.

"It's a jammer," he explained briefly. "While we disarm this thing, hopefully we can jam any incoming radio frequency signals. For heaven's sake, don't use your phone, sir," he added, looking at Antonio.

At that moment, the second officer returned from his visual inspection of the vehicle. He said nothing, but a quick shake of his head to the senior man confirmed to Antonio that these were highly skilled, well trained professionals. They worked well as a team.

"We are evacuating the building," Antonio confirmed to him. "But the fastest evacuation we've ever done is thirty minutes." He looked at his watch. "That means we need another twenty-five."

The first officer had completed his scan of the vehicle's cargo using a lightweight instrument that looked like an extended selfie stick. He shook his head at the senior man, indicating he had found nothing.

"Okay, this could be rigged. But we can't take the chance and wait to find out. We'll have to unload the cargo. If we can separate it, and find the detonators, we can reduce the magnitude of any explosion."

"Sir," he said, addressing Antonio. "I don't have many men—they're all deployed around the demonstration sites. But we don't need you here. Please leave the building immediately," he ordered.

Antonio ignored his command.

He threw off his jacket and said, "We're in this together. Tell me what to do."

He saw that the others were lifting the paper sacks, carrying two at a time. Half-running, they carried them away from the vehicle, placing them at various parts of the parkade, as far apart as they could.

Antonio followed their example, selecting an area away from the others.

"Put them on the ground gently," yelled the senior bomb squad officer. One of the officers was already on his knees, slashing open the paper sacks, while the others unloaded the vehicle.

Somewhere in there, Antonio knew, would be the firing mechanisms.

Minutes later Xavi was at his side lifting paper sacks, taking them away from the main pile loaded on the back of the truck.

"We have to isolate the detonators," the senior officer yelled to them.

Then he heard running footsteps. Two additional members of the bomb squad were sprinting towards them.

The senior officer nodded and spoke quickly to them.

One of them took out a knife and started slashing at the paper sacks. The other helped move the remaining ones away from the truck.

Antonio stopped, perspiration pouring off his whole body. His shirt was soaked. He glanced at his watch. The evacuation would take another ten minutes, at minimum. He saw the senior officer nod his confirmation. Without pausing for breath, the men went back to work.

"I have one, sir," shouted his colleague running with the detonator to an empty stall. He put it on the ground, isolating it away from the sacks, and ran back to open another.

The senior officer inspected the detonator and shook his head. "They're old—and unstable," he shouted. "Take your time," he ordered.

"Number 2," shouted another officer, walking rapidly with a detonator in the opposite direction.

"I have another one," shouted another of the bomb squad, a few moments later.

"Keep looking," commanded another of the bomb squad. "If this stuff goes up, it could still make a hell of a mess."

Several other bomb squad members arrived.

"No disrespect, gentlemen," said the team leader, almost out of breath, to Antonio and Xavi. "We can handle it from here. Both of you will be needed upstairs." He indicated the stairs with his thumb. "Go please."

"That was a crazy thing to do," he said as Antonio picked up his jacket and Xavi wiped the sweat from his forehead. "But thank you both." He smiled a brief grin before getting back to work ripping open the remaining paper sacks.

Antonio nodded to Xavi.

"Thanks, amigo. Let's get out of here."

Tired, but charged by powerful surges of adrenaline, they leapt up the stairs to the lobby.

The evacuation was full swing when they heard the muffled explosion.

Within a minute, a thin cloud of smoke came up through the elevator shafts, as the fallout from the contained blast reached the main floor.

Antonio saw another member of the bomb squad head down the staircase. "We just came up," he told the man. "Get down there and come back to me immediately with a situation report. Do you understand? I'll wait right here."

The bomb squad man paused for a second then, recognising Antonio, saluted briefly. He ran down the staircase.

Antonio and Xavi switched their phones back on. Antonio's rang immediately. The call-display said it was the senior bomb squad officer.

Before answering it, he looked at Xavi. "Amigo, report directly to the chief as soon as you can. I'll give you a call when I know anything more."

"We guessed correctly this time," the officer informed him. "'It wasn't booby-trapped but we did find a remote control wrapped in sticks of TNT among the last few sacks.

"We evacuated the immediate area just seconds before the explosion," he said, sounding relieved, but exhausted.

"The jamming device probably helped, but the person detonating the load must be very close. The explosion was minimal—some minor damage to the structure. Luckily, everyone's fine.

"Thank you," he added, before calling off.

Antonio slumped onto the floor. He did not know it until later but, between them, they had lifted over two thousand kilos of amatol in the half hour they had been down in the car park.

More than a tonne of high explosives.

Sweat dripped off his body. He wiped his forehead and dialled Maria.

"Got to make it quick," he said, when she answered. Rapidly, he summarised the situation for her. "Just want you to know, when you hear the news, that I'm fine. Talk later," he added, and called off.

This time the attack had been a near miss. But the job wasn't finished. He dialled Carmel in Security.

"How are you?" he asked her, lapsing into Catalan. "That was great judgement on your part, Carmel. All of us owe our lives to you.

"Look, we need to get after the perpetrators..." he started to say.

She interrupted him. "I'm already emailing photos from the tapes I've got," she said. "The photos are fuzzy, but they identify the two men. Do you want me to issue them to our patrols, sir?"

He knew then that she had disobeyed the evacuation order and remained at her post. He shook his head.

For her to do that—a single mother with a son at home. He wiped the thought from his mind. "You're amazing, Carmel. You really are amazing." He paused, as he processed what she had told him. "Yes, get them distributed without delay," he said. "We may still be able to catch those bastards."

Antonio's voice trailed off as he slumped against the wall to the floor.

His phone dropped out of his hands, and he passed out.

Escape

Earlier, with his unwilling passenger, the driver of the stolen vehicle had accelerated up the ramp and exited the building.

Their progress out onto the streets had been slowed by police cordons. In his pocket, the driver carried a remote-control device. He planned to activate it as soon as he could get sufficiently clear of the immediate area. Stuck just inside his jacket, his gun was available if anyone tried to stop them.

Knowing the active range of the device, the driver knew his challenge was to make a safe escape—but not move too far from radio frequency contact with the explosives truck. He had planned for various scenarios. Emerging from the car park, he looked at the crowds and the areas the police had marked off. He chose his backup plan.

The public car park he had selected a few days earlier faced the Mossos' building.

Steering aggressively through the crowds blocking the entrance to the car park, he had driven the stolen car to the lowest level. With the local businesses closed, the car park was empty, except for a few parked cars.

"I'm not going to kill you—we have an agreement," he said to his passenger, as he pushed him towards the back of the car and told him to climb into the trunk. "You'll be safe here."

Before he slammed the trunk closed, he levelled his gun and put a bullet through the Mossos transcriber's head.

Avoiding the elevator, he climbed the stairs to the street.

The surging crowd, moving towards Placa d'Espanya and past the Mossos' building, was larger than he had expected. Moving to one side, he took the remote-control detonator and activated it. Moving back into the centre of the street, he could see the entrance to the Mossos underground car park.

He pressed the button.

Swept forward by the crowd and a group of street musicians, he strained to hear the noise that would confirm he had been successful. He looked for smoke, expecting to see the windows of the Mossos building blow out. This, he knew from his experience and the information he had received about the test explosions at Palmyra, would be followed by an implosion of the structure. Expecting to witness its complete demolition, it was best to keep a safe distance, he thought.

There was nothing. He cursed the Bluetooth technology and moved further forward. The thick mass of crowds and the jostling almost caused him to drop the remote.

Again, he pressed the button.

He cursed again. He should have set a timer on the load, he told himself. Normally, he did.

Now he was dangerously close to the Mossos' building, but unable to get through the throngs of happy demonstrators to the underground car park entrance.

Deciding another course of action, he turned and fought his way back against the crowds.

Climbing up the stairs of the parkade, he arrived at the top floor. He cursed again. Blocking his view of the area, a large group of young people was busily taking photographs of the demonstrators in the streets below.

At the next lower level, he tried the remote again. It had no effect.

He went back out onto the street knowing that, somehow, he would have to get nearer to the car park.

If he were one of the zealot jihadists, he thought ruefully, there would be no question of personal safety. He would have detonated the vehicle while he and his passenger were underground, in the Mossos' car park.

That was not a sacrifice he had been prepared to make; anyway, he had been completely confident in his ability to trigger the explosion from outside the building.

Pushing towards a less crowded side street, he received the blast of a trumpet in his ear. He grimaced at the demonstrator, who smiled back at him amiably—and kept blowing the instrument.

He gave his remote another try. Within seconds, he saw smoke billowing out of the underground car park, before he was swept along by the crowd.

He had expected to hear a much larger explosion.

It was time to make his escape.

Inquest

"Through good police work—I would say outstanding police work—and a lot of luck, today we were just able to prevent what could have been a major tragedy," said the chief, his voice cracking with emotion. "I want to ask you to continue to remain vigilant at all times.

"I want to thank all of you. We worked as a team today," he continued. "I will have more to say later; for now, I can't begin to tell you how... how relieved I am that no one has been injured.

"I'll hand over now to the deputy chief for details on how we are handling communications with the media and the public. Thank you."

The noise of shuffling feet and some chairs scraping gave Antonio a chance to check his messages.

One from William caught his eye. *"Boss, come and see me right away"*. It had been sent less than a minute earlier.

"What's up?" he asked, as he entered the room.

William looked up at him and smiled. "I understand that you're the hero who saved the day."

"No, no heroes today. Just a very smart and brave woman and a lot of very lucky people—myself included," said Antonio, shaking his head. "So what do you have for me?"

"Carmel gave the alarm at around 10:45 a.m., and the evacuation order was given a few minutes later—right?" asked the young hacker.

Antonio nodded. "Why, what do you have?"

"We always monitor the chatter before and after these events. Nothing surprising there. It's standard practice," he began.

"When I came back in the building, and I made sure I was one of the first back in, I did a chatter search. The noise started soon after 10:00 a.m. our time. There were distinct patterns between Barcelona, Morocco and Syria. Given what we know on this case so far, that's not a surprise to you, boss, is it?"

"But you do have a surprise for me, don't you, William," stated Antonio, his vocal chords still sore from his experience in the underground car park. It was not a question.

William keyed in some numbers on his keypad, and pointed to a monitor near where Antonio was standing. "Read these messages for yourself, boss. Some of our friends in Madrid were talking about the bomb an hour before it was discovered. And they weren't talking to our security forces."

"Which friends exactly?" asked Antonio, scanning through the emails.

"Your friends on the list. I have been keeping an eye on them since you gave me a copy of that CD. It seems, from what you are seeing on the screen in front of you, that they knew about the bomb—and had no intention of alerting the Mossos."

"Are you sure this is not a hacking job, William?" asked Antonio. "Someone spreading disinformation? Wasn't that the type of thing your former group specialised in?"

He hoped he didn't sound too negative to the young man.

"Well, it could be disinformation, boss. But I can tell you, it was domestic. I looked at the access strings, and they seem genuine to me.

"The chatter came from Madrid."

The General Takes Stock

The General was livid.

Sitting alongside Carlos, they had watched the news together in disbelief.

Instead of the TV news coverage they had expected, they were watching a series of interviews which described the bomb attempt as a foiled terrorist attack, in which Mossos' police officers had shown considerable bravery. The bombing attempt had pushed news of the N9 independence demonstrations to the sidelines.

Carlos' eyes narrowed; he saw that the lines on the General's face were set hard. A deep frown creased his forehead; his lower lip protruded, forcing his chin outward in a display of stubborn defiance.

Several other men in the room glanced nervously at the General, waiting for him to give his opinion. Without a word, the General stood up and paced across the room—eventually standing with his back to them, punching his fist into the palm of his other hand. It was not a violent motion, but rather, an involuntary response of a man wrestling with a multitude of issues spinning through his mind.

It was a stance that he had seen the General adopt many times, and he knew better than to interrupt.

"We cannot allow this single, isolated setback to deter us from our purpose," he said eventually; his voice was clear and confident.

"We will find out what went wrong, and move ahead."

There was a spontaneous outburst of applause from the men in the room, but it was not certain whether this was an accolade for the General's uplifting words or relief from those present that finally he had pronounced his opinion.

The General continued talking for a time, before taking the chauffeur aside. "Luis, find out from Robles what went wrong. I want some answers—and I want them now."

Ten minutes later, the chauffeur returned; he spoke quietly to the General. "The Chief Inspector would like to speak to you by phone, sir."

Raphael Robles was careful to avoid any suggestion of overreaction. He explained what he understood had happened, based on information the Mossos had shared with the National Police, and GEO in particular.

"Mustapha is anxious to put this behind us," Robles assured him. The nervous edge in his voice was obvious.

"To change course at this point would not be understood well by our friends," he added.

"I see," said the General.

Minutes later, he spoke again to the chauffeur and instructed him to meet directly with Mustapha's people. "We must continue," he said. "Do what is necessary, Luis."

The Terrorist

"You failed," said the chauffeur.

Ahmed had spent the past several hours watching media coverage of the attempted bombing of the Mossos' headquarters, and scanning his iPhone. The news was interspersed with coverage of the N9 independence march.

It was clear from the reports that the Madrid government considered it the work of international terrorists—although al-Qaeda had not claimed responsibility. The Catalan president supported the same conclusion.

There were few details of why the attempt had been botched. The government, however, had announced new restrictions at airports and travel near important buildings—and the media had whipped up a frenzy in Spain's major cities.

Ahmed wasn't concerned about not knowing right away what had gone wrong. They would find out the details soon enough, he thought, from al-Qaeda sympathisers in the police and security services.

For now, he needed to know what the General wanted to do.

"Yes," he replied eventually, speaking in Spanish to the chauffeur. He paused, not wanting to dilute the impact of his admission.

"We have the backup target," he suggested.

"I am instructed to tell you that no further action should be taken—not until the situation is clarified. Is that understood?" asked the chauffeur. His tone was not overly critical.

"Yes," Ahmed confirmed.

He was relieved; there was an absence of censure.

It was hard to grasp that the explosives had not achieved their purpose. The same quantities had worked well in Palmyra, and several others sites. He had checked all the materials himself. The detonators had been a little old, but they were perfectly adequate; he had worked with worse in the past.

The radio signal had not malfunctioned, so what had happened, he asked himself.

He thought back to his initial visit to the underground car park with the Mossos transcriber, and wondered if there might have been a better location for the explosives. Had the man perhaps betrayed him in some way?

He doubted it. Anyway, the man was dead now.

Ahmed, sitting at his table, watched as the chauffeur moved slowly around the room. Not far from his reach, his gun was available if the meeting turned nasty.

He did not feel apologetic. In a sense, the bombing attempt had achieved some of the General's objectives—it was clear from the news reports that Spaniards had been badly spooked.

"The money?" he asked the chauffeur.

"'Ah yes," the man answered quickly, "the money."

Ahmed waited, sweating.

"The General sees no need to alter our business arrangement," said the chauffeur.

Ahmed's facial expression did not change. Inwardly, this news was an incredible relief. He had not known what to expect. He often had been perplexed by the cultural preference of western societies to censure failure and non-performance: it was endemic throughout their businesses.

He had feared the worst at this meeting. If he had been heavily criticised by the General, he would have dreaded telling his masters in al-Qaeda. They would not have understood such a reaction.

This news was quite satisfactory.

His natural caution, reinforced by what the imams had taught him, was to be patient and prudent. He waited, anticipating that the chauffeur might follow on and announce some new terms and conditions—or try to extract some concessions.

Now, it seemed there were none.

This really was quite satisfactory.

In a way, Ahmed was not surprised. The General was a veteran of many campaigns in North Africa. His work must have given him an understanding of the culture of the Maghreb and Arabia.

Such loyalty would be rewarded. It would be reciprocated a thousand times, thought Ahmed.

He did not entirely trust the chauffeur, but he admired him. The man had proved himself to be an asset in the partnership. Weeks ago, when Mustapha had called him, with the orders to eliminate the Civil Guard officer, the chauffeur had carried out Ahmed's instructions without hesitation.

The courier had turned out to be a double agent; it was essential to remove him from the network. For that, Ahmed was grateful to the chauffeur.

Now it seemed there would be no recriminations over the failed bombing attempt; they would move on to the next step in their joint plans.

"You have replaced the courier?" the chauffeur was asking him. When Ahmed looked puzzled, the chauffeur repeated his question. "We need another courier. Has Mustapha replaced him yet?"

Ahmed was not slow-witted, but the question had taken him by surprise. He did not want to admit to the General's man that he had not received instructions from Mustapha about who would replace David Casals. It would be embarrassing to admit such a thing. After the mistake that he already had made today, he wanted to reassure the chauffeur that everything on their side of the partnership was well organised.

"My brother," he heard himself blurt out—and immediately regretted his haste.

The chauffeur's eyes narrowed. "Your brother?" he asked.

Ahmed nodded his head vigorously. "Yes, he is a good courier. It will work well."

On the chauffeur's face, Ahmed could detect the doubt that was in the man's mind.

He smiled, then waited in silence.

"Alright," said the chauffeur, turning to leave. "But we don't want any repeats of what happened last time."

Ahmed began to shake as he watched the sneer develop on the chauffeur's mouth.

"Make sure of it," ordered the chauffeur, as he walked to the front door.

Without looking at his watch, Ahmed was aware that within a few hours he would have to speak by phone to Mustapha. It was not an experience he had been relishing.

Now, with the need to explain his hasty commitment of the new courier, he dreaded what Mustapha would have to say.

This morning's incident had taken an unfortunate turn. It would not be repeated. Ahmed would make sure of that. Now he would have to explain his actions—to the leader they all revered and feared.

Ahmed Calls Mustapha

After the chauffeur left, Ahmed's brother came out of their shared bedroom.

"It went well," the younger man said.

"Better than we were expecting, little brother," replied Ahmed. "You heard. The General is not angry."

His brother moved cautiously towards the window, keeping out of sight, as he searched the street for any signs of danger.

"They respect you, Ahmed."

"It is because they need me, I think, little brother," replied Ahmed, examining the clip on his automatic.

"What will you tell Mustapha—about the new courier?"

"That was an error. I should not have said it." Ahmed began to look worried.

"Maybe it is not such a bad idea, Ahmed. After all, I am willing to help. If you do not apologise to Mustapha—if you propose it as your recommendation—perhaps he will be pleased."

"You don't understand the job of the courier, little brother. It is dangerous. It requires certain skills."

"Danger is not anything that is new, you know that, Ahmed. Give me a chance; I will learn the skills of which you speak."

Ahmed looked at his younger brother. The boy was still a teenager. Young, good-looking and naive about the world—despite the hell he had lived through in Syria.

"It will be Mustapha who tells me what to do," said Ahmed eventually. His nervousness was now evident in his voice. For the second time in ten seconds, he glanced at his watch.

The apartment had a few items of cheap furniture; still, it was more than they had been used to in recent years. Ahmed walked over to a suitcase that sat flat against the wall. Unzipping it, he took out three cell phones and carried them to the table. Laying them parallel to each other, he put his hand on each one in turn. Silently he said a prayer asking for Allah's guidance.

Leaving the red-coloured one on the table, he put the other two back in the suitcase.

They had been modified to eliminate GPS tracking, and had auto-encryption functions. Mustapha and he would speak in Arabic. They were aware that their call most likely would be tracked by the security services.

Once activated, Mustapha insisted, the cell phones be used immediately and then destroyed.

Diego Hears the News

I had not heard from Antonio for some time. Then I heard the news.

Surveillance of the General and his gang had been taking up a lot of my time. Not just that, but Raphael Robles seemed determined not to give me a moment's relaxation; he piled other work on me. I had no time to think about the Barcelona homicide case.

We had people watching the General and everyone else we had identified as being at the lodge that night, plus a few more influential people who were associated with them. It was taking a lot of manpower—and we were under pressure to produce results.

Our surveillance had yielded nothing so far. The condesa must have been having problems bugging Carlos' and the General's laptops with the rootkit we had given her. Days later, and it had not yet been activated.

I was beginning to worry that we had overreacted to some of the information that the condesa had given to us.

We knew that some of it was absolutely accurate. We had found traces of materials in the outbuildings at the church in Lleida, which we were certain were being used to make amatol. Inside GEO at least, we were sure that we were dealing with a domestic terrorist case. We had worried that a bombing attempt would be made, but we had no idea where— except that it would be in Catalunya. Barcelona was an obvious target.

Our problem was that we did not have enough evidence to arrest the General and his people solely on the basis that they were vaguely associated with it. It's not illegal to store bags of fertiliser, and it's not illegal to transport it.

Any lawyer worth his licence would be able to throw us out of court if we had tried to hold anyone on suspicion. If we had arrested high profile, well-connected people like the General, all our careers would have been shortened by our superiors—very promptly.

We knew by then that Father Damien had been murdered; the old boy had not died from an accidental overdose. The builder was missing. We couldn't tie either of them to anyone specific.

The case had been going cold.

Raphael Robles was beginning to get concerned about continuing to hold Francisco Rioja, the journalist, in custody. There was nothing we could charge him with—and he was beginning to object noisily about being kept in detention. The promise we had given him, of an even bigger scoop than he already had soon wore thin.

I told him that it was protective custody; he could be a target for the General's people if they knew about the incriminating photographs he'd taken of them. But, after a few days, he wasn't buying it anymore.

News of the attempted bombing of the Mossos' building reached me when I was at the gym, just starting on my workout. I had taken an early lunch. When the news came up on the TV screen, I grabbed my phone and called into headquarters for details.

My first thoughts were for Antonio, Xavi and the chief. Soon the news came through that there were no injuries, which was incredibly fortunate. I was relieved no one was hurt. I called Robles, but he was out of the office.

The attempted bombing was being portrayed by the politicians—and the media—as an al-Qaeda plot. The media's storyline was that al-Qaeda had used the cover of the N9 independence demonstrations, and reduced security around the building, to bomb the Mossos' building.

Of course, it came out later that some Syrians were involved in the failed bombing attempt. The Mossos found the body of their transcriber, and a Moroccan girl came forward asking for police protection for her family. The story of the Syrians, and the girl's affair with the Mossos transcriber soon became known.

Several days later, we received the lab analysis results; they confirmed that the explosives materials used in the Mossos' headquarters underground car park were identical to the traces found in the outbuildings at the church in Lleida.

We tried to establish some connections between this and the General, but there wasn't a direct linkage that we could identify. Of course, later we found out some things which would have changed our minds—had we known.

On the afternoon of the bombing attempt, I received a text from Antonio. He didn't say much, so I planned to call him later to talk. By the time I got back in the office, Robles had returned, and he had other work for me. It was the next day before I talked to Antonio.

In the meantime, I heard about his and Xavi's role in disarming the bomb. Crazy people, those two, but incredibly brave.

My respect for them, and for the Mossos, notched up a level. To do that, Pretty Boy had balls.

Chapter 11

Daniela Settles In

A few days later, Xavi walked into Antonio's office... expecting to find his partner.

Antonio wasn't there, but Daniela was. She was standing next to his filing cabinets searching through some files. Xavi thought she seemed startled by his sudden entry.

"Hey Xavi," she said rather too quickly, dangling some keys in the air. "The boss asked me to pick up some files. How's it going with you?"

Xavi smiled thinly, and dropped off the package he had walked over from the registry to deliver.

"Just great," he replied to her question. "How do you like it here, Daniela, compared with the Civil Guard?"

She placed her finger against her mouth, and pretended to ponder the question. Then, with a laugh, at the same time flicking her hair over her shoulder, she mused, "Let me see... Ceuta versus Barcelona... Ceuta or Barcelona. Mmm, tough choice, man."

She swept past him, a little too closely thought Xavi, and flashed her eyes at him. "See you." She gave his elbow a squeeze.

It was an innocent enough exchange, but it bothered Xavi. He wondered how she had Antonio's keys. Normally, his partner was very particular about whom he loaned his keys to—and who had access to his files. On a hunch, he called Antonio's cell. "Where are you, amigo?"

"Just coming back upstairs from William's office. I had to deliver something for him... to keep him happy," chuckled Antonio. "What's up?"

"I can't find my copy of the Casals file," lied Xavi. "Can I borrow your keys, and look at your copy?"

"Sure, but I think Daniela has them. I'll ask her for them if you want."

"No, it's not urgent. Don't bother. I'll check my desk again. By the way," added Xavi, anxious to move on, "we want you and Maria to come over for dinner. What's a good night?"

"That would be great, amigo. Don't the girls normally arrange these things? You and I never know until we're told," he chuckled.

"Ask Maria, and see what she wants to do. It's Pilar's birthday soon, so I'd like to give her a surprise."

Xavi looked troubled as he walked back along the corridor. Antonio's mention of William spurred a thought in his mind. The more he thought about it, the more ridiculous the idea forming in his mind seemed to be. He tried to shut it out, but the idea persisted.

On a whim, he went to the elevator and rode it down to the floor where William had his office. Xavi had visited the talented geek many times. He couldn't figure how William could produce the great results he did from a workplace in such total chaos. There was equipment and wires everywhere.

He didn't quite know how to begin the conversation.

"What's troubling you, Xavi?" asked William, displaying more powers of social observation than Xavi normally gave him credit. Xavi guessed that his hesitation conveyed a level of uncertainty.

"How would you feel about hacking into someone's computers for me?" he asked eventually.

"Depends whose it is, I guess. For you, Xavi—sure."

"Daniela," said Xavi, watching as the surprise spread across William's face.

"Wow," was his only reply. "Has the boss okayed this?" William turned to face him.

"It's better that he doesn't know about it," said Xavi, trying to sound matter-of-fact, but he could hear the uncertainty in his own voice.

William looked at him, not sure what to say.

"I like my job here, Xavi. To go behind the boss's back... I don't know. Could you get the chief or someone to authorise it?" William suggested, his face scrunched in mock pain.

Xavi realised that he was on a dangerous ledge. Now he began rapidly rethinking his request. Hell, I'm becoming paranoid, he told himself.

"Look, William," he said after a few seconds. "Let's forget it for now. Just don't mention it to anyone, ok?"

"My lips are sealed," William smiled kindly, as Xavi got up to leave.

The episode depressed Xavi. He knew how to recognise the signs of a witch hunt—and that definitely was what he was engaged in.

He could trust William's discretion.

But already he had started to wonder if he could rely on his own judgement.

Friends Help Out

Pilar stroked the back of Xavi's neck, and moved her hands over to massage his shoulders. "You're worried about him, aren't you, *carinyo*?" she asked gently.

He didn't need to say anything for her to know the answer. Pilar knew that her husband's loyalty to Antonio was founded on their long friendship, extending from the time they were kids at school together.

298

Xavi had been small for his age—a genetic trait that he had never outgrown. But in the fights they got into in the playground, it was always Xavi who had been alongside his hero—taking, and delivering, the extra hard punches that, more often than not, had turned the contests in their favour.

Pilar sensed the same street fighting determination in Xavi's emotions this evening. She knew his despondent mood was something he needed to work through for himself. She kept quiet, not venturing an opinion. Patiently, she waited for him to resolve the conflicts she sensed were preoccupying him. He was his own man. It was, she reminded herself, important for her to be supportive, but not to interfere.

"I think I'll talk to Isabel again," he announced.

"What will you say to her?"

"She'll be happy to help," he answered. "Together, we have to find a way to carry it out—without Antonio discovering anything."

"You are convinced about this woman, aren't you?" encouraged Pilar. "The new female officer that Antonio has hired."

Xavi nodded, reaching behind his neck to take Pilar's hand. "It's just a risk I'm going to have to take," he said, still speaking his thoughts aloud.

"For Toni's own good."

****

"How's my dad?" asked Isabel, searching Xavi's face.

"The same as always," said Xavi gently. "The chief spends far too much time at the office," he added.

"Mama should slip a couple of blue pills into his dinner; then she could exhaust him in the bedroom," smiled Isabel without much humour. "Tell Toni to get her to do it."

Xavi laughed. He loved Isabel's irreverence.

She was such a fun member of the family: she'd always injected life and vivacity into their relationships. Isabel… invariably outrageous, always unpredictable.

He grinned at her, but his thoughts were that it was sad to see their family torn apart like this.

"No breakthroughs with them, I suppose?" he asked.

"They didn't mind about Julia and me. They accepted that," said Isabel. "But my dad would rather I had stayed as an unemployed teacher than to see me doing what I do now."

Xavi put his hand on hers. When he had arrived at her apartment earlier, Isabel had been out. Julia had opened the door and welcomed him inside. "She won't be long; she's just across the street."

Xavi didn't have to glance outside to know that Julia meant the hotel. It was an upscale place, maybe even four stars, he recalled. Like many, its management was willing to supplement the revenues by renting rooms on a four-hour basis. They kept their jobs that way.

"Four hours is a lot. My guys never take that long," Isabel had told them brazenly over dinner one night. "It's all over in two hours—and most of that time they spend sleeping." There had been ripples of laughter around the table.

"They wake up feeling guilty and rush home, making sure they pick up flowers on the way," she giggled. "Anyway, while they're sleeping it off, I can catch up on my messages."

They had known she was exaggerating. In all honesty, her johns were not always that tame; everyone at the table knew that. Anyhow, it was a good story and they knew she was telling her friends not to worry about her. She could handle it.

Xavi and Julia had heard the door key, and Isabel had come in.

"Hey, you two," she had smiled, kissing Xavi first, then hugging Julia. Her partner had quietly scanned Isabel for any signs of physical damage. Satisfied there were none, she had gone back to her fortress in the kitchen.

"Give me five minutes," Isabel had smiled at Xavi. "I need to shower."

She came back with her tousled hair still dripping wet, held up with a towel over her head. Her white gown was a shiny silk import from a trip she'd made to Rome. It showed off her slim, well-formed figure; her long legs were muscled and tanned.

Xavi noticed that the silk was damp in places she had not dried. Her nipples thrust forward, provocatively spilling out across the garment's narrow lapels. He felt the stirrings of emotions that had never quite gone away.

When she was a teenager, her outgoing personality already was well developed. Isabel was incredibly popular among the girls as well as the boys. They followed her everywhere.

As a teenager, he had dreamed about her many times. Those became long nights because, no matter what he did, the thought of her drove him wild. The more he tried to banish the haunting image of her from his head, the more it forced itself back into his consciousness.

She controlled his body and his emotions, just as she did with so many of their friends.

He had lusted after her in ways that he dared not confess to anyone, least of all even mention his sinful intentions to the priest at Saturday confession.

There was a time when, as young teenagers, Antonio had caught Xavi looking at a picture of the three of them. It was a photograph taken by his parents. "You like my sister?" Antonio had seized on his friend's weakness and teased him unmercifully.

Xavi denied it vehemently, and the two boys had ended up wrestling on Xavi's bedroom floor until his mother had shouted loudly for them to stop.

Antonio's discovery was still a point of embarrassment for Xavi, even today. His desire for her had intensified over the years, but somehow they had never dated—except as part of a larger group.

As teenagers, Xavi suspected she knew about his infatuation. She would deliberately tease him—sometimes, when no one was looking, running her hand between his legs. The feeling became so intense that, one night at a movie, she massaged him to a glorious finale… well before the film had ended.

He had heard her husky deep-throated laugh. In the darkness of the movie theatre she handed him a paper towel she had been using to hold her drink.

Xavi fretted for the rest of the film. His emotions were confused. He hated that she took delight in his embarrassment. But he also prayed that when they got up to leave, please God, their friends would not see the large patch of wetness that was still spreading across the front of his jeans.

They had never made love. Nothing quite as intimate and carnal as their shared eroticism at the movies ever happened again. It was a concupiscent, lascivious and deliciously shared moment that neither of them ever spoke of—but nor would they ever forget.

He had watched her in the following months as she dated his friends. When they walked as a group, he would see her throw her long hair back over her head, turn and smile a conspirator's smile at him.

The anticipation and promise of their secret passion was even more powerful than that of lovers who had consummated their lust. The possibilities were still limitless. Expectations remained boundless. Their unmet desires fuelled even greater passions.

She flirted with the boys and, in retrospect, he guessed she had with the girls too, wielding a power of control that kept them trapped like bitches in heat, legs splayed, flattened to the ground, mounted by an insatiable desire. He felt his emotions being destroyed.

His instincts had told him to take his rivals aside and beat them into a pulp. He wanted to punish them for the agonising thoughts his imagination created. It tortured him to think about what the other boys were doing with her.

Then, in her late teens, she came out.

The tortured memories his imagination had built up for all those years suddenly were without any foundation. The truth was that Isabel preferred women.

It was as though a huge block of granite had been lifted off Xavi's neck—as if Zeus had suddenly forgiven Atlas and taken the burden of the heavens from his shoulders.

He understood her much better now, and became her close collaborator. Their youthful intimacy became the foundation of a mutual affinity and friendship that no sibling or twin ever could match. Xavi was the first person, apart from her lover, to whom she had confessed her secret.

Late into the night they had talked and cried together. Bolstered by Xavi's understanding, and emboldened by his unreserved support, she had gone home and announced casually to her parents, over breakfast, that she would be leaving—to move in with her girlfriend. That was long before Julia.

****

"I can't do it," William shook his head. "I can't go behind the boss's back."

He turned away from his screens and looked directly at Xavi. He could sense the detective's anguish.

A few moments lapsed. "I could ask Kung Fu to do it," he probed. "That way, it couldn't be traced to us."

Xavi's mood brightened slightly. Perhaps this was a way forward.

"'What are you expecting to find, Xavi?" William continued. "I should give Kung Fu some parameters—something for his searches."

"That's part of the problem," said Xavi, his facial expression revealing his uncertainty. "I don't know."

William looked pained. "Gotta have something to narrow down the searches, Xavi. You know the drill. As they say in our business, 'There's nothing worse than having a client who doesn't know what he wants.' No offence, Xavi, but you are asking me to put my neck on the line here," William continued.

"You're right," said the detective. "I guess I'm looking for something that will point a finger of suspicion at her."

"Daniela is an officer with the Mossos; she's part of our team at Homicide," said William stating what both of them already knew—and feared.

"It wouldn't be the first time we have had to place one of our own under surveillance," said Xavi, feeling ashamed.

"No, but it's the first time we will put the boss's girlfriend under surveillance—without authorisation," said William, trying his best to soften the harshness of his statement.

Xavi sat thinking for several moments, his head bowed down looking at the floor.

"I could ask Kung Fu to look for anything unusual," suggested William eventually. "You know, a quick scan, look for patterns."

"Thanks, William," said Xavi, getting to his feet and walking towards the door. His voice sounded sad.

"Just, please, make sure we keep this away from Antonio."

Antonio and Maria

Maria twirled her fingers through Toni's hair, and looked abstractly into the mid-distance. His head lay on her lap. He began to snore gently. It was good for him to relax, she thought, but really she would have preferred to talk.

His breathing became much deeper, and the prospect dimmed. It was late in the evening; her thoughts and emotions drifted randomly. She knew she was not being unreasonable.

It seemed that something always seemed to get in the way. Every time she had a chance to talk to Toni about their future together, something else intervened. It had been eating away inside her for a long time.

She didn't think he was avoiding the subject deliberately. He seemed content with things the way they were, seemingly oblivious to her concerns about where their lives together were heading.

Was he simply refusing to talk, she wondered, as she gazed down on him. Gently, she moved her index finger over the lines of his face, tracing its contours. It was a kind face; she remembered that was her first impression of him.

So long ago—now nearly eighteen months. She doubted that he knew exactly how long they had been together and, really, it was not important. He was a good man in more important ways.

To his credit, he had remembered their anniversary this year—although perhaps with some prompting from his mother—or maybe Xavi, briefed by Pilar. She smiled at the thought, amused and with affection.

He had been under a lot of stress, and she tried hard to avoid adding to it. The result was that they had hardly spoken about her job interview and her partnership opportunity in Madrid. The thought made her feel sad. Really it was something they should decide together.

She lifted her hand and brushed away two large tears; they were soon followed by others. She blinked her eyes rapidly, not wanting to smear her mascara. An errant tear escaped and fell on the side of his face. On reflex, he brushed it away, but the quick motion woke him up.

He looked up at her. "You're crying?"

She shook her head "no."

He lifted up his hand and wrapped it around her neck, pulling her down to him. She went easily.

They kissed for a long time, each surrendering to the other. Maria could feel her heart pounding. She was at her happiest like this: they were together.

Eventually, he pushed her away from him—yet, it was gentle and caring.

"You were crying," he said, in a tone both kind and insistent.

"It's nothing," she said, repeating the words that women have uttered for generations, when they really mean the exact opposite.

"It's everything," he corrected her. "Tell me what it is, sweetheart."

She shook her head again. Surely, he knew? He's a smart guy. Let him work it out for himself.

"Is it something you want to talk about?" he asked.

She shook her head, looking away from him. The time for playing games was over; their lives together were too important for that.

By now he had pushed himself into a sitting position. He took hold of her shoulders and squared them towards him. "Tell me," he said.

She could feel her heart racing. Large tears started to roll down her face; there was nothing she could do to control them. The unspoken conflict forced its way to the surface. These were no crocodile tears; they came in a deluge. As she cried, her abdomen pulsed and her shoulders shook. She cried the tears she had not cried since she was a teenager.

'Whoa," he said, with surprise. "Where did all this come from?"

She had pushed her face into his shoulder. Now she sobbed, wetting the shoulder of his shirt smudging it with her makeup, emotions made more intense by their closeness. She could smell his smell; she wanted to be part of him. Sobbing, she pulled him even closer with a strength that was not lust, but pure wanting. Her need to be with him was so deep that it hurt.

Gently, he eased her away so he could look at her face. Her mascara had migrated and he laughed gently at the sight of it. Maria knew that she had abandoned herself to him. She had nothing more to give; now it was up to him.

He took out a cotton handkerchief he was fond of carrying, gently wiping her cheeks, now becoming red, as the salt in her tears stung her skin.

"You look a mess," he laughed, kissing her on the nose.

In turn, she laughed, realising he had chosen to kiss the only part of her face that was not wet with tears and smeared mascara.

"We need to talk," he announced.

She burst out laughing, with a sense of relief that was palpable. She had never understood why men were so slow to figure out their women. What goes on in their heads? she wondered. They have such little understanding.

"I'll fix us some drinks," he announced, again taking full control of the situation. "Then we can relax."

Maria tried to stifle the derisive laugh that rose from deep in her abdomen—only managing to brunt its force, converting the sound instead to a noise that resembled a squealing pig. It had taken months to get him to this point, and now he had found another reason to delay.

He woke at 3:00 a.m., awakened by the church bell of nearby St. Agustín striking the hour. Maria was deeply asleep. He covered her bare shoulders with the bed sheet. Making no noise, he got out of bed and moved carefully into the kitchen.

Taking the milk from the fridge, he drank straight from the plastic bottle. He sat down at the wood table, elbows raised, resting his forehead in his cupped hands.

The night had reunited them as a couple. Yet, now, he felt strangely indifferent to their renewed vows—questions answered for her, not so for him. They returned to haunt him, doubts nipping at the heels of his nascent emotional closeness to her. Veiled whispers from the shadows—an underworld of phantoms and demons skulking in the deep precincts of his mind, sowing seeds of discontent where, only shortly before, a blissful sense of fulfilment had taken root.

A few hours ago, it had seemed so right to him. Now, he felt unsure. Squall clouds of hesitation swept in… not driven by any lack of willingness to commit to her, but a distrust of himself—the darker side of him.

Taking another drink of milk, he became lost in his thoughts, wondering what was missing between them. What magic was it that allowed couples like Xavi and Pilar to co-exist seemingly blissfully like one, he asked—as if, through some wizardry, the answer might be revealed conveniently and instantly to him, conjured in a flash from nowhere. Why, he wondered, was it so easy for them, yet so difficult for him?

On his phone, an incoming message buzzed. The noise echoed loudly against the walls of the kitchen, intruding on the peacefulness of the night-time silence like a clumsy thief breaking into the room.

It was from the girl. "*What are you doing?*" asked the terse message.

He stared at the screen for a few moments, aware that, in just those few seconds, he had admitted to himself a longing desire to see her.

There was something insolent about the message, yet also something intimate—a message that declared there were no barriers of time between them. It suggested an intimacy which was unsubtle in its promise of something much more.

He found himself composing a response in his mind. It wasn't smart to reply, he knew, but it was what his carnal desires drove him to do. He was aware he was reacting like an adolescent schoolboy receiving a flirtatious note from an attractive girl.

Antonio thought about Maria sleeping in the next room. He would ignore the message. He could take care of it in the morning. Yet…

Antonio keyed in his reply to the girl. *"Not much. How about you?"*

Her reply was almost instantaneous. *"Want to come over?"*

He thought about her invitation, then glanced involuntarily at the door of the bedroom where Maria was still sleeping. Disregarding the alarm bells going off in his mind, he keyed in his reply: *"Can't…"*

"But do you want to?" asked the swift reply.

Antonio had already posed the same question to himself, and was aware of his answer. He was already involved in this deeply; should he commit himself further? He tinkered with the thought for several seconds. Hesitatingly, he keyed in the cautious words, *"Not unless you have further information on the case."*

He looked at the unsent message, imagining how she would feel when she read it, then deleted it.

She had messaged him in the meantime. *"Don't worry, I'm deleting everything… I miss you."* She had added an emoji: a smiley face with a moustache.

Antonio laughed. He wanted to reassure her—to tell her that he missed her too, that he wanted her. It just wasn't very sensible to text it to her.

"Call me at my office in the morning." He considered the words before finally pressing "send*".*

She didn't reply.

He waited for a few minutes, then put down his phone... feeling a surge of disappointment. It was an empty, hollow feeling in the pit of his stomach. The excitement and intimacy of their text exchanges had vanished.

He looked at his reply to her. It sounded officious. He felt like a prick for having sent it. She was taking as much risk as he was by texting him. He had protected himself, but his careful words had placed her in a potentially compromising position. He re-read their whole conversation. She had told him she would delete it. His reply was telling her, in effect, that he didn't believe her—that he didn't trust her.

That wasn't what he had wanted to say. Annoyed with himself, he started to drink the remainder of the milk from the plastic container. It had lost its chill, and the warm milk tasted sour—like his mood. He walked to the sink and poured the remainder of it down the drain.

His disappointment of a few minutes ago was now replaced with irritation. He was annoyed at himself for his poor handling of the situation. He wanted to crunch the empty plastic milk container, compacting it into a tight ball with his hands. Instead, he placed it quietly in the recycling. He felt disgusted with himself.

Picking up his phone, he went back to bed.

Death of an Investigative Journalist

I did not agree with Raphael Robles' decision to release Francisco Rioja. It seemed to me that the photos he'd taken of the General and his gang at the lodge were highly incriminating. It was logical to assume that Rioja would be a target once he was released.

Not just the General's gang. The Madrid government would not want to see Rioja's photos in circulation either—although I suppose that the prime minister could have used them to help support his policies against domestic terrorism.

My advice was ignored, and Rioja was released late at night. That was earlier this week. Within a few hours, we had a report that he'd been found shot dead at his apartment. I really wish we had kept him in protective custody. We would have needed his testimony if we had been able to establish a case against the General.

What worries me, too, is how it happened so quickly after his release. We had confiscated all his photos and impounded his camera equipment. We were entitled to do so because the photos were part of our ongoing investigation.

In any case, his apartment had been ransacked. I don't know what they found there, but we were confident that any evidence of what went on at the lodge was safely under lock and key, and in our possession.

His death was reported in the newspapers as likely being drugs-related, but the tabloids passed on the story and it caused very little stir.

It was investigated actively for a few more days, then reclassified as inactive, from where, if nothing else turned up, it would be placed eventually in the unsolved crimes files.

I had my suspicions about the condesa. Certainly, she had a motive—even though she had resigned just a few days earlier from government. But I wasn't convinced that she had anything to do with Rioja's death. It just didn't fit.

Daniela Searches for Aladdin's Cave

Daniela had scanned the map several times, trying to guess where the chauffeur might be hiding the stolen truck. In her mind, she had developed a schedule of the timelines. She was confident that she had correctly identified the overall area but, within that, she acknowledged it might be concealed anywhere.

She knew she would need more information to pinpoint the location.

Looking again at the copy of my report that she'd taken from Antonio's filing cabinet, she checked off all my observations. I am a conscientious report man, and she was pleased to see that my analysis was very thorough... with my evidence well documented. Good solid detective work, Daniela said to herself.

She liked my attention to details, such as my examination of the builder's van found near the stonemason's yard where the truck had been stolen. In my report, I had noted that the driver's seat had been adjusted for a tall person. Knowing that the builder was short and stocky, that implied the builder was not driving his own vehicle when it had been abandoned—which, in turn, led to a number of possibilities

It also told Daniela that if it was the chauffeur who'd been the driver of the builder's van, he would not have had time to drive it—or the stonemason's truck—very far. She was convinced she was dealing with a fairly small radius of distances from the buildings at Father Damien's church.

The only fingerprints that the forensics report mentioned were those of the builder. When she had re-examined the photographs that Father Damien had taken, she had confirmed that the chauffeur wore leather gloves. Through interagency cooperation, the photo file had been made available to her using her Mossos-issued access code. She could tap into a restricted number of files on the National Police network in Madrid—and that file was one of them.

The question she needed to answer was 'where' the truck containing the gold was hidden.

She no longer had privileged-access status to the Civil Guard online networks that she'd enjoyed as an officer within the service. Taking a risk, she had emailed a friend in Ceuta who worked in the same department as she had. A favour, she asked—which her friend was very happy to provide.

She had just read the texted reply: there were no records of the chauffeur's service record on file at the Civil Guard—just his birthdate and military ID number.

On a hunch, she did a search of the national statistical database of births, marriages and deaths. It yielded nothing of relevance. She reversed the input data, entering his birthdate. For the whole of Spain, the search yielded several thousand names. She immediately eliminated all females, reducing the list by just under half, but still many thousands.

Daniela knew that she would have to narrow the search parameters. She eliminated all entries which indicated deceased, married or divorced persons, but the list remained formidable. She carried out a geographical screening, eliminating all birthplace locations except those in her immediate area of interest.

The list had shortened to three males, none of them the name of the chauffeur. Where to go next, she wondered?

What if, she speculated, forming an idea that would take her along a very different search path...

Taking note of the names of the three males born on the same day in the area, she shut down the open screens in front of her. Going back into the Mossos network, she searched for a file that would provide the codes she would need to get access to the Catalan government public database. Within a few minutes, she was scrolling through the birth and names records.

It was fortunate that she was fluent in Catalan, she thought. It made the cross-referencing process very much easier.

When she found it, she felt a thrill of excitement. It was immediately obvious that two of the males could be eliminated from her search. A note alongside the third entry indicated that the chauffeur had changed his name, in his early twenties, to Luis Rivera.

"*Déu n'hi do*," she exclaimed, lapsing into Catalan. "Brilliant."

Using an online map, she zoomed-in to the place where he had been born, finding a small village called El Canos, about twenty minutes drive from Father Damien's church near Lleida.

She could not believe her good fortune.

With a further search, the screen zoomed in on an isolated farm which, when she Google-Earthed it, showed a series of stone buildings. She looked for signs of habitation and continued her search over the immediate area for about twenty minutes until she was confident she knew the terrain, roads and pathways. A plan already had formed in Daniela's mind.

****

They had an agreed communications protocol and a code word for when they needed to talk or meet.

"We don't need the project any longer," she told him excitedly. "I know where the source is located."

His surprise was so evident that she had to repeat what she'd said.

When he understood, he too was excited at first but, as their conversation continued, his tone changed. "It makes no difference," he told her. "We are committed. It has to work—it is our best chance."

Both were aware of the need to avoid using words and phrases that would be flagged in phone-tapping filters used by police.

He did not fully believe his owns words. In truth, the project was not going as their client, the General, had planned. Even before the condesa's visit to the lodge, the grand plan had begun to unravel. The General had cautioned him that collateral damage would have to be sustained—as in any kind of warfare. In something as complex as this, setbacks were inevitable, he reassured Raphael Robles. The General had told him: please tell that to Mustapha—he understands. These things are temporary.

Now Daniela was telling him that all his efforts in support of Operation FERROL had been rendered pointless. It was hard for him to accept—agonisingly hard. He had so much committed to it personally.

"We should meet, and talk, on something so important," he ventured, still trying to absorb the implications of what she was telling him. "It is not simple," he added, although it was unnecessary to say.

They talked for a few minutes more, but it was evident that Daniela was becoming frustrated with him.

"We shouldn't do anything that might prejudice our efforts," he found himself telling her, by way of a warning. She thought he sounded old and worn out, as if he had aged suddenly.

She said nothing.

"Let's meet," he said again.

"Alright," she replied, and shut down the cell phone, in the knowledge they had a well-established arrangement for face-to-face meetings.

She removed the SIM card, broke up the phone, and threw away the pieces. Overkill, she thought, but you could never be completely sure.

At this time of night, her journey to the farm at El Canos would take less than an hour, she estimated.

First, she had a stop to make on the way.

****

Ahmed had received fresh instructions from Mustapha. He would be sending a girl to talk to them Mustapha had said. To

315

Ahmed, that meant Mustapha had not fully accepted his recommendation regarding the new courier. The girl would talk to his Ahmed's brother and evaluate the situation, Mustapha had told him.

A girl? Ahmed was disgusted. He felt he was being belatedly punished for his failure. He felt slighted. Yes, he was familiar with western societies and the strange way they did things. He himself was quite liberal. He had lived abroad. Selective emancipation of women was widespread, even in parts of his own country.

But for her to be placed in charge of the couriers? Privately, he questioned Mustapha's judgement. It was not wise; in fact, it was a foolhardy move—in his opinion.

He glanced again at his watch. She would be arriving any minute. He looked over at his little brother sprawled out on the floor playing with a new app on the phone he had pickpocketed that morning in the supermarket. Ahmed had made sure the device was safe and untraceable before he'd allowed the boy to keep it.

He blamed himself for involving his little brother—if only he had not been quite so hasty in his response to the chauffeur, he chastised himself. It was his fault his little brother was being put in this situation. There were plenty of other agents he could have recommended, but the chauffeur had spooked him.

He recognised the coded taps on the apartment door. The building had no outside security—a feature that he had regretted several times.

He kicked the legs of his little brother to get his attention; the boy moved himself off the floor and sauntered away—selecting, out of survival-experience, a wall to lean on that was not visible from the entrance. Ahmed took out his automatic, and opened the door.

She spoke to him in fluent Arabic.

He was so surprised by what he saw that he almost neglected his normal routine of checking outside on the landing. He waved her inside.

Obviously, she was a Westerner, yet she conducted herself with the submissiveness, grace and charm of a well-bred Arab woman. Ahmed was enchanted; he had not expected this.

It was evident that his little brother shared his assessment of this beautiful woman. She did nothing to tantalise them—she was far too elegant, yet her mere presence in the room had the same effect. Both of them had seen attractive and seductive females before, mostly at a distance; this exceeded them all—a stunning beauty, so captivating that, surely, she must be an apparition.

Ahmed strove to regain his composure. She had been sent by Mustapha. He must remember his manners—and be gracious.

"Tea," he said quickly to his little brother, with a snap of his fingers.

As the boy shuffled off to make it, Ahmed saw that the boy too could hardly remove his eyes from her—almost stumbling into the small closet space which served as their kitchen. Ahmed lifted a chair from the table and placed it behind her with a respectful bow of his head. "Sit... please," he invited.

He was conscious that he had stuck his automatic in his belt. Embarrassed, and with exaggerated care, he placed the weapon aside.

They drank their tea mostly in silence, in an atmosphere of mild awkwardness during which Daniela, without communicating anything in words, provided Ahmed with a dignified interlude to regain his composure.

During this time, she was aware that the wide-eyed boy— he couldn't be much more than in his late teens, she thought— was unable to take his eyes off her. He had a strong attractive face, set against long eyelashes and deep brown eyes, while

317

his long hair was swept back—like that, she fancied, of a young Assyrian warrior. He looked directly at her, without any apology, clearly mesmerised by her allure, yet confident of his own looks and almost provocative in his bearing.

Had Daniela's purpose here been to evaluate the boy as a courier, as Ahmed believed, he would have been perfect in the role. A less-likely looking criminal would be hard to find. But that was not her intent here tonight. For her requirements, she needed an accomplice—someone who could drive, and handle a gun. He was ideal.

"Mustapha sent you," said Ahmed, with a diplomatic smile. "This is my little brother," he added, as if she was walking into the room for the first time.

Another round of nods and smiles ensued, during which Daniela decided that Ahmed was being far too polite and that she had to direct their conversation.

"Mustapha has considered your proposal—and he wishes for your brother to be our new courier," she announced. She glanced over at the young boy. "We believe your choice is a good one."

Ahmed was delighted, but he frowned slightly when she added, "However, we have an urgent mission which will require him to travel with me for a short time.

"You must understand that you, Ahmed, would be our first choice, but the police have your photograph; travel will be too dangerous for you."

She stood up. "I regret that we do not have much time. He must come with me now."

Ahmed's eyes darted between Daniela and his younger brother. Finally, he nodded. "Yes, I understand. It is good."

Ten minutes later, Ahmed's younger brother sat in the passenger seat of the car that Daniela had rented for the journey. As they drove onto the autovia he sat quietly, his body at an angle so that he could watch her.

"We have an important mission; you must do as I say," she said after a time.

He nodded. "What do you wish me to do?"

She looked over at him, and took the next exit into a garage. She did not need fuel and parked the vehicle in the shadows at the back of the building, away from any CCTV cameras. "Wait here," she said, and returned a few minutes later with some drinks and snacks.

"Good idea," he said, reaching for a soda.

"Leave them," she said, snatching it out of his hands. "I have a better idea."

She kept his hand in hers, and pulled him towards her. As she stroked his hair, she felt his body stiffen and he moved closer. Lifting up her sweater, she put his hand on her breast and kissed him. It was a rough kiss of pent-up desire, forcing her tongue into his mouth. He gasped, and pulled her closer to him.

"Not here. In the back," she whispered in his ear, twisting her tongue and biting, which only served to inflame him more.

It was a cool night, and the car windows soon steamed up.

Awakened by the rhythmic movement of the car in the shadows across from the truck stop, a long-haul driver was treated to a very enjoyable display of the girl's bare backside moving rapidly up and down. After ten minutes, he was in full admiration of the prowess of her partner. This was certainly something to tell his trucking friends, he resolved—when he reached his destination in the morning.

****

Daniela drove the car through the deserted village, and stopped at a junction she recalled from the online map. From here, she remembered, the farm would be about another kilometre, slightly uphill to the west. A few minutes later, pulling off the road, she recognised the shapes of the farm buildings. She reversed and parked the car several metres up a gravel track.

Walking several more metres, she breathed a sigh of relief when she saw the lights in one of the rooms of the farmhouse. With luck, it might be the chauffeur, she thought. Without luck, it might be someone else—perhaps a caretaker. She doubted it; the chauffeur would not want to take the risk of revealing the new location of Aladdin's Cave to anyone else. A dog might be another proposition, she fretted.

She would need to reduce the odds against herself and the boy. A diversion was needed, she decided. Of course, there was always a chance that she was wrong about the location, but she had a plan to determine if she was right or not.

Flicking open the trunk of the rental car, she extracted from a sports bag two automatics and two pairs of night vision goggles borrowed from central stores at the Mossos' headquarters. One of these, she gave to the boy and showed him how to adjust it. The other, she put on herself. She gave him an automatic, showing him the safety release. He nodded, indicating he did not need the instruction. She pushed her gun into her waistband and winced as the cold metal dug into her trim waist.

Indicating to the boy not to talk, they climbed the track to the house, stopping short by fifty metres. Crouching down, she took out a dog whistle and blew it hard several times. No sound that humans can hear was made, but the high pitch note audible to dogs had an immediate impact.

Inside the farmhouse, a dog began to bark wildly. Immediately, the lights inside were extinguished and the front door of the building opened. Looking through her night goggles, Daniela could see the chauffeur's profile clearly. She was correct: she had the right place. Now she needed to know if the chauffeur was by himself. The night goggles would pick out anyone. Soon, the dog settled down and the chauffeur went back inside. It seemed he was alone. The lights went back on.

She motioned to the boy to follow her back down the gravel track. Speaking rapidly in Arabic, she described her plan to him; he grinned and nodded enthusiastically. This time, they split up. Taking care not to arouse the dog, she moved to the back of the farmhouse from where she could see the back door. The boy was already positioned at the front.

Putting on her night goggles, she followed the same process with the dog whistle. Again, the lights were dimmed, then extinguished. Alerted this time, the chauffeur emerged from the back of the farmhouse with his gun; he left the dog inside, still barking.

The night goggles gave Daniela an unfair advantage. Able to see him perfectly, she came up behind the chauffeur and stuck her automatic into his lower back. Minutes later, she and the boy had tied up the chauffeur and locked the dog in a back room. They would be secure there until the police found them, she figured.

The stonemason's fully-loaded truck was parked in a locked out-building—with the keys still in the ignition. She left a single gold bar at the chauffeur's feet—knowing he would have to explain it to the police.

Two hours later, followed by the rental car driven by the boy, Daniela had locked the door of the garage of her late aunt's house. Until she decided to move it, the truck would be safe inside. She had no good memories of this place, and her aunt had not bequeathed it to her. The woman had died suddenly from a stroke, without leaving a will. As her only relative, the local magistrate had signed over the deed to Daniela on the day she became twenty-one. For once, the place had been useful.

On the short journey back into Barcelona, Daniela handed several thick bundles of used euros to the boy.

"Tell Ahmed that we will have further need for his and your services, but not yet. You should both return home, and use the money to stay safe. Mustapha will be pleased. May Allah be with you."

She kissed him, as he got out of the car near his apartment. He gazed at her, wondering if she would allow him to remain with her. But she waved and drove away... leaving him alone, standing in the dark.

Tonight, she would drop off the rental car. Later, she would return the borrowed equipment. The Mossos' firearms release forms would note that no ammunition had been used: just a routine night patrol, the sergeant-at-arms would record in his inventory report.

Before showering and returning to work, she would make an anonymous call on a street phone and urge the local police to make a visit to the farm.

She doubted the chauffeur would be very talkative.

Madrid: Newspaper Accuses the Spanish Government

"Damn," exclaimed the aide to the prime minister. It was 5:00 a.m. The call he had just received got him out of bed in a less than a second. He went online and found the newspaper headline. The story took up the whole of the front page, along with several photographs.

Quickly, he dialled the PM's unlisted cell phone. The man was tired, having gone to bed at two o'clock after returning from a European Monetary Fund emergency meeting on Greece and a euro-loan. He was grumpy, but by the end of the day he would have a lot more to be furious about.

The aide read it to him: "**Spanish Government Implicated in Barcelona Bomb Attempt.**"

Swiftly, he recapped the newspaper's story. There was a picture of several well-known politicians, along with separate photos of Carlos and the condesa. The story said that they had been taken at the Count's lodge. Most serious of all was a photograph of a former minority party leader standing in front of the 20-N fascist flag. He was surrounded by several well-known former bankers and business leaders.

The aide checked his laptop again. None of the other papers carried the story. Clearly, it was an exclusive. He recognised with dismay the writer's name. Francisco Rioja was no friend of the government. Worse still, the man was well known as a maverick, investigative journalist—an asshole and a left-winger, but a good writer who checked his facts. He was not popular, but over many years, he had earned the begrudging respect of his peer group.

But Rioja had been found murdered in his apartment, the aide told the prime minister.

The newspaper's editorial also covered the story, and promised a follow-up with even more lurid details the next day, he told his boss. The editor accused the Spanish government of complicity in the thwarted bombing attempt on the Mossos' headquarters in Barcelona.

According to the editor, evidence that the government's minister of infrastructure, the condesa de la Santa Maria, was involved drove yet another nail in the coffin of a bankrupt and corrupt government. It called for the immediate resignation of the prime minister and demanded an independent judicial enquiry into the national government's involvement in the mercifully foiled bombing attempt.

"You had better get over here right away," ordered the PM angrily, and cut the connection.

The aide's phone rang again. He recognised the number as one of the prime minister's staff. Answering it, he said abruptly, wanting to cut off the caller's first sentence, "Yes, I know about it. We need a complete lockdown on any government comments about the story until he orders us to do otherwise. Look after it, and don't screw it up—you understand? Call me when you've done it, to confirm."

Next, he called a news station that he could trust.

"Holy saints, Roberto," said the station chief when he answered the call. "You didn't tell me this crap was going to hit the fan. Is Rioja's story true?"

"Jose-Luis, as soon as I have something, I will call you—first on the list, I promise. But right now, you need to help me. I need to know how far this story got out."

"Got out? You must be joking, my friend," answered the station chief. "That newspaper had an exclusive. They've syndicated it in advance to every major left-wing media outlet in Europe. Reuters and Associated Press had it two hours ago.

"I hear that CNN and NBC have it on the early-afternoon news in the States. This isn't a pussycat. It's an angry tiger, and it's already well out of the bag.

Chapter 12

Maria Decides

Maria sat with her back to her desk, staring out of the office window. She would give the draft letter one more reading, then express-courier it to the senior partners of Torres Sanchez in Madrid.

Get it done, and get on with your life, she told herself. She had made up her mind—almost.

Why was she hesitating?

Her conversation with Toni the night before had decided things for her. She knew that she was committed, and so was he. Yet...

Concentrating on the letter, she had ignored the message alerts on her phone. She swung her chair around to face her desk, and glanced at the accumulation. The most recent one was from Pilar, asking if she had time for lunch today.

Maria already had a lunch commitment with a business colleague. But she badly wanted another woman's point of view. Scrolling through her messages, she replied to her colleague's lunchtime confirmation request, pleading an urgent matter and asking to reschedule.

Pilar was not showing yet, but her body movements already were more careful and laboured. She seemed to overcompensate for the as-yet very small extra burden she was carrying, thought Maria, as she approached the table.

"How's baby?" she asked, as Pilar sat down.

They chatted for a time and ordered lunch. Conversation soon swung around to Madrid.

"What have you decided?" asked Pilar quietly, leaning across the table.

"Antonio and I had a long talk last night," Maria began.

"And?" asked Pilar excitedly.

"I'm not going."

Pilar's face lit up with an expression of happiness that was wonderful to witness. She grabbed both of Maria's hands across the table and squeezed them, nearly knocking over a glass of water in the process.

Soon their meal arrived.

"I know Toni's been acting out of character for a time," said Pilar in between mouthfuls.

"How do you mean?" asked Maria, immediately seeing a look of alarm flash across her friend's face.

"Well, it's just that you've told me he hasn't been himself," Pilar answered. She sounded defensive.

There was something in the way her friend made the comment which caught Maria's attention.

Perhaps she was being too much of an attorney, used to questioning witnesses to unearth subtle nuances and half-truths, she cautioned herself. Yet, she felt there was something in Pilar's voice.

"Has Xavi said anything?" she probed, keeping up her close examination of Pilar's facial expressions. "I know he's very loyal to Toni. I'm just wondering if he has said anything to him—you know, about us?"

Pilar's face seemed to relax with a palpable sense of relief. Maria did not miss the significance and she resolved to pursue it.

"Xavi said that Toni has been very worried about *why* you wanted to take the Madrid job. He said that Toni can't understand why you'd be interested in it," said Pilar.

"You know why," Maria responded, with a slight irritation in her voice. They had talked it over several times.

Pilar reached across the table and put her hand on Maria's. "You know men," she said laughing. "They miss the obvious; they imagine all kinds of things."

"What did Xavi say that Toni was imagining?" she asked a little bit too quickly, immediately regretting her tone. It sounded like she was interrogating a witness in the courtroom.

Now it was her turn to squeeze her friend's hand. "I'm sorry, Pilar," she added much more softly, "it's just that sometimes it's hard for me to know where I stand with Toni. You know that."

"Toni's the same way, I think," said Pilar. "But you said that you worked it out between you last night?"

Maria scrunched up her mouth. "Last night it seemed that we did. This morning I wasn't so sure."

"Has he asked you...?"

Maria shook her head vigorously. "You'd be the first to know if he had. Has Xavi said anything else?"

She hated this subterfuge. Why was she searching so hard, asking her friends for scraps of information—clues as to how Antonio felt about her? She resented how it made her feel like a reject.

She couldn't help herself; there had been something that showed on Pilar's face. Perhaps it was something in her eyes. Maria was trained to pick up such signals. It was part of why she was so effective in her profession.

"They're very busy on the case they're working on," said Pilar. "You and I both know what a strain that can create. Does Toni talk to you about it very much?"

Her friend's words unsettled Maria. It seemed to her that Pilar knew something and was unwilling to tell her about it. She recognised diversionary tactics when she heard them. Pilar's obfuscation disappointed her.

She felt that her friend was letting her down; she had thought they were much closer.

Pilar was incapable of telling a deliberate lie, she was certain of that. Perhaps she shouldn't take offence. After all, if there was anything really serious going on, her friend would say something.

Maria was familiar with the Catalan culture. They were wonderful people, and great fun, but they could be very clannish. Sometimes Toni and Xavi would lapse into a conversation in Catalan—mostly because the language expressed better than Spanish something they wanted to say.

Pilar and Xavi were the same, and spoke Catalan at home. Maria could pick up most of the meanings and some of the Catalan nuances. Being from Cordoba, her knowledge of their language was imperfect. They didn't intend it, yet sometimes she felt she was an outsider.

She tried a different tactic. "Do you think there is another woman involved?" she asked.

The rapid dilation of Pilar's pupils confirmed the worst.

"Who is she?" asked Maria quickly, anxious to press the element of surprise.

Her friend swallowed, and took her hand. "I don't think there is anyone. Xavi wouldn't tell me much, but I do know that Toni is not having an affair. If he was, I would tell you. You know that."

Maria believed her friend, but she was determined to find out every detail.

"Somehow, Toni found out that Sergio had been in Barcelona. Someone from the squad saw you two having coffee together. When you didn't mention it to Toni, he assumed the worst."

"He thinks I'm planning to take the job in Madrid—to go back to my ex?" said Maria with a loud gasp of exasperation. "How can he be so stupid? Does he feel threatened by my career?" she protested, already knowing the answer. It was something she had worried about since they'd first met. It was crazy really, she reflected, because she and Toni had already

328

worked through that conversation: he had said he fully supported her.

She noticed that Pilar was biting the corner of her lower lip, uncertain what to say next.

"It's Sergio he's still worried about, isn't it?" Maria said. Months ago, they'd had that conversation; obviously, it was still an issue for him. She shrugged her shoulders. It was something he would have to get over.

"Where does the other woman come in?" she asked Pilar brusquely, no longer caring how she sounded.

Pilar put her hand back over Maria's. "I can only tell you what Xavi has told me. There really is no one else but you. But when Toni thought you were going back to Madrid—and to Sergio—he figured your relationship must be over."

"So you don't think—Xavi doesn't think—that there is another woman?"

Pilar shook her head and looking pleadingly into Maria's eyes. "If there was, and if Xavi told me about it, I would tell you. You are my best friend."

"Toni is always surrounded by women," said Maria in a tone of resignation. She didn't feel reassured about what Pilar had told her. It would take some more thinking. She was glad now that she hadn't signed and sent the letter already.

"You're so lucky to have Xavi," she smiled at Pilar. "It's absolute hell being on the market."

Both women laughed, but for very different reasons.

"Maybe you should propose to him..." suggested Pilar with a conspiratorial wink, which Maria had never seen her do before. Her friend had a darker side after all.

She managed a weak smile.

Daniela's Workout

Adrenaline rushes of the past twenty-four hours had left her tense and anxious. She had turned in the guns and equipment at 6:00 a.m., as the night shift for the city's Mossos squaddies was ending. It was normal and routine. Now she headed for the gym.

Daniela smiled pleasantly in response to the usual jocks, ignoring the attentions of one who recently had become a little too persistent. Positioning herself out of his way, between two older women already sweating heavily on the treadmills, she inserted her ear buds as a 'do not disturb' caution to other possible suitors.

She needed to think.

Raphael seemed determined to try to make the General's plan work. She had pleaded with him, but could not shake his resolve. He's too invested in it, too committed to what he had helped create, she concluded. His words to her as a young girl rang in her ears. "Daniela, we are all foot soldiers; the jihad is what matters."

She didn't believe in jingoisms; she doubted she had ever fully believed in popular causes. They struck her as being simplistic—far too naive. Underneath them always lay evil, and further layers of suffering. She had a better way—other plans.

Antonio need not know about the money—about Aladdin's Cave. He was too much of a conventional policeman, too entrenched in Catalan society, to be able to see beyond what it was—a step on the way to an important end. But he was a good man, certainly clever and—yes, quite honestly—attractive.

Just a few things stood in the way.

Adjusting the pace on her treadmill, she sprinted hard for several minutes finally breaking out into a heavy sweat.

Coasting, she continued to think through her plans, refusing to think back, to inquest her actions, shunning all thought of becoming defensive and paranoid about her personal safety. Her mind could process the risks quite adequately, she reminded herself. She wasn't foolhardy. There was no need to panic and keep looking over her shoulder.

After taking a long cold shower, she felt fully refreshed and went to work.

****

"Do you understand women, boss?"

Daniela posed the question as she and Antonio drove back to the office.

Antonio smiled. "Not well, but better than most men I think." He seemed surprised by her question. "Why do you ask?"

"It's none of my business, but you seem a bit preoccupied these days. I wondered if it was anything to do with... well, something at home."

"Not really." His response was a little brusque.

"A lot of men don't understand women—at all," she continued, undeterred. "They get a lot of wrong things right, and the right things badly wrong. I'm speaking in the abstract, of course. You're probably different, boss."

"Well, I suppose it depends on what you mean by the right things and the wrong things, what they are. I'm just saying," Antonio replied.

"Women know," said Daniela, with finality in her voice. "We're caregivers. We like to look after our man."

"And, as men, we are the providers," smiled Antonio, sounding benevolent. "It's a man's world, after all. Maybe it shouldn't be, but it is."

"Do you think you could accept the woman being the provider, boss?" she asked, swerving the car slightly to avoid a moto coming in from a side street.

"It's never really come up—as an option, I mean," said Antonio. "I don't know. Family comes into it, I suppose," he added, thinking of recent conversations with his dad about Maria. "You know—the lifestyle you can afford, as a couple."

Daniela wanted to tell him that she thought families were very much overrated. Surely it was the relationship with your partner that matters she wanted to argue, but said nothing.

"Let's say that if the two of you had all the money in the world—all you could possibly need—don't you think it would be alright for the woman to be the providing partner in the relationship?"

"I don't think that's the kind of relationship Maria and I have," said Antonio, missing the wince of pain that shot across Daniela's face.

For a time, there was no further conversation.

"Do you miss David?" he asked eventually. "I hope you don't mind my asking."

She shrugged. "It was a tragedy what happened to him. It really was. He was a nice person. I'm not sure, though, that we would have lasted together."

"I'm sorry to hear that. You've been through a lot in the past few months, Daniela. More than most people in a lifetime."

He glanced over at her. "Do you think…" his voice trailed off.

"Do I think it would work out between the two of us, are you asking?" she completed the question for him. "Well, certainly not with Maria around, that's for certain," she added. "Men are cowards in relationships; women are much more sure of what they want.

"You know, boss, women want to know that their man wants them. That's why a lot of women like aggressive men—

332

men who take what they want. They'll put up with a lot of shit to get that."

'Nice guys finish last, you mean?" said Antonio, losing interest and taking out his phone.

"Exactly," said Daniela, angrily shifting lanes and causing the cars behind to blast their horns.

The Crisis Abates

"I think we've contained it, don't you," said the Prime Minister. It wasn't a question, and he was not inviting answers.

"We won't know the lasting impacts until the next opinion polls results," said the aide, "but it looks hopeful."

"Well done, prime minister," chimed in a well-known toady. The PM ignored him.

"How many of those people have they arrested so far?"

The aide wanted to have some private time with the PM, but it was difficult to pull him away during these caucus meetings. "The police want to talk to you about that, sir," he pronounced the words carefully and, with a movement of his eyebrows, signalled to the PM that further conversation on the topic might not be wise.

"We have to remember we have other things to talk about, other business to conduct," said the PM, catching his meaning and turning to address his inner circle. "I'm going to hand over this meeting to the Deputy, and ask you all to treat this whole episode with dignity and sensitivity.

"For those of you who don't understand what that is, it means that I'm imposing a gag order on each of you, telling you not to talk to the press, to the media. I won't tolerate any speculation. The police are perfectly capable of dealing with this criminal element, this terrorist threat to our constitution.

"Does anyone in this room have a problem with that?" he asked.

"Good," he said, as silence prevailed. He left the room, his aide following closely behind.

Dinner with Daniela

"The food was superb," he said, pushing his plate away, sitting back from the dinner table and stretching his legs. "You're a good chef, Daniela."

"Thank you," she acknowledged, smiling. Hers, too, was a polite statement—not what she really wanted to say to him, or what she wanted them to talk about.

A real talk, so she could find out how he truly felt: about her, about them, about their future.

The two of them together: a couple that now could do anything—thanks to her.

She had been unsure about inviting him to dinner, but it had seemed the only way.

Daniela knew he liked her and wanted her. That much was obvious. From the first day they'd met, at the army camp in Istanbul; from the first time they had looked at each other, she had known he was special.

She had watched him carefully. All the signs were right. It was ridiculously simple really. She wanted to say to him: "*Just give up your life and come with me.*"

How difficult was that to understand?

"You never did tell me how you got to Syria," he said, studying the rim of his wine glass.

For a moment, he saw in her eyes the look he'd seen in Turkey, when she recalled her time in the war zones of Syria and Iraq. It was a haunting ghostly look, as if she was passing out of one world into another... entering a place of alien beings; a land of inhuman unspeakable things: violence so

334

terrible and indiscriminate that mankind had abandoned all hope.

"I could," she said, barely whispering, "if that's the most important thing for you to know."

In truth, it was not. He was jealous of Jamal. In the days and weeks after meeting her, Antonio's emotions had been in turmoil; he couldn't stop thinking about her.

"You don't believe me, do you?" she asked, deliberately wanting to provoke him.

Antonio moved closer to the table, and to her. Their eyes met, perhaps in the first honest moment of the evening. "I believe you, Daniela—of course, I do."

"Then what's stopping you, Toni?" Her eyes becoming moist.

He reached forward and took her hands in his, their eyes still locked in a mutual desire for honesty. "I think it's that I don't understand you."

"Could you love me?" she asked, in the voice of a young girl.

It felt to Antonio as though someone had felled him in a single blow—a punch delivered to the pit of his stomach—robbing his body of all breath, leaving only a frantic need to gasp for air, just to survive.

She sounded so vulnerable, so fresh and innocent. The laugh that escaped with his tears was gentle and pleading, a capitulation tinged with angst and desperation.

"Oh God, Daniela—if you only knew."

"You have to tell me, Toni," she said, wiping away a large tear that was running down his face.

He tried to fight away his emotions, failing in the attempt.

Daniela sighed. She was tired of being the one who always took the initiative. She wanted him to be strong, demonstrative and assertive.

"You asked about Syria, but instead I will tell you about Jamal," she said, playing with her blue sapphire necklace. He

335

had noticed it when he'd arrived for dinner and had complimented her on it.

"He gave me this," she said. "He was one of the most compelling men I have ever met. He had a presence that belongs only to a god.

"You couldn't say it was just his laughing eyes, although when he stared at you, it seemed to be with appraisal and an amused detachment. You couldn't say it was his bearing, despite a physical presence that makes most other men step aside. You could not say it was his voice, even though his deep earthy tone sounded like music—at least to me."

"Yes, I understand very well that you liked him," said Antonio, fascinated, but unwilling to tolerate, without some protest, more stories about her lover.

He saw the flash of respect that crossed Daniela's face.

"Toni, I have not told this to anyone," she began, with a shift in tone, "but part of my field assignment for al-Qaeda was to complete the hawala transaction. The money from Spain was for such a large amount that the hawala document had to be transmitted separately to Damascus. It was my job to carry the code word to Jamal—to complete the transaction."

"And to obtain the document that confirmed he had received it," Antonio added. "I am familiar with the system, Daniela."

His emotions of a few minutes ago had gone, now replaced by his policeman's instincts.

"Is there any other information you have not mentioned?" asked Antonio.

"Nothing important," she answered, biting her lip.

"You know, I should go," he said looking at his watch.

"I don't want you to go."

She had disappeared into the bedroom and came out a moment later.

"How about one more glass of wine?" she asked, looking into the fridge. "No more white. Is red okay?" She pulled the cork out of a half-opened bottle sitting on a side table.

"Alright, just a quick one." Antonio looked again at his watch.

A few minutes later, he started to feel much better; his energy level perked up and Daniela also seemed to have a new lease on life. She laughed at almost everything he said, and applauded his stories. He was feeling a lot less inhibited.

Who cares what happened with Jamal in Syria, he reasoned. Daniela was a beautiful woman; the guarded emotions he felt towards her were meaningless.

As they stumbled towards the bed, she fell over trying to throw off her clothes. They sat on the floor, laughing at nothing in particular. Life was good. He leaned over and kissed her. It was impulsive and unrehearsed, but it triggered an explosive response in Daniela. She began to groan like an animal, her pleasure manifesting itself in her complete abandonment to his demanding lips.

It was a shared passion that had its origins in the interview room at the military base in Istanbul. Lustful urges that both of them had suppressed over many weeks since they'd first met. Emotions laid bare by the raw sensuality of the moment, the pure freedom of one body locked in almost perfect harmony with the other.

They entered worlds of vivid colours and fleshy, hedonistic, carnal gratifications. A pulsating universe of glorious galaxies and sudden falls, plummeting into deep black holes of seemingly endless emptiness, only for their senses to snatch them away and carry them up and outwards to a bright, brilliant white light. A starburst, followed by another, and yet another—each more profound than the last.

Antonio's mind was racing far ahead of his suddenly unresponsive body. His frame began a cold sweat. Shivering and nausea followed. Neither of them recognised the signs.

"It's Maria, isn't it," stated Daniela, slumping onto her back.

Antonio forced himself to speak; his body was shaking. He could not overcome the sensation of wanting to grind his teeth.

"Oh God, you look awful," she cried in alarm. She kneeled alongside his now convulsing body. "Toni!" she screamed.

She ran naked to the kitchen to find her phone. "Xavi, it's Toni," she yelled when he answered.

"He's at my place. He's passing out. I need help."

Daniela Meets Isabel

Xavi and Isabel arrived at almost the same time. Isabel kneeled down and leaned over her brother, his body lying flat on the floor. "'Hi, sis," he managed to say, his eyes bloodshot and watery.

She put her nose close to his mouth, immediately recognising the distinct smell. She looked up in anger at Daniela. "What did you give him," she demanded.

Daniela opened her bedside drawer and handed a small bottle to her. "It was only a tiny amount," she began to say. "It's mostly the wine that's doing it…"

Isabel shook her head in disbelief. "Didn't he tell you he has allergies?" she glared at the girl.

Daniela's face told Isabel what she didn't want to admit.

"He didn't know you were giving it to him, did he?" interrupted Xavi, almost spitting out the vehemence he felt towards the girl. "You just slipped it to him."

Xavi looked closely at Antonio, and felt his pulse for the third time. "He's okay, but he's going to have a hell of a hangover after this."

"I'm taking him to my place," said Isabel, trying to put the clothes back on her brother. "We'll have to keep a close eye on him."

Daniela looked flustered.

"That was a stupid thing to do, Daniela," said Xavi shaking his head. "I don't know what Toni will want to do about it; he can decide. But you mustn't say a word of this to anyone, understood?"

Daniela, holding a folded sheet around her body, nodded. Her contrite look did nothing to appease the others.

"Get him a glass of water," Isabel ordered.

While Daniela's back was turned, Isabel took several metal objects out of her pocket and displayed them to Xavi. He looked at them without saying a word and nodded. Their communication lasted only for a few seconds, and was over by the time Daniela returned.

She lifted the water to Antonio's lips; he gulped it greedily.

"Where's his jacket?" demanded Isabel, walking towards the closet. Daniela pointed to it with a movement of her head.

"I'll help you downstairs with him," called Daniela, as Isabel reached under the kitchen table to pick up Antonio's shoes.

"Don't bother," said Isabel irritably. "You've done enough damage already."

Antonio, his shoes now back on, was being helped to his feet by Xavi. He grinned at his partner. "Amigo, what are you doing here?" he giggled and lurched towards the door.

"I need to use the washroom," said Isabel.

As she came out, Daniela was standing there. "I'm really sorry…"

Isabel began to move past her, their bodies touching in the confines of the narrow corridor. Daniela put her arm on Isabel's shoulder. "I know I shouldn't have…" she started to say.

339

For several seconds the two women looked at each other, Daniela's wide eyes pleading with Isabel.

Isabel put out her hand and gently caressed the nipple that was erect and inviting.

Then with a violence that had no warning, she slammed Daniela's body back against the wall in a movement that caused the girl's head to whiplash. Her mouth opened in astonishment and her eyes blazed.

"Bitch." Isabel almost spat the word into the girl's face. Then she turned and walked away.

Minutes later, as they travelled in the elevator down to the street, Isabel asked, "Is he ok?"

"He'll be fine," said Xavi. He gave her a reassuring smile.

"Did you plant them?" he asked.

'Yes," said Isabel. "I put those listening devices in places that she will never think of."

She leaned forward and kissed her brother, running her hand gently over his flushed face.

"I hope he fires the bitch."

Where is Maria?

Xavi looked down at his coffee cup, unable to find any words.

Antonio's mood matched that of his partner. He swirled the remaining liquid around his cup and put it down without drinking. The day had turned grey, and low clouds were scudding across the Barcelona skies. It felt like winter.

"When's she leaving?" asked Xavi eventually.

"I don't know," said Antonio, pretending it was a speck of dust that he was wiping away from his eyes. "She won't return my calls."

Xavi was silent for a moment. "Is she still in town?" he asked.

Antonio shrugged his shoulders again. "She'd packed her bags and was gone by the time I got home. I've called everyone, but no one knows anything."

"Or she's told them not to say anything to you—about where she is," said Xavi, no longer caring if he hurt his friend's feelings. Toni needed a good dose of reality, and now it seemed too late for that.

"I can't figure out where she's gone," said Antonio, his voice flat and unhappy.

"We're the Mossos, for goodness sake," said Xavi a little too loudly. "With our resources, if we can't find her—who can?"

"Where does Pilar think she might be?" asked Antonio, repeating an earlier question.

Xavi shook his head and said nothing. "If she's really going to Peru, we could check with the airlines," he suggested. "Or we could locate her from her cell phone," he added.

"I don't think she wants me to contact her."

"Toni, are you dense or something?" came the explosive reply from Xavi.

His partner looked up in surprise. "Ok," he said slowly. "I'm not that stupid. But she's making it very difficult for me to find her."

"Possibly, amigo, that's exactly her point. You need some help here," he added. "Toni, for someone who otherwise is so intelligent, sometimes you're as dumb as a mule."

Xavi scrolled over his phone screen and keyed in a number. He spoke for a few minutes, giving instructions.

Within five minutes his phone rang. He listened, nodding as the caller spoke.

He reached over to Antonio and took hold of his partner's phone. He keyed in some data and handed it back.

"Maria is staying with a girlfriend. William was able to track down the address. Here it is. She hasn't left for Peru yet, but you only have two days."

"I've been stupid, haven't I?" said Antonio after a pause.

It wasn't a question, and Xavi didn't need to answer it.

"I'll take a taxi and go over to see her right away."

"Not to put too much pressure on you, amigo, but remember that we have work to do." He glanced at his watch. "We have to get going." He glanced at the bill, leaving some notes on the metal dish.

"Can you give me a few minutes?" asked Antonio, starting to text Maria.

He made several false starts before he seemed satisfied with the message he sent.

The Flower Shop

"We have to pick up Daniela before we go to the academy," Xavi reminded him. He was relieved to see that Antonio showed almost no response to the mention of Daniela's name. Thank goodness for that, he thought, as he parked their squad car at the kerb outside the Mossos' headquarters.

Daniela seemed to be in a good mood, and chatted excitedly as they headed towards Sabadell.

As they drove along Carrer de Valencia, Xavi pulled the squad car to a stop alongside a flower store. "Ok, amigo," he said, "if I have to lead you by the nose, I will. Come with me."

He strode inside the flower store, followed by a puzzled-looking Antonio.

"Ok if I come?" asked Daniela, walking alongside Xavi.

"Sure, you can help choose," he said without enthusiasm.

"What's the occasion?" she asked.

"Antonio's going to buy some flowers for his girlfriend," said Xavi. "Aren't you, amigo?"

The two men walked hesitatingly along the numerous racks of flowers and plants. With the help of one of the assistants, Antonio chose a large bouquet of red roses.

"Boss," said Daniela, "if these are for your girlfriend, you need to get real." She removed the modest bouquet from his hands and walked back along the displays, selecting additional flowers along the way.

"Here," she said to Xavi, "hold these." She thrust the already huge and still increasing bouquet into his arms.

"What's her favourite flower, boss?" she asked Antonio, who shrugged. As a centrepiece, Daniela selected five of the most beautiful and expensive blooms in the store. The assistant's face creased up in amusement. The resulting bouquet was huge—and sensational.

"We need to have these gift-wrapped and delivered as soon as possible," said Xavi. "Delivery today, please."

"Time to pay for them, amigo," he said to Antonio, whose face had lost some of its despondent look.

Antonio pulled out his wallet and paid. Gazing at the huge bouquet, he managed to crack a smile for his colleagues. "Thanks for your help."

Antonio gave the delivery address to the assistant.

"She'll get these by tonight," said Xavi. "The rest is up to you, my friend," he told Antonio.

Returning to their vehicle parked on the road outside, Daniela stopped. "Sorry, boss, I need to go to the ladies room. Do we have time?"

Antonio nodded. "Thanks, Xavi," he said, as they settled inside the car and waited for Daniela. "I should have thought about flowers for Maria." He offered Xavi a high five. "I appreciate the heads-up, amigo."

While they were talking, Daniela had gone back to the counter and was speaking to the assistant who was still trimming the stalks and wrapping the huge bouquet."

"Could I check that address?" she asked.

"There," said Daniela. "We thought we had made a mistake. But I've corrected it now," she said, penning in a random street address and a different district, erasing all trace of the original.

"It would be terrible if we didn't deliver them to the right person, wouldn't it?" she laughed, as the assistant nodded and thanked her profusely.

Events Start to Make Sense

Raphael Robles had taken a few days leave—something to do with a family crisis, his secretary said.

I could have done with his help; it had been one hell of a day.

Not just that, but I had wanted to talk to him. I had a few questions for him that had been rolling around in my mind, and which needed answers. Some of the things that had been going on just didn't add up. I figured that would have to wait until he got back.

Since early this morning, we had been getting a lot of flak—from everywhere—about the Rioja photographs. We'd heard that the public prosecutor had interviewed the editor and writers at the newspaper that broke the story. The Editor told him that Rioja had been killed before he could give them the full story, but he had emailed them a few of his photographs in advance.

Apparently, he wouldn't divulge any more details or photos until they had struck a deal for financial compensation. He was looking for a lot of money, they said.

After he was found murdered, they decided to run with the story anyway. Problem was, said the editor, they didn't have much copy to go with the story, so they had to guess at it. They'd probably invented a lot of what showed up in the newspaper. They always do.

I knew better than to say anything. Let the newspaper run with all that sensational stuff, I thought. They don't have any credibility, those people. They were lucky that the public prosecutor didn't charge them for withholding evidence.

Anyway, some of our boys took another look at Rioja's apartment. In his mailbox was an envelope he'd mailed to himself. Somehow, the sneaky man had made himself a duplicate disk of the photos we'd confiscated from him on the night we'd interviewed him and the condesa. Some people have criminal minds.

The Prime Minister's office was all over us for not having figured that one out. Still, the government didn't seem to be coming out of it all that badly, judging from the media reports I saw.

I was more worried about real things.

We were just winding down on the Rioja debacle, when we had a report from our people in Lleida: they had found and arrested the chauffeur. It had been an anonymous tip.

I called immediately to tell them to keep the man under lock and key until we could interrogate him. There would be nothing worse than having some junior officer releasing him through apparent lack of evidence.

"You checked all the farm buildings?" I asked, already knowing the answer. The money was long gone.

Our armoured convoy bringing the chauffeur to Madrid was scheduled to arrive in about an hour, I noted, checking my watch. I want to nail that bastard.

I was thinking my exercise routine for the day was a lost cause. I hadn't even had a bottle of water yet today, and the coffee from the machines in this place is undrinkable. Maybe I could head down to the canteen and pick up a late breakfast, I thought.

No chance. Minutes later, I received a text from one of my colleagues that Carlos, the condesa's husband, had read the newspaper story and suffered a stroke. Did I want to come over to the hospital, my colleague asked, in case he regained consciousness and could be interviewed. About an hour later, I heard Carlos had died.

Let's face it: when things go wrong, they all go wrong—at the same time.

I really could have used Robles' help.

Then I got a break. We had a lot of people under surveillance, and then we received a big surprise. We obtained a major new lead that we were not anticipating. It really changed things; all of a sudden, a lot of things started to click into place.

I delegated another officer to look after the new intel we were receiving. My focus that afternoon had to be on interrogating the chauffeur. We knew that, if we could get the information we wanted out of him, we could nail the General and his gang. That was our top priority.

This isn't the place to get into details about the pretreatment we put him through, but he was a tough person to crack—a product of his military training, I suppose.

He was so loyal to the General, you almost had to admire his resistance during the interrogations. I'm not sure we got a lot out of him on that score—certainly not the full story. The only information he seemed willing to give us was about the girl, as he called her. If it hadn't been for the break we had received a few hours earlier from the surveillance team, I wouldn't have figured right away who he was talking about.

Daniela was not the lily-white super-heroine we had all been fooled into believing.

She had stolen the money. I was determined to get it back, but that could wait for now. The intelligence feed we were now getting had put us directly on the trail of Mustapha. Based on the new information we were harvesting, the border patrol picked up Ahmed. He was in possession of a considerable sum in clean, used euros. The girl's name was revealed when the border guards interrogated him. We weren't able to trace his younger brother.

I wanted to apprehend Daniela and pump her for information about what she really knew—which, almost certainly, was a lot more than she had revealed to us before. I was over-ruled by the new senior officer who had taken over from Raphael Robles; I'll tell you about that later.

"Let it run for now," our new boss said. "We need to unearth as much of this al-Qaeda network as we can—before they shut it down."

I did something I have never done before: I disobeyed a direct order and texted Antonio. He may have been a bit of an asshole, but I couldn't let him continue without knowing.

He needed to be warned about her: she's dangerous.

The Road Ahead

Hours earlier, Antonio had returned from Sabadell to the Mossos' headquarters and dropped-off Xavi. Antonio had gone up to his office to collect the presentation materials he'd be showing shortly. Now he and Daniela were heading downstairs to the car park, with a deadline for attending a recruitment meeting down the valley.

Antonio was anxious to get back so he could see Maria. He realised that he had been stupid. He couldn't even blame peer group pressure. It seemed that almost everyone wanted their relationship to succeed.

He'd texted the message to Maria just after lunchtime; she was sure to have it by now, he guessed. Xavi's suggestion of the flowers had been brilliant. They were being sent to where Maria was staying with her girlfriend. They'd be delivered very soon.

Antonio was confident that Maria would be knocked off her feet by his romantic and extravagant gesture. They would get together. He would apologise and set the record straight. He'd talk her out of going overseas. From what everyone had said to him, it wasn't really what she had wanted to do anyway.

At the weekend, they could visit the jewellers together.

Antonio wondered why it hadn't occurred to him earlier. Perhaps it was just the strain of work, and all that had been happening, he told himself. His parents would be delighted— and, who knows, maybe there might be grandchildren before too long. Yes, for Antonio, things definitely were starting to look up.

At the time, he hadn't said anything to Xavi, of course, but he had been pleased by Daniela's reaction in the flower shop. He'd been grateful to her for taking charge of the flower selection. After last night's dinner, he had questioned if he had been wise to recruit her onto their team. He still had a lingering headache and couldn't recall a lot of the evening. This morning he had figured that, because she was so young, she'd been a bit stupid. In other ways, she had shown such promise, so he had decided just to let things go. It was less embarrassing for him that way.

In any case, the bouquet of flowers they had ordered for Maria was of such beauty and size that even he had been taken aback.

Yes, everything was going to work out well, he congratulated himself.

As they made their way through the Mossos underground car park towards his BMW, he saw a vice squad colleague who gestured to him. "I need a minute, Toni," he said.

"Damn, I left my phone on charge in the office," said Antonio patting his pockets and realising his mistake.

He turned to the colleague, "Sorry, Miguel, we'll have to catch up later."

"Finish your conversation. I'll go back up for it, boss," offered Daniela.

"That would be great—thanks," Antonio smiled, and continued his conversation.

She showed her badge to the security guard and rode the elevator up to the sixth floor. Antonio's office was spacious, she noted once again. But it needed a plant or something to make it more like home. She would pick one up from the market—as a surprise for him, she decided.

Glancing around his desk, she looked for his phone.

Disconnecting it from its charger, she glanced idly at the screen. It was password protected, of course. She laughed, and recalled his password from memory. It had not been difficult to memorise: he had been so trusting.

There were several new email messages and two texts. One from Maria was marked urgent. She ignored it and scrolled through the departmental messages.

Several marked *high-security* caught her attention. She emailed copies to herself.

Just then, a text came through from Diego. Daniela frowned as she read it; her face flushed, as she scrolled through his warning to Toni about her.

Carefully, she deleted the transmission string. It was not a fool-proof method of erasing, but it would give her more time to think about her next move.

Rattled by Diego's text message, but otherwise satisfied with her efforts, Daniela glanced at her watch and started to head back to the elevators. She didn't want Antonio to become impatient waiting for her.

On an impulse, she paused and opened the text message from Maria.

"Toni, I love you so much. I agree with you. Let's start again – a fresh new beginning. It will be just like the old days. Call me quickly. I cannot wait to see you. You have my heart. I am all yours. M."

Daniela read the message twice and scowled. Then she stabbed the delete key and watched the message disappear from the screen. With a quick finger movement, she sent it to the trash box. Once again, she repeated the deleting routine inside the recycling bin.

Within seconds she had removed all evidence of Maria's message.

As she approached the car, Antonio was finishing his conversation, shaking hands with his colleague.

"I'll drive, if you like, boss," she offered. "You can get some work done on the way."

As she manoeuvred the gearshifts, smoothly guiding the vehicle through the outer city streets towards the freeway, Daniela watched as Antonio scrolled through his messages. He did so several times; gradually his buoyant mood from earlier seemed to deflate.

For a long time, he stared out of the passenger window saying nothing… lost in his own thoughts.

It seemed to her that Antonio's mouth gradually turned down, like that of a young schoolboy denied something that he was sure would be his. Suddenly, he seemed very young and vulnerable, she thought.

Shifting into high gear, she guided the car into the high-speed lanes of the autopista.

Now that she had left the traffic behind, she allowed herself a quick smile.

The road ahead was clear.

From here on, there would be nothing to stop her.

Chapter 13

Epilogue

It's important to have friends.

They're predictable most of the time—but sometimes the unexpected happens. One of them does something we were not anticipating; our lives change in ways we couldn't have imagined.

Antonio was lucky that way; he had good friends.

Xavi's suspicions about Daniela were based on his gut instincts. There was no evidence to support his distrust of her. He was worried enough that he talked to Antonio's sister, Isabel. They couldn't prove anything against Daniela, so they recruited William to do what he does best—listen at peoples' electronic doors.

At National Police headquarters in Madrid we knew all about William, of course.

Why wouldn't we? We have one of the best electronic surveillance systems in Europe.

Besides, no matter how smart you are, there is always someone who's smarter. One of the hackers working for us is just as smart as William. He had been tracking him for months. Every operative has a distinct pattern, and our expert reported to us every move that his adversary made.

It had been a tactical decision by Raphael Robles to leave William in place. That was a smart move by my former boss. That's how we found out about Daniela's extra-curricular activities.

It turns out that, despite the affection between them, she hadn't been in love with David Casals.

With the trauma that she went through as a kid, I doubt she truly loves anyone—not in the way most people do.

Until she met Antonio and fell for him, the only man in her life was Raphael Robles. Her aunt was complicit in the abuse that went on for years, but Robles treated her well. Setting aside the moral judgements of society, the facts were that Daniela and Raphael developed an amazing relationship—he became her lover and mentor. At an early age, he had captured her mind.

Raphael had never married. He and Daniela lived together. With her gift for languages, he insisted she should complete her education. It was a complex relationship which would take someone like Freud to figure out.

Raphael had always been something of a maverick. His beliefs about Middle East politics enthralled her. His vision captured her soul. She didn't need a fanatic's view of the jihad, or a terrorist group like al-Qaeda, to focus her thinking. In her view of the world of the future, she already was well ahead of them.

Raphael didn't come up on the radar screen when the Civil Guard recruited Daniela, when they did a search on her background. There's no reason why he would, really. The Catalan police unknowingly were sitting on that information—her juvenile case files.

His family has been part of upper class Spanish society for as long as Spain has been a country; he has impeccable credentials. We had just not looked in the right place—to trace his connections with al-Qaeda.

Together, he and Daniela weaved a scheme so intricate that I'm not sure we will ever unravel it fully. He was the architect of the connection between the General's Project FERROL and al-Qaeda. He brokered the deal to import al-

Qaeda terrorists—planning to destabilise Spain's democratically elected government.

Project FERROL would have continued right under our noses, if it had not been for David Casals. He was smart enough to figure it out, and savvy enough as a policeman to leave us a well-blazed trail to follow. Antonio found the CD in David's locker, and after that the General's scheme started to unravel.

It's been said many times: "politics makes for strange bedfellows." Before the information from David Casals, we thought that the General and Carlos, and their powerful Francoist friends, were merely throwbacks from the past. All talk, no action. Brandy, cigars and teary-eyed reminiscences from the Generalissimo's years.

We should have known better.

What we didn't know about were the slush funds those old boys had been accumulating over the years. Almost all of the money came from corruption—and a lot of that was from the construction boom in Spain.

The money changed everything. Those old guys weren't capable of lighting a firework at a New Year's celebration without their hands shaking. But the money purchased them a deal with al-Qaeda. It was a business deal. Who says that jihadists are not smart business people?

Al-Qaeda would supply the explosives experts, recruited from their friends at ISIS. They are in the destruction business on a daily basis, improvising explosives from almost any local sources. Why waste time on inexperienced volunteers, when you can access the expertise of one of the best trained, and most vicious, bunch of criminals the world has ever produced? Those operatives from ISIS have no morals and no emotions. They're just killing machines.

Mustapha had a brilliant mind: pure evil. Who would have guessed it was Raphael?

The General and his cronies were only too happy to sign the deal with the devil. After a successful trial run at Palmyra, al-Qaeda operatives in Spain targeted the Mossos headquarters with enough improvised explosives to blow the building out of existence. They chose Catalunya's special day—when the injuries among the independence demonstrators would have been catastrophic.

In his warped thinking, that would turn the tide against Catalan separation. Four or five other targets over the next year would have destabilised the economy and the government. In no time, those old boys figured, Spain would be ready to reject its flirtation with democracy and Europe, and get back to the good days—a not-so-benign dictatorship.

We hadn't anticipated that kind of alliance between normally sworn enemies. It's changed the way we think. As the Arabic saying goes: *'The enemy of my enemy is my friend.'* They know.

The Prime Minister did a good job of convincing the country that jihadi extremists were responsible for the bombing attempt in Barcelona. Certainly, that was a very convenient outcome for the Spanish government already fighting a major scandal and lack of public confidence.

Raphael Robles did not emerge well from his close association with the General. He's serving a life sentence somewhere. Wherever it is, believe me... it's remote. He won't be publishing his memoirs for a long, long time.

What happened to the others involved in Operation FERROL? The prime minister took a brave decision and let the General and a few of his high-profile cronies walk away in return for their silence. If you were cynical, you might be tempted to say that he couldn't afford to lose another election over an even bigger scandal.

I really don't care. Those old guys may be walking around free, enjoying whatever years and memories they have left. But they can't take a crap without asking my permission.

Besides, as the Prime Minister himself said, if we give Catalunya and the Basques anything more to target politically, we shouldn't be surprised if they pull together enough support—and separate from Spain.

Democracy won out this time. Who knows about the future? Within Spain, the appetite to go back to some of the old ways is still strong. When will the next crazy fanatic get it into his, or her, head to try to move the political goalposts? After all, this is Europe.

What happened to Antonio's friends?

Xavi's concern about his partner, and the blossoming relationship Antonio was having with Daniela, led Xavi to seek help from Antonio's sister, Isabel. That's a very Catalan thing to do. The two of them recruited William to hack into Daniela's laptop. I'm not sure if they thought they'd find very much there—perhaps enough to get Antonio to break off the relationship. They were seriously worried about Maria.

Of course, Daniela wasn't going to leave anything incriminating lying around. Raphael had schooled her better than that.

We were puzzled when they started to hack into Daniela's computer. Why would the Mossos spy on one of their own officers, we asked ourselves. Especially, after we had confirmed that the intel she gave us in Turkey was first class. She was not on our watch list.

It was still a puzzle for us until Antonio's sister planted the listening devices in Daniela's apartment. That was done very skilfully. At National Police headquarters, we didn't have to lift a finger. It was the breakthrough we needed. She led us directly to Mustapha (a.k.a. Raphael).

That's ironic because Daniela had gone to great lengths to protect him. Her story about Syria was true in all respects, except one. She found out that Jamal knew the true identity of Mustapha. That rang alarm bells for her. If Jamal knew, she figured it wouldn't be long before someone else, like Michael O'Flaherty and the CIA, found out.

We just sat on top of the new intelligence and reaped a harvest of new information. Within hours, we found more about Mustapha's network in Spain than we would ever have discovered otherwise. We let it run for a time, hoping to find out more.

In our business, it's important to know who the bad guys are—and the good guys, for that matter. More important, is knowing how long to let the bad guys run before hauling in the net.

We didn't get that part right. Daniela is still out there somewhere. The student became the master. Along with her, the slush fund disappeared.

By the time we got there, Aladdin's Cave had been completely emptied out.

She led us to the General's chauffeur; he's another who won't ever be back on the streets.

We will get her eventually. We do... almost always.

In the meantime, somewhere out there is a very smart—and rich—young lady.

One thing I *can* tell you: this thing is not over yet.

CPSIA information can be obtained
at www.ICGtesting.com
Printed in the USA
LVHW041451210120
644288LV00013B/1322

9 781786 296788